The 'EMERALD [illegible] novel. The idea for it fi[illegible] when working in Cyprus in 1980. It was not until the autumn of 1989, however, that he began to write the book in earnest, re-writing some earlier false starts and developing the storyline and characters.

He has written the novel in his spare time while working as Chief Executive of an agricultural trade association, negotiating key issues on behalf of his members with the European Commission in Brussels.

After being awarded his doctorate in agricultural science he worked for a number of years in Belfast from 1971, and later spend much of 1979/81 in Cyprus. He now lives with his family in East Anglia and is Chairman of the Suffolk Coastal Conservative Association Political Committee.

DEDICATION

The EMERALD APHRODITE is dedicated to the people of Cyprus, in particular, to those who have been refugees in their own country since 1974, with a special thought for those with members of their family who have been listed as 'missing persons' for all these years.

A KYRIAKOU BOOK

First published in 1991 - paperback edition
by K.P. Kyriakou (books & stationery) Ltd
P.O. Box 159 Limassol, Cyprus
Telex 2836, Fax 05-371706

The characters and situations in this book are entirely imaginary and bear no relation to any real person or actual happenings.

ISBN 9963-7617-8-X

ROGER DAWSON

The Emerald Aphrodite

KyriakouBooks

ACKNOWLEDGEMENTS

The author thanks the following people for their contribution to the completion of 'The Emerald Aphrodite':-
Evripedes Angastiniotis - for his friendship and hospitality over more than a decade of business and leisure visits to Cyprus, without which it would have been impossible to write this novel.
My Mother-in-Law - for her encouragement to continue and complete the writing of this novel.
Sally Ruffles & Geoff Holbrooke - for their diligent and thorough checking of the typescript.

PROLOGUE

The early morning air was clear. Too clear for Anna Haduanois. As she drew back the shutters of her southern Nicosia home her eyes could not avoid seeing the mosaic-like Turkish flag of painted rocks on the southern slopes of the occupied Kyrenia mountains that dominated the skyline of the last remaining European divided city. This constant reminder of the partition of Cyprus was particularly poignant to her today. It was Sunday 14 August 1994, tomorrow she would have been a refugee in her own land for twenty years.

Each year she had marked the horror and distress of that summer war by making a journey, to her it was a pilgrimage, to be as close as possible to her home and memories. Today would be no exception, and as usual she had resisted her daughter's attempts to drive and accompany her. She would go alone and spend the day in silent remembrance of all she had lost, in particular she would pray for her son who had been 'missing' for every one of those long years.

Her first son, Philipos, was born in Athienou in 1950. Like most of the villagers his father was involved in farming. By 1953 he had bought his own land some miles north of the village and had begun to develop a pig farm. During the years when Philipos was at school in the village he often saw little of his father for weeks on end. After feeding his pigs in the morning he would disappear, sometimes returning during the early hours of the morning, sometimes not returning for days. Then his mother had taken him and his little sister to help feed the pigs before they went to school. One day his father did not return at all.

First a husband lost in the battle to end colonial rule and three young children to support, then a son listed as missing and another wounded in the war against Turkish annexation. This had happened just when for the first time she had begun to make her own life, freed of the responsibility for her children. She had left her village home in Athienou and moved east to the expanding resort town of Famagusta, to seek a new life in that new town full of hope. And she had succeeded. After learning her trade, first as a cook, then as a manageress, in several of that resort's cafes and restaurants she had become, several posts later a housekeeper at the Golden Sands Hotel, the four star showcase of that golden coast. With her savings she had purchased a new flat, which had been her pride and joy. After losing so much of her life to tragedy she had still not been content. On the day of the Coup she had opened her own restaurant in a new frontline building. The future had now seemed secure. Despite the final cease-fire call on 16 August, when her part of Famagusta had remained free, she had had to flee for her life as the Turkish army had shown no mercy in its crude aim to destroy the will of the Greek Cypriot community by capturing its most prized economic assets. The remainder of Famagusta had fallen too, following terror bombing of tourists and Greeks alike by Turkish jets.

All this, and more, much more, came flooding back into her mind as she left Nicosia that morning. She started early to avoid as much of the traffic heading for the southern coast as possible, the next day was also a public holiday to mark Independence Day. She, like many, many more had little to celebrate. Driving past Lymbia she looked up to the tiny church on top of the hill overlooking the village, still occupied by Turkish troops and closed to villagers. Despite the many hopes there had been for a settlement there had been none. All the children and young people of the village had ever seen of their church was Turkish soldiers using it as a base, look-out and shelter. The bloody Turkish invasion of 1974 had been at its fiercest in this area and Lymbia itself had seen heavy fighting. The nearby Turkish Cypriot village of Goshi had been raised to the ground, some say as a reprisal for the war and the bombing, others saying it had been done by the fleeing Turks themselves, as they left for the nearby British base at Dhekelia. The real truth was that many ordinary families had suffered enormously, while business had been rejuvenated and the national economy had grown from strength to strength on the fruits of reconstruction and resettlement. The lessons of 1945 had not been lost on the Greek Cypriot businessmen, losing a war could create tremendous opportunities and vast fortunes.

But the price had been high, very high, unacceptably high, to the Cypriot population as a whole, in particular to the hundreds of thousands of individuals like Anna. The armed forces of Turkey had used the pretext of a Coup in Nicosia to invade the island and pump in vast quantities of weapons of war and soldiers. This build-up had all happened during the space provided by peace negotiations in Geneva. Then, despite the continuing talks and in defiance of the Security Council of the United Nations, and despite the restoration of constitutional Government in Nicosia and the overthrow of the dictatorship in Athens, the Turkish army had systematically expelled a quarter of a million Greek Cypriots, selected simply because of their race, language and culture, from their homes, from their land, from their jobs and from their businesses. Those who had not been willing to flee from the forty percent of the island treated so brutally, had been forcibly ejected, or worse. Thousands had simply disappeared, many of whom had been slaughtered and buried in mass graves, the women having been raped first. Relatives had never learnt the fate of their loved ones. Anna had survived herself, but had had to desert her home and had had to live with the agony of her missing son for twenty years.

The earlier battle for freedom from British rule in the 1950s had been very confused and untidy. The Greek Cypriot leaders had fought for Union with Greece, ENOSIS. Some would have settled for independence first, allowing them to unite with Greece at a later date. The Turkish Cypriots, just under twenty per cent of the population, at first were unconcerned. Certainly they did not want to be ruled by the eighty per cent of the population who were Greek, even less did they want Union with Greece, but neither were they particularly worried by the prospect. The majority saw themselves as Cypriots first and Turks second. The British, in those post-war days when that country was struggling to remain a world power, wanted Cyprus as a military base. This seemed even more important after Colonel Nasser threw their army out of the Suez canal zone base in 1954. Cyprus was the natural place to relocate. It was British sovereign territory and no one could throw them out of there. The Suez crisis of 1956 had made these Cyprus bases seem even more important. Not only was it important in their eyes to remain in the area, but the delay caused to the Suez invasion force by the absence of troop loading facilities in Cyprus made development of, not retreat from, these Cyprus facilities seem even more important. Had it been possible to embark the invasion force in Cyprus, instead of Malta, then the whole canal could well have been seized, just as Eden had planned, well before international opinion forced a stop to the British and French action. The history of the Middle East could have been very different.

Until the mid 1950s there had been no real Greek Cypriot leader who had the overwhelming support of the population. Makarios III changed that. His role in the development of events during the second half of the 1950s remains an open question. Nominally he led the fight for Union with Greece, eventually he accepted independence and undoubtedly enjoyed the power this gave him and his role as an international figure. Whether all along he had sought independence and power and had just used the ENOSIS movement to help him achieve it must remain a real possibility. Certainly he was, towards the end of his life, fighting a resurgence of this feeling with his attacks on the reincarnated movement, EOKA 'B'. Makarios knew that if there were any real moves towards union with Greece then Turkey would invade and partition Cyprus as it had threatened to do several times. It was in the end rebel elements of the National Guard, led by their officers from mainland Greece who bombed the Presidential Palace, temporarily replaced him with Nicos Sampson, a militant

ENOSIS activist, thus playing into the hands of Turkey, providing that country with the justification it had always sought in proceeding with an invasion of and division of the island in 1974. The truth was that Cyprus had been used by the United States as the means of replacing the military dictatorship in Greece; Greece had been led to believe by the US that if they absorbed Cyprus then the US would prevent Turkey from intervening, as they had done before. In fact the US knew that Turkey would invade and thus discredit the Greek Government, leading to its overthrow within days. The only partial failure of the plan was the escape of Makarios himself.

The Turkish Cypriot community kept a low profile during the first stage of the struggle in the 1950s. They knew Turkey did not want the borders of Greece extended any further along the soft underbelly of that country's shoreline. This community was used by the British in an attempt to prevent any change to the status of the colony. They were brought into the equation in line with the time honoured policy of divide and rule. The British successfully involved Turkey to veto ENOSIS and help justify the British position. With independence and Union with Greece out, there remained only the continuation of British rule or partition as a solution. If there was to be any change partition was seen as being the desirable option, certainly by mainland Turkey, if not by the Turkish Cypriots themselves.

There is no such thing as a Cypriot race. There are Greek Cypriots and Turkish Cypriots. They are from different racial groups, have fundamentally different religions, Greek Orthodox and Muslim, and two very different languages and cultures. Few Greek Cypriots spoke Turkish and a minority of Turkish Cypriots spoke Greek. Many Cypriots spoke English and that was the language they used to communicate with each other. The Turkish Cypriots tended to find themselves with the more menial jobs, often working for Greek Cypriots.

Another difference in Cyprus, as compared to many countries with divided populations, was that there were very few areas of the country which were exclusively the territory of one group or the other. There were Turkish villages all over Cyprus, just as Greek villages were scattered over the whole island; the larger villages, towns and cities had Greek and Turkish areas. There was no separation of population between North or South, East or West. Any solution involving partition, therefore, would have meant a huge movement of both populations to achieve separation. Few of either group wanted to see such an upheaval.

One of the main aims of the EOKA campaign of the late 1950s was to make it impossible for the British to maintain the status quo in Cyprus. General Grivas, the leader of the military side of EOKA, who the British never caught, was fighting for ENOSIS, Union with Greece. Makarios' objectives were more complex. Not being able to catch Grivas, and believing Makarios was the real leader of EOKA the British removed him from the island, into exile in the Seychelles. This left Grivas to continue the fight in his own way without Makarios there to temper some of his followers' wilder excesses. Eventually Makarios had to be released; brought into the negotiations and handed the power he had probably always sought for himself. He, like many other leaders who rose to power, including Banda, Kenyatta, Julius Nyreere and others, was able to add the letters 'JB', Jailed by the British, after his name.

Eventually all sides had had enough and a formula for a settlement was worked out. Even Grivas was persuaded to end the military fight. It was the Athens government's Foreign Minister, with his Turkish opposite number who began the initiation of the final solution. At a series of meetings, beginning in New York, and culminating in Zurich, an independence formula was agreed. No Union with Greece, no partition, but the end of colonial rule. The Greeks got control of the new Republic's government, the Turks got safeguards, thirty percent of the Government, the Parliament and the civil service, together with an effective veto through the vice-

President. The British retained several large sovereign bases along the southern coast of the island.

This system had never worked. Effectively there were two Governments operating in parallel at both national and local level. Makarios, who became the first President, frustrated by the Turkish veto and his inability to wield the power he thought rightly should be his as Head of State proposed changes to the Constitution. He addressed his changes to his Turkish Cypriot vice-President, but the veto came not from him, but from Turkey itself. Eventually there was Turkish inspired inter-communal fighting in yet a further attempt to achieve partition. This was prevented from engulfing the whole island only by the intervention of British troops from the sovereign bases, followed by the United Nations, those same British troops forming the largest contingent to this UN force. The Turkish Cypriot leaders established their own mini-state in several areas and forcibly encouraged many Turkish Cypriots to leave their villages to populate these enclaves and provide some justification for their leaders' action. Despite inter-communal talks, led by Glafkos Clerides for the Greeks, and several Turkish threats to invade the island, there was no settlement and from 1963 Makarios held real power over most of the island, with the exception of the Turkish Cypriot enclaves. The situation was only ended by his temporary overthrow in 1974, followed by the invasion by Turkey, which effectively forced the partition of the island. The less than twenty percent of the population who were Turkish Cypriots went to the occupied northern forty percent and the Greek Cypriots to the free southern sixty percent; a situation that had remained unchanged to the present day. Makarios returned to the island a few months after the invasion and was reinstated as President. He resumed the inter-communal talks with the Turks and had he lived may have reached a settlement, he had the strength and support to do so, his successors did not.

The United Nations had maintained a 'Green Line' right across the island from August 1974. Few, if any, Greeks had been able to go north, Turks were not allowed by their leaders to travel to the south. There were some privileged people, journalists, foreign residents in the North and an increasing number of curious tourists, who had been allowed to cross at the only crossing point, the Ledra Palace Hotel in Nicosia, but most citizens accepted the fact that no border crossing was possible.

The Greek Cypriot Government had maintained its international authority and despite its blockade of the northern ports of entry had not succeeded in changing the situation. More than 250,000 refugees from the north of the island had been settled in the south, whose economy had remained strong. However, most of these displaced persons had only one aim in life, to return home.

One of the odd results of the 1974 Turkish invasion was the ghost town of Famagusta. During the fighting the Turks had paid no heed to Security Council resolutions in the absence of additional pressure from the United States. They kept fighting and extending their area of control despite being ordered by the toothless UN to stop. Having taken the old town of Famagusta, which was inhabited by approximately 5,000 Turkish Cypriots, making about ten percent of the town's population, they continued towards the holiday resort area of the town with its complement of high-rise apartments and hotels. The Turkish airforce bombed Famagusta mercilessly. The innocent civilians had no choice but to run for their lives. The result was swift and complete, 40,000 residents, plus many thousands of summer tourists staying there that hot August, fled, leaving Famagusta deserted. Turkey had never intended to take the whole town, but it was theirs by default. Ever since August 1974 the new town of Famagusta has been held up to the Greek Cypriots by the Turks - totally deserted, with decayed food still on the tables from interrupted meals, never occupied, as the rest of the north - as a bargaining counter. "Give us everything we have stolen in the North, effective partition, and a confederal, bicommunal Constitution and we will give you Famagusta back", was the Turkish offer.

There had been a series of abortive talks and several apparently serious attempts to reach a settlement. First Makarios himself met, and had seemed to reach an accord with Rauf Denktash, the Turkish Cypriot leader, less than two years after the end of the war. After Makarios' death his successor, when he felt strong enough, met with Denktash under the chairmanship of Kurt Waldheim, UN Secretary General. At Nicosia airport in June 1979, they announced a ten point agreement with a great fanfare, it was never implemented, the two sides having subsequently failed to agree about what the agreement meant. Agreement was again close when the two sides met in January 1985 at the UN in New York and almost agreed a new Constitution, this time the Greek Cypriot President couldn't bring himself to sign away the property of his refugees, the talks failed. The election of a new President in 1988, promising at first, did not lead any nearer to a settlement. The Greek Cypriot government had allowed themselves to believe that since, in their view, they had right on their side they would prevail. They had a series of United Nations' resolutions condemning Turkey and ordering their withdrawal. In fact the Cyprus debate had become a routine annual event at the General Assembly; and they had effectively blocked international recognition of the 'independence' of the Turkish Cypriot mini-State. Many Greek Cypriots had, however, become convinced that they would reach their own individual ends first. It was in this context that the Cyprus Liberation Movement had been born. The CLM was by no means a rebirth of the original EOKA, despite the EOKA history of many of its members, it was felt politically more acceptable to establish a new and unconnected organisation.

The publicly recognised leader of the movement was a businessman who had been active in EOKA and held the rank of Major in the Greek Cypriot National Guard Reser-ists. He had made his fortune later, from the years of re- peace that had allowed the tourist industry to flouriish it did, particularly during the mid 1960s after Harold Wilson's government in Britain imposed a fifty pounds foreign currency allowance on British holidaymakers. This allowance did not apply when travelling to countries inside what was then called 'the Sterling Area', a group of ex-colonies and Commonwealth countries, most of which were too distant from Britain, for example the Caribbean, to benefit from this concession. However, two countries that were not too far away built a tourist industry on the basis of what was regarded in Britain as a mean and miserly measure designed to hurt the rich who took their holidays abroad. In fact it had no effect on the rich who could afford to travel further than the Costa Brava or Majorca. For Cyprus and Malta the measure was of real benefit. They were not too far away for a holiday flight, and the existence of the restriction on travel to other countries in the area allowed them to charge higher prices than they would have been able to if the British had been as free to spend their holidays in France, Spain, Italy or Greece.

Savvas Patriches had benefited enormously from the development of the tourist industry. He had acquired a chain of hotels and apartment blocks in all the popular resorts, particularly Kyrenia and Famagusta. The result was he had lost more than most in the invasion of 1974. Even if there was a settlement it seemed unlikely that he would ever see the return of his property in Kyrenia, but his hopes had been raised many times that Famagusta would be returned. He now believed this was most unlikely in the absence of some event or events to bring the Cyprus problem back onto the front pages of every world newspaper, particularly those in the United States. If there was enough trouble to threaten their interests they might well decide to force the parties to a settlement. Since Famagusta was merely a bargaining chip in the hands of the Turks it followed that any settlement would see its return to its Greek Cypriot owners. He resolved that he must play his full part in making this happen and had readily agreed to become the figure-head and military leader of the

CLM.

All this and more had been swimming through Anna's mind as she drove towards what she still regarded as 'home' that Sunday morning. She used the motorways until she arrived at the British base at Dhekelia. Instead of turning right through the garrison she carried straight-on up the hill, following the signpost that still read 'Famagusta'. That road followed the northern boundary of the British base, which also served as the southern extent of the Turkish conquests. For much of the journey she was within a few yards of occupied Cyprus and found the experience very strange, but somehow not depressing. Akhna was distressing though. As the road looped to the south around the deserted and decaying small town in which her daughter had taken so much interest, she could not help seeing the dereliction and waste. "A monument to what?" she wondered. It made her think about the fate of her own home, and for once she was glad it was impossible to get as close to Famagusta as she was to Akhna.

Just before she turned left towards Phrenaros, near the British Middle East radio listening base at Ayios Nikolaos, she passed within twenty yards of a Turkish army sentry post, and saw out of the corner of her eye a soldier stepping into it. That was the closest she remembered being to the enemy.

It was still not eight when she arrived at Dherinia and the village streets were still quiet as she went down the hill as far as the border checkpoint, through which only United Nations Forces were allowed to pass. Turning right, in less than a minute she had stopped the car outside the village, on a side road sloping gently downhill towards the east. A few hundred yards away the deserted resort of Famagusta filled her horizon. Beyond the high rise hotels and apartments was her home. This was as close to it as she had been for twenty yar

As she got out of her car she was surprised to he name.

"Mrs Haduanois. Good morning. I needn't ask why you are here. Had we known we could have travelled together."

It was Savvas Patriches. She had first met him twenty-five years ago, when she had worked for him in Famagusta. Then, after promoting her and valuing her greatly as an employee, he had not stood in her way when she decided to open her own restaurant. Instead he had helped her, given her some almost new furniture and other restaurant items that he was replacing. Then, she had lost touch with him, until the last few years, when her daughter had begun to see a lot of him. She claimed it was only politics that drew them together, but as a mother she had still not lost hope that one day her daughter may marry. Perhaps they may grow closer...

"Thank you, but every year I force myself, just once, to make this journey, and it's so upsetting that I would not be company for anyone, its best to be on my own."

"I've always felt the same, until recently. But I've come to the conclusion that it's all very well us all keeping our silent grief to ourselves, that way there will be no end to it. It's time we all got angry, together. Your daughter has convinced me of that. I pledge to you now Mrs Haduanois that before the anniversary next year year I will invite you to lunch in Famagusta as an honoured guest in the hotel where you became one of the best employees I ever had. Now, let me take you away from this depressing site and buy you breakfast further down the coast."

CHAPTER ONE

Set astride the mouth of the Lagan, where it changed from a modest river into the wide sea lough that had formed the basis of the city's former prosperity, Belfast appeared peaceful and tranquil. In contrast to the world headlines that September of 1971, it looked quite normal and indeed attractive. There were no large columns of smoke identifying the latest car bomb, nor burning buildings from last night's riots. The British Airways Vanguard crossed the lough to the north of Harland and Wolf, their huge crane being an unmistakable landmark even from 4,000 feet, and headed across the rolling green hills of the Antrim countryside towards the largest fresh water lake in the British Isles. Over Lough Neagh the vibrating Vanguard dipped its wing, began to tremble, and turned through almost a full circle. Helena Haduanois, on only her second ever flight, was terrified. She was sure they were going to fall sideways into the water. But reluctantly it seemed, this carthorse of an aeroplane, a stretched version of the successful Viscount, gradually levelled out, shaking even more until, it seemed, it was bound to fall apart. But nevertheless it crossed the shore and carefully touched down on Aldergrove airport's new runway, sending the hundreds of rabbits that inhabited this corner of Ulster, scurrying for cover. Although some twenty miles from the city, Aldergrove had recently taken over as Belfast's airport from Nuts Corner, an airstrip some two miles away that even eighteen years later would fool a perfectly competent pilot into landing his passenger jet there by mistake, after aiming for Aldergrove.

Only eighteen years old, Helena had arrived in what was, to her, a new land, to begin her student days. She had travelled from the beautiful, but troubled Island of Aphrodite to the cooler, equally beautiful, but yet more troubled, Emerald Isle. Despite her youth Helena had the maturity of sacrific[illegible] and determination. Her mother's sacrifice and her ow[illegible] termination. She was tall for a Cypriot girl, but othe[illegible] average build, with stunning green eyes and dark brown hair, but her skin had remained largely untanned and fair. She was an indoor girl, who, had she paid the attention to herself that she had to her books, could have been very attractive.

Despite of, or perhaps because of, the troubled times in Northern Ireland Queens University of Belfast had maintained, and even strengthened, its academic reputation. But to do so it had to work even harder to encourage the best potential students to attend. Few outside the troubled Province eagerly sought a place at an institution, however good, in that riot torn city. To anyone living outside its boundaries it seemed that every other car must contain a bomb, that on every street corner there must be a riot. But although there was trouble, death and destruction on the streets, much of the population of that once splendid city, went about their business in a completely normal manner. Children went to school, people went to work, housewives did their shopping. The only areas of life affected for those living outside the few areas of the city controlled by sectarian forces, and marked red in Building Society offices, were the routes they travelled and the pubs they frequented.

Queens University had determined to attract a continuing proportion of good overseas students, even if attempts to attract more than a handful from across the water in Great Britain, seemed doomed to failure. Their first and obvious source of students, and the additional welcome finance they brought, was the British Commonwealth. In addition to the virtually universal use of the English language, many in these countries, especially in the newly independent, so-called 'New Commonwealth' countries, saw the trouble in Northern Ireland as merely reflecting the last days of Empire that they themselves had so recently experienced. Certainly to Cypriots there were many parallels to their own situation just a few short years earlier. Recruitment from that island had been as successful as from any other country.

It was not only those at Queens University who saw parallels with Cyprus. Interviewed on Ulster Television in the fall of 1971, the Director of the Northern Ireland Tourist Board, when asked about that year's disastrous reduction in visitors to Northern Ireland, drew his own parallel with Cyprus. He had said;

"I am optimistic about the future of the tourist industry. As soon as these temporary 'troubles' are behind us then we confidently expect to see a significant increase as compared to the last full year before civil disturbances began in 1968. One only needs to examine the record of Cyprus. Following the establishment of relative peace there has been an almost exponential growth in their tourism. We are sure the same will be the case here in Northern Ireland."

The interviewer failed to point out that the main attraction of Cyprus was its climate, an advantage Ulster did not have. Nevertheless there existed an affinity of thought between the two countries.

Helena's mother had sacrificed everything for her three children, and with the help of her family she had managed to send them all to high school in Nicosia, where they had become fluent in English and had taken and passed English examinations, in Helena's case the Oxford Examination Board's GCE 'A' level examinations in Biology, Physics and Chemistry. Her grades, however, had not been good enough to gain admittance to either Oxford or Cambridge, but she had been attracted by the active steps Queens had made to encourage her to apply to its School of Agriculture. Believing that it must be advantageous to go to a University that actually seemed to want her, rather than one which set an obstacle course in the path of potential undergraduates, she had accepted the place offered. She therefore set out for Belfast that late September morning in 1971. Had she known when she made her decision to accept Queens' offer that internment without trial would be introduced for terrorist suspects on 9 August, and that flames would then erupt from all corners of the Province within hours of the decision becoming known, then she might have reconsidered. But having made her choice she stood by it. That was Helena. Her character had been formed by the life her mother had been forced to follow after her father's death. It had been very hard. Born in 1953 she had been three when her father had been killed. Although his death had never been properly explained she had discovered that his only bullet wound had been in his thigh. He had died from being beaten. Her bitterness had increased as she had become older and made no allowances for the fact that two British soldiers had been killed by terrorists close to where her father's body had been found. One day she would honour her father's memory, but first she had to educate herself out of the closed village community in which she had been brought up. If she did not do so then her life may not be much better than her mother's had been. She would be trapped into children and village life. That was not for her.

On the bus from the airport to the city, as it swept down the hill into the top of Crumlin Road and onto the Ardoyne, she had her first view of the city at ground level. Just a few short weeks ago that area of small streets had been a mass of flames and fleeing residents. Cranbrook Gardens consisted of little more than a row of burned out little houses. Depending upon which version of events was believed, the residents, Roman Catholics, had either burned their own houses and fled to avoid them being taken over by the Protestant community; or they had been literally burned out. Either way it had been a human tragedy. Could this happen in Cyprus again, or was today's long-held truce more soundly based, wondered Helena.

She decided to take a taxi from Great Victoria Street bus station to the University, although it was little under a mile away. Her luggage, although very sparse compared to home-based students, was nevertheless too much for her to carry alone for that distance. As the taxi pulled out to turn right towards Donegal Square she saw the tall building on her left, the Belfast Europa Hotel, that was home to journalists covering the continuing story of Northern Ireland. It had become newsworthy itself. Because the journalists, whose home it was would surely cover any attack upon it to the maximum extent possible, there had been many such attacks. The latest attempt had almost succeeded, a large bomb with the most sophisticated anti-handling devices yet seen, had been placed in the lobby. It had taken the British army officer charged with the task of defusing it almost twelve hours of painstaking work in an evacuated hotel, awaiting its fate in dignified silence, to succeed once more in saving it for a future, more successful attempt a few months later.

Queens University was very much a part of the city. Sited in an inner suburb the campus was compact, a village within a city. Helena was lucky to have found a place in a student hostel on the edge of the campus, part of the incentive package she had been offered to attend. Her first term flew by. It was a totally new experience and new life to her, but she buried herself in her course work. Hers was a happy department. Under the genial eye of Professor James Dodd the Agricultural and Food Chemistry Department was one that actually liked students, it did not just see them as a necessary irritation, as an obstacle to the more important and satisfying field of research, but as human beings wanting to learn. The students responded positively to this by no means universal attitude. Helena made few close friends in those early months, but no enemies. It was fascinating for her to learn the attitudes of her fellow students to what were universally regarded as 'the troubles'. They had begun three years earlier following a civil rights campaign in which many Queen's students had been involved, but now they had gone beyond intellectual unrest and campaigning, but were still nevertheless regarded as a temporary aberration that would soon end as both sides sought a respite.

On the surface, the student body tried to remain distanced from violence. It was often regarded as a very working-class phenomenon. But she was very shocked and surprised to gradually learn how very hardened attitudes had become even amongst those who it might be thought had the education to see and understand each other's point of view. She was regarded as a potential friend by each community. Neither saw her as antagonistic, nor a threat. Just as the few English students and staff were regarded as being on neither side, so she was an outsider to convert to their point of view. She had once been asked whether she was a Catholic or Protestant Greek Orthodox.

When in the company of a mixed group of students the conversation never turned to the 'troubles', it was a subject a cross-community group seeking to live and work together in harmony did not mention. It soon became clear why this was so. Each group, when on its own with her, would soon turn their conversation to the political situation. They each believed that right was on their side and became surprisingly bitter about the other community. There was little or no meeting of minds. Each person could be placed within a few seconds of speaking by someone from the other side, it was eerie, even with a common language it seemed just as easy to identify Catholic or Protestant as it was at home to separate Greek or Turk. The tribal terminology intrigued her, say Northern Ireland and you were a Protestant, the North of Ireland and you were a Catholic. These were not the only two terms. Ulster was generally used by Protestants. The 'Six Counties' was virtually a term of abuse used to describe the only six counties of the thirty-two in Ireland which had been partitioned off to remain in the United Kingdom and which made up Northern Ireland, was used by Catholics. Generally, Loyalist referred to Protestants and Nationalist or Republican, to Catholics. One of the most emotive of all was Londonderry and Derry. They were the same city, but Loyalists never used the shortened version, and Nationalists never included the 'London' prefix. It was not a very United Kingdom, she used to think to herself.

When Helena had first left home she had decided not to return until the June of the following year, to have a full nine months away and to save the cost of returning to Cyprus. As Christmas approached she began to feel homesick and had second thoughts. Christmas had always been special to her, a family event. What would she do that year, could she manage to spend it alone? Just as she was becoming increasingly concerned, and even began checking what student discounts might be available to her should she decide to return home for three weeks, she became much closer to several Irish girls. They were working to organise a Christmas Ball at the hostel and were glad of all the help they could enlist. Helena joined them to take her mind of her homesickness. Soon she had virtually taken over the organisation. Once her mind was set upon achieving an objective it became her single-minded obsession. She did not have a partner to the ball. Not because she wasn't asked, but because having organised the event she was equally determined to remain free on the big night to make certain that everything worked as she had so carefully planned. It did. It was the best Christmas Ball that the student body had ever held, entirely because of Helena. One of the friends she had made, one who had gratefully taken a back seat and enjoyed herself rather than working, became closer to Helena and asked her to spend Christmas at her home in Derry. Helena accepted and gratefully abandoned her thoughts of travelling home, since that meant her money would surely last through to the summer and the end of the academic year.

Christmas passed peacefully and quietly. Helena was content. It was New Year's Eve that marked the most important turning point of her young life. At the local Bogside dance, which she and her friend had decided to attend, she met Sean O'Neil. Like so many twenty year-olds in Derry, he was unemployed, despite being highly intelligent and having seven GCE 'O' Levels.

Having had no possibility of employment, yet no incentive to ask his mother to support him for two more years at school, then college, at sixteen he had drifted for a year around the streets of Derry with his friends. It was therefore no surprise that he had become a member of the IRA at seventeen and when the Provisional IRA had split from the main body, he went too. The IRA had become too political for many. Those who were determined that only war would be effective, left to form the 'Provisionals'. He was no different from many students she knew in Belfast, except he was clearly more worldly-wise and mature. She fell for him that night, but succeeded in fending off his amorous advances. He would have dropped any other girl for that reason alone. Believing himself to be a soldier at war, engaged in a serious and dangerous struggle, risking his life and liberty, he considered he had a right to expect any girl he asked to meet his manly desire. Not Helena though. She was different. So different that even he was prepared to wait, not for long perhaps, but wait he did.

Helena had intended to return to Belfast early in the New Year but she saw something in Sean that made her stay. Here was a young man of her generation who was prepared to fight for his country's freedom at the risk of his own life. Just like her father had.

He still lived at home and despite the fact that she was not a Catholic and foreign he took her home. His mother took an instant liking to this young Cypriot girl. She seemed serious and tough minded, loved her country, and intended to return, so was not likely to catch her son for whom she still had high hopes. Neither was she a Protestant.

Sean and Helena spent the early days of that January together. Although he remained on active service, he had been given no task to perform since before Christmas. One night he was. Helena noticed a change in him. He became tense and she suspected the truth. Eventually he answered her question. Yes, he had a job to do; to steal or hijack a car, take it over the border into Donegal, stay with it until dawn, collect a package, and to bring it back into the city. She refused to leave him, determined to taste something of what her father had felt during his missions. After a heated argument he had conceded. After all it was against every order to have told her at all, he could not afford to risk that she could be picked-up and questioned before his mission was completed. Thus he allowed himself to be persuaded that it was in everyone's interests that she accompany him.

It was a little after five o'clock when they walked out of the Bogside towards the city centre, each carrying a small bag containing nothing more sinister than some sandwiches and cans of drink. He had decided, since she was with him, to obtain the car as easily and with as little trouble as possible. No bravado this time. Having reached the bomb-damaged main shopping street where many of the shops were still boarded up, he had led her towards the corner of William Street and Strand Road. There he waited, watching the newspaper stand twenty yards further down the road. Drivers began stopping their cars on their way home from work to collect an evening paper. Leading her by the hand they walked towards the newspaper stand.

Turning to her he said;

"Act perfectly normally, don't jump or move suddenly. We are going into that shop doorway. Hold me tightly and kiss me, but I want to able to watch the street, so try to keep your head out of my line of sight."

It was as if they were glued together in a passionate embrace. He had great difficulty in concentrating on his task. He would have preferred to concentrate on her, just as she was doing with him.

"How long can I stand this, why couldn't you act like this last night." he thought.

Perhaps it was the excitement, but had he responded this time she wouldn't have stopped him. To her it was for real.

When he thought he couldn't stand still any longer he saw what he was looking for. The red Ford Cortina that had just drawn up grabbed his attention. It had no passengers, only the driver who had got out and walked around the front of the car towards the newspaper seller. But he had left the engine running.

Sean said quickly, quietly and seriously,

"Follow me round, wait by the boot. I'll open the door and check the back on that side to make sure it is not locked. As I get in open the back, throw yourself in, close the door. When

I move follow."

It worked like a dream. He had the door open, put his hand round the back of the seat to check the back door lock was up and jumped in. She was so quick that she had her door closed before his. They were moving before the owner noticed. He was too late, his car would soon be a mere insurance statistic.

Sean turned left into Strand Road, halted for a moment and told her to climb into the front and put her arm around him, then headed for the border. Driving swiftly, but not excessively so as to attract attention, they crossed the border and were in Muff ten minutes after setting off. Having arrived in the Republic they could begin to relax.

His orders were to be at a certain farm just outside Letterkenny at five the next morning. He checked the fuel. No problem, at least seven gallons, enough for the round trip and plenty to spare to keep them warm during the night. The night; where would they go? He had to keep in the clear. There were rumours that the RUC and the Garda swapped information about stolen cars, no need to ask for trouble. He had about an hour for certain.

"You can take your arm away now, we are safe," he said to her.

"But I want to hold you," she pleaded.

He smiled, "We have all night for that. Let's find somewhere safe."

He headed for Letterkenny, located the address he had to find in the early hours, so there would be no mistake, then made for Millford. Arriving at Millford he found a track which led to a quiet foreshore on the edge of the sea lough. They would wait there.

"Let's have dinner," he said taking a sandwich and a can of coke from his bag, breaking the thick sliced cheese sandwich in half, "I'm famished."

"I couldn't eat a thing, but I need a drink," she said taking out one of her cans of beer. "I'm as dry as a bone."

After they had finished he began to shiver. It was a cold, wet and windy night on the shores of County Donegal. The north westerly wind had not touched land since leaving the Greenland ice cap.

"I'll put the heater on again," he said moving his hand towards the ignition to start the engine.

"No," she said, "later, someone might find us if they hear the engine. I will keep you warm. Let's get into the back, we can be closer then."

He took the ignition key out and put it into his pocket. Then they opened their doors and were both nearly blown off their feet by the blast of freezing drizzle that hit them. Together on the backseat it was not only affection that drove them together, it was the need for shared bodily warmth.

Never in her wildest dreams or fantasies had she ever imagined that this would be how she would lose her virginity. Because lose it she was sure she would. She wanted him, yes. But like this? She knew there was no choice. Even if she had wanted to she could not hold him off all night. So why try? No, if it was going to happen then she would want it too. It would be better that way. Why should she feel guilty? She had wanted him an hour ago after all.

She took him in her arms and kissed him with all the energy she had. This time she had the initiative. He was taken aback and it was a few moments before he responded. When he did she knew this was it, but she was determined to keep the initiative she had, and sat astride his legs unfastening his shirt as he attempted to pull her sweater over her head.

"No, it's too cold without it," she said, "wait."

She then put her arms behind her back, expertly undid the clasp and pulled her bra out from under her sweater.

"There, there's no need to take it off now," she said, taking his hands and placing them underneath it. She gasped as his cold hands searched her chest. She had the initiative now and kept it.

Her hands moved down his bared chest, working on his belt and trousers. His also moved down, but with her astride his legs he could make little progress without her assistance. This she was determined to give only at her own pace, not his.

After what seemed hours to him she lifted herself up and removed the obstacle. Still slowly she eased herself towards him and moved down onto him.

She stayed on him long after he had finished. They really did need each other's warmth now, but it soon got too cold, even though they were so close. She climbed off him and said.

"We can risk running the engine now I think, don't you?"

They both adjusted their clothes sufficiently to brave the arctic conditions outside for a moment. Soon the engine had warmed enough for the heater to become effective and they could no longer see their breath condense in front of them.

"I'm hungry now, I'm going to have that sandwich, won't you have a beer this time?"

"No, orders. We must not drink on active service."

"What about making love? Do you have orders about that?" she smiled. "I'm going to have a beer, it gives me strength."

Later, he couldn't resist the temptation for a second time. Then they slept uneasily for a few hours. Before dawn he awoke for the last time, becoming tense and nervous, checking his watch every two or three minutes. At last it was a quarter to five. He started the engine and drove off towards Letterkenny, driving off the road across the fields to his destination. He gave the signal he had memorised with the headlamp flasher. Instantaneously both doors were opened violently and they were each pulled out and pressed into the mud.

"You were to come alone. Who is this girl?"

He couldn't breathe, so how could he speak. He began to panic. It was only when he began to stop shaking that his head was released a little, enough to breathe, could he speak?

"She's my girl," was all he could manage.

They were both roughly pulled upright, spitting mud out of their blocked mouths.

"You were told to come alone. How do we know who she is? We nearly shot you both, two people in a car that's supposed to carry one means trouble. Since it's your first time we let you live, but her, how do we know we can trust her, we ought to shoot her.

At that Helena began to kick out at her captor, catching him very painfully.

"Stop." ordered the man holding Sean. "No more of that or you will die. Now."

Sean didn't believe she would be killed if he was allowed to live. They knew that if she was his girl he might turn them in. He knew that. They knew that. They would both live or both die.

Wanting to be rid of their package into his car rather than keep it too long themselves they decided to risk it. But the second man made a slight adjustment to the package.

"Here are your orders. Obey them this time. Not a minute before, not a minute later, park the car at eight o'clock outside the Guildhall in Derry. Get out, walk slowly and naturally away. Go home. Stay there all day. Get it?"

"Yes." said Sean, not wanting to prolong the discussion any longer than necessary.

They were cleaned up, so they would not look suspicious in that almost new car, and held captive until seven, then roughly returned to the car, now containing its package, and left.

Sean retraced his steps, but was too anxious not to be late. He had arrived a few minutes too early, but could not risk a circuit of the city centre to waste another five minutes due to possible road blocks and checks. So he parked. They got out and, while the Guildhall clock was striking eight times, from the next street there was an enormous explosion.

She held onto his arm and said softly,

"That was meant to kill us both." It was a statement of fact, not a question.

"Yes." was his anxious reply. "It's no good hiding, I know them all here, they know me. But I am sure trying to kill us wasn't authorised. I can square it, we are not so hard here in Derry as them over the border. They will not try again, not here."

He was right. His own commander was very angry, more angry than him, about the attempt on one of his own men, and the needless slaughter of his own fellow citizens who were killed before his own bomb warning could even be telephoned.

"The murdering bastards. One day they will pay for that." he had said. "just keep out of sight for a couple of weeks, that's all."

Sean did just that. He spent a lot of time with Helena and decided to return to Belfast with her, camping out in her bedsit. Then at the end of the month it was time for him to return home and they went to Derry together for the week-end. This time she stayed at his home, not her girlfriend's.

Since she was to return home that Sunday evening to be in Belfast on the Monday morning she did not want to join in the mass protest demonstration taking place. He had stayed with her. They heard its noise from the relative peace of his mother's flat. The rest of the family had joined in, it would have been noticed if they had all been absent.

In the late afternoon it happened. Her world fell apart. They heard screams from outside. He took a look and rushed to the stairs. She watched. The crowd of demonstrators were being pursued by soldiers. His family were amongst them so he had gone to join them, to help if needed. Then the shooting started. Helena did not know who was shooting at who. She saw men fall and couldn't bear to look any more.

Thirty minutes later she knew the worst. Sean was dead. Shot through the head. He was not the only one. Twelve more bodies were found. It was Sunday 30 January 1972. Bloody Sunday.

CHAPTER TWO

That day, 30 January 1972, marked a turning point in the history of Northern Ireland. It led directly to the ending of the devolved Government at Stormont and the appointment of an English Secretary of State for Northern Ireland. A change from Protestant rule to colonial rule.

For Helena it was an even greater tragedy. Six weeks later it was confirmed that Sean had left an heir, her unborn child. She had returned to Belfast after the funeral to continue her studies, but it had been a struggle to concentrate. Then she had begun to fear the worst. Now it had been confirmed. What was she to do? Her mind was in turmoil, first her father, now her lover, killed by a British soldier when fighting for their country. Her determination to avenge her father was redoubled, she matured overnight and began, not to dream about doing it, but to plan it.

That weekend she returned to Derry and told Sean's mother, Mary, about her condition, who, to Helena's delight and surprise, had smiled with joy. She had persuaded Helena to have the baby, not to have an abortion, and to let her, bring up the baby as her own. She had lost Sean, so she wanted to start again with his child. Helena had agreed willingly, she did not want an abortion. She could remain at Queens until the end of the summer term, stay in Derry for the summer and after the baby was born return to Belfast during the autumn term. She need not miss more than four to six weeks of the term.

She did not tell anyone else that she was pregnant, especially her mother or anyone from Cyprus. In June she had written to her mother explaining that life was much more expensive than she could afford and that she had decided to stay in Ireland to earn some money during the summer. She explained that she would be able to earn enough to save sufficient for the following year. Although very sad at the news that she would not see her daughter, her mother was pleased that Helena seemed determined to make more of her life than she had the opportunity to do until very recently. More than in most other cultures, the ambition of the Greek Cypriot was not so much for him or herself, but for their children.

Helena returned to Derry for the summer. She experienced the trauma of operation 'Motorman', when on 31 July, converted British Centurion tanks broke down the barricades to the Bogside and other areas that had preserved them as paramilitary 'no-go' areas since Bloody Sunday. Recognising the overwhelming superiority of the forces brought in for the task, the IRA leaders had decided to offer only token resistance. Most had escaped south of the border the day before, when it was clear such an operation was planned.

Sean's mother Mary, fearing that Helena might get involved, and thus endanger her grandchild, had sent her to friends of hers in the Republic for the month of August. It was during this period in the summer of 1972 that Helena had become acquainted with some of the key strategists of Provisional Sin Fein, the political arm of the Provisional IRA. In her condition she had sought no romantic entanglements, but being regarded almost as a widow of one of their soldiers, she had gained their trust and friendship, especially when they learnt that her father had been killed by the British.

Although sympathetic to the cause for which Sean had died, she began to question the purpose of such killing.

"Why do you bomb and kill? How can that possibly help you achieve Irish unity?" she had asked innocently.

The most politically aware of her hosts had replied with words that were to remain with her and haunt her for the next twenty years.

"Because we need to advertise the cause. Coca-Cola can afford an advertising budget of millions of dollars worldwide. Then they only reach a proportion of the population, those who bother to read or listen to their message. Just imagine how much it would cost to buy the headline story in every newspaper and every newsbroadcast every day, as well as the acres of newsprint and hours of documentaries that provide additional background. If it wasn't impossible it would cost billions to buy the sort of coverage we are achieving every day. If the media took no interest and didn't report anything we did, then there would be no point in doing it. It is unfortunate that it costs us some casualties, such as your Sean, and a few totally innocent people are hurt or lose their lives. But compared to war their numbers are minute. You ask, why do we do it? Low cost advertising, that's why"

Several of these contacts she was to retain and develop during the next twenty years and more. She had effectively become a key member of the IRA team during that summer, but active involvement was then some years away.

Mary and Helena agreed to name the baby after Sean if it was a boy. Her son was born in Altnagelvin hospital on 15 October 1972. She had agreed with his grandmother that she would leave his upbringing entirely in her hands, as if he were her own son. Helena would be able to see him whenever she wished, but would allow the child to regard Mary as his mother.

She returned to Belfast on 1 November and with the understanding of her Department took up her studies again immediately. She remained in Belfast during the Christmas vacation, only spending Christmas Day itself in Derry, catching up on her course work. The next eighteen months passed quickly. She became a normal student, if there can be such a person, and returned to Cyprus for six weeks in July and August 1973, returning to Belfast early to begin her final year's study. Her final examinations were successfully negotiated in May 1974 when she obtained the only first-class degree on her course. Deciding to stay for the degree ceremony on 4 July, she went to Derry to spend some time with Mary and Sean. She was convinced that she had done the right thing. Little Sean was doing so well and Mary had regained some of her lost youth with her new family. Yes it was best for all three of them for her to stay away from the child and become a distant cousin who only occasionally saw him. While there she received an invitation to the South to renew her friendship with the people she had met two summers earlier. Being very grateful for the financial support she had received on a regular basis ever since, she was happy to accept and agreed to meet on Monday 15 July.

Clew Bay as seen from Westport Co. Mayo is one of the most beautiful scenes in the British Isles. It was while she was eating breakfast in a small hotel overlooking the bay with her three republican friends that she heard the news on RTE radio that there had been a Coup arranged by the Athens dictatorship in Cyprus earlier that morning. First reports said that President Makarios had been killed. Later in the day as she followed the story on the BBC World Service it became clear that he may have escaped to Paphos. Her immediate reaction was to return home to her family, but a few phone calls made it clear that this would not be easy. Nicosia airport was closed and even if it were not, it would be almost impossible to get a seat. She could fly to Athens and try to return by sea from there, but it was not certain. No, she would stay and fly back on 23 July as she had planned. The situation would be clearer then.

For the next few days her attention was two thousand miles away as much as her hosts tried to show her the delights of their native land, a land they were determined would one day be united, whatever it may take to achieve that aim. Then on 20 July came the news she had been dreading. The Turkish army had invaded and begun to divide her native land. From that moment she and her hosts had more in common than ever they had imagined. Their struggle to unite their divided islands, once under British rule, now nominally independent, would be joined together. The Emerald Aphrodite was born.

It was September before Helena saw Cyprus again. With Nicosia airport closed, she had made the long sea journey to Limassol from Athens. Her mother was safe, a refugee, but safe. However, her brother Dimetrios was missing and Philipos, her elder brother had been wounded. She did not know what the future would bring. Although she had her degree her job had been destroyed. She had been due to begin work as a poultry nutritionist at the largest integrated poultry production company on the island near Kyrenia on 1 September, but that dream lay in the ruins of that once fine enterprise. During her stop-over in Athens she had visited the Greek sister company, a partnership with the English feed manufacturer Spillers and poultry breeder, Ross. There the prospect of employment in Athens had been held out to her, once the company had reviewed its future plans following the disaster it had suffered. That suited her well enough, it allowed her time to help rescue the fortunes of her family, particularly her mother who had suffered and struggled enough.

Helena knew of her family's plight before she left Ireland after a series of difficult telephone calls to London, Athens and Nicosia. As she was leaving, her Republican hosts had given her a large bundle of ten pound sterling notes. It was a gift they had said, to help her rescue her family from disaster. She knew that one day she would be asked to repay that gift, but not with money, but in the circumstances of the summer of 1974 she was grateful to accept it. When she counted the money later, she found it amounted to more than ten thousand pounds.

"Use it wisely," they had said. "Build a future for you and your family."

During her stop-over in London she had deposited nine thousand pounds in a Barclays' external account, bought nine hundred pounds worth of travellers cheques and was still left with more than six hundred pounds in cash.

As she stepped off the ferry in Limassol she still had more than five hundred pounds in cash together with her travellers cheques. Even in early September, less than three weeks after the war had ended, Limassol was beginning to change. Overnight it had become the only port of entry, for people as well as goods. The dock area was chaos, but despite this, trade was beginning again. Food had to be imported, quickly.

Twenty percent of the population had stolen seventy percent of the agriculture, together with that year's harvest. A quarter of a million refugees were a sufficient problem in themselves, a shortage of food and medicine would cause famine and epidemic amongst the people who were needed to rebuild the nation.

Having plenty of cash to hand, not that she intended to waste it, she decided to find a taxi. Cyprus now had more taxis than ever; many refugees had managed to get out of the north with little more than the clothes on their back, and their car. That was their only asset, so they put it to work. It became a taxi overnight and its owner became a cabby. Many families began their journey back from the depths of despair by taxi.

Helena had no difficulty in finding a driver willing to take her to Paralimni, where her mother had sought refuge, despite the area still being considered as less than secure. Many still feared a final Turkish push to clear the south eastern corner of the island of Greek Cypriots. The journey took almost three hours. Life in Cyprus had not even begun to recover from the trauma of July and August. Many of the villages, such Leopetri had more than doubled their populations, and everyone seemed to be either on the streets or travelling the roads.

When mother and daughter met again after more than a year they hugged each other and both cried openly. Neither were concerned about lost property and belongings. A missing son and brother were all that they thought about.

"I just want to know whether he is dead or alive," cried her mother.

"Has there been any news about any of them, " asked Helena.

"Very little, they say that nearly three thousand are listed as missing. We don't know whether they are prisoners in hospital, or dead." she paused and held her daughter. " A few of them were seen being marched towards Kyrenia on the Turkish television, but only about twenty."

"Where was he lost?" asked Helena.

"Somewhere on the Nicosia - Larnaca road, trying to keep it open," she began to cry again, "it was after even ... those Turks," she had difficulty even voicing the word, "...had accepted the last cease-fire. They had agreed to stop fighting and they still wanted more..."

"What about Philipos?"

"He will be out of plaster this week. I will go and fetch him and take him...no I can't take him home, he has lost his flat .. Oh, Helena you seem so strong. I'm so glad you are home. You went away a girl and became a woman so quickly. I was sad the first time you came home, now I'm glad. Oh, Helena..."

Helena let her cry. She knew her mother had probably tried to be strong and not to show her feelings, just as she had in 1956. Now she seemed to feel she could let go. It was for the best.

Later Helena had said quietly, but firmly.

"Tomorrow I am taking you away from here. Away from the memories, away from where you can see where you lived. We will go to Nicosia and I will see what I can discover about Dimetrios. Then we will find somewhere to live. I have some money. Later we will visit Philipos and see when he can come home."

He mother nodded. Helena had taken over, she would always be the strong one now.

"You know Helena I'm so proud of you. With all this happening I haven't even told you. Your father would have been so proud, he was a farmer and you ... you have your degree in agriculture. For a son to follow in his father's footsteps is one thing, but it is really special when it is his daughter. Well done my girl. By the way did you learn to drive, because I did and that's the only thing I managed to bring with me, my car."

"Oh Mamma, you never told me you were driving and had your own car. Yes I learnt in the holidays. I have a Northern Ireland licence. We can drive to Nicosia tomorrow."

"I'm not sure," her mother said, "it's very difficult to get petrol now. To get any you have to pay a lot of money."

"That's OK I have money, I worked hard and managed to save a little." she said, not wanting to disclose how much she had, nor especially how she had obtained it.

The next morning they left early. Two months ago Nicosia was less than one hour away, now the journey took three hours via Larnaca and the crowded Nicosia to Limassol road.

Helena tried all she knew to gain information about her brother. Failing to learn anything from her own Government she even tried the British High Commission. Although sympathetic they knew nothing, but she did plead with them not to allow the Turkish Cypriots who had sought refuge in the Sovereign bases to leave for Turkey, or the north, without co-operation from Turkey on the question of missing persons and prisoners. Her plea fell on deaf ears. A few months later, without any concession or humanitarian gesture from Turkey, the Turkish Cypriots were embarked onto British naval vessels at Akrotiri and shipped to Turkey, from where they were ferried to the north of Cyprus. That episode, together with the failure of the British forces on the island to prevent or limit the invasion, which they could have readily done, was a cynical act of British Foreign Secretary James Callaghan. Had the Heath government remained in power a few extra months in 1974 and not been defeated in February 1974 there is little doubt in many Cypriots' minds that their island would still be united. Britain's failure to act in accordance with her treaty obligations to Cyprus demonstrated more than any other single act the depths of that country's decline in those pre Thatcherite days of despair.

With Nicosia so full of refugees it was also difficult to find an apartment. It seemed impossible. Empty property was occupied by the refugees, quite rightly Helena thought, they have nothing. The more she thought the more she became convinced there was only one answer. She had nine thousand pounds in London, why leave it there when they had nowhere to live. Her decision was made. In one afternoon she agreed the purchase of a house complete with furniture for five thousand pounds sterling from an elderly couple who had decided to join the rest of their family in London. A deal was done. Most of the payment would be made in sterling in London. To satisfy local authorities the legal transfer would be completed with five hundred of the travellers cheques she had. Not only were the couple delighted to sell to an eager buyer, they offered to share their home until they could find a way to leave.

So, from the second day of her arrival back in Cyprus, Helena had secured a home for her mother, herself and Philipos. They were one of the lucky families, they had a home, but how could they be happy with a missing son and brother. Was he alive, was he wounded, was he being tortured, would they ever see him again, would they ever know? Their new house was just off the main road into Nicosia from Limassol, near the Cyprus Hilton. To take their mind off their problems, and to celebrate their agreement Helena took her mother and the couple to the Hilton for a meal that evening. Although tinged with regret it did mark the end of the beginning as far as she was concerned.

The next morning they left for Paralimni to collect her mother's few possessions and later Philipos from hospital in Larnaca. His fracture had healed and his wounds had knitted together sufficiently for him to walk out unaided. He would need extensive physiotherapy to rid himself of crutches, but she could afford that too. How much she began to appreciate the help from that other divided Isle. Could she ever repay it? She knew the call would come, but not when and how.

Helena was determined to stay in Cyprus, not to move to Athens, as she had the prospect of doing, now her chance of work near Kyrenia was ended. But how would she find work with so many refugees and the economy devastated? There was no rush, but her money would not last for ever. What did she have to offer? A first class degree in agricultural science. What did Cyprus need to support the population? Food. There must be a way of marrying her expertise with her county's need. Indeed there was. She had spent some time during her final year in Northern Ireland with the Province's largest integrated poultry production company. They had helped her a great deal in providing facilities for her to complete her honours project in their company. She knew there was an unused capacity on their farms and factory just outside Dungannon, and decided to enter the import business with the little capital she had remaining.

The next week went quickly. By injecting her surplus cash held in London and after engaging in hard credit negotiations, of which she had no experience, with Dungannon, she had her order accepted. A first consignment of five thousand frozen chickens. It had been hard to persuade them to grant any credit at all since the British Export Guarantee Scheme had placed Cyprus on their blacklist, a bad credit risk. The hard nosed officials really did know how to hit someone hard when they were down, she thought. It was only her personal knowledge of the people that persuaded them to relent and take a commercial risk, without an export guarantee. Thirty percent down, with the remainder to be paid after thirty days were the terms she obtained. Hardly generous, but possible.

As soon as flights could be arranged and co-ordinated so that the transfer to the Viscount shuttle service to Larnaca could be organised through Athens, they arrived. Marketing presented little problem, demand was high. She engaged two school friends to handle distribution and within six months had succeeded in increasing her capital significantly and more importantly to her, helped her fellow citizens to find something to eat. But she was the first to recognise that the trade could not last. Home production was increasing again, so she diversified her sources and began to wholesale local produce through her established distribution channels. Through the years she never built a large business, but sought to exploit short term demands and as they began to be satisfied, changed track again. Despite her modest success she remained depressed at the future prospects. No progress was being made towards reuniting the island. The division began to seem ever more permanent, but there was always some hope. Discussions were always on the horizon, but nothing was ever achieved. When the airport agreement of May 1989 failed to be implemented she decided there was only one way forward, to begin to plan it herself. That meant money.

That same year she was delighted to agree to join her brother in a joint venture with an Englishman who knew Cyprus well. Although she could never trust the British after Derry, he was the best option to provide the new company with the necessary expertise. The international nature of the company would make it credible. It would also provide her with the legitimacy she now needed. Her import-export volumes were not sufficiently large to provide the sort of cover she was going to need. This was because she had been asked to find a way to repay her debt to the IRA. They wanted guns, ammunition and explosives. Helena's job was to find a way to supply these items to them through suitable external accounts and by providing shipment cover through totally legitimate exports out of Limassol port. The discovery of a consignment of arms aboard the Claudia the previous year had convinced them of two things. That they needed to buy from a 'clean' operator, otherwise leaks and information would seep back to London or Dublin; and that Limassol was still the best possible port to use, they had slipped up, but it could work. Helena was their answer.

She had largely financed what nominally began as her brother's business in its early days through an interest free loan to the company, and a second one to Philipos to enable him to purchase his share. The two Cypriots had thirty-five percent each, the Englishman had the maximum allowed to be allocated to a non-Cypriot, thirty percent. Her role, right from the start, had been that of financial director, but she had also taken on the control of the administrative affairs of the whole business. She was thus in the best possible position to launder IRA money and provide cover for the export of arms to Ireland.

CHAPTER THREE

The Tristar climbed through the September drizzle and headed towards the climbing sun. It was powered by Rolls Royce engines, the very same engines that had been saved from the liquidator by the uncharacteristic nationalisation of one of her predecessors in 1971. She allowed herself a wry smile, was it through thinking of her colleagues managing without her, or was it a smile of anticipation?

Clare had succeeded. She had slipped away almost unnoticed. It had been very difficult to arrange and typical of the woman that she had done it herself and not relied upon others to arrange it for her. A late evening trip to the 'tied cottage' in the Chilterns was not unusual. A 7 a.m. departure from Chequers in her own 1970s TR7 had left everyone, including her detectives, guessing. Despite their efforts Clare's planning had paid off. She had lost them in the Chiltern lanes as they had attempted to follow her at a discreet distance. She had taken the M40 at High Wycombe, joined the M25, then the M4, and was in Heathrow before her shadow had left Penn. She took her bag and left the car in the Terminal One short-stay car park, walked, not to the VIP lounge, but to the British Airways office next to their ticket sales desk in Terminal One, and found Ray Whitehead waiting for her as arranged.

Clare Spencer was to most of her country a truly remarkable young woman. She was of average height, not too slim, but fit in both mind and body. In all she did she presented an air of cheerful confidence. Her rather dark blond hair contrasted with her light blue eyes which alone were sufficient to gain her the attention of everyone she met. Aged only thirty-seven, she was the United Kingdom's second woman Prime Minister and the first of her sex to come from the Liberal Democratic Party, or any of its many predecessors. Her rise to power had been meteoric. Finding herself at thirty-five, single and an out of work victim of the previous Government's program of closure of small rural schools, she had allowed herself to be persuaded to stand as a Liberal Democrat candidate in a by-election, held soon after the General Election, in her home constituency of North Avonside. Having played an active role in her local Party for much of her adult life, beginning in the heady days of the Alliance, persuading her had not been a difficult task. It was the dismal showing of the Liberal Democrat candidate in the General Election that had caused the local Party to seek a new candidate. Following the 1983 General Election the Government had suffered a series of reverses, the most notable having been the loss of the Trade Minister, the Party Chairman who had guided them through the election campaign, followed two years later by Westland and the loss of two more Cabinet Ministers. Then in 1990, in the midst of turmoil over the so-called Poll Tax and European integration, Margaret Thatcher, Prime Minister for more than eleven years, had been cynically ejected and replaced by the softer face of capitalism. By comparison with more recent events, each those episodes had been, in the words of a former Prime minister 'a little local difficulty'. Such was the climate, and being able to marshal all their resources into one constituency, the Liberal Democrats had been determined to win and further embarrass the Government. It had not helped the Government's cause that the reason for the by-election was the forced resignation from the Cabinet and Parliament of the previous MP.

Shocked as she was to find herself suddenly catapulted from being an unemployed teacher to the only woman Liberal Democrat MP she threw herself into her new role immediately. She was never out of the headlines, partly because she was news, mainly because she made a very attractive picture.

Clare had her own policies and beliefs. She believed in the market economy with a human face. She knew it was necessary to generate the wealth necessary to provide the sort of education and social services she wanted. To some, her evangelical promotion of an entrapreneurial spirit was almost 'Thatcherite' in its vigour, to her it was the key to providing the Government income she wanted to spend. Although several of her policies were portrayed as right-wing by her opponents, it was her belief that the main hindrance to a wealth-generation philosophy in Britain was inherited wealth. From her own experience she knew that the best brains were anaethetised by being sent through the public school system and into the Establishment. The security provided to them by their parents' wealth resulting in little need to make their own individual contribution to the generation of wealth. In the Establishment they talked and compromised, devised positions, but made little happen. It was no accident that many of the new businesses that had developed to become household names, had as their prime motivating force, someone from outside the Establishment, someone who had not inherited wealth and power.

Her policies were designed to end once and for all the class-based system and included the re-introduction of a capital transfer tax, but this time one that actually worked, one that made it virtually impossible to pass on wealth to the next generation, not one that could be by-passed. Secondly she had advocated the abolition of all tax allowances and employee national insurance contributions, using the money saved to reduce tax rates to a lower band at the same level as VAT, and a higher rate at 25%. Tax would be payable on every penny of income, just as it was on a box of matches. Additionally she had suggested the abolition of child benefit, which had its history as a tax allowance, for children over five years old, and instead, replacing it with the payment of an educational voucher to all parents which could be used at any school, including private ones.

The overall aim of this group of policies was to make it necessary for every individual to reach his or her full potential, to generate their own wealth. No one would be able to have an easy life on the basis of inherited wealth. By introducing low tax rates everyone would have the incentive to achieve high disposable incomes. To break the Establishment, just as the Unions had been broken during the eighties, she would make it possible for all to afford the Public Schools, so that only the best brains were accepted. All these policies were important to her, but not her driving force, which remained her deep desire to create a peaceful world and to find a way to rid mankind of weapons of mass destruction and war. Her involvement in direct action had ended, not because she was any less committed, but because she had become disillusioned with such methods, believing success would only come through constitutional political action.

When, within a few months of her election her Party leader had had to resign in tragic circumstances, she was nominated in the leadership election by a group with whom she was sympathetic and who were determined at all costs to prevent one of the leading members of the Party, whom they disliked, from being elected. In their view Clare would split his vote. Not only did she split his vote, she captured the votes of the ordinary party members who comprised the electoral college leadership election system of the British Liberal Democratic Party, the nearest in British politics to that found in America. So she astonished all political observers by becoming a party leader almost as soon as becoming an MP, and she was only thirty-six years of age.

The rest of her rise to power was perhaps even more remarkable. Naturally her election brought her and her Party even more public attention. The Party's standing, as measured by opinion polls, continued to rise and was standing at a little over thirty percent when another unexpected General Election was called. The scandal that had led to the by-election and her entry into Parliament did not die away, it got worse. It could not be shrugged off, it became like Watergate. But now the Government only had a slender majority. During the final winter of that Parliament the Government had been so preoccupied with these problems that the Unions had totally reasserted and rekindled their power. The Prime Minister had had no alternative but to call a General Election early in May, to coincide with the 1994 Local Elections.

Of the 630 seats in the House of Commons, 250 of them

were won by the Liberal Democrats, 189 were won by Labour, 157 by the Conservatives, 12 by the Scottish Nationalists, with the rest taken by the Ulstermen and others. The Conservative Prime Minister's seat was lost in the biggest electoral disaster ever for the Party in southern England and the Government resigned at once. The Queen duly invited Clare Spencer, the leader of the largest single Party to form a Government, an invitation Clare was happy, but overwhelmed, to accept.

From the moment of her adoption as a Liberal Democrat candidate for a 'safe' Conservative seat, to her call to the Palace had been less than eighteen months. Never had anyone risen so quickly with so few problems. Never had anyone so inexperienced been asked to form a Government in modern times. It took her a full two weeks to get an agreement on the formation of a majority Government, she had been most unwilling to risk losing everything so soon by going to the House with a minority Government. Neither of the old major Parties were initially willing to join her band of totally inexperienced Liberal Democrats. It did not help that the Conservatives were without a leader in Parliament. There were discussions between Labour and Conservative about the possibility of forming a 'Grand Coalition" in order to keep out the Centre. They both knew that one of the first pieces of legislation they were committed to introduce was proportional representation. If this were to go through then it was unlikely that either of them would ever again be able to form a single-party Government.

Clare spent the first week after the election in talks with the Labour party, they at least had a leader with whom she could talk. Their talks were very difficult, common ground was hard to find, certainly for a Parliament that would last more than a few months. Clare knew that she needed much longer than that since she fully expected the Conservatives would find a new leader and would recover much of their lost ground in an early election. She had to prove that a Liberal Democrat led Coalition Government could and would work, for this she needed a few years, not months.

The breakthrough came when a former Conservative Cabinet Minister, still an MP, with a newly enhanced reputation and stature after the humiliation of his Party's last Government, from which he had been sacked, led a delegation of like-minded members to the Prime Minister Elect. He persuaded her that there were more than 75 Conservatives who would support him in backing her, rather than seeking a Grand Coalition with Labour, with whom they had nothing in common. Personally supporting proportional representation on the grounds that an extreme Government of either persuasion would not then be possible, he felt that enough support could be found to form a majority Government. A deal was done. Ex-Defence Minister Edmund Stead became Foreign Secretary - and within two weeks officially leader of his Party, and a new Government, a genuine Liberal Democrat/Conservative coalition, was formed. Clare relied on Edmund's support in putting together the Cabinet and eventually agreed on ten Liberal Democrats and nine Conservatives. The Deputy leader of her own party, and her former rival, Dr Roger Evans, became her Chancellor of the Exchequer.

Clare had arranged to meet Ray Whitehead at Heathrow since she knew him from her University days in Bristol when they had once been quite close friends. He had dropped out of teacher training to join British Airways as a computer operator and was now the personnel manager responsible for cabin staff at Heathrow. Clare had invited Ray to Downing Street a few days earlier on the pretext of asking him to meet and assist a Commonwealth airline chief seeking British assistance in recruiting pilots. Clare had explained to Ray that she was making a trip on Friday and wanted to do so without any attendant publicity, she just wanted a few days holiday away without the Press following her everywhere. Ray had arranged to be in the particular office she headed for, which was well away from the patrol of the resident Press Association correspondent, seeking news of the comings and goings of prominent people.

She pinned on the BA pass Ray had arranged for her, lifted her lightly curled hair under the flat BA regulation female hat, added a pair of dark glasses and walked across the concourse, Ray carrying her suitcase. They seemed to the casual observer like any other two staff members carrying out their normal routine and reached Gate 23 ten minutes before boarding would begin for BA 583 to Larnaca.

The 09.00 hrs Tristar to Cyprus was not fully booked. Less than 150 reservations had been made and there would be a dozen or so standby passengers. For most people the holiday season was over, but the airlines kept their full summer capacity on this route until towards the end of October. Ray had blocked her a group of six seats in the Club Class so she would not be obliged to enter into casual conversation with other passengers. He had also decided it was necessary to take the crew of the Tristar into his confidence. BA crews knew that they had to be discreet about certain passengers, so this was not an usual request. Ray had emphasised the importance in this instance by implying that crews that couldn't be trusted not to disclose such information might be more appropriately transferred to serve a few months on the Belfast shuttle service. It was not necessary for him to have said more.

The doors were closed and she settled into a port side window seat and relaxed for the first time that morning, reflecting upon how she had managed to escape for this week away. Oh, how she was looking forward to it.

It is not easy for a Prime Minister to delegate everything, but she had insisted. By forging a Coalition Government she had effectively had to accept two powerful deputies, one from her own Party, vastly more experienced than herself, the other from the Conservatives; the Chancellor of the Exchequer and the Secretary of State for Foreign Affairs respectively.

On Wednesday she had arranged a late evening working

dinner for the three of them. They had dealt with the problems of the past few weeks, when each of the other had had a holiday, and had looked forward to any obvious potential problems that might occur while she herself was away. Towards the end, after coffee had been served she astonished them both by announcing;

"From the time I leave here on Thursday evening to my return on the Saturday of next week I am determined to have a real break, to get away from everything and everybody and recharge my batteries. Under no circumstances should anyone, least of all either of you, try to contact me; in any case it is my fervent hope that no-one will be able to find me if they should wish to contact me."

"That's most unusual, in fact without precedent". faltered Edmund Stead, "You can't mean it."

"I do mean it, I'm quite determined."

Her Deputy Leader, former Foreign Secretary himself, Dr Roger Evans, thought to himself that at long last it would be he, he whose ambition for the job she held had no bounds, who would be in charge. Remembering the phrase of one former Prime Minister 'A week is a long time in politics' his mind began to race through the decisions he could take and actions he could start that she would find impossible to stop on her return.

Clare continued,

"To put either of you in charge would be wrong. If it were Edmund, then rightly the Coalition as a whole would feel betrayed that I had handed the Government back to the Tory's. If it were Roger it would be equally wrong since Edmund's party agreed to serve in my Government and some of them, with all due respect to you Roger, would not serve you."

"I have decided that you will jointly be in control. The Cabinet Office will be informed that only instructions which they know to be decisions of you both will be implemented. The Press will also be so informed - after I have left - so they do not pursue me to see where I am going, before I've left.

This announcement was greeted in silence, then Edmund said,

"Very well, Prime Minister, it is not the way I would have dealt with this matter, but I respect your right to do it in your way and I fully understand your desire to get away for a truly private holiday. I can disappear on the estate, but you haven't got that opportunity."

"Prime Minister, we are partners, not only in Government, but in the Coalition. Now you are handing over half of this job to the leader of a Party who was our enemy in the election. I must protest and ask you to reconsider not delegating your authority to myself, your real partner."

"Roger, you do protest too much. My decision is final.

The next day Clare wrote the Press announcement concerning her holiday and called Edmund over so she could hand it personally to him. Of the two deputies it was Edmund she really trusted and admired. She knew all about Roger and what he would have attempted had she left her Chancellor in sole charge.

The Press statement said,

"The Prime Minister, The Rt. Hon. Clare Spencer, MP, is on holiday. She left Downing Street at 8 p.m. yesterday for an undisclosed destination. In her absence she has delegated all, and she wishes to emphasise the word 'all', her duties and functions jointly to Edmund Stead, Foreign Secretary and Roger Evans, Chancellor. Any matters requiring Prime Ministerial decisions will be taken by these two men acting jointly, or will await the Prime Minister's return to Downing Street. The Prime Minister has instructed her staff and her colleagues not to attempt to contact her during her absence. She has not informed them where she will be spending her holiday.

"The Prime Minister wishes it to be known that she believes it to be essential that in order for her to be able to carry out her duties that she be enabled to have at least one week per year to herself, and that such a break will ensure she is able to serve more effectively for the remainder of the year. In this context she asks that the Press make no attempt to find her, and warns that if this request is not heeded, then all reporters and journalists from any organisation on who's behalf attempts are made to locate her, will be excluded from all Governmental and Party briefings for a period of twelve months.

"The Prime Minister undertakes to listen to the BBC News at least once each day and in case of National or International emergency will return or make contact with her colleagues immediately.

"Her Majesty the Queen, on holiday at Balmoral, has been advised personally by the Prime Minister of the Prime Minister's statement and wishes."

"You can't really mean you are going to issue this," said an astonished Edmund Stead.

Clare smiled at him and said softly in her most seductive manner,

"No, you will issue it for me, at precisely 10 o'clock tomorrow morning."

Knowing there was absolutely no doubt that she meant every word he nodded, and murmured,

"We came together in the most difficult circumstances and I know you have been more than fair to me so I will follow your wishes. And Clare, I do hope you enjoy yourself, you deserve it after the last six months," he smiled.

Spontaneously she did something she had never done before with or to any of her political colleagues. She threw her arms around the neck of an astonished Edmund Stead and kissed him fully on the lips. They were together a fraction longer than she had intended, she really liked and admired him and was thanking him for everything. He froze, not knowing whether to respond or draw back.

"Sorry if I embarrassed you," she smiled impishly, "I just couldn't resist you."

He cleared his throat, tried to look serious and began to move towards the door, saying,

"At 10 a.m. sharp tomorrow morning, unless I hear from you to the contrary, this statement will be in the hands of your Press Office."

With that he shuffled out, not knowing quite what to think. It is one thing having yet another woman as Prime Minister, its quite another having a young sexy one, he thought to himself.

On Thursday evening Clare phoned Her Majesty at Balmoral telling her what she intended, offering to tell the Queen exactly where she was going. The offer was not taken up, Clare was wished every joy while away with an understanding of how she felt. Did she detect a touch of envy in the voice from Scotland?

Her staff knew she was going on holiday. All they knew was that late in the evening she would be leaving for Chequers. She had packed only two suitcases, one larger than the other, plus a much smaller overnight bag. Her staff saw these cases into her official Jaguar and it was almost 8.30 p.m. when the sleek black car paused for the gates at the end of Downing Street to be opened, so that it could leave and enter Whitehall.

Fifty minutes later it swept through the gates of the magnificent country house, set on the north western edge of the Chiltern Hills to the north west of London. As they were travelling along the drive Clare leaned forward and spoke softly to her trusted personal chauffeur, Anne Davis,

"Anne, don't drive up to the front door, go round the back first, I want to see if my car is OK and put one of my cases into it to save taking them both into the house."

Sure enough her bright red 1977 Triumph TR7 was still there looking quite immaculate. The previous weekend she had taken it out of the garage and deliberately left it outside, making sure no keys were available for anyone to move it back inside. As soon as the car stopped she got out, opened the car, returned to the Jaguar and selected the largest of her suitcases from the boot and placed it carefully in the TR7, making sure it was locked securely. Just as she was getting into the official car again someone came out of the house and politely enquired why they had come to the back.

"Just wanted something in my car," said Clare cheerfully, being careful to be ambiguous, not untruthful.

Waking early, Clare threw the things she needed into her overnight shoulder bag, dressed and quickly ran downstairs, saw no-one, and was speeding down the drive in her car within another minute, much to the consternation of the detective mandated with the job of being her shadow, who was not expecting her to drive off without warning. It was another two minutes before his white Rover sped down the drive after her.

Knowing her detective would not lose sight of her if he could avoid it she had meticulously planned her route last Sunday afternoon, but had avoided travelling along the exact route and had made sure a different detective had been on duty from the one she expected to be her shadow on Friday morning. Part of her plan involved cutting through a private housing estate at Hazlemere, near High Wycombe, when she knew she was out of sight, then skirting Penn she dropped down to the A40, turned back through Wycombe before joining the M40, by then she was well away. Her detective had totally lost her and was in Amersham before he realised he had.

She decided to make one phone call from Heathrow while she was getting ready in the small BA office. Although she would have preferred to call Edmund she called Roger to make him feel important and gave him one last instruction, to make certain that her detective, who she quite liked as a man, was not disciplined in any way for losing her. She would deal with the matter at a higher level on her return and did not want this one junior detective to be made the scapegoat. Detectives shadowing Prime Ministers did not expect to be deliberately lost in the way she had used.

Clare knew that she couldn't hope to escape for as long as a week. She knew that not only the Press, but the Security Services, would make every endeavour to trace her and would succeed. But, she did hope that she would have a few hours, if possible a few days. That there would be no fuss on arrival and that she would get to her destination without her normal entourage. That would be something, she thought. There was another reason. Before becoming Prime Minister she had been one the fiercest critics of the Security Services. She had hated them since her Aldermaston days. Nothing was going to give her greater pleasure than causing them to suffer the embarrassment of losing her. She might even use it against them now they worked for her, on the basis that if they couldn't even organise the security of the Prime Minister, then radical change at the top was necessary.

She gave Ray the keys to her car and asked him to call Chequers the next day and have someone collect it.

Clare had studied at Bristol University. It was there that she had met graduate student Richard Rowland. They had been more than close friends for much of their time together. Clare had been an undergraduate while Richard had been studying for his Doctorate. They had found themselves neighbours after her first term and had become very close. Clare had been active in Union politics and had been much more radical and left wing at that time. In particular she had been very active in campaigning for nuclear disarmament before Cruise Missiles became an issue at a time when this cause did not receive much public attention.

After University she had remained in Bristol to complete her teacher training, then obtained a post in the small town of Thornbury, north-west of the city. Richard had left Bristol before Clare finished her training, having married a girl they had both known well as a friend and had moved to Northumbria. She had cried for days when she discovered that he had married. He had only really started a romantic attachment to his new wife after Clare had refused to fly off to Spain with him for Easter, preferring instead to help keep up the dwindling numbers at the Aldermaston demonstration. After their row she had not seen him again until he had been married six months and his wife Barbara was expecting their first child.

She had obtained a more senior post in a smaller school five miles to the east. After two terms they had decided to close her school. Clare had led a campaign trying to organise demonstrations and petitions, but all to no avail. The teachers in employment were too frightened for their own jobs to have supported her campaign.

Throughout her teaching career Clare had continued to live in the Clifton area of Bristol, a village within a city that she had grown to love during her student days. Despite some close encounters she had never married and had begun to worry that she may never find anyone to compare with Richard. He had never asked her to marry him, perhaps he had been too frightened of her tough personality, exhilarating in short bursts, but easy to live with? She knew Richard had thought not. There was no doubt though that they had loved each other. Anyone who had seen them together, first as students, then later during Richard's frequent trips to the West Country, both before and after he had become involved in Cyprus, would have concluded that they had a deep love for each other. They would have been right. Now at last she had agreed to spend some time with him in Cyprus. The fact that she was doing it just as secretly as he was, made the anticipation even stronger.

Once the seat belt signs had been switched off, she took off her BA hat and pass. The flight was uneventful with a smooth touchdown just before 2 p.m. local time.

CHAPTER FOUR

Sir Rodney Longbotham, head of the Security Services, picked up the phone and listened with an expressionless face. He was horrified at what he learnt.

Thirty minutes earlier he had received a visitor, the Cabinet Secretary Sir Mark Salisbury, who he invited to join him for morning coffee. Sir Mark had begun by handing Sir Rodney the Press statement at that moment being printed on the Press Association's teletype machine, which within the hour would be broadcast on the 12 noon news summaries around the country. Clare Spencer had done it again, this time though it was not that she had made news by her presence, but by her absence.

The information he had just received was the second piece of disturbing news that had reached Sir Rodney that morning and it was no surprise when Sir Mark enquired after he had replaced the 'phone:

"How on earth did your people manage to lose the PM in the Chilterns this morning? It is profoundly disturbing that we seem unable to keep tabs on our own PM. What hope is there when we try to keep tabs on other people's?"

"When we are keeping someone under surveillance we do not lose people. But we do not expect our own PM to deliberately try to lose her shadow at 7 a.m. in the morning. If anyone is determined enough they can lose one car, it seems the stupid bitch accomplished that with some ease."

Sir Mark asked what progress was being made in trying to re establish contact with the PM. It did not occur to him that he was taking it for granted that this should be done, and that there was no question of acceding to her wishes and not attempting to trace her.

Sir Rodney answered the unasked question.

"Of course we must find her. We shan't let her know we have found her when we do, but find her we must. What if someone else, someone hostile, found her first and took advantage of the situation, with us having no clue as to her whereabouts. It would make us look real fools, and worse. No, for the reputation of the Service we must know where she is and observe her until she returns. I don't care about her, but I do care about the reputation of the Service."

"Quite so. Where do we start?"

Sir Rodney ignored the word 'we'.

"I have already started and narrowed it down very considerably. She lost my man north of High Wycombe. From there she could, and probably did join the M40, either towards the M25 or Oxford. She did not pass the A41 junction with the M25, or join the Oxford Bypass. There was an accident on the M25 just south of the A41 turnoff and she couldn't have got through there before we arrived. I had men at the A40 - Oxford Ring Road junction before she could have reached it. That leaves the M25 to the south. I don't think she would be heading to London, wants to get away from there after all, so that leaves the M4 to the west, the south coast, Heathrow or Gatwick. Have asked the Airport Authority for passenger lists of all flights out of both airports between 8 and 11 a.m. this morning. Expecting them at any moment now. Special Branch in Bristol has been alerted and are covering the motorways and having her old haunts in that part of the world thoroughly checked."

"I'll leave the matter in your hands then. Better return and try to keep the peace between Edmund Stead and Roger Evans, Evans is hopping mad that she didn't leave it all to him, then she had the cheek to phone him just after 8 a.m. telling him to make sure her detective didn't get in trouble for losing her."

"What time did you say she rang."

"Just after eight."

"Don't suppose he got any clue where she was phoning from?"

"None at all."

"I'll wager it was from one of the airports, probably Heathrow at that time."

Fifteen minutes later Sir Rodney was staring at the passenger list of BA 583. A phone call to Heathrow and some not so gentle pressure by a Special Branch man based there had extracted an admission from BA's personnel manager at Heathrow that he had assisted the Prime Minister to evade detection and was amongst the passengers on the list he had in front of him. He made a call, on the secure satellite link, to one of the British sovereign bases on Cyprus.

It would be touch and go whether Charles Noble, holding a unique position in British Intelligence, seconded to Cyprus with the rank of Captain in the Royal Marines, based at Akrotiri, would have time to reach Larnaca before the plane landed, so that he could follow her and determine the final destination. It was possible she might be intending to fly on to Cairo on the Cyprus Airways 14.35 hrs. flight, being a history graduate she might be planning to visit the ancient sites in Egypt.

After Sir Mark had left, Sir Rodney walked to the cabinet, reserved for times of stress, and poured himself a large vodka. The news he had just heard over the telephone had been bad. The worst. It seemed that when he received the message to hasten to Larnaca, Charles Noble had been on the point of transmitting a report based upon his carefully constructed intelligence network that the Cyprus Liberation Movement, the CLM, a Nationalist organisation they knew little about, were preparing to take action of somekind that weekend. He did not know all the details, only that a large number of off-duty Greek Cypriot National Guard servicemen were gathering near Paralimni that evening on the orders of the leadership of the CLM, not for their health he was sure. With next week's United Nations General Assembly debate on Cyprus due, for which half the Greek Cypriot Government were already in New York, he believed the CLM maybe planning something spectacular. And now Clare Spencer would be likely to be there.

"What a mess." he thought.

Charles Noble was a rather special sort of man. He had been the first man ashore on the Falklands, if Pebble Island counted as part of the Falklands. The Special Boat Squadron had been his aim, even during his undergraduate days at Edinburgh University, where he collected a first in electrical engineering on an Navy scholarship. Brought up in Tobermoray on the island of Mull, islands and boats, of all kinds had always been his fascination and after serving his two years in the Navy to honour his obligation he had achieved his transfer. Setting foot on that island, north of West Falkland in 1982, was almost a boyhood dream come true, but much colder. He had watched every film he could find on the war in the Pacific from 1942 to 1945, fascinated by the way first one side, then the other, had hopped from one island to the next. Now it was his turn.

What irony it had been. With the Argentine base well alight, totally destroyed, lit by blazing Pucaras and fuel, he had fallen badly into a large ditch in the soft water-logged ground. Running at speed as he had been, the crack as his leg crumpled beneath him had been audible to those of his colleagues within fifty yards. It was a dejected and despondent Charles Noble who had sat on Ascension Island three days later, his leg now in plaster, but still very painful. It had seemed a world away from that early morning raid. He knew then there would never be another for him.

Ten weeks later, when it was all over his C.O. visited him at Stoke Mandeville Orthopaedic hospital.

"Now Charles how are you?"

"Can't wait to get out of this place and back to work, sir."

He knew then, although he wouldn't admit it even to himself that it was the end of his adventure in the SBS. He might always have a limp, his leg would not recover either its movement or its strength. His C.O. knew too, and he knew his C.O. would know. After a few minutes of polite conversation the C.O. said:

"Charles, I know what this leg business must mean to you. Believe me I really do, same thing nearly happened to me in

South Armagh, but I was lucky. I also know how valuable the rest of you can be to your country. I've arranged for a friend of mine to visit you tomorrow morning, rather odd chap really. Don't get angry with him, just listen to what he has to say. If you like 'phone me afterwards, here's my home number. Goodbye Charles, I'm proud that you served under me, your action on Pebble Island, before your injury, probably saved hundreds of lives of our men. Those Pucaras would have wreaked havoc at Goose Green."

The next day a young middle-aged man with steel rimmed glasses, and dressed in a top of the range Marks and Spencer grey suit, sat down alongside him.

"I'm Henry Johnson, Bob Chandler asked me to drop in for a chat," the accent was unmistakenly Liverpool. "Let me say something about me first, don't expect you to jump at a scouse offering you a job blind. Was in the Marines, got thrown out 'cause I couldn't see in the dark. Got sent to Cheltenham, GCHQ, they thought I could hear even if I couldn't see. Bob was my first C.O. Known him ever since. If he says you're good, then that's good enough for me. Didn't want to let them invalid you out, so he transferred you to MI6. When you get out catch the first train to Cheltenham. Ask for me."

With that he got up and left before Charles had a chance to catch his breath to say anything.

Charles had done exactly as Henry had told him, he hadn't much choice, he needed a job and with no experience of civilian life after university, with so many unemployed, he would not have found that easy; in any case he had been transferred, so was actually employed by MI6. Four years later, in 1986, he had been sent to Cyprus, still employed officially by MI6, as he was operating abroad, but with a direct link to the head of MI5. As cover he had been given a Commission in the Royal Marines. His primary objective had been to ensure that there was no penetration of the sensitive listening facilities there. His work had routed out two separate rings of Soviet bloc infiltration into the local staff of the bases, his only failure had been his inability to get sufficient evidence to secure the conviction of the servicemen involved in one of these rings. It was he, through the extensive networks of contacts he had developed, who had first reported to London on the formation and ideals of the CLM.

Nevertheless his primary objective had always been a return to full fitness and active service, a dream he had never lost. His chance had come in the summer of 1990. Following the breakdown of the attempt by Saudi Arabia to mediate between Iraq and Kuwait he had warned London on 1 August that an attack on Kuwait was imminent. He had gone further, much further than the CIA, and warned that the attack would not be limited to the capture of the disputed oilfield and islands at the head of the Gulf, but would attempt to seize the whole of Kuwait and incorporate that small state into Iraq itself. It brought no satisfaction to him to have been proved correct. Indeed he had been very angry to learn that a British Airways flight had been allowed to land in Kuwait at almost exactly the hour he had predicted would see the start of the invasion. Nevertheless he had not expected this single event would have led to his spending the next six or seven months away from Cyprus, playing a vital role in the liberation of Kuwait.

To him it had been tinged with irony that he had been based in a small country that had, sixteen years earlier, itself suffered an invasion condemned by numerous Security Council resolutions, but that he had been transferred to help implement similar, but more recent such resolutions calling for the liberation of another small country that had similarly been invaded by a more powerful neighbour. Charles had been ordered to join his old unit as civilian liaison officer. He was the link between the intelligence services and the military, being one of the very few who understood both and knew how vital each was to the other. He had not been expected to become involved in any action himself. Nevertheless he did. Partly through choice, partly through circumstances. On the night of 20 February 1991, less than sixty hours before the land war was to begin, he had found himself ashore in Kuwait City. While most of the Special Forces in his sector were concentrating their efforts on confusing the Iraqis into believing an amphibious assault was imminent, he had already landed on a very special mission, a mission that was being undertaken at the direct and specific request of the Emir himself.

The image of Kuwait in the eyes of the outside world had become the twin landmarks of the Kuwait Towers. Two large futuristic towers holding large globes over the sea-front. One was a simple water tower, the other held two globes high into the sky, one of which carried a revolving restaurant and the country's television transmitter. The Kuwait Government knew the oilfields would be set alight by the enemy before they withdrew, and could do little to prevent this from happening. They also had reason to believe that their primary landmarks and their main drinking water facility, would suffer a similar fate and be destroyed, making normal life in their desert kingdom impossible. This they took every step to prevent.

It had taken Charles twenty-four hours, but he had succeeded in defusing all the charges in and around the twin towers in such a manner that his work was not readily noticed and the charges were not re-set. Then under the cover of darkness he had slipped quietly into the strangely deserted British Embassy, where he had sat out the last few days of the liberation and retreat of the defeated Iraqi forces. He himself was liberated on the following Wednesday, the day the Kuwaiti forces had re-entered the city, by men from his own unit. The only publicity this had ever received was the announcement on the same day that a group of British marines had entered the Embassy to clean it up and make it ready for the return of the Ambassador. At the time it had seemed strange that this had been seen as a priority of the marines, but to provide added justification for their presence the British Prime Minister had publicly announced, when welcoming the liberation, that the Ambassador would indeed return the very next day.

Having returned to his previous post in Cyprus he had become regarded as an invaluable link to the always potentially unstable region he monitored. Now it seemed he would again become closer to a return to active service than he had anticipated. It had not been until almost 1 p.m. local time, 11 a.m. in London, that Charles had received his call from Sir Rodney. He had been horrified to learn that the PM was en route to Cyprus that very day. What a time to choose, he thought. Not wanting to waste time, he had listened to Sir Rodney's instructions that he was to get to Larnaca, follow the PM, and discover her final destination. He had not discussed the report he had been preparing to send to London, except to say that a report relevant to today's events was being prepared for transmission and that Sir Rodney should read it himself as quickly as possible, as soon as it was received over the secure facsimile line at Cheltenham via the MoD satellite. With that he ended the conversation, picked up Steve Bradshaw, his young assistant and potential replacement in Cyprus, jumped into his Rover, which left at high speed in the direction of Larnaca.

The British sovereign bases on Cyprus cover 99 square miles along the southern coastline of the island. One is at Dhekelia, just to the east of Larnaca, the other complex of bases is west of Limassol, the largest being Akrotiri, the only one able to be effectively sealed off from the rest of the island. Dhekelia borders both the Greek and Turkish Cypriot sectors and the only route to the holiday resorts of the south eastern corner lies through its heart. A similar situation exists in respect of Episkopi to the west of Limassol, the only main route to the south of the Troodos mountains to the developing resorts of the south and north west of the island, Paphos, the Baths of Aphrodite, Pissouri and Petra tou Romiou, passes through that base. It was for these reasons, and the facilities that could be provided at Akrotiri, that Charles Noble had insisted he be based there. He wanted to be able to ensure he could not be observed carrying out his work.

Akrotiri was unfortunately for Charles the wrong side of Limassol, rather than joining the Paphos motorway at Kolossi he made the mistake of deciding to go through the town. The expansion of Limassol since 1974 had been to many Cypriots beyond belief, it was said that they had built a new, bigger, Famagusta at Limassol. Even before then it was one of the few towns where the original bypass, built years earlier, had become the main shopping street. The area by-passed, the port area of Limassol was now less crowded than the old bypass itself. Well aware of this fact Charles left the base, first headed towards Kolossi, the site of the castle featuring on many souvenirs of Cyprus, turned right at Phasouri continued through the citrus groves, since the salisbury of Morphou in 1974 the best orange and gratefruit growing area left to the Greek Cypriots, and into the old part of Limassol close to the old port. Just as he had negotiated the old Turkish Cypriot sector of Limassol, now mainly occupied by Greek Cypriot refugees and their families and littered with small businesses repairing and making most items one could imagine, and was about to pass the Amathus Navigation building across the road from the seafront, he met his first real problem: a convoy of six slow moving container lorries leaving the port area and passing, in the outside lane of the harbour road, a continuous line of parked cars in the inside lane. With a steady stream heading towards him there was no way past for Charles, until they reached the traffic lights a few hundred yards before the Churchill Hotel. Rather than following the lorries to the left, taking the shortest route to the Limassol - Nicosia highway, he took the outside lane at the lights and carried straight on past the Churchill, through the main tourist area of Limassol, before turning left towards the motorway, just before he reached the Amathus Beach, probably the best beach hotel in the Mediterranean.

It had taken him more than thirty minutes to reach that point from leaving his office and it was now 1.25 p.m., only thirty-five minutes before the scheduled touch down of BA 583. He had forty-three miles to go, thirty-five on the dual carriageway. As he left the Nicosia motorway at Kophinou he had twenty minutes left for the final eighteen miles, but his average speed would be reduced. Allowing for customs and baggage he might just have enough time for his purposes. Despite its status as an international airport Larnaca had not been served by noticeably better roads than it had been in 1974 until 1991. Too much permanency could have given the impression that the Government never expected to recover Nicosia airport. Then the highway to Limassol had been hurriedly constructed. Unfortunately for Charles the section closest to Larnaca had been built in such haste that it had been closed earlier that year for urgent repairs. Six miles from Larnaca he had to return to the old road.

Nearer Larnaca, between the old Limassol road and the sea, was Larnaca free port. A consignment of Israeli figs had been received by one Cypriot entrepeneur two days earlier. By working his packing plant for forty-five hours continuously, two containers had been filled with crates containing boxes of figs that would soon be filling the supermarket shelves of Jeddah and Riyadh. Labelled 'Aphrodite' and stamped 'Produce of Cyprus' such operations were one of the commonest ways round the boycott by most Arab states of any Israeli goods or products. Neither the opening of trading relations with Egypt after the Camp David accord, nor the Gulf War of 1991, had interrupted this lucrative trade. Many Cypriot businessmen had amassed large fortunes by creating an acceptable origin for all types of Israeli goods, then exporting them to the Arab world. Such trade was no secret, both sides saw it as in their mutual interest and the Cypriots as an acceptable intermediary.

After a series of frantic phone calls Sodieruis Petrou had persuaded, if that be the right word, the shipping company owners to delay the departure of the Hellenic Adventurer by two hours and as the containers left his factory his drivers had orders to be alongside the ship in Larnaca harbour no later than 2.15 p.m. It was then 1.55 p.m. Each driver had been promised one hundred Cyprus pounds bonus if they made the deadline. As the first one left the Free Port he looked to the left, saw nothing, looked behind to see his mate was closely following, looked right and pulled out making a right turn towards Larnaca. As he was completing his turn he heard, above the noise of his engine, a horrific squeal of brakes, then saw a black Rover alongside him on the nearside heading into the orchard. Mindful of his bonus he did not stop to investigate, both containers sailed on the Hellenic Adventurer later that afternoon.

The first thing Charles Noble remembered afterwards was oranges everywhere. They had been shaken off the tree into which their Rover was now firmly embedded. Charles had seen the lorry, was about to pass it on the right when he was horrified to see another following it, closing the gap he had intended fill. He had had no alternative but to head into the orchard on the left, which he might have negotiated had his front wheel not hit a large boulder, this sudden jolt threw the car straight into the nearest tree.

Charles himself had received a nasty bang above the temple and did not remember anything until more than five minutes after the accident, but his assistant had been trapped until he had been freed by the firemen based in the Free Port across the road who had heard the crash and been on the scene within two minutes. All this had taken more than an half an hour. By the time they got to Larnaca airport in a passing taxi half the passengers from the Tristar had left the airport. There was no sign of Clare Spencer.

He did not notice a Cypriot, in his early thirties, with an expensive looking Canon camera slung over his shoulder, walk out of the terminal, cross the road into the car park and head off towards Larnaca in a green Fiat Tipo.

CHAPTER FIVE

As Dr Richard Rowland climbed down the aeroplane steps at Larnaca International Airport three days before the arrival of Clare Spencer's ageing Tristar, he had surveyed the scene in his usual way, trying to decide which direction to take in order to avoid the yellow airport bus. Until the late summer of 1979 there had been no buses at Larnaca airport. The quickest across the tarmac was the first in the queue for passport control. Richard had used this bus once, which had resulted in him standing for thirty minutes behind those who had managed to get out first. Now he just avoided it and those directing passengers onto it, pretending to understand neither Greek nor English. It had always worked. Tonight was no exception, he walked straight towards the bus, only changing direction at the last moment to avoid being herded onto it. He was second through passport control, going through the section marked 'visas for payment', knowing that the sign discouraged most people from that gate, but that it was just a normal gate, but one where visas could be bought if required. Having successfully entered Cyprus all that now remained was for him to wait to see if his luggage had followed him from Newcastle, surviving the trip through Heathrow.

As he waited, and if things ran true to form it would be a short wait, he looked at his fellow travellers as they joined him at the baggage conveyors. Larnaca was one of several airports Richard knew where most of the luggage arrived before its owners had managed to get past the immigration officers. Sometimes it was more than forty-five minutes before everyone was was through, bags began arriving within ten, often as little as five minutes. The efficiency of the airport staff being negated by officious officials.

Richard had visited the divided island about eight times a year. He had done this for the past sixteen years, but had never been to Cyprus before the 1974 war, so had never used

Nicosia airport. He often wished at times like this that he was at that deserted airport, only ten minutes from his luxury penthouse in the centre of the city. Once he got out of the airport he would still be at least forty-five minutes from 'home'.

The baggage had started arriving, but still only a handful of passengers had got to the right side of the barriers. He was lucky, his bag was among the first dozen out. He picked it up and walked straight out through the green channel without any challenge. All the customs men in their brown uniforms were standing around in small groups waiting for the bulk of the passengers to begin moving through. That was when their real work began, sorting through dozens of Marks and Spencer bags in the suitcases of the visiting expatriate Cypriots. It had never ceased to amaze Richard that with all their entrapreneurial skills at successfully developing import substitution industries, Cypriots remained subconsciously convinced that anything made abroad, particularly England, was better than anything made locally. Perhaps it was the still-remaining sense of inferiority from their colonial past, more probably it was their desire to be 'one-up' on their friends and neighbours. Either way it had the effect of causing most customs men to avoid the obvious tourist and concentrate their efforts on their fellow Cypriots, whom they knew only too well.

Once outside Richard walked straight past the welcoming parties, waiting to meet their long absent brothers, sons and daughters, or friends just getting away to the sun for a few weeks from a wet English September. He walked past the taxis just getting ready to look for business, and remembered the night he had vowed never to get a taxi from Larnaca to Nicosia again. The flight had been delayed and eventually he had arrived at four in the morning. The man with the book, who paired off people with taxis, had taken him to one, opened the back door, woken the driver from his deep sleep on the back seat, and told him his destination was Nicosia. Richard spent the whole journey in the deepest fear, the driver had never really woken up. He talked to him, opened the window, lit his pipe, but nothing worked. His worst moment came when the driver took the old road to Lymbia by mistake, rather than going a few hundred yards further up the old Nicosia road to the junction to the new road. It was not possible to continue on the Nicosia road directly, since it passed through Turkish territory. The old Lymbia road is narrow, hilly, twisting and has steep drops to the valley below. Despite not sleeping during the flight Richard was so filled with a mixture of fear and relief when he reached his flat, that he just could not rest, never mind sleep.

As he walked across the airport forecourt that night he felt very relieved to be driving himself to Nicosia. He reached the third row of the car park and sure enough his gleaming new Mercedes Coupe was still there. Seeing it took his mind back to the day when he had collected his old Mini from Limassol port, some fourteen years earlier. Spending so much time on the island alone, and with the cost of cars being so high, he had arranged for this old second car to be shipped out from England. Had he not done so he would have either had to stay in Nicosia, rely on Philipos for his every move, or hired a car when he needed one. When he brought it to Cyprus it would have worth less than four hundred pounds in England, but would have cost more than double this in Cyprus and it had only cost a hundred to ship out. It was a decision he had never regretted. The freedom it had given him over the years had been priceless. Now when the business had become successful and he had been able to afford to replace it, he sometimes had regretted losing his old faithful friend to a Nicosia scrapyard. He had used to worry about the ambiguity of the import regulations as he had first imported it on a temporary basis, getting extensions every few months, and worrying about the next time. Eventually, as is usual in Cyprus, a friend of a friend had gone with him to the Nicosia customs house and they had arranged a permanent import licence. As usual everything had fitted neatly into place after needless worry.

He opened the door, threw in the suitcase onto the backseat, the briefcase onto the passenger seat, turned on the radio, tuned it to the BBC World Service, and after remembering which side of the steering column it was on, put the key into the ignition. Would it start after its four week rest? It was his lucky day again, first time.

It had been less than twenty minutes since the aircraft had touched down, one of the quickest ever from landing to driving away. As he turned right out of the car park and headed for the dual carriagway across Larnaca's famous salt lake, he wondered if the rest of the trip would run so smoothly. Somehow he had his doubts. It was going to be an exciting and very memorable stay. How often had he tried to persuade Clare to come with him, he had lost count. Now at last, in a few days she would be here. The fact that she now had the position she had and was still aiming to keep her visit a secret, made it doubly exciting.

Traffic was very light and he was through Larnaca and onto the Nicosia road in less than five minutes. Despite being more than twenty years since the 1974 Turkish invasion of Cyprus it was still not possible to drive to Nicosia by the shortest route, which went through the Turkish occupied sector, but a new motorway to Nicosia had been built in 1990 to meet the Limassol-Nicosia motorway, built in 1984, at Perakhorio. These new motorways had been desperately needed since the closing of the main port, Famagusta, to Greek Cypriots, in 1974.

Richard had visited the 'north' only once, in 1988. He had been appalled by what he had seen. It had been like entering a time warp and moving back several decades. To Richard, the Turkish province of northern Cyprus was exactly that, a poor region of mainland Turkey and a convenient training ground for the huge army presence that seemed to him to totally dominate life and movement in that part of the island. It was impossible to travel more than a few miles without encountering an army convoy, or being directed away from a forbidden military zone. Neither could he understand why they had stolen so much, the best tourist areas, the most fertile and productive land, when they could not use it. Much had lain derelict for twenty years. Land that had been breadbasket of Cyprus had now returned to nature as if the science of cultivation and modern agriculture were of an alien planet.

Richard was reflecting on all this as he left the motorway and entered the southern suburbs of Nicosia. His route took him directly towards the city centre, past the Hilton hotel, and onto Makarios Avenue. Just before Woolworths he turned right and on the right there was his apartment block. He parked the car at the rear, took out his luggage, entered the building and ten floors later he left the elevator and stood outside his penthouse.

It looked just the same as he had left it four weeks earlier. What a change, he thought to himself, from the days when he used to return to find the ash trays were still full and four week old newspapers lying about. Success certainly had its compensations. Suddenly he felt very tired, although he thought of ringing Philipos to say he had arrived, he didn't.

Lying in bed five minutes later he thought briefly about the next two weeks. Meeting Clare in three days, and how deeply was Philipos really involved with the CLM - the Cyprus Liberation Movement? He knew he was, he thought he knew the timing, but not what they planned.

At Larnaca airport most planes arrive and depart in the early morning or late evening, except during the busy tourist months of July and August. Most of the mid-day flights are local ones and the number of staff on duty is the lowest of the day. In the early days of the airport at Larnaca Richard had often been met by his Cypriot agent and been taken through the VIP route of entry. As it had become a much busier airport, and he became more independent, that had no longer been possible. However, he knew Marcos Koumides, one of his friends at the airport from those early days, and stepfather of Philipos' cousin, Costas.

"Marcos", he said the next afternoon, "I have a very dear friend of mine visiting Cyprus for the first time tomorrow.

Many years ago, when I first came to Cyprus, I was met at the aircraft steps by my host, then taken through the VIP route of entry. I have always remembered that first impression of real friendship and hospitality whenever I think of Cyprus. I would like Clare to have that same memory. Can you fix it for me?"

"What time is the flight in?" enquired a dubious looking Marcos.

"It's the 2 o'clock Tristar from London."

"OK, that's expatriate, no problem my friend. Not too busy then and security isn't as tight with a London flight. I'll fix it for you. Any friend of yours is a friend of mine."

"I'll come to your office about 1.30 p.m., if that's OK," suggested Richard.

"No, let's meet at 12 o'clock and go for some lunch and you can tell me how Costas is getting on," replied Marcos.

"Thanks, I'd like that. One other point, her name is Clare Spencer, she tells me she gets into all sorts of problems with a name like that these days! But she hates people always saying, are you the real Clare Spencer?"

"Point taken Richard, I'll make sure no-one makes remarks like that tomorrow."

They agreed to meet at noon on Friday, then welcome Clare off the plane. She would be met at the aircraft steps, whisked through a passport check by a good friend of Marcos and there would be no embarrassment over her looks or her name. They would agree that she did look like the 'real' Clare Spencer. She had been quite definite that she would not travel on anything other than her own passport to gain anonymity, and she would not lie about her real identity if challenged.

During the 1970s Richard had been a Technical Manager with an American-owned poultry breeding company which was based in the North Eastern corner of England, in that vast empty area between Newcastle and the Scottish border. This was a part of England that many, perhaps most, Englishmen didn't know existed. They thought when Hadrian had built his wall from Carlisle to Newcastle to keep out the Scots he had defined the border for all time, and that anything north of the wall must therefore, by definition, be Scotland. It was a mistake the Scottish Nationalists also made in the mid-1970s when they were campaigning for Scottish independence and control of Scottish oil. They overlooked the fact that the border ran from the Solway to Berwick and that if the line were continued out into the North Sea in the same direction, then much of the area due east of Aberdeen, near the edge of the British sector, where the oil was located, then became part of the English, not the Scottish sector. The realisation of this fact had much reduced the enthusiasm of some of the more thinking Nationalists, and was one of the reasons for the dropping of the 'Scottish oil' campaign, which itself was the end of the growth in Nationalist support, from which it never recovered.

This area had been chosen by the Broster Poultry Corporation of Maryland due to its unique geographical advantages. With European headquarters located in Berwick-upon-Tweed, and breeding farms on either side of the border, it could export from Scotland if disease in England made English exports unacceptable, and from England if the situation were reversed. Being so far from the major centres of population, the area had a very small poultry population and therefore, there was much less chance of disease coming in from outside their own farms. They had made all their own feed in a huge complex just south of the Scottish border.

Richard's job had been to oversee all technical activities which could have an influence upon the output of the poultry farms under their control, world-wide. He was judged on the number of day-old chicks obtained per hundred breeding chickens. Many of these chicks were exported to other parts of the world, in particular Europe and the Middle East. They were not ordinary chicks, they would not be grown for forty-five or fifty days before finding themselves deep frozen or cut into the ever more popular chicken portions. They were the elite, they were the parents and grandparents of the final product. The farms near Berwick produced parent and grandparent stock for a quarter of the world. Where grandparent chicks were exported they, in turn, produced parent chicks for that local market. Richard had had the responsibility for seeing that these overseas farms produced results comparable with those in England and Scotland.

During Richard's travels assisting new agents in various countries start their own parent farms to supply local farmers, he had become particularly attracted to Cyprus. Whenever he had visited the Middle East he had always managed to find some excuse to stop-over on the island. Broster had an agent in Cyprus, but he was small by any standards and did not really justify such frequent high powered technical servicing. The justification for such stop-overs used by Richard was simple. It reduced his travel costs very considerably. By buying a return air ticket to Larnaca in England, then buying flights in Cyprus to any part of the Middle East from Cyprus Airways, very considerable sums could be saved as compared to purchasing direct flights in England. For example the cost of a trip to the Gulf could be reduced by almost one half, and such a procedure was perfectly legitimate and did not involve the use of any 'bucket shop' or tickets of dubious origin. With this justification his employers never had any objection to these slight extensions to his trips.

In fact, during his visits to Cyprus Richard had been secretly planning his escape from his multinational masters with Philipos, a Greek Cypriot farm manager whom he had met on his second visit, and Philipos' sister Helena, who had already built a modest business distributing Cypriot produce, both in Cyprus and now overseas. The plans had begun to be hatched in 1979, and were implemented during 1980. Richard had seen for a long time that as sophistication in poultry production grew during the 1980s and into the 1990s there would be an increasing demand for turkey meat, in addition to chicken meat. Such an expansion would require turkey breeding farms, now almost non-existent outside North America and Western Europe. He, together with

Philipos and Helena, had planned to establish a huge turkey breeding operation in Cyprus to supply the whole of the Middle East with day-old poults and fertile hatching eggs. Richard had negotiated all the necessary agencies and contracts with a Belgian turkey breeder, a German hatchery and a British feed manufacturer. They had even managed to persuade the Belgians to allow them to market the turkeys under their own brand name, and the Germans to provide a limited amount of the financial backing. Helena had developed her contacts in Ireland over the years and had recently successfully negotiated a technical service agreement with a large poultry processor to provide them with the expertise they needed to promote the fast-growing turkey-portion and processed-product market.

They had had a great deal of trouble finding a suitable company and brand name for the obvious reason that the name 'turkey' was the same in English as the name of the country 'Turkey', and with forty thousand Turkish troops occupying almost forty percent of Cyprus, the inclusion of that name would not have proved too appropriate. The name they had eventually settled upon was 'Cypropoult', this indicated both the Cyprus connection and the involvement with young turkey poults, as opposed to mature turkeys. The Cyprus Government Ministry of Commerce had taken some persuasion to accept the name, since they would not automatically accept, without good reason, the use of the letters 'Cypr..' at the beginning of any trade name.

During the first few years things had not gone too well. Then just when their initial difficulties had been overcome the Gulf War had caused them very serious problems. Their business in the Gulf States and Jordan slowed to a trickle, and the future had looked bleak. But all that was behind them, and now, at the end of their fourteenth year, Cypropoult was reaping the rewards of all the hard work. The first few months had been the worst. Richard's ex-employers had reacted angrily to his leaving on the grounds that they were considering a similar venture. They had, in fact attempted to do so and had poured money and expertise in to accelerate their own plans for a world-wide turkey operation, beginning this expansion in the Middle East. They had reduced their prices and increased their incentives to agents, in an attempt to buy a large market share in advance of Cypropoult reaching the market with hatching eggs and poults. Pressure had been put on the Cypriot authorities by Broster's agent in Cyprus to create difficulties for Richard in his attempt to be allowed to work in Cyprus, and to Cypropoult itself in its attempts to get export licenses. Fortunately Philipos' and particularly Helena's, connections had proved stronger and all the necessary permissions had been obtained. Richard often wondered who some of these connections were. If there was a crisis or problem it would be Helena who would remark:

"I think it is time I went to see my friends again."

But she never did say who these 'friends' were and was very evasive when asked. The world-wide thing was, it always seemed to work.

More recently the three of them had established a new venture. They had entered the rapidly growing tourist market in Cyprus with a company called CyproVilla. This was not merely yet another construction and marketing company. Although they took every opportunity to market properties to their vast number of contacts throughout the Middle East, they had seen a gap in the market which they were proceeding to exploit. Until recently there were vast numbers of visitors in Cyprus for much of the year, taking advantage of the longest sand and sea season of any Mediterranean island, but there were few leisure activities. There had been no golf courses and no water parks, to take but two examples. CyproVilla was in the process of changing this. Their first golf course was due to open in March and their first water park in May.

During the early months and years Richard had been in Cyprus almost as much as he had been in England with his family. It had been hard and lonely. There had been many times during the first year or so when he was almost on the verge of bringing his wife and family out to Cyprus to live, but each time there had always seemed to be some convincing argument against it. First, it was an absolute lack of money and the only way would have been to sell his house in England to cover his borrowings and raise the cash for the move. He had never felt justified in doing this. Then there was the feeling that permanently moving to Cyprus would have left him technically isolated from all the advances constantly being made and which he kept in close touch with by attending all relevant conferences in England. Perhaps most importantly, he simply liked England, he liked to see his family happily settled, his wife a full member of the local community and a part-time dentist at the local health centre and his two children happily settled with their friends in the local school. And then there was Clare... So for these reasons, and others he wouldn't even admit to himself, he was just a visitor, not a resident and had now firmly decided against the permanent move and was concentrating his efforts on the design and construction of his villa being built on the coast just north of Fig-Tree-Bay at the south-eastern corner of the island. It was to be one of the most luxurious on the island, overlooking the coast to the east, and the new golf course to the west.

Now fourteen years after the start of the venture Richard had settled firmly into the routine of flying to Larnaca every six weeks, spending four weeks in Cyprus and the Middle East, then returning to Northumbria for two weeks, before beginning the cycle again. In the school summer holidays the Rowlands spent at least six weeks in Cyprus as a family. The present visit was the first after the long summer one, during which he had learnt that Philipos was closely linked with the CLM, the Cyprus Liberation Movement. In fact it had been Barbara, his wife, who had first suspected something when talking to friends at Ayia Napa early in August. Richard had followed it up and learnt a little more, but the real breakthrough had come later. He was in Orunda one day with Philipos at the village cafe. Now Richard had been, unknown to Philipos, secretly trying to learn Greek. He knew enough to have been able to have followed a conversation Philipos had had with his cousin, Costas, now a colleague in CyproVilla. This conversation had shocked Richard, he had learnt about the CLM in some detail, and more worrying for the future, the fact that Philipos, and probably Costas too, were leading members.

It seemed the CLM was an underground group of Greek Cypriots dedicated to the recovery of the Turkish occupied area. They had lost patience with the lack of any progress that had been made by the UN over twenty years and were modelling themselves on the early days of the PLO, but intending to be much more effective in achieving their objective. It was their aim to carry out actions designed, not only to gain the maximum possible international publicity, but actual territorial gains, and it seemed they had planned some action during the autumn. Richard had kept this information to himself, frankly being afraid to do otherwise. By this time Clare had agreed to the visit in late September, he had considered cancelling it, but how would he explain such a cancellation to Clare. He could not tell the truth, that would be betraying Philipos, and after trying to persuade her to visit Cyprus for years the last thing he wished was to stop it now. His head told him to postpone it, his heart told him there may not be another chance if he did. His heart won. Clare would be arriving on Friday.

CHAPTER SIX

For Helena, the decade of the 1980s had been one of organisation, of building the structures that would form the basis of future action. She organised cover for shipments to Ireland through her own import/export business, which she brought into Cypropoult as a subsidiary company named Cyproport, a clever combination of the 'Cypro' prefix and the end of the words import or export, but which could easily be confused with the name of a company set up to trade in port wine. Her exports were of traditional Cyprus produce, in particular red wine, sherry and grapefruit. The packing cases were specifically designed and produced for her by Sodierus Petrou in Larnaca. As with his Israeli trade, Sodierus did not mind what the business was, provided it was profitable to him. Being in the free port area he had easy access to imports through Larnaca, but in his early days he had found it necessary to prepare his own packaging for security reasons. That self contained wing of his factory was the ideal place to prepare laminated wooden packing cases for the export of wine and citrus fruit. Without careful chemical analysis even the most detailed inspection of these plywood packing cases could not identify or discover the plastic material which formed the centre of the three ply construction of a small proportion of the cases he manufactured.

These cases had found their way, without challenge, for more than twelve years to a legitimate and long established fruit and wine importer to the north of Dublin. This company had a separate contract with another Irish business for the disposal of all its packing materials. An important aspect of the contract was that all packing materials, without exception, were handed over. Since this paid very handsomely there remained every incentive for every scrap of material to be handed over. Checks were made that this was so, and there had never been any shortfall.

That route worked well enough for flexible plastic explosive, but not for guns or ammunition. Then it had come to her in a flash. Citrus pulp. Since Ireland had joined the European Economic Community traditional animal feeds, barley, wheat and maize had increased in price to a huge extent. The economics of the Common Agricultural policy being designed to encourage the production of huge quantities of highly subsidised cereals and the creation of the infamous cereal mountain. But by increasing the price of these traditional materials those same policies made their use as animal feed totally uneconomic, reducing their use and thus further increasing the size of those same cereal mountains. This had become a severe problem by the mid 1980s, even though action to reverse the process did begin to have some marginal effect by the end of the decade.

Helena had studied the Common Agricultural Policy as part of her degree course at Queens so she was well aware of these peculiar effects. One of these was the incentive created to find substitutes for the expensive cereal that was being piled up in mountains. The first such material was tapioca or manioc. Much of the prosperity of the port of Rotterdam had been based upon this lucrative trade, as was the economy of Thailand. More recently other materials were being imported to replace both cereal and manioc after a ceiling had been placed upon imports of manioc from Thailand and China. Maize Gluten, imported from America became ever more popular, until the Americans found that since it was impossible to export maize to the EEC, due to import levies, but possible to export the levy-free by-product, maize gluten, then it then became profitable to convert maize to maize gluten and flood the market with that product. They became greedy and increased their price. Then there was an even more peculiar situation, maize gluten substitutes were produced in Rotterdam from imports of such materials as rice bran from the Far East, such a ludicrous business had to come unstuck, which it did towards the end of the decade when some of this rice bran had been contaminated with lead and fed to thousands of cattle throughout Holland and England with disastrous consequences to consumers of milk.

However, at the beginning of the decade Helena saw through these potential consequences of the trade and saw the answer from which she would profit, Citrus pulp. An excellent cereal replacer without any of the pitfalls of other substitutes, one that she could establish first.

She had arranged for her Irish opposite numbers to establish an animal feed ingredient importing company at Cork. The rest had been easily accomplished. Some loads were sprinkled with ammunition, which was extracted by magnets in the purpose built warehouse outside Cork. Other shipments contained strategically located guns of all types. To the outsider this was a legitimate business. The citrus pulp was an economic import for Ireland and that business was quite profitable in its own right. Supplying the IRA was a bonus.

During these years she had visited Ireland most summers to keep her contacts alive, and importantly to watch her young son grow to adult life. When he was ten she had agreed with Mary that they should tell him the truth, that she Helena was his real mother. By that age he had accepted Mary, so it was relatively easy for him to see her as his grandmother, rather than his real mother. He never appeared to do other than accept the news as a fact of life, he had always loved Helena and continued to do so. The relationship never became, for either of them, that of mother and son. During her visits to Ireland Helena always spent a few days in Westport, where she met her Irish customers, and made a brief visit to Dublin where she met the public ones, those who bought the commodities she openly exported to Ireland. When he was sixteen Helena took Sean with her to Dublin and persuaded the wine importers to employ him as a trainee buyer. Since they bought at a significant discount on market prices, this they readily agreed to do. Two years later, in 1990, she invited him to Cyprus and took him into her confidence, but while there she kept his real identity from the rest of her family and her business associates. She told him everything, wanting him to understand why her father and his father had died, and how one day they would together begin to make others pay for those deaths.

It would not be easy and she had no definitive plan, but had begun to lay the groundwork in the mid eighties. Although always remaining in the background it was her organisation that had led to protest demonstrations on the Green Line. Having begun in a small way these were designed to keep the issue alive and a dynamic one with the younger generation in Cyprus, those who had never seen the lost lands and to whom Bellapais was only a name on a wine bottle. Her most effective tactic had been to arrange a large demonstration somewhere along the line, somewhere known in advance to the press and media, and encourage demonstrators to walk across the Green Line as if it did not exist. Turkish soldiers did resist, but not with firearms. That demonstrated a point at least. Her most successful events were arranged outside the village of Akhna. The bypass to the south of the village was in the British base of Dhekelia, but the houses themselves were deserted, the village was in Turkish hands. A Greek village that rapidly became an archaeological site, like Currium, but with much more meaning, since its former inhabitants could see it decaying, but could do nothing. They had reoccupied Akhna twice, making world headlines each time by being shown retreating in the face of Turkish armed force. One day, she had determined, there would be no retreat. It would be the Turks who would do the retreating.

After the new President elected in 1988 had failed to break the deadlock, Helena became ever more fearful that the cease-fire line really would become a permanent border. This conviction was reinforced when the divisions in Europe began to fall after the Iron Curtain had been melted down in November and December 1989. In Europe the great powers were involved, in Cyprus they were not and nobody seemed to care that in Cyprus there was a border across which far fewer people were permitted move than had ever been the case between the two Germanies or across Berlin. This feeling of hopelessness was further reinforced when Turkey actively supported the stand against Iraq, making it less likely that any useful pressure would be placed on Turkey over Cyprus, particularly by the United States or the European Community. There had been more United Nations' resolutions calling on Turkey to withdraw from Cyprus than there had been calling on Iraq to withdraw from Kuwait, but it had been Kuwait, not Cyprus, which had been liberated after only a few months of occupation. As her feeling of realisation and resentment grew at decades of occupation, so did her determination to break the deadlock. The only real joy she had had was watching with real pleasure the financial collapse of Polly Peck, a company that had been built upon, and had profited from, the occupation of the north of Cyprus. She was delighted that the money she had spent on the covert public relations campaign aimed at the British financial institutions in respect of the ownership of property in the north, had been money well spent.

Nevertheless, that had been a very small victory which had only further reduced the economic viability of occupied Cyprus. More, much more had to be done, and she had been determined to play a leading part in doing whatever was necessary to achieve freedom for her country. It was her initiative that had established the Cyprus Liberation Movement, and it was at her insistence that its name was in English, not Greek. No one outside Greece or Cyprus had really known what the initials EOKA had stood for, but everyone knew what the PLO represented. This time it would be different, the CLM would have a real meaning to the whole world.

Although her brother did not share her conviction, which she regarded as almost 'Thatcherite' in its clarity, he was nevertheless persuaded that she was right and must be supported. His contacts in the Greek Cypriot National Guard were important in the early days of the CLM. It was he who introduced her to Major Savvas Patriches, who it later emerged had befriended her mother many years earlier. He became her front man. Her experience and knowledge of the IRA helped her structure the command. Few people, only she, the Major and Philipos, would know everything. The rest would handle their individual tasks. She was the real leader, but was content to exercise this through the Major. He carried more credibility with the team leaders. Armies were still a man's world. Her brother would be her right arm. The Major was seen as chairman of the board and Philipos managing director, but Helena retained financial control and remained the real power source within the CLM.

Her main aim throughout had been to avoid getting involved in minor terrorist actions, despite their publicity value. She was determined that when they did act it would be decisive. It was no part of her plans to be the subject of public and world anger at the slaughter of innocents, however noble the cause. She had learned that from Ireland -killing and violence could be a useful form of 'low-cost corporate advertising', but in making real progress they were totally ineffective. Her objective had been to work towards the twentieth anniversary of the invasion and occupation, and to build up the organisation of the CLM with that in mind. But which date was she to regard as the most important? The Coup, the invasion, the start of the second round on 14 August, or the cease-fire and the effective division of the island on 22 August? During the preceding years all efforts had been devoted to securing this organisational strength, to ensure that much of the National Guard became an integral part of the organisation in all but name. It had been a remarkable achievement that by the beginning of 1994 this had been achieved. Her initial plan had been to mark the anniversary of the capture of Famagusta with its recapture and plans were set in hand designed to achieve that primary objective. However, early in June she learnt something that changed everything. She had made it her business to know everything about Richard Rowland after Costas had told her about his relationship with Clare Spencer. She had him watched, his calls recorded and his mail intercepted. She had known of his long standing invitation for her to visit Cyprus, and like everyone else could not believe it when she became Prime Minister. Now she redoubled her efforts to know everything. When Clare confirmed to Richard that she would visit Cyprus at the end of September, Helena knew before Richard.

Having set the plans in motion she was delighted to discover that the United Nations General Assembly debate on Cyprus was to be brought forward and would coincide with her plans. Even if Clare Spencer found some last minute reason not to visit Cyprus there was ample reason for the new date to be a perfect alternative.

In mid-June Helena flew to Ireland. This time her son Sean accompanied her to Westport. Yet another important aspect of the overall plan was finalised. She had more than repaid her debt to the IRA, now she would begin to collect some of the credit she had deliberately built up over the years. Having concluded these plans it was agreed that Sean would make all the arrangements, he resigned his job and was officially appointed as Cyproport's EEC Distributor.

Major Patriches had looked across the room at the assembled central committee of the CLM. It was Friday July 15 1994. Philipos Haduanois and his sister Helena were on the platform with him; the only other members of the small executive committee who had developed the plans he was about to announce. Helena and Philipos' cousin Costas Koumides was also present. The Major spoke slowly and carefully, gone was the obvious passion in his voice, replaced by quiet determination:

"Fellow Cypriot soldiers. We have spent many long hours in this room, our staff have worked for two years making and devising plans. Until today you have rejected them all as being too dangerous, likely to be counterproductive, or with some similar excuse. You are all successful men and women. Is it that you are frightened to take any action at all in case it interferes with your comfortable life style, with your hunting, your seaside villa, your mistress... A few of us have devised a strategy, a plan, it is going to work, those of you who do not want to be involved, please leave now, either you will support us or we will do it with anyone who will support us. We did not convene the CLM as a talking shop, the time for talking is over. When we return in ten minutes time I expect those of you remaining will be with us, will want to see the memory of 1974 erased, and will be willing to concentrate all their effort on that objective."

When the executive committee returned to the basement room, the former night club and restaurant of the Cleopatra Hotel in central Nicosia, they found none of their eleven colleagues, ten men and one woman, had departed. Whatever their doubts, they, like him, believed that if they did not act they would never see their former homes, villages and property again. They had used this room for most of their meetings, Savvas Patriches had acquired this hotel to begin again, its former owners had undertaken extensive refurbishment in 1983, this had included the construction of a swimming pool and reorganisation of the restaurants. Before the basement night club had been modernised his purchase had been completed and it had now become the offices and meeting rooms of the CLM. The Cleopatra was a modest city centre hotel, much favoured by the less affluent visitors from the Middle East and Eastern Europe. It made a perfect cover for the headquarters of the CLM.

"So, no one left," observed a serious, but delighted Savvas.

One replied for them all, "Everyone is of the same mind, we must proceed, some are less sure of your methods, but think it better to have some influence by staying, than none by leaving."

"Very well. Today July 15 sees the twentieth anniversary of the Coup, which we all know was followed a few days later by the Turkish invasion. In August it will be twenty years of stalemate. The Turks have taken our land, our homes and our businesses, they are not going to leave voluntarily. On Monday 3 October the twentieth United Nations General Assembly debate on Cyprus will begin. It is time they had something new to debate."

"There is another small country in this world with similar problems to our own. It is a country with a majority and a minority population, it is a country that has been artificially partitioned by forces sympathetic to the minority. It is a country where the majority have the internationally recognised government, but a part of their country is occupied by foreign troops sympathetic to the minority. It is a country where people speak of the problem as being religious, but it is not. It is a country where the real difference between the minority and majority is a racial, not a religious, difference, just as it is in our country. There are some differences between the two situations. There both racial groups speak the same language, that is one reason why the problem is seen as religious, not racial. Here we speak different languages. There the majority group does not have the theoretical backing of a 'mother' country, as we have Greece. The country of which I speak is the island of Ireland."

"That country was partitioned in 1921. It remains partitioned in 1994. Do you want this to happen here in Cyprus? No, of course not, but if we allow it to continue much longer it will. You may say that in Ireland men, such as us, have been fighting to end partition ever since 1921, and an intensified struggle has been going on since 1969, with no useful result. That is true enough, we must learn from their mistakes. For this reason we have been holding discussions with the leaders of today's IRA, the leaders of yesterday's IRA and with leaders of the minority Protestant community, the latter not being aware of our views tend to believe the Greek Cypriot has something in common with the Ulster Protestant, whereas we see it the other way round."

"We have learned a great deal from these people. We have also helped them a great deal, this help began well before the CLM, remember the Claudia, that shipment of arms from Limassol which was discovered, we are proud to say that no more consignments from Cyprus have ever been discovered, they have all got through. They are now willing to repay some of this debt to us, as you will learn soon, gentlemen. We have also learned that small scale terrorist actions have no benefit. It is only major actions, and the threat of many more that bring results. They learned that in 1972 when there was almost open civil war. That led to the abolishing of the Parliament of the minority, Stormont, and talks between terrorists and British Ministers, even their Prime Minister. Nó, our action must be such as to force countries such as the United States and Britain to reopen the whole Cyprus issue and, if necessary, impose a solution on the Turks in order to protect their own interests."

"We have ten weeks. Our strike will take place immediately before the General Assembly debate; Saturday 1 October is the date we should each etch on our hearts, that will be the end of the beginning of the latest phase in the struggle for Cyprus."

"It is not sensible to go into all the details now, these will be refined during the next six weeks on a need to know basis. We shall need two thousand five hundred men, five hundred here in Nicosia."

The Major went on to explain the broad outline of the plans for 1 October, plans which were much more ambitious than most of the Central Committee had ever envisaged would be proposed. Philipos and Helena were the only ones present who had previously known what they had just heard, Helena having largely devised the plans. The others were amazed at the audacity of what they had just heard. Costas knew all about the Irish connection, but there was one aspect that had come as a complete surprise to him. He had not realised the full international implications of their plans until that meeting. Could the plan work? Yes he believed it just might, but he knew it would cause consternation in Washington when they read his report of this meeting, how would they react, would they see advantage in it proceeding or would they order him to find a way to sabotage the plan. The next ten weeks were going to be interesting and dangerous weeks, that was for sure.

On the Thursday, 29 September, Helena reflected on the meeting that had been held in mid-July at the Cleopatra in Nicosia. Major Patriches had read her script brilliantly. There would be no return now. Each man had his own tasks to perform, his own organisation to secure. Everything had to be made to run like clockwork. Richard Rowland had arrived in Cyprus and Clare Spencer was to meet him the next day. Her plans for alerting the world's press to Clare Spencer's presence had been made, as had the plans for a special welcome for the Prime Minister. Yes, so far the plans were proving themselves. But the major actions were still to begin. All those years of determination were close to fulfilment.

CHAPTER SEVEN

Helena's only problem was Costas. Why was he taking such an interest in Clare Spencer. His job had been to act as her liaison with the airport, why had he avoided that particular job and involved himself in the sea journey to the east coast? It did not make sense to her and she was deeply suspicious of anything that did not. But he had been insistent that Clare Spencer had to be handled personally by one of the top people, even at the expense of changing plans at the eleventh hour, despite her having previously agreed to his presence at Larnaca airport and Limassol the day before to begin the entrapment. She had decided to accept his insistence with the minimum of argument, without expressing her real fears and suspicions. She had, however, arranged for someone she trusted implicitly to be with him at all times. Nothing must be left to chance.

Costas remained an enigma to Helena. He had only been ten years old in 1974. She had had little to do with him until he returned from California in 1987 with his degree in economics. Then his stepfather, who had worked very hard from the beginning to establish Larnaca airport as an international airport in its own right, had approached Philipos to see if there was a place for his son in Cypropoult.

Helena had reluctantly agreed. She had never been convinced that he would be totally loyal, he was too independently minded a young man. Costas had worked closely with Helena on the legitimate business, so that she could concentrate on the Irish trade and the CLM. Against her instincts it had become necessary to make Costas aware of the CLM and its aims, mainly so that it would be possible to continue to keep its close association with Cypropoult from Richard Rowland.

It came as a relief to her when they agreed to put Costas in charge of CyproVilla's new projects, that kept him largely out of her hair, especially since Richard was taking a particular interest in that division of the company so that effectively Costas would now be working for Richard, not Helena.

Costas himself had always felt something of an outcast and consequently had become very much a loner. This had begun when he had been told that Marcos was not his real father, but that his real father had been murdered by extremist nationalists as an informer in 1965. He resented it more than he had ever said. After all, he had been working for the legitimate independent Government of Cyprus at the time. His execution was quite different in character from that of those who had worked with the British before independence, they were traitors, his father was a patriot. His family, had, however, been so embarrassed, that when his mother had married Marcos she had not only changed her name, but the name of all her family.

Costas had gone to California to study at San Diego in 1983, glad to have some space away from what was to him the claustrophobic atmosphere of Cyprus and family. The turning point for him came in 1984 when he was at the Olympic Games at Los Angeles. The authorities were paranoiac that there could be a terrorist attack along the lines of that which had ruined the Games at Munich. As a suspicious alien he was picked up by the FBI and subjected to intensive interrogation.

He had been held for three days when a new interrogator visited him.

"Costas Koumides, Mm, quite a history I see. Cousin virtually a member of the IRA, one of their best assets outside Ireland. Father executed by a bunch of terrorists," the man said as he handed him a piece of paper, "know what this is sonny?"

"No", said a shaken Costas, " What Cousin? What do you mean - IRA?"

"Don't come that one on me, sonny. One thing is for sure, you are not stupid, quite bright in fact, I see reading this report from San Diego. For your information it's a deportation order. You have been classified as an undesirable alien.

You are not a citizen, so no appeal. That's it. First British Airways flight out, booked through London to Larnaca."

Costas' world fell apart. Why him? What did it mean? What could he do? Arguing would not succeed, so he tried to play along with his interrogator.

"Sir, I have three cousins, Philipos and Helena Haduanois, and Dimetrios, who has been officially listed as missing for ten years. Either Dimetrios has turned up with a new identity, which I do not know about, or Helena made connections when she was at University there. But if she had do you think she would have told anyone? No, sir, what you say about my father is true. The bastards killed him for doing his job for the Cyprus Government, the sort of job you are doing for the United States. One day...." he did not finish, thinking it would not be very helpful for him to express the resentment he felt. "But as for a cousin involved with the IRA I can't believe it is Philipos, so it must be Helena, and it's news to me."

"Even if you are telling me the truth, why should I believe you? It is much easier just to get you out of the USA, then we can be sure." With that he left the room, saying, "I'll be back in less than two hours to tell you when you are leaving."

He returned in less than fifteen minutes.

"We're thinking of changing our minds. Washington wants us to prosecute, they think we are taking the soft option by just deporting aliens. They want a case to give publicity -to act as a deterrent to others like you to stay away from Los Angeles during the Games. Now tell me, where did you get this?"

He held out in his hand a thin pencil like object. Costas looked puzzled, and even more worried now, he had never handled one, but he knew what a detonator looked like. They were framing him all right and there wasn't anything he could do about it.

The interrogation went on for another twenty minutes with Costas beginning to become desperate. He had no rights, none at all. Then another man joined them, took the first man on one side and whispered a few words. The first man left. The tone of the second one was different.

"Now Costas it seems you are in real trouble. You know what it could mean, ten years at least. Well, there is another way."

He spent the next hour explaining. The relief on Costas' face was complete, but nothing to what he felt inside. He had just been recruited into the CIA, or at least had become a potential recruit. Not only would he remain free, he would have all his University fees paid by the Government and would receive a small salary - pocket money they called it -to him it was a small fortune. He would be made for life. All he had to do was to finish University and spend his vacations at a CIA camp. If he succeeded, which he was sure he would, he was to return to Cyprus, get a job with Helena and report everything back to the Athens office. And he would be paid in Switzerland. That is exactly what had happened since his return to Cyprus in 1987, seven years ago. Until now it had been routine.

When he reported on the CLM plans for 1 October 1994 he was excited and nervous. His reports became more frequent. For the first time he began to receive orders regularly. Then, after his final report, he had received a personal visit and had been given his final orders. Could he manage to get the plans changed? Could he get to Clare Spencer and stick with her? How would he explain it? Could they handle Nicosia without him? It had been difficult, but not quite as difficult as he had expected. Perhaps Helena was finding the pressure too much. No, that would be too much to expect, after all it had been his business to get to know everything about Helena for seven years. But, and there remained a 'but', did she suspect him? Suspect him of what? No, that was stupid, but he couldn't be certain. He would have to be careful, doubly careful now.

Early in September the Oval office desk had been covered with photographs of a foreign politician. President Sam Fowler, now Commander-in-Chief, after spending a frustrating apprenticeship as Vice-President, was deep in thought, his CIA chief, together with the head of one of its important overseas offices, remained silent. It was left to the Chief of Staff to ask the obvious question.

"How are these snaps of scruffy, untidy youths relevant to the President?"

He had been hand-picked for his ability to keep the business of Government working, while the President indulged his tendency to become totally engrossed in some issues, while remaining bored with others. This particular issue, he suspected, might be one in which the new President decided to take a real interest.

The more junior CIA staffer spoke first:

"What you see Mr President are a series of photographs taken during the years 1975 to 1978 depicting demonstrations against some of our military bases in the country concerned by groups of fanatics, mainly students. We identified the students at the time, their names have been in our subversives database ever since. One of the subversives has just become the leader of the Government of one of our most trusted allies. We have prepared a plan to deal with the matter in a highly advantageous way to the USA. It will guarantee the removal of this person from Government and her replacement by a leader we know and trust. With your permission I will outline the broad principles of the operation. It will also have other major political benefits."

"Quite an undertaking", observed the President

"Remember the Bay of Pigs", interjected the Chief of Staff, "not to mention the Irangate fiasco".

"OK, that's out of court. On the Bay of Pigs Eisenhower planned that as a legacy to Nixon. Kennedy won and wouldn't go all the way with it. Needed Nixon to have won in sixty, then it would have worked and Castro would have been got rid of thirty-four years ago. When I back something I back it all the way."

"That's what I'm afraid of", thought the Chief of Staff.

"Please carry on", invited the President.

"We've found her Achilles heel. Sex. When she first got

elected we dug out her file and found her boyfriend mentioned. We've traced him too. Seems he's got himself involved in a business venture with a group of nationalists - terrorists. Stroke of luck really. That could have been enough itself, but it gets better. She's still seeing this old boyfriend and he's happily married. At first we thought it might be enough to stop there, spot of blackmail would have worked well enough. I told you it got better, seems he's invited her to join him - for a sort of holiday -overseas with this bunch of terrorists and she's, you'd better believe it, agreed. Don't suppose she knows they're terrorists though, their intelligence service doesn't even know."

"It might be better if you were to merely outline the politics of the plan to the President, avoiding too much detail, then he can quite legitimately deny knowledge of any details if he is ever asked", suggested an increasingly concerned Chief of Staff.

"OK. Well we've infiltrated these nationalists. Got a man right on the inside there, very close to the top. He works for the local business in which our friend's boyfriend is involved, that's how we know about her holiday over there. They have planned something big to coincide with her visit."

"When we gave the green light to the Stepfather in 1974 for the Coup against Makarios in Cyprus it went wrong, he escaped and the British flew him to London. But we still succeeded in opening the door for Turkey to invade Cyprus and partition it, despite the fact that they were so incompetent that the UN nearly stopped them before they had done the job. Anyway it had the desired result, the Colonels in Athens were seen to have gone too far by their own army and were overthrown. But because Makarios survived to appeal to the UN personally, we had to stop the Turks at the Attila line, there wasn't time to let them annex the whole island as we had hoped they would. By leaving the Stepfather in control of the Cyprus Government they have been a damn nuisance ever since. They won't accept the facts. Now if we arrange for them to be seen to assassinate the Prime Minister of England they'll get the blame and will lose any support they have left. Turkey will have every justification for occupying the rest of the island on the pretext of restoring order. We will be able to openly support them, and so will England if the Turks have the sense the make the right noises about going in to bring the terrorists and assassins to book."

"Are you sure? This operative of ours, can't be traced back to us can he?" asked the President.

"Quite sure sir, family still live there, he's related to the two at the top, cousins. Nothing points to us. Only reason he works for us is that more than thirty years ago another bunch of terrorists, ancestors of the current lot, tried his father on trumped up charges, then tortured him to death. Hates 'em all for it. Would do anything to get back at 'em. Expects us to help him."

"Right gentlemen, I suggest we meet again when this is nearer action. Best of luck. I'm with you all the way."

The two visitors left the Oval Office and the White House, one to Langley, Dean Lawson to Dulles Airport to catch his plane back to Athens, to be nearer the action. The President smiled, action at last. This time he was going to enjoy it, he wasn't the Crown Prince anymore, this time he was in charge.

CHAPTER EIGHT

From the moment of his arrival on Tuesday, Richard had been waiting in eager anticipation for Friday to dawn. Not that his trepidation about the visit of Clare had been in any way diminished by his researches during the last few days. They had increased.

He had gone out alone early on the Thursday evening. First he had spent a quiet two hours in the bar at the Cyprus Hilton, including the Happy Hour, an early evening period when all drinks purchased were supplemented by a similar free one. First introduced into the Mediterranean by the Cyprus Hilton in 1975 this practice had now been copied by every hotel bar around the coast from Marbella to Rhodes. Then, after relaxing for a while in the lobby, watching the Cypriot high society pass by, he walked down the corridor to the Coffee Shop, or as the Hilton preferred, the Fontana Amorosa. It was in that very room in 1978 that the infamous PLO murder had taken place. An event which had led directly to an even more serious shoot-out between the Cypriot forces and the Egyptian version of the SAS at Larnaca airport and the subsequent severing of all relations between Cyprus and Egypt for several years.

That room had many memories for him, some delightful, others less so. It was there that he had had his first taste of Cyprus back in 1977. After being driven from Larnaca feeling exhausted, he had been introduced to the family of his host and was invited to join them for a meal, an evening that had been so enjoyable he had forgotten his tiredness. That same room had seen the conception of Cypropoult in 1979. Philipos and he had spent a long evening over a meal developing a casual remark into a concept. Now fifteen years later it was that same room. He ate alone, admiring an atmosphere that could be created with such a simple design. Traditional Cypriot furnishing, adapted for modern use and comfort. Genuine artefacts from the Cyprus Handicraft Centre were placed unobtrusively throughout. These handicrafts were all handmade in the traditional manner, but co-ordinated by an agency of the Cyprus Government to ensure the survival of the traditional village crafts in a modern economy. Demonstrating that the entrapreneurial skills of the Cypriots did not end in the Private Sector of the economy. Perhaps that was because most civil servants were also businessmen in their own right, they worked for the Government during the standard hours of 7.30 a.m. to 2 p.m., then spent the afternoon and evening starting, running and developing their own business. It made for a vibrant economy. The Civil Service benefited since they gained real commercial experience and expertise, and enterprise gained through the start up of small businesses upon which their owners were not dependent for an income. Richard pondered that such a model could well be worthy of transportation to some of the more developed and mature economies of Western Europe. He also wondered whether Clare's radicalism would entertain such thoughts.

Clare, how he had longed for so many years to be alone with her for more than the occasional stolen night in Bristol. These dreams were about to come true, just as Cypropoult had done those long years ago, and just as CyproVilla would do in the future. Or were they? He had been so excited at the prospect that the warning signs had all been ignored. But how could he credibly have suggested a postponement? After everything he had told her about the island of Aphrodite, and the numerous invitations to spend time with him here, he could have have no excuse to suggest anywhere else, and he knew that postponement meant the end. How could someone like Clare, in her position, manage to arrange something similar twice? Neither could he have told her the truth about his fears, that would have meant betraying his friends, which even if they betrayed him he would not do. He had wanted her so much that he had agreed to her suggestion that she come at the end of September. She needed a real break after two so hectic and exciting years, a break after the election and the formation of the Government, after her Party

Conference and before Parliament's November resumption. No, it had to be now or never. Tomorrow she would arrive. He knew he should 'phone her that moment, but equally he knew that he would not and the die was cast.

He knew that his relationship with Clare had to end, especially now that she was Prime Minister. In fact it had almost ended as a relationship, it had been more than two years since their last night together in Bristol. They both knew it could not continue; but they both wanted to have some time, time to end it in their own loving way, together.

The first extra clue had come that very morning. He and Philipos were together in Philipos' office overlooking Nicosia and the forbidden Kyrenia hills to the north. They had taken these offices in 1984 after deciding that they had to move into the city from the farm to be near the various Ministries for such things as export licences. Cypropoult occupied the top three floors of the block which had been built on the site of one of Nicosia's fast disappearing traditional buildings, which had housed the Date Club restaurant before it had moved to the Hilton suburbs. It had also been essential to be located in the city to take care of their increasing number of overseas visitors. They had to be ultra-careful in respect of visitors to the farm since isolation was essential to prevent the introduction of disease to their valuable flocks. Their farm was ideally situated from the point of view of disease control, but not convenience. Although quite close to the city it could not be reached by a direct route, which crossed the neutral zone, a bulge in the 'Green Line' around the airport, policed by the United Nations. To get to the Cypropoult farm meant a detour of more than a dozen miles, around the airport to the south, before heading back north, then east right up to the UN zone. In addition to its ideal position, due to its isolation from the point of view of disease control, because it was so close to the Green Line they had been able to buy it at price they could afford, way back in 1980. A similar farm would have cost them more than double in most other parts of the island.

He and Philipos were trying to solve what seemed an

intractable problem of timing. Their new water park was to be finished in May, in time for the 1995 tourist season, but the authorities were being difficult over the supply of water. They had decreed that it could only be filled with water during the winter, in the summer the water pipeline capacity was insufficient, it all being needed to supply the hotels and apartments around the coast. Philipos wanted to go ahead with sea water, Richard was concerned that the extra corrosion caused would more than wipe out the revenue benefits. Still in the middle of an unresolved dilemma the phone had rung, after to listening for a few moments Philipos answered in Greek:

"No, Costas you must remain here in Nicosia.....I do not want to speak of this on the telephone, you know the rules."

".....Helena is good, but not good enough to do it all alone....."

He looked, somewhat anxiously Richard thought, directly towards Richard, who began to rise.

"That is my concern.......Famagusta is the easy one, we do not need you there, you must be at the airport.......they must be able to see the runway from the air above Ercan...."

"Look, come here at 2 o'clock....."

With that he replaced the receiver a little more heavily than was strictly normal, and he looked up at Richard who had stood, as if to leave, but had remained, appearing to stare out of the window towards the north.

"Ah, my friend one day I shall return to Kyrenia", he thought aloud in Greek, "perhaps sooner than you think."

"That was Costas, he's going to try to get them to agree to allow us to take a water feed from the golf course to the water park for a few months", he lied in English.

Richard had been puzzled. He had not understood all the conversation between Philipos and Costas, but he had understood sufficient to know that it had been important enough for Philipos to lie to him, which in their business relationship of fourteen years had been rare. He had assumed it must have been about the CLM plans. Famagusta and Ercan, what could it mean? He had asked himself that question dozens of times in the past few hours.

He began to put together all he knew. Firstly there was to be a large Greek Cypriot National Guard reunion weekend on the east coast. The weekend was to be strictly for the men, no wives were to allowed. It was the end of the holiday season and the owner of the Golden Coast hotel had been persuaded by someone important in Nicosia to unload his bookings into Ayia Napa Hotels, safely round Cape Greco. The area round Protaras had some of the best beaches in southern Cyprus, and the Golden Coast near Pernera had both a fishing shelter and an excellent sandy cove to itself. Then there was the reference to Famagusta, just a few miles to the north of Protaras, across the Green Line. What puzzled him most was the reference to the airport, particularly to Ercan. Ercan was an illegal airport, formerly an RAF airfield it had quickly been brought into service by the Turkish Cypriots in 1975, just as Larnaca had been by the Greek Cypriots. It now served as the North's link to the outside world.

It began to make some sense to him, but not complete sense. It seemed there was to be some sort of action against Nicosia airport, perhaps the reference to Ercan was connected with a worry that the Turks would use Ercan as a base to attack them. If so why did they want it to be seen from above Ercan?

Gathering a large group of well trained, hand picked ex-sevicemen a few miles from Famagusta might make some sense if their aim was to attack the ghost town, but he couldn't see how they could achieve this, perhaps they were just intending to stage a large demonstration as the women had done under Helena's leadership when they had walked across the Green Line near Nicosia and at Akhna. Because if they were intending to attack where would their weapons come from? One of the peculiarities of the divided island was that the British Dhekelia Base cut right through the southern free part of Cyprus and bordered both the 'North' and the sea, with the only access to Ayia Napa, Paralimni & Protaras being through the Base. Since, strictly speaking, there was no dispute between the Turks and the British the border between the British Base and the Turkish sector was not policed at all effectively. One of the roads through this British sovereign territory ran ten yards from the 'North' for a distance of several miles, either side of the deserted and abandoned Greek village of Akhna. There were no obstacles to anyone crossing between the two. In fact it was not uncommon for Turkish troops to cross the road, wave down passing motorists and demand cigarettes and other items. The sovereign base authorities did however operate random and thorough checks of people and goods, much to the irritation of many innocent tourists forced to pass through the base. It would therefore be difficult to get a large consignment of weapons of any kind through to Protaras or Pernera, without the risk of being discovered.

He was still pondering and trying to put the jigsaw together as he walked down Makarios III Avenue on that most pleasant Thursday September evening.

Richard left Nicosia about half past nine on the Friday morning. He did not head straight for Larnaca by retracing his steps of the previous Tuesday night/Wednesday morning. Instead he followed the dual carriagway almost to Limassol and half an hour after arriving at his interim destination, left for Larnaca International Airport, arriving just before noon. He was waved through into the staff car park, on announcing that he had an appointment with Mr. Koumides.

Marcos Koumides was waiting for him in the lobby of the VIP suite, to where he had been directed.

"All our VIPs are at the UN in New York so I thought we could use it for your VIP", he smiled. "Don't worry Doctor Richard, there are no Press here today."

Richard was taken aback, recovering quickly he said;

"I told you she was Clare Spencer, but...."

"Costas has told me all about your Clare, your secret is safe with me"; he said somewhat unconvincingly.

Richard had been particularly careful not to talk about Clare in Cyprus. But he had broken his rule once, just once, not in Cyprus, but to Costas. The two of them had spent a week together in the May of the previous year researching the water park idea in Spain. Knowing that there were two very successful such parks within 20 miles of each other on Spain's Costa Brava, Richard had suggested he attempt to learn everything he could about them so they may profit from the mistakes of others, rather than make their own. Costas had been the obvious person to go with him on two counts. It was the intention of Philipos and Richard to give Costas the responsibility for the day-to-day management of CyproVilla, and during his time studying in San Diego, California, Costas had spent much of his time with Hispanics and had become a fluent Spannish speaker. The two water parks they had visited were 'Water World', near Loret de Mar and 'Aqua Park' near Playa d'Aro. They had stayed at the four star Costa Brava Golf Hotel during their visit, and had spent some time looking into golf course irrigation systems both at the course next to the hotel, at the magnificent new Mas Nous Course and at the championship course near Pals.

It had been late one evening after a particularly enjoyable meal with one of their Spanish hosts at the best restaurant Richard had found in mainland Spain, El Tinars, that Richard and Costas had joined a party of golfers on holiday from Suffolk. Part of the conversation had centred on how someone like Clare Spencer could get into Parliament, it had been just after the by-election. Much later, after the party from Suffolk had retired early, because they were to tee off at 8 a.m., Richard had talked of his love for and relationship with that same Clare Spencer to a curious Costas. Hardly remembering what he had said, he had sworn Costas to secrecy the next day, and the subject had never been mentioned again.

If Costas has told his father, who else has he told, wondered Richard? Not only did Costas know about Clare, his father knew she would be in Cyprus today, so Costas would know that too. And he was on the executive of the CLM....Too late, the plane was due to land in less than two hours time, even now she would be over the Adriatic and there finally was nothing he could do.

They had an uneventful lunch during which Marcos had told Richard of the plans to complete the development of Larnaca airport. As an old RAF airstrip it had been pressed into service after the closure of Nicosia Airport. Being determined to restore communications between Cyprus and the outside world, Larnaca had been the obvious choice. Although the short runway could not accommodate jets, the loan of two Viscounts by British Airways had allowed a link to Athens to be established within weeks. When no quick solution seemed probable the runway had been extended and the main trunk route to London had been re-established using two Boeing 720B jets, short-range versions of the 707. Continuous expansion had been carried out in a piecemeal fashion ever since, and now there was in place a primitive international airport handling much of the tourist traffic using Cyprus. Since the Cyprus Government had never been prepared to regard the loss of Nicosia airport as permanent, much of the building at Larnaca had been temporary, prefabricated buildings, providing visitors to the island with a most uncomfortable entry and departure. Now it had been accepted that even if the day were to come when Nicosia airport was recovered, there would still be a need for a major international airport at Larnaca to handle the tourist traffic destined for the southern, and in particular south-eastern, coast resorts. Larnaca airport was now regarded as a permanent institution and its development could be progressed on that basis.

After they had drunk their cup of Greek coffee, known outside Greek Cyprus as Turkish coffee, Marcos had suggested they visit the control tower to see what progress BA 523 was making. It was 1.30 p.m. and it was ahead of schedule, crossing the coast west of Paphos. Twenty minutes later they watched as the Tristar made a 360 degree turn over Larnaca Bay, lower its landing gear and begin its final approach. After landing without incident, it began the long taxi from the edge of the salt lake towards the terminal. As it approached, Marcos and Richard walked out of the air-conditioned terminal into the unexpectedly hot and humid September afternoon. They watched the two yellow airport buses and two sets of steps made their way towards the designated parking slot. Before the steps could be put alongside the forward and aft cabin doors, the cargo door was open and unloading had begun.

Once the main doors had been opened the chief steward ran down the steps and handed the manifest to the waiting official. A few moments later, seen only by Richard and Marcos, but barely noticed by any other airport staff, history was made. The Prime Minister of the United Kingdom of Great Britain and Northern Ireland set foot on the soil of an independent Republic of Cyprus. Yet another tourist had arrived to swell the numbers of foreign visitors that record summer. This one was to receive more attention than most.

Clare was totally relaxed. She was not in the least apprehensive. She had no reason to be. Determined as she was to taste freedom again, she knew she had only a very few hours, perhaps the weekend if she was lucky, before she was found. She would make the most of it and as she almost ran down the yellow airport passenger steps, Richard had rarely seen her look happier. He did not really know how to welcome her, she decided for him.

Recovering from finding himself carrying her weight as well as his own on his legs, as she pressed herself against him, grabbed him tightly and took her own feet off the ground, he heard her whisper in his ear;

"I'm expecting the Island of Aphrodite to live up to its reputation, so I hope you're still up to it!"

"They don't seem to have changed you yet - make sure they never do - but please do keep your feet on the ground! I'll welcome you properly later", he replied equally softly into her ear, "get down everyone's watching."

Releasing himself from Clare's practised grip, Richard

said,

"Marcos, Marcos Koumides, may I introduce you to one of my best friends, Clare Spencer, Clare and I were at University together..."

"Don't believe him Marcos, I was a young student when he was an old graduate student, you mustn't think he could possibly be as young as me," Clare joked.

The ice was broken. Neither made any reference to Clare's position, Clare not knowing herself whether Marcos either knew, or had recognised her.

"Miss Spencer", Marcos began.

"No, Clare please," she interrupted.

"Er, Clare, as an honoured guest of my good friend Richard, and since it isn't being used today - we don't get many important guests to Cyprus when most of our Government is in New York -", Marcos ambiguously remarked, "you will enter Cyprus through the VIP lounge. If you can give me your passport please, then it will only take a moment once we are inside."

Clare handed him her passport, issued eight years earlier in Cardiff. It was one of the old blue British passports, not one of the new, less substantial, burgundy EC passports. She had not used it since becoming Prime Minister, having been issued with a new Diplomatic version, and it still stated her occupation as 'teacher'.

"If you could tell me your address in Cyprus for the immigration card...."

"Initially, at least the Amathus Beach", interrupted Richard.

"Oh, are you not taking Clare to Protaras, or Ayia Napa, we - I mean I - thought that with your villa nearly finished...," said Marcos, wishing he hadn't said anything.

"No, not at first. Clare must experience the best that Cyprus can offer first. Anyway, it is a better centre for exploring the island on a first visit," commented Richard.

The 'we' was very significant, thought Richard. Marcos must have been discussing, probably with Costas, where they would be staying, and it seemed they had jumped to the wrong conclusion. "Good", thought Richard, "as they will all be in Protaras they might leave us alone."

They refused all kind offers of refreshment and by 2.20 p.m. had loaded Clare's two bags into Richard's car and were leaving the car park. They did not see a younger man walk up to Marcos, shake him warmly by the hand, and set off to walk towards his Fiat Tipo in the nearby public car park.

As the Mercedes turned right out of the airport complex and onto the road alongside the salt lake, neither did they pay particular attention to a Lordos coach closely followed by a taxi, seeking to overtake the coach. They did notice, however, that there had been a nasty accident outside the gates of the Free Port and that one of the vehicles involved had ended its journey amongst the oranges.

Clare looked across at Richard and smiled, "Do be careful, it might be difficult to explain if we had an accident like that and the police got involved." For the first time he could ever remember she was talking like a wife, not a girlfriend or misstress, perhaps she had changed. He hoped not too much...

CHAPTER NINE

As recently as the early 1980s the Amathus Beach Hotel had stood alone. Then it had pride of place on an otherwise almost empty coastline. Facing due south, as seen from the sea it was an impressive architectural pioneer. Built in a step-like fashion it caught the mood of some of the more famous archaeological sites of Cyprus, the grand Roman amphitheatres of the past. Even its name, taken from the nearby temple of Amathus, itself a mecca for enthusiasts, seemed totally appropriate and added to its prestige as a member of that exclusive club, the Leading Hotels of the World.

By contrast, when arriving by road it was different. All that was seen was a totally impersonal, grey concrete building, that equally could have doubled as an unimpressive city centre office building, even one containing Government offices. This was Clare's first sight of the Amathus. It was Richard's second that day. As they drew up outside he produced two keys.

"I called in earlier today and checked-in", he announced, "thought it might save some embarrassment if I took the two suites in my name. I stay here myself for a weekend during most of my trips to Cyprus so know them quite well and nobody even raised a question about why I wanted two, rather than one, suite this time".

"Always the efficient one, do you always think of everything?" enquired Clare, "what name were you going to give for your guest - Miss Smith!"

"Part of their reputation comes from their being so discreet", he smiled.

"Is it always so awfully hot - its nearly October. I'm melting, can't wait to get my clothes off".

"All in good time, patience girl", he laughed.

As they walked towards the main door the duty porter rushed through and grabbed Clare's case from Richard's hand.

"No, really its OK, I've already checked in, this is just an extra case I had in the car", Richard protested.

"Sir, you are our guest, I carry the case", was the insistent reply, "your room number sir?"

"S201", surrendered Richard.

As they walked through the lobby Clare gained her first impression of the wonderful vista and the peacefullness, almost grandeur, of the public rooms. Modern, yet tasteful, very light, but not bright, with the south wall almost completely glass looking over the gardens towards the marina and the sea beyond. She caught her breath, saw the porter disappearing off to the right towards the transparent tunnel connecting the main building with the block of 36 suites, and turned quickly herself, grabbed Richard's arm and followed.

The block of suites had been added to the main hotel in 1980 in a style that complemented the original building. Each one was large, very comfortable and faced the sea, and had its own lounge leading out onto an extensive open balcony which could not be overlooked. Richard had taken two, S201 & S202, adjoining. When Clare had agreed to come to Cyprus at last they had never discussed accommodation or where they would stay. She had been quite happy to leave all the arrangements totally to him, he had always proved so capable of getting details right. But she had been inwardly very curious to learn what he had arranged. Was it to be his flat in Nicosia, would his villa be finished, would it be a hotel, one room or two rooms? She was pleased with his choice - two individual suites, but with an interconnecting door, which at that moment, she noted, was discreetly locked on her side, but not his. She could get into his room, but unless she unlocked her side he could not do the reverse.

Richard gave the porter a £10 note, when he would have been happy to receive much less. Waving off his thanks he closed the door and walked out to Clare who was standing on his balcony.

"You've had a long flight and must be very tired, do you want a rest, or are you hungry?" he enquired gently.

"I should be tired, I should be hungry, but nothing has hit me yet. I am very hot and will take that shower and get into something cooler", she announced.

"Fine, I'm happy with a drink for now, I'll sit out here with something from the mini-bar until you're ready, then we can decide", he replied.

They turned around and went into his room. Clare hesitated, then turned towards the connecting door, although she had noted it was locked on her side, she still tried it.

"It's locked", she said, "where's the key?"

"To protect you my love from the unwelcome advances of an old man! You'll have to unlock it from your side if you trust me".

"Really Richard, do you think I would have come all the way to Cyprus to spend a week with you if your advances would be unwelcome?" she laughed as she moved towards the door to the corridor, "relax, we're together now, I'll only be fifteen minutes". With that she opened the door and went into her own room via the corridor.

After taking a beer from the mini-bar Richard picked up the phone and ordered a bottle of champagne.

"What the hell", he thought, "its not often I'll ever have Clare to myself". He demanded it be brought up immediately, hoping it would arrive before Clare returned. Then he dialled an outside line and called his secretary in Nicosia.

"Any messages?" he enquired.

His expression grew more thoughtful as he listened to the reply.

"If he calls again just say that you have spoken to me and passed on the message, and that I will be in touch just as soon as I can", he said, "will call in again on Monday, Bye".

With that he replaced the phone, and most unusually for him, did not give a contact number. With their main business being the production of live animals it was a seven, not five, day week, twenty-four hours a day. Anything could go wrong, feeding problems, disease, export transport delays, etc. Normally Philipos could always be contacted, but when he was in Cyprus, Richard had always considered it only fair that he take weekend responsibility and relieve Philipos of it for a few weeks. Not today though.

There was a knock on the door, which he answered and to his relief the champagne had arrived before Clare.

"Put it on the table in the lounge area, please", he said as he walked across to where he had left his wallet to extract another £10 note. "Let's have the staff on our side, at least", he thought. The waiter offered his thanks, very genuine they seemed, they exchanged pleasantries about the exceptional humidity for late September and the likelihood of the first thunder of the autumn, and Richard closed the door behind him.

As he was returning towards the middle of the room he heard a click, then saw his connecting door open, Clare had unlocked her side and walked through.

She looked gorgeous and seductive. Her wet hair seemed longer and laid across her shoulders. She was wearing a soft, blue cotton beach wrap, with nothing on her feet. Clare was not the most naturally attractive young woman imaginable, she would not have won a beauty contest, nor could she have been a model. She was rather too strongly and firmly built. Neither was she at all unattractive, in fact when she wished, she could make herself stand out across a crowded room. She regarded herself as perfectly normal, her figure was in proportion and her weight was not excessive for her height. It was her eyes that had always attracted Richard, they were clear and very blue, sharply defined against her light complexion, but determined, and at all times deeply seductive.

"Clare, I know it's only mid-afternoon, but I ordered a bottle of champagne to celebrate...", he began.

"Richard, I didn't come all this way just to drink champagne", she protested softly, "I can drink that every night back home at some reception. I came here for you".

She walked over towards him, and as he took a step towards her they looked into each other's eyes, her left hand grasping his right hand tightly while her right arm stretched up and clasped his neck drawing him towards her. He responded with his free hand and she released his other hand, her freed hand moving to his chest and quickly and expertly unfastening his shirt buttons. When this had been done with what seemed to be one movement, she threw open his shirt and pulled the tie cord on her beach robe revealing that to be the only garment she wore. Then she held him firmly to her with both arms and a moment later took her lips away from his.

"Didn't you say that most people in Cyprus take to their beds for a siesta in the afternoons?" she enquired,"I'm beginning to feel that I need one now, won't you join me"? she added impishly.

He picked her up and carried her across to the large bed, laid her on top and by the time she had pulled down the covers and eased herself underneath, he had removed the remainder of his clothes and was beside her.

Later, much later, after they had both taken a late, short siesta together after all, they sat out on the balcony watching the sun set over Limassol, holding a glass of champagne in one hand. They had for the first time for many years been real lovers. Not two persons each taking advantage of the other for their own pleasure. Sitting there together they both wished that the world would stop at that moment. That the sun would stay forever hovering over the town and that tomorrow would remain tomorrow.

Richard was the first to break the spell.

"You must be starving, I am", he said.

"It always did make you hungry", she teased, "we could always go back to bed and eat each other".

"You're such a romantic at heart, but...."

"But I could never let the heart rule the head for long, is that what you were about to say?"

"Perhaps", he mused. "Do you want to eat at all? Do you want to go out? Or should I order something to be brought up here?"

"Let's go out", she decided. "I'm free at the moment, the

Press haven't caught up with me. Even if they do discover where I am, they won't get here tonight, but by tomorrow night it may be different. Let's go out and enjoy ourselves - we might have to spend the rest of the week locked in these rooms - in which case we can spend all the time in bed then." she added cheerfully. "I just want to be an ordinary person again for one night".

"Right, I'll take you to have one of the best steaks in Cyprus, then afterwards, well, we can decide later. Go and get ready - nothing formal, just dress as a tourist, and I'll phone and make sure they keep a table for us".

Twenty minutes later they left the Amathus and joined the old Nicosia road, just half a mile from where seven hours earlier Charles Noble had left that same road to join the motorway.

They drove towards Limassol, past the developed holiday resort to the east of the town. Darkness having just fallen, the area had come to life with coloured lights and neon signs. This was the very worst of the post-1974 tourist explosion that Cyprus had seen. From 1980, when it had become clear that there was to be no quick return of Famagusta, expansion had been almost exponential and the result was all too clear. As in much of the Mediterranean the very atmosphere and character that had attracted the original visitors had been destroyed and a totally new urban resort had been created. For a few years business boomed and much money was spent and made. Then disillusionment set in, the peak was all too quickly past and attempts were made to retain numbers at the expense of quality. Finally a plateau was reached and everyone began to strive for quality, which all were then agreed, was the answer. At the moment Cyprus had passed the boom and was now nearing the edge of the plateau; that same plateau that many of the popular Spanish resorts had fallen off some four years earlier. In CyproVilla Richard hoped that they were anticipating this new more mature demand and that they would be ready before the rest.

After passing through this area they reached the old

Limassol sea front, which had largely remained undeveloped and unchanged. They turned right at the traffic lights and found themselves on the old by-pass which now formed one of the town's main thoroughfares. About a mile further along, after a slow journey through numerous sets of lights, Richard suddenly, without warning, turned left into what seemed to Clare to be an ordinary residential street. She had noticed, as they made the turn, a small, very ordinary looking cafe or bar. He found a parking place, they got out and Clare took Richard's arm as they walked back towards the corner. She was surprised when he led her up a few steps from the road into that same cafe she had noticed. As they entered they passed the cooking area, behind a display cabinet containing a large quantity of fresh, uncooked steak.

"This is it?" she asked with a disbelieving look on her face.

"Yes, welcome to Scotties, the best steak house in Cyprus", he replied.

Being expected, they were taken to the table in the corner by the window that Richard had requested when he had phoned earlier.

"What did you expect?" he enquired of her.

"When you said the best steak house in Cyprus somehow I suppose I imagined something more impressive looking, look even the waiter looks less like any other waiter I have ever seen, and can they really, in that tiny space, cook it perfectly? There isn't even a proper sign outside, how would anyone who didn't know about it ever find it?" she offered.

"Scotties is an institution here, part of the establishment. It never changes, but believe me it is the best. I remember coming here once in 1979 and the place had been burnt down. It was such a disappointment, and yet despite the opportunity to change it he rebuilt it exactly the same as before."

He ordered for them both. Clare was indeed impressed by the succulent fillet steak cooked to perfection. She was less impressed by the Othello Special Reserve red wine he had chosen to drink with the meal. She did not know how on earth Richard managed the massive T-bone he had ordered for himself.

"I see you are trying to build up your strength - frightened a week like this afternoon might be too much for you"? she seductively enquired, while at the same time reaching over and kissing him.

Neither of them paid any attention to a bright flash just at that moment, subconsciously assuming it was the first flash of lightning from the expected thunderstorm after such a hot and humid afternoon, if not from the electricity that flowed between them.

By the end of the meal they had both decided that they didn't want to go on elsewhere, but to return to the Amathus. Instead of going straight up when they arrived back, they went into the northern end, the quiet end, of the lobby lounge and ordered French coffee. Richard had found that in Cyprus there were three types of coffee, Greek coffee, French coffee and Nescafe. Greek coffee was served in the traditional small cups, Nescafe was served in the form of a jug of hot water together with small packets of powdered coffee, as a sort of self-service catering exercise, and French coffee, a jug of excellent percolated coffee. He always chose French.

As they were waiting for their coffee they both looked more serious. Richard was trying to decide whether to tell Clare a little of what he knew about the CLM and Clare was wondering whether and how to tell Richard her real reason for coming to Cyprus. They both decided together, each leaning forward and speaking the other's name. That broke the ice and they laughed together. They were saved a further attempt by the waiter who brought their coffee and mints.

Clare spoke first.

"Richard, today has been one of the most thoroughly enjoyable I have had for a long time, but I do want to speak seriously to you about the future. Perhaps not now, but soon, perhaps later if we are both not too tired."

He decided; "I've something important I ought to tell you, but I didn't want to spoil today". Checking to see that they were not within earshot of anyone else, he continued: "I am very worried that there may just be some terrorist action here in Cyprus within the next few days. You know that I have got to know a great many local people here, I work with them every day, and I do understand some Greek. It may be putting two and two together and making five, or even six or seven, but from some conversations I have overheard the CLM, the Cyprus Liberation Movement, seems to be planning something. I thought about getting you to cancel you visit since obviously it could embarrass you, being here in the island at the same time. Seems it is connected with the UN debate next week, twenty years after the first one after the partition. I have no idea what they are planning", he lied, "but I think it will be this weekend. If you want to catch the morning plane out I am sure I can arrange it...I am sorry Clare I should have stopped you coming, but I thought, worried, if I did then I may never see you again.."

"No, Richard I'm glad you didn't. This afternoon was worth any number of problems later. No, I am not going in the morning. If the worst comes to the worst I can always say that I had been tipped off something was going to happen, and wanted to be on the spot to direct our forces based at Akrotiri and Dhekelia. Mrs Thatcher always made a good picture driving a tank, perhaps I could try a helicopter".

"Hadn't thought of that, they'll never believe you though". he said. He thought, then thought again and decided not to tell her that he was sure those planning the CLM operation knew she was in Cyprus.

They talked for about ten minutes more while they drank their coffee. Richard did tell her a little more, that he suspected they were going to try to recapture Famagusta. Clare had felt that might not be too bad since at least that town was now deserted and that few if any civilians could be endangered.

"What did you want to talk to me about", he asked.

"Not now, perhaps later. Lets go up and finish that bottle of champagne if it hasn't gone too flat. I didn't drink much of the wine, too heavy for me, so I want a night-cap."

"No, it will be flat, this is a special occasion, I'll order a new bottle". As good as his word he called the waiter over and order a bottle of their best to be delivered to room S201 at once, and made sure of it by producing another £10 note.

In the moonlight of the half moon shining straight onto the balcony from the south he could see the edge of the retreating storm. To his eyes on this night of fulfilment of long held dreams, Clare shone as brightly as the moon.

Starting her second glass from this second bottle, Clare began;

"Richard, my love, I want to talk to you. I didn't know whether to wait until our last night, but perhaps now after what you have just told me we don't really know which night will be our last together. It's so difficult to put words, deepest thoughts and feelings to someone you love, - yes I've always loved you - but never as much as today. And yet - yet it seems so easy to say exactly what I want to say in politics - even to those who have a right to believe they know far more about the subject than I do. I suppose its confidence - it's hard to be really confident about feelings and innermost thoughts."

A horrible thought flashed through his mind - "she's come to have one last fling, let me down gently and end our relationship." he began to think, and his heart sank.

"What I have discovered more than anything else since moving into No. 10 is how really lonely I am."

"Surely not - that's the last thing I would have thought was possible in a place like that, isn't your biggest problem getting any time alone, any peace at all?"

"That's how I thought it would be. But when all those Red Boxes have been dealt with, when I retire to the flat, I have no one. It's not easy. I'm all on my own. How can I ask someone to come and have a bedtime drink with me, it would be the talk of Whitehall, whether it was a man or a woman. 'The News of the World' has already set people wondering - attractive, unattached and unmarried at thirty-seven - I'm sure it will not be long before stories start appearing suggesting, not overtly of course, I might be a lesbian. I wish it were different. Why should politicians be any different from anyone else. If I was a pop star or a TV newsreader it would be good for my image if I had a live-in boyfriend, or was seen on the arm of someone different every night. But a Prime Minister...?"

They were sitting on the lounge sofa in Richard's suite and she moved closer, put her arms around him and began to cry.

"I want to change things, I want people to regard politicians as normal people. We are. I'm the same person I was standing in front of a class of kids." A watery smile appeared. "After all standing at the dispatch box isn't very different from facing a classroom full of schoolboys."

"At least you have a shoulder to cry on tonight," he said trying to encourage her to continue, "but why are you telling me this, how does it affect us?"

She continued to find it very difficult to get to the point of what she wanted to say to him.

"All those years in Bristol after you had left just flew by. I was involved in my work, with the Alliance until 1987, and then I travelled a lot in the holidays. Yes I had men in my life, but they were not important. I was never serious. I could never forget you. About seven years ago we teachers had to read all the AIDS propaganda produced for schools and that made men even more unattractive, especially any single men left in my generation. Then suddenly I was standing for Parliament and to everyone's surprise, including my own, got elected and became a headline story that ran and ran. You know the rest."

She released herself from him, took her half empty glass, stood up and walked towards the glinting moonlight streaming through the open balcony door. While still looking away from him she continued;

"I want a husband and I want a baby before it's too late, " she blurted out.

He was speechless and before he could think of anything to say she went on;

"Of course I want you, you are the only man I have ever loved and I don't think I could love anyone else as much or in the same way. But if I can't have you then I am determined to find a man I like who will have me as his wife. I'm thirty-seven and I've no time left, it has to be now or never.

She turned to face him, looked him straight in the eyes and said seriously;

"This week can be the beginning...or, and with all my heart I would hate it...the end. You must decide. Not now, not tonight, but soon. Don't answer now"

She walked over to him, bent down, kissed his numbed face and added, "I'll leave you for a few minutes, but will be waiting for you. Whatever the future holds for us let's at least enjoy what we have left of this week together."

She straightened up, walked through the door to her room, leaving both doors ajar.

His mind was in turmoil. He reflected that it could not be easy for her either. "That's why she said what she did over the meal earlier," he thought. She had asked him bluntly why he had never asked her to marry him all those years ago, they both knew the excuses he had given had been just that - excuses. But surprisingly, perhaps, he thought, she had never pressed him, until tonight, and he had never volunteered...Tonight, for the first time he had told her the truth. He had answered her straight question.

"Because I wanted a wife for myself and a mother for my children and you would have been neither. A lover, yes, a wife and mother, no."

Surprisingly it had been the sort of answer she had been expecting and she had not appeared at all troubled or insulted by the answer, in fact she had joked about it;

"And if you had married me we could never have afforded to keep you in steak so that you could have satisfied my enormous appetite as a lover, so it could never have worked anyway!"

What was he to do? To give up his marriage for Clare? Or to lose Clare, perhaps for ever? His marriage was not unhappy, if not exciting. He wondered though how stable it would be if he lost Clare. The excitement she added to his life allowed him to be content with a good businesslike marriage. Yes he had cheated Barbara, but it had been in her interests as well as his own, at least that was what he had made himself believe. Without Clare they may not have lasted the course this long. Did Barbara know? How could he know, he couldn't ask her could he? What would happen if he lost Clare? Would he lose Barbara as well? Should he give up Barbara and throw everything into a fresh start with Clare? What about the children? No, it was an impossible choice to make, but one day one he would have to make....

He shook himself out of his thoughts as he heard Clare sobbing again. He had never, never seen her like this before. She hadn't even seemed particularly bothered about the CLM and what they may bring. As he went into her room he saw that she was lying across her bed, her head almost buried in the pillow, she had thrown off her dress and shoes, but still had her underclothes on. He took off his own shoes and shirt and lay down beside her, putting his arm round her back and shoulder. She turned to him, burying her face in his chest.

"What have I done," she sobbed, "I've spoilt everything. I so wanted just to enjoy this week, but too much champagne got under the facade, made me say what was underneath. I do want you, but not at the risk of losing you."

"I do understand, whatever else, whatever may happen you must know that. I'll always love you too. I'm not going to try to answer you now. It's been a long, wonderful and most unusual day - one I'll never forget. We'll talk again in the morning."

They held each other closely, she sobbed herself to sleep and he drifted in and out of sleep, but was awake when the sky began to lighten. As the curtains had not been closed it got brighter more quickly and she stirred, then awoke. Then they were lovers again.

CHAPTER TEN

It was almost 9 a.m. local time. He had ordered breakfast for two at 9.30 on his balcony. Leaving the bathroom he saw that a complementary copy of the Cyprus Mail, an English language daily broadsheet, had been pushed under his door. The front page hit him like a bullet. The headline read: 'President in Talks with Fowler Administration.' That was not what he noticed. At the bottom of the page there was a small story under the headline 'Largest Ever Reunion Today', which went on to describe briefly that reservists and former members of the National Guard were meeting near Paralimni today and had completely taken over the Golden Coast, one of the largest of the hotels on the east coast. It also quoted several Swedish tourists who had been found alternative accommodation at Ayia Napa, as having been delighted to accept a complete refund of their holiday costs, together with complementary accommodation for the remainder of their stay. That story confirmed one of his worst fears, and made him worry even more about the implications of the message he had received from his secretary yesterday afternoon, which he had deliberately ignored.

It was the third item that really shocked him; a picture. A picture of a couple enjoying a romantic meal together under the headline: 'British Prime Minister in Cyprus.' The short piece under the picture told the facts briefly, but accurately:

Attractive Clare Spencer, surprisingly elected as British Prime Minister in May, is seen here enjoying a meal at Scotties in Limassol with Anglo/Cypriot businessman Richard Rowland. It is not known where Miss Spencer is staying in Cyprus, neither the Cyprus Government nor the British High Commission in Nicosia were prepared to comment.

Clare had heard his half suppressed yelp of surprise and by the time he had finished reading, was standing beside him.

It did not need him to point out to her what had shocked him. She saw, and to her what she saw, seemed to take up the whole front page, a picture of herself leaning over a dinner table, looking at her most seductive, with her mouth opening, just before she had kissed him. In the picture it seemed that she was about to devour him.

Suddenly it was Clare the politician, not the lover. She glanced at the clock and dashed for the radio, saying;

"Let's see if the BBC have got hold of this yet."

In Cyprus, unlike most Mediterranean islands, it was not difficult to find and receive the BBC, a short-wave radio was not necessary, good reception could be obtained on medium wave on the simplest radio. This was because the BBC maintained its Middle East medium wave relay station on the island. She was just in time to catch the fourth item on the 06.00 hrs GMT, 9 a.m. local time, BBC World Service News, which immediately preceded Newsdesk, the morning news magazine programme. The announcer said;

"The British Prime Minister, Miss Clare Spencer, announced in London yesterday, Friday, that she has taken a holiday to an undisclosed destination. She had asked the media to respect her privacy and allow her to take a complete rest. But following an item in today's Cyprus daily papers, which was picked up by the newsagencies in London, showing her dining out in Limassol, Cyprus, Chancellor of the Exchequer, Dr Roger Evans, has issued a statement. He asked the media to continue to respect the Prime Minister's privacy; adding that he knows the British people will make allowances for the relative inexperience of the Prime Minister in diplomatic matters, and asks the Government of Cyprus to accept his apology on behalf of the British Government for any embarrassment caused by the unexpected and uninvited arrival on its territory of the British head of Government. In answer to a question, he also added "I am sure one cannot assume any relationship with her dinner-date other than that they are just good friends."

"The bastard," cried Clare.

Richard saw on her face the ice cold determination that had got her to the top of British politics. She lifted the telephone and dialled a UK number, one of dozens she carried in her head at instant recall.

"Edmund", she said when it was answered, with no preliminaries, "have you heard what Evans has said?"

"Clare, I've been up half the night with reporters on the phone, yes I've heard what he said on the 6 a.m. news, I'm expecting the Today programme might phone him, or even me, and do a live interview."

"Don't wait, Edmund." she ordered. "Listen."

She then quickly and concisely told Edmund the truth. Even about Richard and what the relationship really was. It was no good expecting his help unless she was straight with him. She then suggested what he might care to do.

Ten minutes later the Newsdesk anchorman said:

"We have a late item on the Clare Spencer story. A few moments ago we spoke to Foreign Secretary Edmund Stead on the telephone."

"Mr Stead," the reporter began, "what is your reaction to discovering that the Prime Minister is in Cyprus..er, and the circumstances of her appearance last night."

"Clare Spencer is the most brilliantly unconventional Prime Minister this country has had this century. She is undoubtably the right person in the right place at the right time. No one else could have put together the strong Government as well as she has done, the rest of us have too much history as baggage. She is new and the country needs her. But, it needs Clare Spencer as she was, a vibrant lively young woman, not Clare Spencer exhausted and overwhelmed by it all. No one can work seven days a week, twenty-four hours a day. She must be allowed to carry on her life as Clare Spencer. I for one totally respect her for trying to do so. As Foreign Secretary, I can say that it would have been more embarrassing to the Government of Cyprus if her visit had been official, or even semi-official. Most of their Cabinet, certainly those concerned with foreign affairs, are in New York. Had they known in advance, someone would have had to remain behind to welcome her."

"What about her..er, implied liaison with married man Richard Rowland." pressed the reporter.

"Clare has known Richard for eighteen years, they were at University together. What is more natural than for her to turn to a close friend to help arrange her holiday in a country where he has extensive business interests in the tourist industry, and then for him to entertain her to dinner?"

"It is reported that in one of the photographs published she was kissing him...."

"Really." interrupted Edmund, "at almost every dinner party I attend, the hostess starts kissing the male guests, and the female guests start kissing the host. If she wants to kiss Rowland or even sleep with him that's her business. It makes no difference to how good she is as a Prime Minister or her abilities as a politician. If she was from the world of entertainment, or dare I say, the BBC, such publicity would enhance her reputation and her value. I certainly welcome the breath of fresh air and honesty she has brought to politics. Perhaps we can all be treated as normal human beings after Clare has smashed some of these outdated attitudes and prejudices."

"You mean you would condone it if she had an affair with a married man?"

"What I would condone would be her right as human being and a politician to make that decision herself. Certainly it would not affect her suitability to be our Prime Minister, either in my eyes, that of my Party, or that of the British people."

"Mr Stead, one final question. How do you react to Dr Evans' remarks in which he apologised on behalf of the Government for Miss Spencer's behaviour?"

"I am sure," replied Edmund carefully and deliberately, "that Dr Evans will become an excellent Chancellor of the Exchequer. I know it is difficult for him, but am equally sure that he will come to accept Clare Spencer's position as Coalition leader and that his, as well as his country's, interests lie in Clare Spencer's success in leading a united Government."

"You do not agree with his comments then?"

"I repeat I have every confidence in Roger's abilities as Chancellor."

"Mr Stead I am afraid we are out of time, thank you for speaking to us so early on a Saturday morning."

"It is always a pleasure to speak to the BBC."

Clare looked at Richard and smiled.

"That should set the cat among the pigeons. With any luck the stories about Roger's remarks and Edmund's support will be a bigger story than you and I by tonight. Evans has shot himself in the foot once too often. Edmund and I can manage without him and his tiny Establishment group in my Party. None of the new intake of Liberal Democrats have any time for him. He was happier with a Party small enough to fit in a single taxi. He'll soon be history and if my instincts are right he will not get much public sympathy for attacking me or my morals. His opposition will make what I am doing quite acceptable!"

Richard smiled back and wondered to himself what the British public would think if they could imagine the scene. That here in Cyprus their sexy thirty-seven year-old leader was pulling the strings of her coalition partners from her married lover's bedroom, dressed only in a pair of brief bikini bottoms and enjoying every moment of it. Now he could see how she managed such long intervals between sex, she got almost as much satisfaction from juggling all the political balls in the air.

There was a knock at the door, Clare ran into her room as Richard let the two waiters in with the breakfast trays. He did not imagine it when they both cast a knowing look at the connecting door standing open.

"About your proposition, "he began, as they ate breakfast, bathed in the hot morning sun. "Has anything really changed? After watching and listening to you this morning I'm still not sure you could ever be a wife and mother. Why not stick to what you do best? - An exceptionally talented politician and an exceptional lover!"

"Richard, most of the hard work has been done. I've had one real objective. Once my proportional representation bill is through the Commons by Easter it's complete. Never again will one Party be able to impose the will of its leader on the country. We will never have extreme forms of Government, changing from one to the other every five or ten years. Everything will have to be sensible and objective. No nationalisation, state control, no large cuts in public services, but sensible public investment. It will have to be a consensus. When I've achieved that I can relax more. I can't get my tax ideas through in this Parliament, I had to accept that in agreeing to accept the Tories in coalition. I will stay on as a chairman, or I will step down. Number 10 can cease to have such a large executive role. I'm determined to have my own life. I want to share it with you. We can both start again, sixteen years late. But if not with you...I don't want to think about it, but I will try. It could never be as good, but it's worth trying."

"When do you need to know? - if it was just me, if I was alone, I would say yes, you know that. But, well, I do have to think of Barbara and the kids..."

"Barbara has had your best years," she replied shortly, "she stole you from me, she has a family, she will not be alone, now I want you back. Let me know by Christmas, no by the beginning of December. If it's 'yes' then we spend Christmas together, if it's no then I want to be able to make other plans. I'm not going to spend another Christmas alone"

After breakfast she announced:

"Come on let's go for a swim, I'm on holiday so I'm going to act like it for as long as possible."

"It's a pity you've got to act out a holiday, it can't be much of a mental break banging heads together in London before breakfast."

"Oh, but I enjoyed that, I probably wouldn't have done it if I'd been there - and it has needed doing for three months now."

"You can't go out like that," he said, leaning over and stroking her bare chest, "this morning's photo was bad enough, but that only made the front page, page three look out!"

This time her face did begin to change colour.

"I had completely forgotten I hadn't put the top on, I was just going to when you shouted out after you had picked the paper up. I won't be a moment."

She returned, respectably covered, wearing both parts of her bright yellow bikini and her blue beach robe, which she had modestly tied. He already had his shorts on, but put on an unbuttoned sports shirt over his shoulders.

"Let's go, we can collect beach towels outside the Coffee Shop."

"What about your wallet and my bag," she asked.

"I'll get a safety deposit box from Nicos on the way out," he replied, "bring it with you and put any jewellery inside first."

He collected his wallet, she her diamond brooch and necklace, the only valuables she had brought with her. They ran down the stairs and through the tunnel to the main part of the hotel. After securing their valuables and handing their room keys into Reception they went down the flight of stairs across the lobby from the desk, to the lower floor, collecting beach towels from the desk next to the external door, beside the Coffee Shop.

They walked out, and with the original hotel pool on their right, headed towards the extensive green lawned gardens populated by widely scattered couples and families making the most of the midmorning sun. They picked their spot, to the western side of the garden, between two trees forming part of a thin row separating the beach from the grounds.

The appearance of the beach was perhaps the least attractive feature of the Amathus. The sand was very dark greyish brown. From a distance it could have been mud. In fact it was as clean as the most golden beach imaginable. Looks were deceptive. Richard walked twenty yards from the spot they had chosen and collected two sun beds. There was no need to rise before the sun here to reserve a beach bed. Even the Germans stayed in bed until breakfast. They laid their towels over them and ran towards the inviting sea. No one had given any sign of recognition.

Clare was an excellent swimmer, far better than Richard. She threw herself into the waves, which were larger than usual due to the previous night's storm, but she had soon crossed to the rock breakwater, which she climbed, then waited for Richard to reach her. When he did, she dived in and raced back towards the shore. They spent three hours swimming and relaxing. They enjoyed every moment, the sun, the sea and each other.

Rather than returning upstairs to dress for lunch they merely walked through the garden to the bar, close to the pool, but attached to the Coffee Shop and enjoyed a leisurely lunch of kebabs, washed down with a freshly chilled, slightly sparkling bottle of Bellapais wine. A brand that was still produced and universally available despite the village of Bellapais having been in Turkish hands for more than twenty years. They indulged in the uniquely English practice of finishing with strawberries, since they were still available well outside their normal season. Richard smiled and told Clare of the time he had commented to his Cypriot host how much he loved strawberries and how he wished he could get them at home in March. The next morning, before leaving for the airport, that same host had arrived with boxes containing thirty-six half kilo punnets of that same fruit for him to take back. How he had managed he did not know, but they had all been safely transported to his home. He had only ever made the same mistake once more - this time it had been lemons and he had been confronted with a twenty kilo carton to carry as part of his luggage.

After coffee they returned upstairs, collected their valuables from the safety deposit box, their keys from Reception and were soon back in their suites. Neither noticed the same young man who had watched them leave Larnaca, who had snapped them in Scotties, sitting gazing out to sea in the lobby, watching their reflection in the glass wall.

"It's time I showed you a little of Cyprus," Richard said, "after we have had a shower and got ready we can go to Paphos. We can see the Tomb of Kings, then go down to the harbour, it's at its best in the early evening."

"Always so sensible, so practical - you will never change will you? Yes, I'd love to go to Paphos later, but first I have a much better idea," she replied walking through the door to her suite, removing first her wrap, quickly followed by her bikini top and bottom. She turned with her 'little girl lost' expression on her face. He hesitated for a moment, but realised he didn't need a second invitation, her appetite changed his desire.

Afterwards she whispered to him.

"Before I came here I used to think so much about you, hating myself for ever having let you go. Now I can't manage without you. I want you for myself all the time."

"If you did have me all the time you might get tired of me. Are you sure you don't feel the way you do just because we are not together all the time, because we only share the good times, the fun and not the boredom, the everyday worries and the irritations that being together would bring.? I need to be sure...."

"We can never be sure of anything, politics has made that clearer than ever. Life, people and events defy any rational prediction."

They lay together for a while longer in silence. He held her closely to him and they both enjoyed being so close and still. Then they took a shower together, remaining for far longer than either had intended, and dressed in smart, but casual clothes.

"Come on, let's go now, it's only four o'clock, we'll be in Paphos before half-past five, then we can see what there is time to do." he said, becoming anxious they got as far away from Protaras, Nicosia and Famagusta as possible that Saturday evening.

As they left the air-conditioned hotel the heat of the afternoon surprised them. Perhaps we shouldn't have dressed for the evening yet, he thought, never mind the car was air-conditioned, although it seemed a pity to close out such lovely weather.

When they had returned the previous evening few parking spaces were available. A wedding reception had just ended and many of the guests had not left the hotel. The only space had been at the western end of the hotel, in the gap between the main hotel and the new block, alongside the glass tunnel. He had reversed into a rather too narrow space, having let Clare out before finally parking. Seeing the car again he was pleased that different cars were parked on either side and that there was room to get in. Clare went straight to the passenger door, waiting for him to unlock it with the central locking, she was not the sort of person who expected car doors to be opened for her. As soon as he had unlocked the car and they had each opened their respective doors, the driver's door of the green Fiat Tipo, and the passenger door of the Mercedes Taxi opened. Richard was immediately pushed from behind against the inside of his door. Clare was similarly pressed against her door from behind. Turning his head, Richard saw the figure of Costas. In a flash he understood. Now he knew why Costas had besieged his secretary with calls that he was needed at the farm. Costas was standing behind him, the Fiat's open door at his rear, the two doors forming a box from which there was no escape. The taxi door was similarly trapping Clare, behind her was a very nervous looking young man dressed in National Guard Private's uniform.

Neither Costas, nor his companion threatened them with guns, although each carried one. Instead they had hyperdermic syringes, held a few inches from each of their victims' thighs.

"Not a sound or she gets it," ordered Costas. "Listen. Slowly, ever so slowly, move towards me, close your door, then walk round the front of your car and the taxi and get into the far side rear door of the taxi. Now."

Richard was too shocked to speak or exclaim, but not Clare. She turned on her assailant and made a grab for the arm that held the syringe. Too late. In one movement the nervous Private inserted the needle, pressed the plunger and put his arm round her head and over her mouth, pulling her head back and preventing all but a stifled scream. He dropped the syringe, and roughly threw her collapsing body onto the back seat of the taxi, as she touched the seat she finally blacked-out. Horrified by what he had just seen, Richard obeyed. He got in beside her and lifted her head onto his lap. Costas and his companion closed the back doors, got into the front, locked the rear doors electronically and with Costas driving, reversed out and were onto the old Nicosia road less than fifty seconds from the moment Richard had first unlocked his car.

To Richard's great relief Clare was still breathing normally. At least it hadn't been cyanide, he thought. Only slowly did the realisation of what had happened begin to finally sink in. The CLM had kidnapped the British Prime Minister. He began to bang on the glass partition separating the front seat from the passenger compartment. Costas spoke into his microphone.

"Sorry Richard. No harm will come to either of you, but tonight we are fighting for the future of Cyprus. We couldn't pass up the opportunity of trying to prevent the British forces attempting to stop us. If we have their Prime Minister they will think twice about interfering. As soon as it's over you will both be freed. In the meantime she might also be useful to us in other ways, she may be a means of communicating our aims and objectives so that they are believed."

"What has your trigger-happy friend done to her? What was in that syringe? shouted Richard.

"Don't worry, she will be round in a few minutes no worse for the experience. It's just a dentist's general anaesthetic, just acts long enough to extract a few teeth. Now I'm not going to answer any more questions. Just look after Miss Spencer, don't let her try anything foolish. Just as she is our link to the outside world, you are our link to her. Your job is to look after her, you will be held responsible for her actions and health. We can talk more later."

They sped along the old main road, which was very quiet at that time on a Saturday. They were making such rapid progress towards what Richard believed would be Protaras, that he was taken totally by surprise when they turned violently off the road and into the entrance to the Limassol Sheraton. They passed the hotel and continued on until they came to an abrupt halt alongside a thirty foot motor cruiser in the marina. Costas got out and walked to Richard's side, his companion unlocked the rear doors and Costas opened the door.

"Get out. No tricks though, we need Clare, but I was originally told to kill you," he lied, "Lucky that I knew you as well as I do, since they agreed I could keep you alive. If you prove me wrong I'll have to follow my original orders. Help me out with her."

They carried her upright between them, holding one of her arms over each of their shoulders. She was beginning to come round.

"Quickly, this way, onto that boat."

Costas led the way, crossing the sloping gangplank they had to go sideways. As soon as they were on board another man, Michalas, Cypropoult's freight manager, removed the ladder and cast off. Back in the cockpit he eased the powerful twin diesels into forward and headed out to sea just as quickly as he decently could, through what seemed to be swarms of windsurfers. The Private, left on shore with the taxi, headed off back towards the main road and the direct route to the action.

To Richard it had all happened so quickly. One moment they were a happy couple off to Paphos, now they were held captive on the high seas heading towards what may come to be regarded a few hours later as the eye of the storm.

CHAPTER ELEVEN

A few hours earlier Barbara Rowland had woken to the incessant ringing of the telephone. It was her mother.

"Have you heard the news yet?" her mother had asked.

Barely awake, Barbara's mind began to race, what on earth could be that important to cause her mother to ring her little after seven o'clock on a Saturday morning.

"No, you know me Mum, Saturdays and Sundays I like my bed too much...," she began sleepily.

"It's Richard, Clare Spencer is with him in Cyprus," her mother blurted out without trying to let her daughter down gently.

"I've told you that it's not natural for him to be away so much. I've always thought he must have other women, but that one, all the publicity, all the humiliation, she's not even a Conservative.."

Barbara couldn't think of anything to say. She didn't hear the rest of what her mother was saying down the phone line to her. Wide awake now her mind was swimming.

Of course she had known about Clare. When she had first discovered that Richard had established contact with her again she had feared the worst. She knew that although Richard still loved Clare, he had married her. She knew why, but she still feared that rekindling the flame would end her marriage. She had never wanted that to happen. Never less than now. She was too old to start again, or so she had told herself. Anyway he had always come back to her, that had been enough. She had heaved a huge sigh of relief when Clare Spencer had been elected to Parliament, and an even bigger one when she had become leader of her Party, and then incredibly, Prime Minister. It would be much more difficult for Richard and Clare to see each other now, or so she had thought, until today.

"What exactly did it say on the news, Mum?"

"That Clare was in Cyprus, that she and 'Anglo-Cypriot

businessman Richard Rowland' were seen dining together last night. Apparently there is a picture of them together in the Cyprus morning papers. Anyway it's caused a real fuss here. Dr Evans was hinting at an affair and that nice Edmund Stead was defending her. Imagine that, defending her, even condoning, it if she were having an affair. Listen to it yourself. What are you going to do?"

"I'll listen to 'Today', then think, Mum. I'll ring you back later, bye."

"Don't be long. If it was me I would get him on the phone and tell him to find a plausible explanation and to deny everything."

"Yes mum, I know you would, but I like to think first, bye."

Barbara replaced the phone, laid back on her pillow and reached for the bedside radio switch, twiddling the knob until she found radio four and 'Today'. She heard the bones of the story at seven thirty, but had to wait until eight for the full story. It was much as her mother had told her, despite her mother's elaboration of the bare facts.

What should she do? Her first and second reactions were nothing. That was until she received her first call, from 'The News of the World', looking for a Sunday exclusive. What would its headline be she wondered; 'Life with the Premier's Lover', or 'Why I Can't Give Him Enough'! Then there was 'The Mirror' and 'The People', but it was the Sunday Times that decided her, even the serious papers were becoming more than a little interested. She couldn't do nothing. This time she would take the initiative. She would save her marriage. After all she was not entirely blameless herself....

Despite this morning's news, or perhaps because of it, she could not help but think back to her one and only affair, only it had not lasted long enough to really qualify for that description. It had been in the early days of Richard's venture in Cyprus. She had not been used to being on her own with two young preschool children as her only company. She could remember it as if it had only been yesterday, it remained one the highlights of her life. Taking the children out one afternoon, not really for their sake, they would have much preferred to have stayed at home and played with their toys, but for her own, she had been desperate just to get out of the house for a while, she had arrived in the Keilder forest. Having taken the forest road towards Keilder Water, she was looking for somewhere safe to stop so she could allow the children to run off their energy. Then it had happened. Suddenly the narrow road that was not much more than a track, was filled with an armoured personnel carrier. Its driver was searching for his troops on exercise and he did not see her in time. Her only option had been to drive off the road, the edge of which sloped steeply away. She avoided the 'tank' as she would later describe it, but at the expense of becoming firmly immobile. The personnel carrier did not stop, simply because its driver did not realise that she was in difficulty, he merely thought that she had moved to the side of the road to let him past, for which he was very grateful. The last thing he would have wanted would have been to have had an accident, he had been told so many times that peacetime armies should not antagonise the civilian population.

In the five minutes that followed she began to realise how deadly, quiet and lonely a large forest could be. She was six miles from the nearest help. What should she do? Leave the children and walk for help? Or take them with her? Could they manage to walk six miles? She decided she could not leave them and was just putting on her nylon waterproof when she was startled by a deep, friendly voice.

"Little Red Riding Hood I presume?"

She turned and was delighted to see a handsome young officer with his platoon of men, all dressed in a smart, blue uniforms.

"Oh, I've never been as pleased to see anyone, can you help me please, your tank forced me off the road, and, well, I can't move it," she said to him with great pleasure and hope.

"Sergeant, see what you can do, see if you can get it back on the road without damaging it, if not we will call up help on the radio."

"Yes sir. Come on lads, let's see if we can get this lass' wheels back on the road," ordered the sergeant.

When he had succeeded, it had posed little problem for six strong, young men, the officer said.

"Madam, I insist upon driving you home. You are in shock and I can see you will need to comfort the kids," he said sympathetically above the crying of her youngest.

To her surprise she had agreed. He asked where she lived and he spoke for a few moments into his radio, ordering a car to collect him from the address she had given him. She did not stop talking during the journey home. Not only was it the relief, but it was not often that she had a captive audience.

He declined her offer of a cup of tea or something stronger, and his car arrived within ten minutes of him delivering Barbara and her children home. She had thanked him most profusely, perhaps too much, she would think later.

On the following Saturday evening he knocked on her her door about eight o'clock. She was surprised, but delighted to see him. Nothing was worse than Saturday evenings alone, as she had told him during their journey home earlier in the week. He had explained to her that he had some time off from their training exercise and had called to make sure she had suffered no ill effects. She had invited him in, the children had already gone to bed, and offered him a drink. This time he accepted, he had been living rough for more than a week. Richard's malt whisky was honey to his lips. She had enjoyed the evening more than she could ever have imagined. The inevitable happened. He had not returned to camp until the next morning.

The following Saturday, his last before returning to Devon, he had taken her out for a meal. She had arranged for the children to stay with a neighbour, rather than arranging a babysitter, so that they could go as far away as Newcastle, in order that she would not be seen locally with another man. They had stayed the night at the Newcastle Holiday Inn, returning home early the following morning. That had been the last she had ever seen of him. They had parted the very best of friends, but had agreed that neither of them wanted anything more and the inevitable complications.

Now, more than twelve years later she still looked back on those two nights as two of the most enjoyable she had ever spent. But she had never done anything like it again. She awoke from her day-dream and immediately decided what she must do. She must fight to keep Richard, otherwise these last twelve years would have been totally wasted.

She ran downstairs and found in the magazine rack the most recent copy of Cyprus Airways' Sunjet flight magazine and found the advertisement for which was looking. Picking up the telephone she dialled a number from the magazine advertisement.

"Amathus Beach," the operator answered in English.

"Can you put me through to Richard Rowland please," she said without hesitation.

"Just a moment please, I'll have to check if he is taking calls."

Barbara smiled grimly to herself. She had guessed right, he was staying there. She replaced the receiver without waiting for any further response. Then she found her address book and dialled a Reading number. As the phone rang out she waited anxiously and nervously, hoping he would be at home. At last it was answered.

"Ray Whitehead."

"Ray, it's two years since we last saw each other, but I want you to do me an enormous favour, it's Barbara Rowland in case you have forgotten me," she said without stopping for breath.

"Barbara....have you heard the news..," he hesitated.

"Yes. That's why I calling. Ray do this for me please. Get me on the first flight possible to Cyprus. When we all went around together in Bristol you must have known how much there was between Richard and Clare. I am going to try to keep him and the only way to do that is to be there. It will be the last thing he will expect and it will show him that I really do care and may make the difference. I am sure the flights will all be fully booked up by now, by the media people, but with your influence...."

Ray couldn't believe this. It was only twenty-four hours since he had helped Clare get to Cyprus. He now knew why -so she could see his old friend Richard on the quiet. Now here was Richard's wife, another old friend, Barbara, who he himself had escorted many times in a foursome with Richard and Clare, seeking his help to join the fray. He had to help her too.

"Of course I will do my best. How far are you from Newcastle, or is Edinburgh nearer? Give me your number and I'll be back to you just as soon as I can."

She told him that Newcastle was nearer and quicker to reach, and gave him her number, adding;

"I don't care what class I am in, first, club, economy, or I don't even mind working my passage as a hostess, just get me there before dinner tonight please."

He rang back in less than five minutes.

"Get to Newcastle airport by ten fifteen, collect your ticket from the British Airways desk. You have only got twenty minutes at Heathrow, since it's not long enough to check baggage through I've arranged for you to be allowed extra hand baggage. Don't take more than you can carry onto the plane. OK?"

"Thanks a million Ray. Yes I can manage it, just. I'll let you know what happens. Bye."

It was just after eight thirty. Newcastle airport was almost an hour's drive away, but at least it was on her side of the city, just off the old A1 road, shortly after the link to the Tyne tunnel branched off to the east, so traffic should not be too big a problem. She made two calls. One to her mother in York, another to her best friend locally. Her mother had been taken aback by her daughter's decisiveness. This time she had had no chance to utter more than the odd word, but she had agreed to drive up to her daughter's home and stay to look after the children and get them to school until Barbara returned. Her friend was the sort who did not ask unnecessary questions. She was delighted to help out by collecting the children before nine fifteen and take them to their Saturday morning football match. Barbara was also grateful that her friend had offered to keep them for lunch and would return them later in the afternoon after her mother had arrived. Although the children were quite old enough to look after themselves for a few hours it was just as well that the house would be empty until her mother arrived, since they may have the Press on the doorstep later. "What would the press make of my mother?" she thought, allowing herself a quick smile at the prospect. After her second call she switched on the telephone answering machine. No more distractions.

Over a quick snack that served as breakfast she explained to the children what was happening, then rushed upstairs, dressed and packed. Her friend arrived five minutes early and she was able to leave for Newcastle on schedule, soon after nine fifteen.

The first part of the journey had gone without incident. Her ticket was ready and waiting, confirmed outward flights and open returns. She paid with her gold visa card, at first being a little taken aback by the price, until she noticed she would be travelling club class. Ray had been right. Time was very short at Heathrow, but she had managed to get off the domestic Newcastle flight first, had run through the underground walkway to Terminal Two in time to check in at the gate for CY 327, the 11.50 a.m. Cyprus Airways Airbus to Larnaca. It was due to land four hours fifteen minutes later, just after 6 p.m. local time. She should be at the Amathus before dinner.

The 'plane was full. How many were media chasing the Clare Spencer story she did not know, but could guess that several were. In fact she recognised one well known television reporter sitting two seats away from her. She had a window seat and sitting next to her was a pleasant young man who had exchanged a few words with her. As they crossed the channel the hostess offered them drinks as aperitifs to lunch. She also left them lunch menus from which to make their selection.

Her young companion turned to her and said,

"I'm not used to travelling Club, so this is the first time I have had a choice on an aeroplane. By the way as we are together for the next four hours please allow me to introduce myself. I'm John Palmer."

Not knowing whether he was a reporter who might connect her name she decided to use her maiden name.

"I'm Barbara, Barbara James, please call me Barbara. To tell you the truth I am glad of the company because I forgot to pack anything to read."

"Do you know Cyprus? This will be my first visit," he remarked as he opened a miniature gin."

"Yes, we go there most years for a summer holiday. It's lovely island, and despite everything the people still like the British. Are you going for a holiday or on business?" she asked, thinking it sensible to find out what she could about him before she said any more.

"To tell you the truth I'm a fairly junior staff reporter on the Times. I'm being sent out there because Clare Spencer is there - I don't know whether you heard the news this morning before you left, but apparently that's where she has gone for her holiday. If you ask me she should be left alone to enjoy it. If anyone deserves it she does, she managed to keep the Socialists out after all. Anyway, since I live in Slough I was asked to get to Heathrow and catch this flight. My senior colleagues are in New York, for last week's summit at the UN and some are staying over for the Assembly next week. All the political boys had left for Blackpool for the Labour Conference, so I got the call." he explained.

"What are you supposed to do when you get there?"

"Just find out what I can and be there to file any story that breaks. It looks much better in the paper if they are able to use a story signed by their own man rather than using newsagency material. Did you hear the story on the news this morning? I didn't, I missed it, I had already slept through 'Today' when they rang. Then I had to pack a few things and get a seat on this flight. I'm supposed to travel Economy until I get promotion, so I hope they pay my expense claim."

He seemed genuine enough to Barbara. Although she did wonder if he was in the right job. A reporter worrying about running up expenses didn't seem to ring true. But perhaps the Times was different, she thought.

"Yes I heard the story. I agree with you she should be left alone."

"I know, but as I am on my way I must try to get some angle on the story I suppose."

The hostess brought their meal. They had both chosen the fresh salmon salad and the Cyprus Aphrodite wine.

"I would never chose a Cyprus wine anywhere except Cyprus. But having some now will help adjust the palate to it," she had observed to him, "it's perfectly acceptable, quite drinkable, but by no means memorable. It needs to be drunk ice cold in the hot sun."

Later, after lunch had been cleared away, they both decided that they had quite enjoyed the wine after all and ordered another bottle.

"Have you arranged anywhere to stay," she asked him.

"No, I was given the number of a free-lance journalist we sometimes use. He may be able to advise me, and perhaps bring me up-to-date on anything that has happened since I left. There may be more news by now."

"Do you really think there is anything to these rumours about her having an affair?" he continued, "as a woman do you think someone like her would risk the scandal? Even in 1994 she must know that it would cause an awful fuss if it was discovered."

"She is an attractive woman, in her position there must be a lot of men trying to get her attention," she added noncommittally.

"I've heard rumours for the last two years - since she has

been in Parliament - amongst the reporters. She gives the impression of being so much in control, a little cold perhaps, that it's suggested that she doesn't really like men at all, that she prefers women..."

"That's not true, Clare..." she stopped, realising what she had done, she had given herself away.

He turned sharply as her words abruptly ended.

"Barbara, you know her don't you? You were very evasive when I asked why you were going to Cyprus. You are going to see her there aren't you." It was a statement, not a question.

She was silent for a moment. Then she decided. She had to talk to someone. Since he had guessed so much it might be worse to try to avoid the issue, he probably wouldn't believe any cover story, even if she could work one out in time. In any case he may be useful to her if she could help him find a story.

"John, I will tell you the truth if you promise not to report anything I say as having come from me, from my lips. If you do promise me that, then I will promise to try to help you find an exclusive story, or at least to steal a march on the opposition."

"OK, I promise," he smiled, "let's drink to it", he said raising his glass.

"My maiden name was James. I am Mrs Barbara Rowland, Richard Rowland's wife. My husband was photographed with Clare Spencer last night. Clare, Richard and I were three members of a group of very close friends at University in Bristol. We always thought that Clare and Richard would marry, but they had an argument and he proposed to me. Clare and Richard did see each other later, I know that. I thought it had stopped when she was elected to Parliament. I thought that had ended it, but it seems I was wrong." her eyes began to fill and she took a sip of wine and wiped her face before she continued.

"It was a shock to me this morning, but I decided to drop everything and come to Cyprus. If I hadn't, anything could have happened, they could be forced out into the open by the media and having gone that far decided to stick together, leaving me out in the cold. This way if I can get there in time

I can head them off. Clare can point to Richard and his wife together and would find it politically difficult to appear to be driving a wedge between a husband and wife. Richard will find it much more difficult to leave me. It could save my marriage and Clare's political career. After all we were all close friends once, perhaps we can be again."

The reporter in John thought about how such an exclusive interview could get him the promotion he coveted. The integrity that he undoubtedly had said no. He had given his word, he would honour it. The exclusive story may come if he stuck with her.

"What do you intend to do first when we arrive?" he asked.

"Grab the first taxi I can find and go to Limassol. They are staying at the Amathus Beach Hotel there, I discovered that before leaving. Look, in return for not quoting what I have just said you can still get a lead on everyone else. Let's go there together, then we are on our own. You will at least be in the right place before anyone else". she suggested.

"Yes please, and Barbara, thanks, the taxi is on me by the way." he replied, thought for a moment, then added, "Just before I booked the flight I rang the office to ask if there had been any further developments on the story. Our Washington correspondent had just called. A source in the intelligence community had tipped him off that something fairly major might be planned in Cyprus. Their nationalists, the CLM, were intent on capturing headlines in advance of next week's twentieth anniversary General Assembly debate on the Turkish invasion, twenty years of stalemate. The Cyprus Government is again proposing that mandatory sanctions be imposed on Turkey for ignoring and not implementing the UN Security Council Resolutions on Cyprus for twenty years. After all, sanctions were imposed on Iraq over Kuwait. This year they have the non-aligned movement and the Scandinavians on their side, so they have a sporting chance of getting their way. Our man wondered if there might be a connection with our Prime Minister's visit, or whether it was just a coincidence.

Said he didn't believe in coincidences. So it might be that there is a bigger story than we realise brewing."

"It might be that they knew she was going. Richard mentioned something about the CLM to me. Some of his business associates are connected. You know about Helena Koumides' women's movement, well Richard is sure that's more than it seems on the surface, possibly more important than the CLM itself which could be only a front. Anyway Helena is Richard's partner's sister. She's an odd character. I've never understood her at all. I don't think she likes the British at all, perhaps that comes from her time at University in Belfast in the early seventies."

"Interesting," said John. "If they knew about the Prime Minister's visit they may have deliberately spilled the beans as it were to get the world's media on the island. Nothing like having an audience present with nothing to do if you want to make news. Is your husband involved, could it be that he is part of the plan and that his job was to get Clare Spencer to Cyprus and get photographed with her?"

That was a possibility that had never occurred to Barbara. No, it wasn't likely, she concluded to herself. Richard would never have done anything to harm Clare, unless....unless he had decided to end it once and for all and this was his way of doing it. She kept those thoughts to herself.

"I suppose its always a possibility," she contented herself with saying.

They spent the rest of the journey at times involved in conversation, interrupted by long silences during which they were lost in their own private thoughts. Barbara began to be very apprehensive. What would she do when she arrived at the hotel? March up to his room to find them in bed together? Sit in the lobby and wait for them to appear? Check-in herself and invite him to her room on the internal phone? No she would pay a porter handsomely to take a note up to Richard announcing her arrival, suggesting he join her for a drink in the cocktail bar. Another thing bothered her. She was dressed to travel, not to impress. She must find somewhere to change before arriving.

John had been sensible enough to bring only hand baggage, split between a briefcase and a soft suit-carrying case containing a few essentials. If he was to stay after Monday he would have to buy a few things. They were therefore able to clear customs before any of their fellow passengers awaiting luggage. Barbara had been well trained by Richard and went straight to the right passport desk, with John in close attendance. They took the first taxi in the rank and were heading to Larnaca fifteen minutes after landing. Their route was the same as that followed by Richard and Clare the previous day. Traffic was light and despite the rapidly darkening sky they were within ten miles of Limassol by seven forty-five. After they had left the motorway, Barbara leaned over and asked the driver to call at the Sheraton first.

She turned to John and said;

"I'm going to use the Sheraton to change. Do me a favour and walk in with me, and as soon as we get into the lobby head for the desk, while I nip down the stairs to the cloakroom to get changed. One person entering alone may attract attention, but if we go in together that will divide their attention. You can think of something to say if necessary. See if they have a room next weekend, anything."

When she returned to the lobby, up the stairs, past the waterfall that dominated the area, she looked very different. She wore a simple, but very attractive black dress. Her hair had been transformed thanks to her skill with a brush and spray, and her make-up was immaculate, topped off with a liberal dose of clearly expensive perfume. No one could have guessed that she had not spent hours getting herself ready for an important dinner party. Even John, fifteen years her junior, was attracted by her now.

"Come on, let's get out of here, we'll be there in five minutes or less," she ordered.

The taxi had waited and they followed the same road, but in the other direction, that the captive Clare and Richard had been driven along in a similar looking taxi some four hours earlier.

As they entered the Amathus' grounds at the eastern entrance, Barbara said to the driver;

"Slowly please, and drive right to the other end, don't stop outside the doors."

She did this so that she could search for Richard's car amongst the large numbers parked.

At first she did not see it, then as they reached the Limassol end she turned her head towards the tunnel linking the main hotel and the new block. Then she saw it. At least he was here, she thought to herself. They hadn't gone out yet, at least by car. She told the driver to stop and thanked him for the drive. John paid him twenty five pounds, five more than he had asked. They collected their bags and walked alongside the back of the hotel towards the main doors and casually walked through. She was momentarily taken aback by the doorman who said,

"Good evening Mrs Rowland."

She nodded and turned to John, "I forgot that they remembered your name here, even if it's years since your last visit. Actually it's only five weeks since we stayed here for a weekend."

There was an anxious looking group of men standing at the top of the steps leading down to the lounge and bar area. Their heads turned to look closely at any new arrivals. By now they had become deeply worried and suspicious of everyone. One man began to look startled, then as his shock turned to recognition he began to move over towards them.

"It may be thirteen or fourteen years, but I never forget a face, and in your case more than a face. Hello Barbara, do you remember me? What are you doing here?"

His name came straight to her lips, after all, she had been thinking about him only that morning.

"Charles, Charles Noble, I could ask you the same question."

At any other time she would have been quite pleased to see him again, but tonight meeting her one and only indiscretion when she had come to shake her own husband out of a much longer lived affair, how ironic. She remembered she had never told Charles about Richard's Cyprus work, about his Cyprus involvement. She had tried to forget she had a husband while with Charles and had merely said that he was overseas on business for a few weeks. She continued,

"Charles, you know my name is Rowland. Well it was my husband seen with Clare Spencer last night. I've come to take him back. By the way this is John Palmer. of the Times, chasing the Clare story. But he is off the record until I release him. We met on the plane."

"Barbara," said Charles softly, "let me buy you a drink. I want a private word with you."

He did not wait for a reply, but took her arm and led her down the steps. She did have the presence of mind to look over her shoulder to John, indicating to him to wait.

Charles sat her down in one of the comfortable easy chairs just outside the entrance to the bar, and after calling a waiter and ordering for them both, sat down himself so that he could still see the main doors.

"Barbara, we have a problem. Clare Spencer and your Richard have disappeared. As I was stationed here in Cyprus, I am acting as head of the British side of the investigation. Tell me what you know." his tone had changed.

CHAPTER TWELVE

As the motor yacht Salamis Dawn passed close to the shore before beginning its crossing of Larnaca Bay, a Cyprus Airways Airbus A310 seemed to almost touch the tip of the boat's radio mast. A moment later flight CY 327 from London completed its final approach to the main runway of Larnaca airport which began on the shore of the Bay. Richard and Clare saw it land as they looked backwards through the transome doors of the saloon in which they were being held captive. Had they known that the airliner carried amongst its passengers Richard's wife Barbara and representatives of the British media they may have given it more attention. They were, however, much more concerned with their own predicament.

The yacht was a Colvic Sunquest 43, named Salamis Dawn by its owner Sodierius Petrou to remind him of his lost home close to the temple of Salamis on the coast, north of Famagusta. The joy of seeing the sun rise each morning out of the calm clear sea off the east coast of Cyprus had always remained a powerful memory. Rather than providing money from his vast wealth to the cause, Sodierus had offered his possessions. His ocean-going barge would now be at anchor off the Pernera fishing shelter, when asked for his yacht as well, he had willingly agreed. Costas had collected it that same morning from its berth in the Larnaca marina before cruising to the Limassol Sheraton.

Michalas had not been the only man on board. Two other men, one a sergeant, the other a corporal, both dressed in National Guard uniform, had been waiting in the saloon. As soon as they were out of earshot of the windsurfers and before Clare had fully regained her senses, one had held Clare's left ankle and attached a heavy steel chain to it, locking it in place with a large padlock. The other man repeated the procedure with the other end of the chain, locking it to Richard's right ankle.

Costas was the first to speak when Clare had recovered sufficiently to understand.

"I repeat, no tricks, the keys to the locks are in Pernera, so whatever happens you cannot escape. That chain would quite easily hold you both on the sea bottom. When we arrive the whole area will be surrounded by the National Guard, so if you are good we will release you both then and treat you as our honoured guests. Until then we have to be sure that even if you had the thought to jump overboard and swim for it, you will think again."

"Why. Why are you doing this to us?" asked Richard, not wanting to believe the obvious reason.

"Tonight will see the beginning of the end, or to quote your Churchill correctly, the end of the beginning, of the fight for a united and free island of Cyprus. Having the British Prime Minister herself with us as we set out on this historic venture, for her to see for herself the start of our struggle, is an enormous insurance policy to have. Don't you think so Miss Spencer?" Costas asked, with great emphasis on the word 'Miss'.

Clare had been thinking very quickly now that her mind had once again sharpened its focus on the situation. She had recalled the discussion she had had soon after taking office with Rodney Longbotham. He had requested a meeting to brief her on those security matters about which the Prime Minister had to know. After completing that part of the meeting he had said to her,

"Miss Spencer, there is another subject I must raise with you. In your position you must be a target for any number of potential assassins, terrorists, even lunatics," he began, and then continued, with his usual diplomacy, "Well, it may sound hard, but if they kill you we have failed and there is nothing anyone can do, it's final. But if you were ever to be taken hostage, for blackmail against the nation, or even for money, there are two points that arise. Firstly, if you will permit me, I would like to offer you some advice on how to conduct yourself. This is gained from our experience of debriefing freed hostages in the past. Secondly, I would like you to tell me from your own lips your attitude to doing deals with such people. Would you want us to negotiate for your release, meeting their demands if necessary, or would you wish us to attempt to rescue you, even at the risk of you being killed?"

Clare had remained silent for what seemed an eternity, reflecting on what had just been said. It was clear he had made a point of asking her, and there was only one answer she could give, which would enable him to abdicate any responsibility later.

"Sir Rodney, whatever my personal views may be, however frightened I may be, you have only one choice, and you know it," she said pointedly, "on this subject I agree with one of my most recent predecessors, nothing is ever gained by giving in to terrorists. I may be more liberal and tolerant than she, but even if I thought differently, which I do not, there is no way I could survive politically, even if you managed to buy my physical survival, if the nation had conceded anything for my personal benefit. No, do not concede one inch, if we are still allowed to talk in inches. But by all means send in the SAS, I'm looking for a strong, active, handsome man in any case," she smiled. "But I would be most grateful for any advice you may wish to offer on how to deal with such a situation should it ever arise, please go ahead."

Sir Rodney had proceeded to explain to her some of the findings they had made. That she must avoid two dangers in particular.

"Miss Spencer you must not be aggressive. I know that is your nature, if you will forgive me for saying so, you do have a strong will. Do not use it to antagonise your captors, it makes them nervous. On the other hand you must not fall into the 'Patty Hurst Syndrome'. Do not become so full of despair that you give your mind to the captors. Do not let their objectives become your objectives, even if they have set a deadline, do not share their disappointment if it is not kept. Avoid becoming too friendly. In other words use your strong will to keep your own mind clear and focused upon the fact that you are a captive, but that you are going to remain your own woman. A cool, but civilised relationship should develop. They must know that they will not capture your mind and that they will not succeed in driving you to desperation."

"Thank you Sir Rodney. I am sure that is good advice, but it is one piece of advice that I hope will never have to be put to the test."

This conversation had raced through her mind as Costas had been talking. Her initial reaction that had led to her being injected had been foolish, she could easily have been killed. She must be more careful. Clare decided to answer Costas.

"Thank you for explaining why we have been taken prisoner. I am sure my presence will make no difference. If I am harmed I have plenty of colleagues all of whom want my job, so it will make no difference to the Government of my country. I do admit though that I was very silly to attack my captor back at the hotel, you could have killed me. You seem to have the upper hand until we are on land again," she said looking down at the heavy chain around her ankle, "It seems there is little point in resisting for the present at least. Relax and enjoy the voyage, I'm going to."

As she finished speaking she turned her head and shoulders round, looked out the saloon window, then put her arm around Richard and kissed him. Richard remained silent. Why had he got her into this mess? And Costas. The last one he would have suspected of playing a leading role. He had always imagined him to be a real loner, not the person to be an activist of any kind. How appearances deceive, that was truer than he had thought?

"Costas, why not tell us everything. Who else should I know is involved in this, I don't imagine you thought of it yourself," he said bitterly. "Why Pernera, what are you going to do with us there? Why would it be surrounded by the National Guard, they don't operate in that part of the island."

He asked those questions, not because he hadn't guessed the answers, now that his suspicions had been confirmed. He asked them so that Clare may hear the answers and begin to understand the real seriousness of the situation, and not just from the point of view of their personal safety.

"You will have to wait until we get there. But I can tell you that Helena is the power behind tonight, but you may have to wait until tomorrow to see her. She will decide what to do with you then," he lied.

It was after eight o'clock when the Salamis Dawn rounded Cape Greco and headed north along the eastern shore of the island. Once a virtually deserted coast, the area was now suffering from serious over development. The gently rising ground behind the shoreline lent itself to tourist developments of all types. A sea view could be virtually guaranteed far back from the shore. Although the season was well past its peak there were still many tourists enjoying a late summer holiday. The coastal road itself was quieter than usual, because the National Guard had established two road blocks either side of Pernera. One was at the bottom of the hill leading up to Paralimni, and the other at the Pernera road itself, south of the side road to the Golden Coast. Traffic was not allowed between these points, it had to make the long journey round the Cape. A third checkpoint, but not a road-block as such, had been established by the road to the Cape lighthouse, in order to filter out any unnecessary traffic that could not demonstrate a need to be in Protaras or Pernera.

It was virtually dark when the Salamis Dawn threaded itself between the convoys of small boats passing between the anchored barge and the jetty. They tied up to the small jetty in the fishing shelter and the Major, who had been awaiting their arrival, stepped on board.

"Welcome to Cyprus, Prime Minister, please allow me to introduce myself. I am Major Patriches, commanding officer of the detachment of the National Guard stationed in Eastern Cyprus. I do apologise for the manner of your invitation to join our little party and operation, but I am afraid it was the only way it could be done with security. Please let me release you from these chains, so undignified for so handsome a young woman, if you will allow me to say so."

Having unlocked the chain he continued,

"Please, may I ask you to step ashore, please. If you will follow my staff, we will have dinner together and I shall explain why it was necessary to bring you here as our guests. Please," he beckoned them to step off the yacht. They did so, with the Major bringing up the rear of the little group. Neither Clare nor Richard spoke.

They followed the two NCOs across the jetty, the National Guard men ferrying items from the barge standing to one side to let them pass. Clare noticed what the men were carrying, boxes of ammunition and rifles, together with various other items which she knew were offensive weapons, but which she did not readily recognise. They climbed the steps and the group walked the short distance to the Golden Coast hotel, which stood on the edge of the sandy cove next to the fishing shelter. Besides being one of the largest hotels on the east coast, crucially it was the closest to Famagusta and was virtually isolated from most of the recent development. That was why it had been chosen by the Major as his base camp.

Outside the hotel literally hundreds of men were beginning to gather together, but they were only allowed a quick glance over their shoulders as they were rushed into the hotel lobby, which was virtually deserted. Entering through the main doors with the reception desk on their right, they turned right, then went across to the main stairs. They walked down the stairs to the restaurant area on the lower floor, where they were expected. In an otherwise empty restaurant a table had been set for four, on the end wall of the hotel. Another table, nearer the stairs, had been set for five. The Major, Clare, Richard and Costas were seated at the first one. The two guards from the yacht, The Major's personal staff of two, together with Michalas were seated at the second. No obvious precautions to prevent escape were visible, but the numbers of men around the hotel made such details unnecessary. The Major continued to treat his enforced guests with the same courtesy as he would have extended to any personal guest of his at any of his hotels. He knew no other way.

"My dear Prime Minister would you like a Cyprus Meze - that is what my men have just been served, or would you like to look at the a la carte menu?"

"Look Major, let's cut the crap. I agree we are your prisoners and we are both hungry, but stop treating us like honoured guests, " Clare said angrily.

If the Major was surprised by her outburst it didn't show for one moment on his face, that is why she had done it, to see what, if any, effect it would have. He turned to Richard, who he had met several times over the years.

"Richard you have such a strong woman here, no wonder she became your country's leader. Although it is not convenient for you to leave now I promise that you will be allowed to leave freely just as soon as the job in hand is completed. We do not wish to make an enemy of Britain again, we need all our friends now. Costas has been asked to make sure all your needs are met promptly, if they can be accommodated, and make your stay as comfortable as possible under the circumstances."

Clare noticed that as the Major spoke, Costas diverted his eyes as if there was something else. She had also become very annoyed with Richard. He had become almost passive, he spoke little and just seemed to accept everything, even now he seemed to be looking forward to his meal. The Major began again.

"We begin at ten tonight. My forces are gathering together in their correct detachments, but we will not move until it is dark. Then we take the United Nations post on the coast, and cut their communications. That should pose little problem, they only fire in self-defence, we know that and they know that. We will bring them here as our guests. Our first major objective is the Golden Sands, my hotel. That is not defended at all. We expect to have occupied the military area of Famagusta in less than an hour, with little or no bloodshed. It should be relatively easy to advance up the beach to their end of the ghost town. The other fronts will begin from Dherinia, one group will head north east towards the coast and the other will head north and when they reach the junction of the small road that links one of these to the British Base at Ayios Nikolaos they will take that road. Our aim is to hold a line from the sea to this British territory. We need to hold this line for about an hour while the rest of my men advance to fill up the gaps behind. The Golden Sands will become our field headquarters. Then it is up to Helena."

"What is Helena going to do then, move the women in behind so the Turk's bombs will kill them too, you don't expect them to stand idly by do you?" asked Richard sarcastically.

"All eventualities have been considered, that is not something we expect to happen," said the Major flatly, "there will be no bombing, nor any serious counter attack. You will be quite safe at the Golden Sands."

"You are not seriously intending to take the British Prime Minister into the battle zone," interjected an indignant Richard who suddenly became angry, "you are not endangering her life by taking her there, it's madness. Of course the Turks will counter attack, by land, sea and by air. Why do you think they have kept forty thousand troops in Cyprus for twenty years? You are all mad, all of you. I thought you would have had more sense Costas than to have got yourself involved with this set of lunatics."

Clare, remembering Sir Rodney's words, kicked Richard on the calf. "Perhaps I misjudged him, perhaps he was just suffering from shock." she thought to herself.

"Major, what purpose can possibly be served by taking me there? No one will know I am there, or believe you if you say I am...." Clare began.

"My dear Prime Minister," the Major interrupted, "look up and behind you."

Clare did so and saw a small video camera pointed at the table, the cameraman seemed to be alone.

"Most of the male staff at the Cyprus Broadcasting Corporation, the CBC, are National Guard reservists. It wasn't very difficult to arrange for an outside broadcast unit to travel down here for the weekend. They have direct access to the satellite networks from their portable dish on their lorry outside. Pictures of our little meal here will go out across Europe at ten thirty. The commentary will explain that you were engaged in last minute liaison with the commander of tonight's action and wanted to see it all for yourself, rather than just hear about it from your office in London. They will also explain that this was the real reason for the secrecy behind your visit here. Later they will set up the unit outside the Golden Sands and show that you are there."

She was very concerned now. What impression could they create. It could be made to sound so plausible, her secret trip, coupled with pictures of her sitting down and eating with the leader of raid. What on earth will Evans make of that, even Edmund will find it difficult to make excuses. Time for reflection, she thought, and remained silent.

The Major caught her mood,

"You must recognise our cause is honourable. We were all so very disappointed when your country refused to meet its treaty obligations to us in 1974. Your prompt actions four years ago, in helping to liberate Kuwait, made us remember again how you had abandoned us in 1974. After all, like Kuwait, Cyprus is a small country which was invaded by a strong neighbour. The Security Council passed resolutions calling on Turkey to withdraw, just as it did in support of Kuwait. But no multinational force, not even the RAF who were already here, came to our rescue. We were abandoned to our fate by you all. Now you have another chance, but this time we are reducing the odds in our favour. We only want to reunite our island, to regain our lost lands and homes. Your country never hesitated under Churchill, nor even Thatcher. This time you can help us, not by fighting for us, but just by being here."

"That is true", Richard interrupted, "but you can never take on Turkey and win, only fifty miles from her shore. They have one of the largest armed forces outside the superpowers. What can you muster tonight against that"? A couple of thousand men, perhaps, no tanks, no air force, no navy. It's suicide and if you force Clare to go with you into the battle zone it's murder".

Clare was grateful for Richard's growing strength and conviction as the Major replied,

"What you say is factually correct. We know that. We have known that for twenty years. That is the only reason there has been peace for so long. It is because we know that that it has been necessary to reduce the odds as I said. This is the core of our strategy. You are part of it, but only part," he pointedly looked at Clare, "but there are other means we are using, which I will not bore you with now. Please do not worry unnecessarily. The Turks will not attack. They will not risk killing the British Prime Minister, not when the RAF are on the island in strength. We will make sure they see the television pictures of you joining us in planning tonight's events. We will make sure they see pictures of you at the Golden Sands. They will be made to think that it is a joint action involving the British forces on Cyprus as well as the National Guard. If we can make them think that, they will consider very carefully before they counter attack, they will hesitate at least long enough for our second blow. Then, before they can decide to attack, we will have forced the UN forces out and established a new Green Line. At that point we will ask for a cease-fire and a new peace conference, a real one this time. Even if we eventually are forced back before they agree to a cease-fire, we will still win, look what happened to Egypt in 1973, they lost, the Israelis got across the canal, but by losing they won the peace conference and got Siniai back."

Clare and Richard exchanged glances, neither had been able to draw out either Costas or the Major on the subject of the 'second blow'. They would not give any information about it. Nevertheless they both concluded that such a surprise attack, coupled with the uncertainty created by the presence of the British Prime Minister and the attention that in itself would attract, might just succeed in achieving their objectives. Turkey might hesitate just long enough. They finished their meal, not that either of them ate very much. Even Richard had not felt hungry when the steak had arrived. Clare had picked at the meze, satisfying her small appetite. The Major rose and announced,

"We are leaving you now. My men will take you upstairs. You have been allocated the best rooms in the hotel, the ones President Kyprianou used to use for his vacations when he was President. First floor, sea view, large veranda, two rooms with connecting door. One is locked into the corridor so we need only guard one. The telephone is disconnected. You have an hour to rest, use it well, it will be some hours before you have another opportunity."

He and Costas left and Clare and Richard were taken politely, but firmly, upstairs and locked in the rooms.

"Oh my God, what a mess, " she said as the door was locked behind them, "I hate being helpless, but what can I do?" Richard held her to him and said nothing, he was thinking, calculating.

"Go and turn on the shower in the bathroom when I tell you, make it as noisy as possible," he began whispering into her ear, "I'm going to see if I can get out of here, but they may hear me trying to open the balcony doors."

"What are you going to do then?" she asked.

"See if I can get down to the ground, then try to get help - at least a message out that you are a hostage, not a free agent, so that will be known to your Government. Those idiots could drag us into a war with Turkey. That's not something you particularly want, do you?"

"Do be careful, it may be the first floor, but it's two floors above the ground, you'll kill yourself, then what can I do? Anyway if you are escaping I'm coming with you."

"No. By myself I have a chance. Two of us would have double the risk of being seen. No you stay here, they won't harm you. It's not in their interests to do that. If I can get down to the jetty, they may have finished unloading by now, and I may be able to find a fast boat and get to Ayia Napa and phone London. Give me a number of someone who will believe me, someone who is important enough to do something."

Quickly, she wrote two numbers on the telephone pad, tore the sheet off, and gave it to him. then went on to say,

"One of them will reach Sir Rodney Longbotham, tell him Clare has remembered the advice he gave her, that she sincerely hopes she is not killed and so ends his problem that way. Tell him I am trying to use my mind to focus on the fact that I am a captive. That should convince him you are who you say you are."

"Go and start the shower now," he said releasing her.

Far from releasing him she strengthened her grip and kissed him passionately. Lifting her mouth from his she said,

"I do love you and want to make love to you now, we have a few minutes."

Very, very reluctantly he pushed her away.

"No, there is no time for that now, plenty of time when we get out of this mess. Every minute counts. Now go and run those taps," he ordered firmly, but regretfully. She did as she was told.

As the noise started from the bathroom he switched off the light and walked over to the patio door furthest from the door, there were two in that special room. "Good girl" he thought as he heard the toilet flush add to the sound of the shower, making even more noise, "she's trying".

He was delighted to find it was not locked. In a flash he was outside and had the door closed again in case it was spotted. As soon as she saw he had gone, Clare turned off the taps in case the guard decided to investigate. Richard made for the seaward side of the large balcony which stretched across the two large rooms, directly overlooking the sea. There was no moon yet and it was quite dark. The National Guard had all left, or so it seemed to him. How many men would they have left behind, not many, he thought. The balcony was directly over the raised area of the lobby, which itself was on top of the large dining room on the lowest floor.

He had noticed on previous visits however that the building had been constructed in steps. He should be able to get down in two steps. But could he manage? The narrower step was the first. He dropped onto the dining room roof, almost silently since he was wearing soft rubber soled shoes. Then he remembered more geography, the ground sloped towards the sea, so he crept along the roof as far as he could in the opposite direction, towards the pool. Then he discovered a very small ledge between the floors and slowly, but steadily, made his way along it until he was at least fifty feet nearer the side of the hotel, and six feet closer to the rising ground. He dropped and in one movement crouched behind a black Jaguar. There were three soldiers outside the main doors, forty feet away, but they had not moved. He had succeeded? Keeping some vehicles between himself and the hotel he moved steathily towards the sea and the sandy cove. He waited there and listened. Nothing. Then very carefully he crept along the sand until he reached the rocks forming the small headland between the fishing shelter and the cove. Trying to keep below the line illuminated by the hotel lights, he climbed around to the fishing shelter. The unloading activity had now stopped and he could not see anyone through the gloom. But, illuminated only by hotel lights, he could see the variety of small boats in the shelter. He had to choose correctly, there was only one chance. It had to be fast, it had to have enough fuel and it had to be easy to untie. He made his choice, the nearest speedboat, one of those used to carry tourists for pleasure trips up the coast to view the deserted Famagusta, he had to risk it.

Reaching the black and white boat he found it to be tied with a double rope. Damn, thirty seconds lost. No matter he succeeded. Now for the big moment, the one of no return. It was death or glory, perhaps literally. He would have to try the motor, if it started he had a chance, if it didn't, the noise would reveal him and shots might follow. The first try failed, his fault. He froze, perhaps it wouldn't be recognised as a boat engine being started. It was, a searchlight hit him in the face.

Second time, success, he raced the engine, turned the wheel and headed straight out of the harbour towards the open sea. He wanted to get as far away from the shore, as quickly as possible. Then, well out of gunshot range he turned south and realised his mistake. A second boat was leaving the shore, he saw against the dark grey background, but it headed south-east, to intercept him. The chase was on, could he keep his lead, or was the other boat faster? It was faster, gaining on him, not quickly, but measurably.

Before he reached Cape Greco. he realised he wasn't going to make it. His pursuers were gaining too quickly now. He could stay ahead until they reached the Cape, but only just. Thinking quickly he threw off his shirt and shoes and found his gas lighter. Within a hundred meters of the Cape the shooting started. Keeping his head down he kept going and in one movement turned the wheel and made for Ayii Anargyri, which commanded the beautiful, unspoilt, rocky bays north of the Cape. Then he turned around and pulled the petrol pipe out of its outlet from the tank. Firing his gas lighter in the general direction of the tank, the petrol exploded into flames as he threw himself overboard. Moments later the boat itself erupted into a blazing inferno, but carried on its course before spilling burning liquid over the rocks as it broke apart. The question now was whether they had seen him jump out. It seemed they had not. Staying afloat with the minimum of movement he saw them circle twice, then head back in a large circular movement towards the north and the direction from which they had arrived.

Although not a strong swimmer, the three hundred yards to the shore were no problem. Climbing ashore, he assessed his position. He was just north of the small church where the coastline, although still rocky, was beginning to flatten out to the north. He headed west towards the junction of the coastal road and the lighthouse road. He saw the men at the road-block, who were questioning the drivers of all the traffic and returning much of it back towards Ayia Napa, before they saw him. Then he crossed the road on the Protaras side of this small group of National Guard. "Damn", he thought. Just as he was across the road, he was hit by headlights approaching from the north. "They must have seen me", he cursed himself as he threw himself behind a convenient rocky outcrop. Sure enough the green landrover screeched to a halt at the point he had crossed, a little more than fifty yards from the corner. He had to move quickly, despite the agony of crossing rough ground in the dark with no shoes. Just then a car drew up at the road block from the Ayia Napa direction. It was a black Ford with red number plates. He was close enough to hear some of the conversation in English between the lieutenant in charge of the control point and the English driver of the Ford. The Englishman had been trying to discover why he could not travel further, in an extremely polite manner. He showed no antagonism whatsoever, even commenting that he was delighted to turn back if that would be helpful to those brave enough to defend Cyprus from its enemies. Richard thought that was an unusual comment to make, unless the Englishman knew something and was trying to draw more information out of the Cypriot soldier.

He heard one of the soldiers from the Landrover getting uncomfortably close, there was no choice, he had to gamble. Gamble that the Englishman would stop and act quickly. By leaving his cover and making a run for the road beyond the corner he would expose himself to fire. Since they had fired at him once he knew they would not hesitate to do so again. Now. It took him forty seconds to reach the road. He had succeeded, the Ford was only moving slowly, less than fifty yards away. He knew its lights would make him a perfect target, but he had to do it, it was his only chance. He ran towards the Ford in the middle of the road. It stopped just as they opened fire. He was hit. As soon as the Englishman saw him fall his training took over, he had seen it before. He killed his lights and jumped out, lifted Richard, threw him into the back and sped away at what seemed to his passenger, suicidal speed. Nevertheless, the passenger reclined his seat and stretched out to tend the injured Richard who had been badly hit in the chest. He reported this to the driver.

"Who are you and why were they shooting at you? he asked Richard.

The passenger leaned forward and whispered to the driver,

"He's dying, won't last more than a couple of minutes," then leant back again.

"Quickly in case I pass out, listen," began Richard, "My name is Richard Rowland, I was captured with Clare Spencer, the British Prime Minister......"

"Oh, my God," said Charles Noble from behind the wheel.

CHAPTER THIRTEEN

Earlier, when Barbara Rowland had suddenly arrived without warning at the Amathus, Charles could hardly believe it. He distrusted coincidences. In fact he had begun to think that Barbara's appearance pointed to a domestic argument and perhaps nothing more serious than a scandal. After her husband had been discovered with Clare Spencer perhaps they had got wind of Barbara's arrival and had just disappeared out of sight. Clare was supposed to be on holiday after all. Then he remembered the syringe. Although he did not know its contents, it had been sent for analysis, he could not accept that there may be a second coincidence.

Barbara soon convinced him that Richard could have had no idea that she was about to arrive. Charles was then certain that it was a kidnapping, and he suspected from his sources, that it must be the CLM and that they may have been taken to the east coast, rather than Nicosia. He put in a quick phone call and then told Barbara he was going to search for Richard and Clare. She had been determined not to be left behind.

"If you leave me I'll tell John and he will have it on the front pages in the morning. Take us with you and you can keep the lid on it a little longer," she had implored him.

Not wanting to waste time arguing, and seeing that she had meant it, he had agreed. After all he did not know Richard Rowland, so she might be useful. The three of them, together with Steve Bradshaw, had climbed into a Ford Sierra 4x4 that he had begged from Akrotiri. He did not know where his chase might lead him, he might need the four-wheel drive. For the same reason both Barbara and John threw their bags into the boot of the car, rather than leaving them behind at the Amathus. They had covered the distance to Ayia Napa in little more than an hour, no lorries today, thank goodness. Charles had insisted on leaving Barbara and John at the five star Grecian Bay Hotel as they passed it. He implored John not to phone in the story, and told Barbara to prevent him doing so as it could endanger her husband's life. They had both agreed that no call would be made. Then he and Steve had set out towards Cape Greco. That had been thirty minutes earlier.

Richard Rowland continued to speak weakly from the back of the car, "The National Guard are planning to recapture Famagusta beginning at ten tonight. Clare is still a hostage, I escaped. You must ring someone called Sir Rodney Long... Longsomething, on this number." Weakly, Richard handed Clare's note with Sir Rodney's numbers to John, then went on, more slowly and quietly.

"They intend to show the world on live television that the British Prime Minister is with them and assisting them. They already have some pictures of her talking to their leader which will make it appear that she is not a hostage. They want Turkey to believe that the Greek Cypriots have active British support to make them hesitate before fighting back...I escaped to get this message....", he lost consciousness, but regained it briefly to utter a few short words, then lost it again.

"We must get him to hospital quickly, he's dying. Do we stop at Ayia Napa, or get him straight to Larnaca. How the hell are we going to tell his wife?" asked Steve Bradshaw, still leaning over the motionless Richard.

"Yes we will stop," answered Charles. "you and Barbara can take him, I'll stay and phone Sir Rodney."

"Too late, I'm afraid he's gone," murmured Steve.

"Look, when we get there you phone London. Then get that reporter to help you with the body, tell him everything then he'll co-operate. Then call the military hospital at Dhekelia, tell them to collect the body and that we will explain later, let's keep it in British hands. I'll talk to Barbara and tell her, somehow," said Charles after a pause, "then you and I will have to begin working out how to get Clare Spencer out. Hell, what a mess."

As they pulled up sharply at the main door of the Grecian Bay, where they had left Barbara and John, they looked at each other, neither was looking forward to their unpleasant tasks. Charles to tell a former lover that her husband had just been killed, and Steve to remove a body from a car and to tell the head of the British security services that his country was about to be implicated in starting a war with an ally.

Charles told Steve to cover the body before going in to make his call. He jumped out and climbed the hotel steps. Barbara, with John beside her, was waiting just inside the doors, opposite the reception desk, in a small area of chairs, conveniently located away from the lounge, for the benefit of those waiting for taxis and coaches. She did not like the look she saw on his face, something she had not seen before.

"John, wait for Steve, then book two rooms, in your name, while he makes a phone call, then help him sort something out please. Barbara, come with me to the bar." They were not requests, they were military orders.

They reached the bar in double quick time, Barbara having to run, down the few steps from the lounge, to keep up with him.

"Barbara, sit down there, please," he pointed to a large sofa. Then he went to the bar, and out of her earshot, ordered two large, straight brandies, then returned across the room and sat down beside her.

"I'm sorry I've been so sharp with you since we returned," he began softly, "Barbara, my dear, I have some bad news, it's no good beating around the bush, Richard is dead. Shot by the Cypriot National Guard while escaping."

"Oh, no," she said simply, "why, why? How? When?"

"He and Clare Spencer were kidnapped and taken to the Golden Coast hotel at Pernera. He somehow managed to escape and was trying to get somewhere to get a message out for help. He jumped out into the road in front of Steve and I, to wave us down. They fired and he fell in front of us. I managed to get out to him and get him into the car and away before he died. He was still conscious and he spoke to us. Steve was doing all he could while I was speeding away hoping we might be able to get him to Larnaca hospital before it was too late. He died before we got here."

The brandies came and he made her drink hers, then she slumped against him.

"Oh, Charles I'm glad I came to Cyprus and found you when I did. This would have happened anyway, even if I had stayed at home. At least I'm here and you were here to tell me. Thank you Charles."

"Barbara, yes I'm glad too, but you must know I can't stay with you. They still have Clare Spencer and whatever you may think of her, she is still head of the Government I work for. It's my job to work out how to get her out, alive if possible."

"Yes I know that." her tone changed. "We can never persuade John to sit on this for long now. There is only one way. The two of us are going to stay with you until this thing is over. If you had taken us with you before I would have seen him again....alive....before...", then she did cry, but not for long.

He put his arm around her, thinking quickly.

"Barbara, look its no place for you, especially now. What if I left Steve with you and took John with me?"

"No, I'm staying with you now. I want to tell her that she has killed my husband," she said bitterly.

Steve and John came over to them, not knowing whether they should attempt to join them or not. Charles beckoned them over and said to John.

"Do sit down John, I want to have a word with Steve."

Charles got up and took Steve over to the bar, telling the waiter on the way to give all four a brandy, and continued quietly, "Did you get Sir Rodney?"

"Yes, he is going to deal with it, but he didn't say how, after all it was an open line. All he said was to tell you to find her and find a way out for her. Then he added that he was putting any British resources in Cyprus at your disposal, he is making it known through the High Commission and Akrotiri that that is the position."

"Did you get him out of the car safely?"

"Yes, we managed to get him to one of John's rooms on a stretcher, had a white coat in the boot so it was easy to pass John off as a medic."

"What about the car, any mess?"

"Very little, his bleeding was internal. I've cleaned it up, no one would know."

"Good man, Steve."

He walked over to Barbara and John.

"John you are in the middle of a big story, probably the biggest you'll ever be involved in. It's Saturday night, you've missed tomorrow's paper, except the very latest editions. Do you want to spill it now and be on your own, or stick with us for the time being and have an even bigger exclusive later?"

"I'll stick with you." he said with no hesitation. "I can see your side as well as mine. You may be right, you may be wrong about having something bigger, but you are not a story now, you are my friends."

"Right I don't like it, but for now at least the four of us will stay together. But first I must decide what to do next. Careful planning is the key."

Charles had been in Cyprus long enough to have a mental picture of the island, its roads and its border, in his mind. He knew what they must do, at once.

John handed him Barbara's bag and the key to one of the rooms he had taken, being very careful to be certain that it was not the one in which they had put Richard's body.

"Come on Barbara, I'll take you upstairs for a few minutes, if you are coming with us you need to change, into a pair of jeans or slacks, do you have something?"

"Yes, what I travelled here in will do."

"Steve, sort out a secure radio frequency to Dhekelia, we are leaving in a few minutes," he ordered.

When they were upstairs he asked again if she would not rather stay behind. She was determined not to be left, she was frightened to be alone. She needed to be with someone she knew, and she didn't care about any danger. Neither did she think twice about taking off her clothes and changing with

Charles present. After all twelve years ago... Neither was Charles prepared to let her out of his sight now, he was sure she would break down on her own, and how could he either leave her, or take her if she did? Then suddenly she stopped.

"Mother - I must tell her before she hears anything on the news. It will get out by the morning. She'll have to tell the children, they must not hear it from anyone else. How do I tell my mother my husband is dead and then ask her to tell her grandchildren that they will never see their father again. Oh, Charles I came here to save him from Clare Spencer. I'd much rather she had him than this." Then she did begin to cry.

Charles had no experience of dealing with emotional problems like this first hand. All he could think to do was to hold her, and in fact that was exactly what she needed most. She regained her composure,

"Barbara, what is you mother's number?"

"It's mine, she's staying with the children."

She gave him the number, he dialled it for her, then passed the receiver to Barbara. She did not waste time, neither did she break down. Her mother was told quickly and factually that her son-in-law had been killed and that her daughter was helping find the assassins.

"Mum, it will probably be on the news tonight or tomorrow, you'll have to tell the kids before they hear it from someone else. I'm sorry to land you with such a horrible job but it's better if you do it than it coming from me over the phone. And, Mum, there's more," she covered the receiver and said to Charles "I've got to tell her," then she continued, "Clare Spencer is a hostage and there may be war here tonight, I can't say don't worry because you will, but I will be careful and call you tomorrow if I can."

Her mother was resilient, but that conversation shook her more than she realised. It was her mother who shed the flood of tears, some of them on behalf of her daughter, some of them for herself, after all it was she who would have to tell her grandchildren that they had no father, but mostly it was for Richard, who she had grown to like and love as if he were her own son, despite her wish that he did, what she would have regarded as a proper job in England, instead of being away so much.

Barbara handed the phone to Charles who replaced it.

"Come on we must go now, otherwise you will blame me for holding you up", she said to him.

Back in the lobby they joined up with John and Steve the four of them went down the steps and got into the Ford. Steve and John had made an excellent job of cleaning the back seat, it bore no trace of Richard's blood.

Charles took the wheel and set off in the direction of the village.

"We'll try another way this time," he observed.

He went through Ayia Napa at speed, turning left by the monastery car park, then right towards Nissi Beach. The car virtually flew along the coastal route, a road that had been little more than a track before Ayia Napa had been developed into the present day resort. Now it was the main road to Larnaca, an investment that had facilitated Ayia Napa's rise and which had been gratefully acknowledged by the villages relieved of the vast volume of traffic it now generated.

He turned right at the junction to Sotira and entered a road that had not been similarly improved. Barbara and John were bounced around on the back seat as he sped towards Sotira, which was crossed in record time. The next destination was Phrenaros, one of the villages that had recovered to its former self since the opening of the new road to Ayia Napa. He had to slow down through the village. Children had begun to play on the streets again and cycled without a care for other road users. Nevertheless he was through quickly, leaving at least two startled cyclists picking themselves up from the edge of the road and shaking their fists at the fast disappearing Ford. From Phrenaros the road got even rougher and their ride even more uncomfortable.

Their destination was Ayios Nikolaos, the British base which extended to the very outskirts of Famagusta itself. Charles drove through the base, only screeching to a halt as he approached the check point which defined the boundary between British and Turkish held territory. It was precisely ten o'clock.

Since Richard's escape Clare had not known what to do. She began to pace around the room, then went to the window and looked out. She could see little through the darkness. Richard had closed the balcony door behind him, but had not completely fastened it to avoid any noise. It was easy for Clare to open it enough for her to step outside in time to hear a speedboat leave the little harbour, closely followed by a second one. Once they had both disappeared around the edge of the bay, and she could see or hear no more, she went inside and closed the door behind her. How long did she have? She could not tell. They had said an hour, but if they had identified Richard, or thought they had, it would be much sooner. The room would be checked out for certain.

She was right, less than ten minutes later her door burst open and Costas entered.

"Where is he?" he demanded.

Knowing there was no point in trying to hide the fact that he was no longer there she stated the obvious.

"He escaped. Did he get away or did you catch him?"

"We will get him. The fool. Those soldiers have orders to stop and if necessary kill anyone, anyone at all, leaving here without permission. We don't want any leaks now everyone has been briefed about tonight. They will get him, but, if they have to, they will kill him, they were hand-picked, they have no inhibitions about killing, even their own comrades trying to get away. That's why they were selected."

"He won't be caught, you'll see, he'll blow your deception out of the headlines," she said defiantly, much more confidently than she really felt.

"I doubt it, it's dark and there is only one of him, we have sent a lot of men to make sure he doesn't get far. Anyway it doesn't matter now, we are almost ready. And to avoid any possibility of you doing anything foolish or trying to follow him, you are coming with us. I am not going to let you out of my sight. Now, let's move."

He pushed her more roughly than was necessary into the corridor. She had no choice but to do as she was told. Had Richard got away? If only she knew, it could help her in the hours ahead.

He led her to a National Guard Range Rover. The Major was waiting for them, he looked more concerned than when she had seen him half an hour earlier. "Perhaps Richard made it", she thought. The Major did not speak to her, but got into the passenger seat. Costas pushed her into the back seat, next to Michalas and got in beside her. The Major's staff driver was at the wheel. They headed towards Paralimni, but at the crossroads, where the main road headed straight inland towards the town, they turned right, past the road-block, towards Famagusta.

The Range Rover made rapid progress up the small and rough coastal road towards Famagusta, past the numerous terraced villa developments built there despite being so close to the line. They stopped half a mile from the United Nations post on the headland, close to the large police centre on the coast, just south of the border. The Major and Costas got out and walked towards the sea, disappearing off the side of the road into the darkness. Ten minutes later they returned.

"Everything is ready. The men will move on my signal. Now Miss Spencer you will see we are serious about this, it's no joke. The radio in Costas' hand crackled. He put it to his ear and listened.

"Something that might interest you," he began sarcastically, "your man came ashore near Cape Greco after his boat exploded. Before we could get to him he flagged down a tourist car, so we shot him. They picked him up, but we understand from Ayia Napa that he was killed, a body was brought into the Grecian Bay half an hour ago."

Clare opened her mouth to cry out, but Costas was too quick, he covered her mouth to muffle any sound. Then he gradually released his hand as she began to cry, uncontrollably, but quietly.

"You shouldn't have told her that, you should have kept it from her for now," reprimanded the Major. "She may have been more co-operative if she thought we had him in our hands."

"Doesn't matter," replied Costas, realising his mistake, "he is dead and can't get a message out, so we have no problem.

The Major took him on one side.

"It does matter, we don't want her to look like a hostage in distress, we want to project her as an active participant. Clean her up, stop her crying. You caused it, you solve it."

"Yes sir," said Costas, silently resentful, but secretly pleased.

Costas took her into the Range Rover and gave her his handkerchief. She was just about to throw it back at him and hit out at him when she remembered Sir Rodney's words again. She took the handkerchief and automatically wiped her eyes, but she couldn't repair her heart so easily. Nothing mattered now. When the opportunity came she would get her revenge. It was precisely ten o'clock.

It was nine-thirty Cyprus time, but only seven thirty in London, when Sir Rodney picked up his phone. On Saturday evenings, Sir Rodney was usually an honoured guest at an establishment dinner party, but following Charles Noble's earlier report that Clare Spencer was missing, he had cancelled his dinner engagement to remain by his phone. He had also suggested to the Foreign Secretary that it may be wise to remain in London, without suggesting exactly why, and he had recalled certain key staff from their weekend. He was surprised to hear Steve Bradshaw's voice, not Charles Noble, and was more surprised that it was on what appeared to be a public open line from Cyprus. Either he was a fool, which he knew no assistant of Charles Noble could be, or it was important. Even Sir Rodney was shocked by what he heard, but so as not to prolong the insecure call, he said the minimum possible, and just listened.

As soon as he put the telephone down he called another number, when the person he was seeking came onto the phone he said;

"Foreign Secretary I must see you immediately, where would it be convenient to meet? I cannot talk over this phone, but would it be best at the Foreign Office?"

They agreed to meet there in fifteen minutes, but before Sir Rodney rang off Edmund Stead asked;

"If it is a matter needing Prime Ministerial authority I ought to call Evans, is it that important?"

"Yes and no." replied Sir Rodney, "yes it is that important, but no I do not recommend bringing Dr Evans in at this stage, it can be regarded as a Foreign Office matter. In any case I understand Dr Evans has gone to his constituency, it would take him hours to get to London, even by air. I did not recommend to him that he stay in London as I did to you sir."

"Very well."

They entered the building together at seven forty-five.

"What is it," Edmund Stead asked. Sir Rodney began;

"Earlier I had a message from Charles Noble to say that he had lost contact with the Prime Minister and that no one seemed to have any idea where she was. Then, just before I rang you young Steve Bradshaw telephoned me from Cyprus. From a hotel in the south east of the island, so I could not prolong the conversation. We have a real problem on several fronts sir."

"Go on," said Edmund apprehensively.

"The Prime Minister and Richard Rowland were kidnapped this afternoon by the Cyprus Liberation Movement. Richard Rowland escaped and was shot, dead. But before he died Charles Noble picked him up and Rowland told him the story. Miss Spencer is a hostage of the CLM. In ten minutes time thousands of the Greek Cypriot National Guard are going to attack the Turkish army in Northern Cyprus on behalf of the CLM. They intend to tell the world that the British Prime Minister has joined them to see the action for herself, that it is a joint action with the British. They hope this will cause the Turks to hesitate long enough, fearing the RAF based at Akrotiri, for them to secure their immediate objectives without serious opposition. They have a video of Miss Spencer dining with their leaders, which I understand can be made to appear convincing, convincing enough that is, to demonstrate that she is intimately involved with them."

Edmund Stead could hardly believe what he had just heard. He knew Cyprus, having visited the island as Defence Secretary in the previous administration some years earlier. It was possible. He called in the duty officer before replying to Sir Rodney.

"Get the Defence Secretary and the Service Chiefs here now," he barked, if they can't get here in thirty minutes tell them to send their most senior deputy who can get here in that time."

He looked at Sir Rodney sharply before adding to the duty officer,

"Get hold of the Chancellor and put him through to me here."

A nod of the head indicated the conversation was over and the duty officer rushed out. Before he had left the room Edmund added,

"See if you can find two whiskeys, large ones, for us when you have finished that. "

When he had gone and closed the door behind him Edmund said to Sir Rodney,

"What about your people, do you want any of them in on this?"

"Two are on their way, will be here soon," he replied.

The air force Chief of Staff, ten minutes later. It was eight o'clock, precisely ten o'clock in Cyprus.

Helena had spent the day in Nicosia, much of it in her city centre office. Although the Cleopatra basement was the official headquarters of the CLM, Helena's offices were the nerve centre, and it was from there that she would direct operations. She had reviewed the plans for that evening many times. It had taken more than twenty years to be in a position to hit back and she was not prepared to see it fail for the sake of a minor hiccup that was foreseeable. It had to succeed. She had spoken on the telephone several times. Costas had called to report that he had berthed the Salamis Dawn at the Limassol Sheraton. The Major had called to report that his force was up to the minimum required strength and more men were still arriving. Helena found it very difficult to resist the temptation to drive to Pernera and see for herself, but she knew that she could not, she at least had to retain her detached confidence and overall perspective, in order to be in a position to remain in control of co-ordination. By late afternoon she did however decide to visit Philipos. Of all her commanders, although he was her own brother he was the one in which she had the least confidence. That was why she had decided that he should lead the Nicosia operation, the one to which she herself would be closest. She had been disappointed when Costas had persuaded her that he should handle the kidnapping, Michalas could have handled that quite easily by himself, and Costas would have been useful as her personal chief of staff, or errand boy, as she would have seen his task. However, the die was cast. Events would soon gain their own momentum and then her role would become paramount.

Philipos's command was quite small, but crucial to the success of everything. Although he had less than three hundred men, they were the best. It had been necessary for them to have been selected for a special exercise, as they had been told, to prevent them from making arrangements to travel to Pernera with their colleagues. Instead they were told to report to the west of the long-closed Nicosia airport, quite near to the Cypropoult farm, installations and hatchery. It was to there that Helena had travelled that Saturday afternoon. The journey had taken her much longer than she had anticipated. The late summer sun and warmth had tempted many citizens of Nicosia to head for the Troodos mountains before the altitude made it too cool, rather than, as on that day, a welcome relief from the heat of Nicosia itself.

It was six o'clock when she arrived. Nearly an hour later than she had told Philipos to expect her. Already he was beginning to brief his section commanders. As she drew up more men were still arriving, although the armoured personnel carriers were not due to leave the camp at Galata on the road to Troodos until after sunset, so they would not arrive until darkness had fallen over the area. Helena was satisfied with what she saw and heard, but was angry with herself for not having allowed for the delay in her arrival. This made her very concerned not to stay too long. She could see that her presence was not likely to achieve any further benefit, so she decided to leave earlier than she had intended, to make sure that whatever may befall her on her return trip to the city, she could not possibly be late again. Everything depended upon everyone being in place and ready at the agreed time, so she took her leave of Philipos.

"Take care sister, this is your show and we won't let you down," her brother began, "I know you don't think I am committed enough, like you are, but I have my family, you have your cause. Tonight your cause is my cause too. You'll be as proud of me tonight as I have been of you for twenty years - only I've often been too jealous to show it. I love you Helena, whatever happens to us all tomorrow I wanted you to know that."

Helena couldn't speak. She had never allowed herself to show any emotion, and she didn't want to speak now since that would have betrayed her feelings. She contented herself with a halfhearted hug and kissed his cheek, but did manage before she turned away,

"Thanks Philipos."

She had not eaten all day so called at a kebab stall near the Cleopatra before parking her car and returning to her office suite. Her two trusted secretaries had already arrived, and she asked them to check that the fax and telex lines were all working. Then, as she preferred her own company, she made herself coffee, switched on the two television channels, the local CBC service, and CNN International; then the two radios, CBC and the BBC World Service. It was difficult for her to know how to pass the time, so she forced herself to watch one of the televisions. It was showing an old World War II film, Anzio, in which the Americans landed virtually unopposed on an Italian beach, only to halt, rather than pursuing their attack, being too suspicious that it was a trap. How appropriate , she thought, was it a lesson? The film ended a few moments before ten o'clock.

The village of Athienou in which both Philipos and Helena had been born was almost due north of Larnaca. Since 1974 it had been almost surrounded by Turkish held territory. In their drive to capture the village of Louroujina, the Turkish army had not only cut the main road between Nicosia and Larnaca, taken the hilltop church of Lymbia, but had also captured the range of hills that dominated Athienou to the north and east. Like Lymbia a few miles away to the south west, Athienou had existed for twenty years under the fixed gun emplacements of a hostile armed force. Although villagers had grown used to this foreign presence on their very doorstep they could never be happy or rest content until it had been removed to its rightful place. Neither were Helena and Philipos the only members of the CLM central committee to have their roots in this part of the Cypriot homeland that had seen the fiercest and bloodiest fighting of August 1974. George Spyrou had never moved out of the village of Lymbia, although he now worked as a banker in central Nicosia. Instead, he made the daily journey into the city, but remained a villager at heart. Following the July CLM meeting at the Cleopatra, at which the Major had outlined plans for the organisation's first major action, George had sought out Helena and Philipos and proposed to them that an action on this central front must be taken at the same time. He had two reasons for suggesting this. Firstly he was concerned that if no action were taken then in retaliation the Turks may well attack the villages of Athienou, Lymbia and Dhali, which were all highly vulnerable and difficult to defend. Secondly, he believed that if they did not try to relieve the pressure on the area of their home they would be abandoning their birthright. To him Famagusta was a candy-floss town with no substance. For the action to be worthy of the movement he believed something must be done elsewhere, nearer to hearts of the true Cypriot than that holiday resort could ever become. There could be no better place than near his own village.

Helena was doubtful at first. She did not consider the second reason was a justification for risking spreading their forces too thinly. But she did concede that there may be merit in his first argument. Philipos was supportive of his sister's view, but she could sense that he had more sympathy with George's overall enthusiasm than she. Therefore she agreed to study the strategic implications of an additional front, and from these studies had emerged a plan of action that she eventually endorsed, willingly, but still apprehensively.

George was put in command of the central front. His forces had been divided into two companies. Their joint aim was limited to forcing the reopening of the main Larnaca to Nicosia road. One company would advance from the south, the other from the north. Their aim was to hold the road, but not to attack towards the villages of Pyroi or Louroujina. The defensive formations around the villages of Dhali, Lymbia and Athienou were to be placed on the highest possible state of alert. Although small, George's force was to be very well equipped. Light tanks were to be made available to him from both the Nicosia garrison of the National Guard, and from the defensive forces encamped to the east of Lymbia.

George himself had chosen to travel with his southern company, that was the one likely to have the most difficult task. It had been agreed that his action could not be the first to begin, but neither could it be delayed by more than a few minutes beyond that at Famagusta and Nicosia in case the Turkish army had time to become alert. It was agreed therefore, that his tanks would begin moving towards their objectives at ten o'clock, which would mean that they would not expect to have to engage the enemy for a further ten minutes.

George mounted his vehicle, a rather old ex-British army Land Rover, flashed his headlights twice as he turned left towards the north at the junction between the Larnaca to Nicosia road and the Lymbia road. At this signal his forces began to move. It was precisely ten o'clock.

CHAPTER FOURTEEN

The Turkish airliner was en route from Istanbul to Northern Cyprus with many British holidaymakers on board, most of them were going to Kyrenia to enjoy an early autumn break. There were 183 passengers on board the A310 Airbus, some families, but mainly middle aged couples returning to a part of Cyprus some had not seen since before the 1974 invasion by the Turkish armed forces.

Since 1974 it had not been possible to fly directly to the northern part of Cyprus. All airlines had continued to accept the Greek Cypriot Government's designation of all ports of entry into the north, including the airport, as illegal ports of entry. They had resisted all attempts to open international routes to the north, threatening to prevent them having access to the south if they did so. Of course the same did not apply to the national Turkish airline, but even they had to route flights via Turkey itself. Flight TK 980 was one such flight and at ten forty-five Turkish time, nine forty-five in unoccupied Cyprus, it was just crossing the Turkish coast, less than thirty minutes from Ercan airport.

Helen Jones was just finishing her second gin and tonic since leaving Heathrow airport, London, and leaned over to touch her husband Robert on the arm.

"Look Bob, we'll soon be there."

Robert Jones was an office manager from Reading who spent most of his working life trying to hold back the march of the microchip into his offices. He enjoyed being surrounded all day by a great many very sexy, attractive secretaries and typists. That was the main perk of his job. He had no intention of giving it up voluntarily if he could possibly help it. His wife Helen was in her way even more attractive than some of his office girls for all her forty five years. She knew all about Bob's attraction for his charges, and about some of his minor affairs. She had got used to the idea some fifteen years earlier after the initial shock. Now she secretly saw that the excitement that it added to Bob's life made him a much better husband. That lesson had been well learnt, she had had similar adventures, making her, in her own mind, a much better wife.

Bob turned to her with a look of anticipation.

"Yes." he said simply.

Helen knew from twenty years of experience of Bob what effect flying had on him and she was glad they had booked an afternoon flight and would be in their hotel in Salamis well before midnight. She felt some anticipation herself, and for the first time for weeks she looked really happy.

Sandra and Pete Wright were a totally different couple. Pete was an export salesman for an international drug company and his job frequently took him to the southern Greek-Cypriot, free part of Cyprus. He was the sort of man who was fascinated more by the things he could not do, or could not have, rather than all the things that his well paid job brought him. Every time he had visited the south he had looked out of his bedroom window in the Cyprus Hilton at the range of hills providing the backdrop to Nicosia and longed to see over them to Kyrenia, about which he had always heard so much from his Cypriot customers. During his weekends in Cyprus he had often gone to the sea and stopped on the road from Dherinia to Paralimni so that he could stare across to the deserted town of Famagusta. As he looked at the rows of empty, high rise hotels he had often thought how much he would like to stay there. He had become so obsessed with the idea of visiting the other Cyprus that Sandra had finally persuaded him to take them all on a week's family holiday. The only time they had been able to manage it was out of the high season, so it had been necessary to take the children off school for a week, it was the first time they had done so.

The trip had taken careful planning since they had had to obtain a second family passport, because a Turkish Cypriot stamp in Pete's would have meant that he would not have been allowed to enter Cyprus through Larnaca again. Neither had he told his employers where he was going. They might have frowned upon him risking their lucrative Cypriot business by going to the north on holiday, since all the hotels in that part of the island were Greek owned, and were being operated illegally by the Turks. Pete had been so many times to the south that he was really looking forward to this holiday and seeing the rest of the island for the first time.

Sandra was a very independent person. She looked after her two small children almost single handed with Pete away so much, and held down a teaching job at the local junior school in their village, one of the dormitory villages of Manchester in the Cheshire countryside. Sandra was a good teacher, and spent a great deal of her own time working for the school, and had done so cheerfully for so long, that her headmistress had granted her a week's leave of absence and insisted she book the holiday, when she had first mentioned the idea to her and the impossibility of going in the school holidays. Her life was busy and full. How she managed none of her friends knew, but manage she did. The weekends alone were the worst.

The trip to Cyprus would provide a welcome extended period of real rest and relaxation, oh, how they were looking forward to a week as a normal happy family. With many couples being together acted as a stimulus, in their case individually they were each complete, vibrant personalities, totally self confident and able to enjoy life to the full, while when together each defused the other into calm, quiet and thoughtful personalities. The two children, Adrian and Joan reflected both of these contrasting aspects of their parent's characters. Adrian, the eldest by eighteen months, was a quiet studious and very intelligent ten-year old. His sister was very much an opposite.

Adrian and Joan, then, were different, had different interests, but when together they were the perfect foil for each other, and on occasions when Sandra's busy life had meant she had had to risk leaving them on their own for a short time they could not have been more sensible or concerned for each other, each helping the other as much as they possibly could.

The children had not been to Cyprus before and were really looking forward to seeing somewhere new, with unlimited swimming. They were all looking forward to what they hoped would be the best family holiday yet.

Sean O'Neil and his companion Sarah sat in a pair of seats at the rear of the plane. It had seemed a very long day already, although they had had little to do. It had been absolutely essential that they catch this particular flight so they had taken no chances. They had travelled across from Ireland via Fishguard on Wednesday, and had reached Bristol that night. The following day they toured the archaeological sites of Wiltshire and deliberately had taken an active interest in all they saw. The Thursday night had been spent at Swindon. Friday was spent in the Thames valley, lunching by the river at Bray and doing much as any other young couple would do on a touring holiday of southern England. They checked into the Heathrow Holiday Inn on the Friday evening, and even borrowed some golf clubs to try the hotel's golf course before sunset.

They were in Terminal Two by ten on Saturday morning, just to be certain nothing could delay them and prevent them from boarding their flight. The next five hours were the longest Sean had ever spent, but he had to remain calm, and he did so. They had watched as an out of breath Englishwoman had rushed across the departure lounge in a desperate attempt to catch a flight to Larnaca, and overheard her explaining that she was making a connection from the recently arrived Newcastle flight.

Sean reflected, once they had boarded their flight, that this was for his mother, he owed her a lot. Neither he nor Sarah had spoken to their travelling companions, Patrick and Ruth, there had to be no connection between the two couples. But each couple had watched to be sure that the others had kept to the prearranged plan.

Sean had known the worst moment would be when his hand baggage was put through the X-ray. Although they had checked it themselves there was always the chance that there were some checks about which they did not have the correct information. He was right, it had been a desperate moment. The security officer carried the bag over to the table and asked him to open it. As he did so he caught sight of Patrick, one of his companions, out of the corner of his eye. When the bag was opened the officer went straight to the radio cassette, as he had hoped. It was turned on and found to work, then put individually through a second machine. The officer looked through the rest of the bag, glanced at the travelling iron, electric razor and a number of minor items. Then said,

"Thank you sir, all seems to be in order. We do recommend that people refrain from taking that type of cassette player in their luggage. Walkmans and small radios separately are preferred."

"I'll remember that in future," replied Sean, as he took Sarah by the arm and walked across into the departure lounge. "We can allow ourselves to have one drink," he said to her, "it's a long time until eight o'clock."

The flight had been largely uneventful. The passengers had not been allowed to leave the plane during its thirty-five minutes stop on the ground at Istanbul. A few extra passengers joined the flight before it took off again without incident. Two of these passengers did give Sean some cause for concern. They had every appearance of being army officers and he suspected they would be returning to their units of the army of occupation in Northern Cyprus, following leave or some other business in Istanbul. Would they be armed? Since it was a civilian flight and Turkey was no longer controlled by the army he doubted if they would have been allowed to carry their personal revolvers on board. But he could not be certain. His life depended upon certainty. They must be watched very carefully indeed, and probably moved before they could try anything.

Crossing the Turkish coast was the signal. Sean got up and let Sarah out, she walked up to the front of the plane, then retraced her steps. As she passed his seat Patrick rose and took his bag from the overhead locker. Sean did the same.

Sarah took the isle seat on her return while Sean busied himself with his task.

Some of the contents of his carry-on bag had taken years to develop, others years and large quantities of cash to purchase. The most important was the travelling iron. Measuring only twelve centimetres long by eight centimetres wide at its broadest point, to the naked eye, and indeed to the average X-ray machine it was a standard travelling iron. A little larger, perhaps, but essentially similar to those taken overseas each year by millions of travellers of all nationalities. It even gave the appearance that it would work, if connected to a power source a light came on and it began to warm on the bottom surface. It did not, however, get hot.

Sean took his bag onto his legs. That particular design had been chosen so that he could work on its contents in the bag, keeping them well hidden from the view of a curious onlooker. He took the iron out of its small box. Below the handle on the top of the body was a small wing nut. This was cleverly designed. It undid halfway on a normal thread, then when it had travelled halfway off the thread reversed, it had to be turned in the opposite direction while gently easing it upwards. While ingenious enough to prevent accidental opening that was the least of the miracles of technology inside.

The handle and body lifted off once the wing nut had been removed. To the casual observer the inside of the base looked like any other flat piece of steel which had had an electrical element pressed against it. The casual observer was wrong. Machined to a tolerance normally found only in the highest of technology, inside the base was the outline of a perfect miniature hand gun. It was such a perfect fit that there was only one means of removing it, pressure had to be applied at a precise point. He quickly removed the gun, then unclipped the steel glove, the mirror image of the gun itself. Underneath was a second element, the one that actually warmed the iron if necessary for inspection purposes. He then removed what appeared to be the main element and replaced it with the actual element from the base. Having removed the items he required he rebuilt the iron so that no one could know its deadly purpose. That was a secret he had had to agree would be protected and not divulged to anyone, in return for being able to purchase two of them for the mission.

Next he turned to his battery operated razor. This was simpler. Inside it contained four AA long life batteries, or so it seemed. In fact only two were real batteries, the razor had been specially adapted to work normally on two. He removed the surplus batteries. From one he removed a perfectly machined, but detachable top. The space inside was of a very small diameter, the case itself being lead lined. Nothing showed through X-ray examinations of these batteries, other than that they were solid tubes. Inside were three beautifully made bullets for the miniature hand gun. He loaded them into it very carefully. Inside the other battery was a thin, delicate detonator, attached to which was a thin wire, about one metre long. He attached the other end to the correct point in the razor. Then he replaced the tops on the dummy batteries, returned then to their slots and slipped the battery compartment lid back into place. It now appeared to be a normal razor, but with a very thin wire hanging from it.

Due to having carefully practised this procedure hundreds of times it had only taken him three minutes. He waited another minute. He and Patrick had agreed four. Ruth, Patrick's girl, then stood up and walked down the plane towards them. The prearranged signal. Then everything happened quickly, as quickly as had been planned. Patrick, who was ideally situated, grasped his opportunity and out of sight of the passenger cabin forced a hostess to gain entry to the cockpit, his arm round her neck with his weapon, which was identical to Sean's, pointing upwards into her chin. Ruth, a former Air Lingus hostess herself, who knew the aircraft intimately, took over the public address system from the hostage hostess. Sean handed to Sarah the material that had served as the main element in his iron, together with the razor and attached detonator. Sean had reserved for himself the fourth role, to react quickly to any difficulty and to immediately deal with it as necessary. He had decided in Istanbul that the army officers he had identified would be his initial objective. They would serve as the two passengers required to demonstrate to the others that compliance was the best option.

It was ten fifty Turkish time when Patrick spoke slowly and clearly to the flight deck crew. He did not move his arm from the hostesses neck.

"Listen please, no one will get hurt if you and your crew do exactly as I say."

Patrick also understood the aircraft well. He had been a maintenance engineer at Knock airport, the one built by the Irish government in the 1980s, despite its own opposition, in the west of Ireland. That was why he had been chosen for the mission.

"Please remember I know exactly what all the controls do and what all the instruments mean. I shall be watching your every move. Do not touch the radio without my permission." He went on. "I want you to make this announcement to the passengers now, in English only."

He handed the paper to the captain, who looked at his hostess and nodded.

"Ladies and gentlemen, we shall shortly be commencing our descent, please fasten your seat belts immediately since there may be some turbulence. My stewardess will give you further instructions."

"Well done captain," said Patrick. "Now let me assure you we are not maniacs. Nor are we intending to ask you to fly around the Mediterranean for the next week looking for somewhere to land. We shall land in Cyprus with only a very minimal delay of no more than a few minutes. Please speak to your controller and tell him this, exactly. No tricks."

He handed him another piece of paper. The captain just nodded, he did not speak, then he did as commanded and called up ground control.

"This is flight TK 980. I have to report a small problem with the flaps, just to be certain I am going to make an approach, but not land at the airport, and circle round. My landing will be delayed by up to fifteen minutes."

Ground control acknowledged, then a minute later came on to confirm a new landing time, fifteen minutes later than the original time.

"Thank you captain, let me explain I have a colleague with a similar weapon in the cabin. We also have a quantity of plastic explosive which is being positioned on the rear hatch. If you overcome me you are likely to cause that to be detonated and to crash the plane. Do you understand?"

The captain nodded.

As soon as the captain had told his passengers to fasten their seat belts Ruth had performed her role to perfection. She spoke to the passengers in her stewardess voice.

"Ladies and gentlemen, please be calm and remain in your seats. We have a small technical problem that will delay our landing for a few minutes. This aeroplane has been taken over by armed hijackers and if anyone makes any sudden movement all our lives could be in danger. I have been asked to tell you by one of those in charge of the aircraft that they are not Muslim Fundamentalists, nor Palestinians, but Greek Cypriots. It is their intention to land in Cyprus after a short delay. You are asked to remain quietly seated."

That announcement was greeted in a stunned silence. It was the signal for Sean and Sarah. Sean had positioned himself to watch the Turkish gentlemen who had joined the flight in Istanbul closely. He moved towards them as Ruth began to speak and one had begun to reach towards the bag under his feet. Sean showed them his gun, hidden in a long wide sleeve on his jacket.

"Come." he had beckoned to them both. They obeyed his order. without question.

Meanwhile, Sarah had been busy. She had taken the element, a cream coloured material with silver streaks painted on it, and pressed it into an oval shape, no bigger than an out of shape golf ball. Then she took it to the rear hatch and flattened it on the handle and pressed the detonator into the plastic material. She walked almost a metre away, holding the razor in her outstretched hand. By switching the razor on she could blow out the hatch, which would suck out into the thin night air anything not tightly fastened down. She was able to seat herself into the crew jump seat and fasten the belt over her body with her one free arm. Now at least she stood a chance, perhaps a remote one, but at least a chance, if she had to detonate the device.

Sean brought the two Turks to the rear hatch. They were made to sit down on the floor in front of it cross legged. They understood enough English to appreciate their fate if they caused trouble. They also noted that it was a very small bomb, and with Sarah fastened to a seat it was not certain that the hijackers would kill themselves if they did detonate their threat. They realised they had no choice but to be careful if they wished to live.

Satisfied that Sarah had the Turks under control, and knowing that she would have no hesitation in switching on the razor if there was trouble, Sean went forward. As he approached the Wright children Adrian looked up and said to him without inhibition.

"If you detonate that bomb it would probably damage the rudder controls and we would be out of control."

Sean was taken aback and momentarily lost his composure, he had not expected to be confronted with the truth by a twelve year old.

"It's OK son," he began in a broad Irish accent, " we don't want to die either, but they don't know that."

"You're not Greek Cypriots, you're Irish, why are you doing this to us?" Adrian continued as if it were an everyday conversation.

"We are Irish, but we really are working for our friends from Cyprus." he realised he had already said more than he should and he gently patted Adrian on the head and continued forward, as he left he turned and said, "don't worry, it will soon be over."

Sean entered the cockpit and explained the predicament of the two Turkish men sitting under a fused bomb by the rear hatch. Patrick left, taking the hostess with him, to watch over Sarah.

"Now gentlemen you will make a normal approach to Ercan. Call ground control and don't try any tricks, but tell them all is now well and you are proceeding with a normal landing at eleven twenty."

It was precisely eleven o'clock, ten o'clock in unoccupied Cyprus.

After Helena had left Philipos' command things began to move quickly. His briefings continued for another hour, then the first of a dozen armoured personnel carriers began to arrive. They were deployed in the correct and pre-planned formation, ready for the order to roll forward. Just as important were the thirty private cars necessary to achieve his purpose. They were made ready and their drivers briefed.

Philipos was not expecting any armed resistance. To achieve their objective they did not have to capture or even enter any Turkish held territory. Their objective was under the exclusive control of the United Nations Forces. The terms of reference of the UN force were for it to be a deterrent, not to engage any belligerents, just as they had stood aside when the Israeli forces had invaded Lebanon, so they would stand aside for Philipos. They were permitted to fire in self defence and the key task, the primary message, of Philipos to his section commanders was to do nothing which could lead any UN soldier to fear for his life. They were all to be approached under a white flag and invited to surrender. A second key objective was to prevent communications between UN forces, and particularly between the UN and the Turkish army, part of which was stationed along the northern boundary of the UN airport buffer zone. This was to be achieved in two ways. Firstly a jamming noise was to be transmitted on UN frequencies from ten o'clock. Secondly the lines from the terminal building of Nicosia airport must be disabled very quickly.

At nine forty-five a group of fifty men set off, on foot, from the airport perimeter. They were to penetrate and infiltrate the airport grounds and cross without detection to the terminal building. They were to be in position by ten o'clock, and they were.

At ten precisely Philipos gave the signal, two civilian cars led the way and stopped at the first UN checkpoint. As the driver began to speak to the Finnish soldier in his UN uniform the post was overpowered by CLM foot soldiers who had been in place. No communications had been possible to warn the rest of the garrison and nobody had been hurt.

The next checkpoint was a mile further towards the terminal. This was taken out in a similar manner by five of the men who had crossed a little earlier on foot. The road was open. That post was at the junction between the airport spur road and the main road along which the CLM were travelling, the continuation of which led straight into the Turkish held sector. Two of the armoured personnel carriers remained there, blocking the road. Two more travelled beyond the terminal building and blocked the spur road which led to Nicosia. The terminal was theirs by five minutes after ten. Only six UN soldiers were on duty in the building and they had been taken completely by surprise. The large steel gates leading out onto the apron were easily opened and the thirty civilian cars quickly sped across the flat ground to their prearranged positions alongside the runway. Fifteen either side at intervals of 150 yards, offset so that there was a vehicle every 75 yards for 2250 yards, enough length to land an Airbus A310 they had calculated. Two armoured personnel carriers drove along the full length of the runway to check for any possible obstructions, despite this having been checked through field glasses immediately prior to nightfall. There were none.

Everything had gone like a dream, how long would they have to hold the situation before the aircraft landed. Marcos had called from Larnaca at nine forty-five, so the schedule would suggest a ten twenty landing, if..... and it was a large 'if', thought Philipos. He had no time speculate, Marcos would not have called if he had not picked up the message from the captain of TK 980, exactly as Helena had written it. He would gamble and stick to the plan. Headlights on at ten fifteen. The two armoured cars along the spur road closest to Nicosia were approached by a white United Nations Land Rover. Two soldiers wearing blue helmets got out and walked towards the obstruction. The Cypriots stayed in their cover.

"Halt. Is anyone in charge?" one called out in a heavily Scandinavian accent.

"Hands up, drop your weapons," came the reply from the shadows. One blue helmeted soldier did as ordered, the other turned and ran towards his vehicle. A single shot rang out. The Cypriot was a perfect marksman. He had not shot to kill, just to disable, to prevent radio contact being attempted and possibly overcoming the jamming. Two Cypriots ran to the Finnish soldier and examined his leg wound and were pleased that it was only superficial. They had no dispute with the United Nations forces. The soldier was carried to the armoured personnel carrier, put onto a stretcher and taken to the terminal where a field station was being set up to deal with any casualties. His comrade went with him. The Cypriot lieutenant having explained who they were and that they would not be harmed further, just prevented from making contact with their headquarters for the next few hours.

Ten fifteen arrived and thirty vehicles started their engines and switched on their lights to main beam. Almost immediately Philipos heard the quiet whine of the twin GEC/SECAM engines that powered the A310 airliner. Then they saw its navigation lights approaching over the city. It was ten seventeen.

The airliner had continued to fly normally through the night and had crossed the Kyrenia mountains without incident, then swung to the east, turning to head towards Nicosia at a point a few miles west of Salamis. At two thousand feet Sean spoke again.

"Switch off the radio. Climb to three thousand feet and continue on your present course."

The captain spoke for only the second time since his aeroplane had been seized.

"That is impossible, we are heading towards the centre of Nicosia, just south of west, we will cross into Greek Cypriot airspace."

"That is correct," said Sean, "Exactly what I had in mind, now please proceed."

As the Airbus flew over the divided city of Nicosia it was precisely eleven fifteen, ten fifteen in the Republic of Cyprus.

Sean spoke again to the captain.

"You will shortly be above Nicosia airport. I want you to circle so that its position can be seen through the cockpit windows at all times."

They had only made a half circle when two long rows of lights appeared from below, marking the main runway. It was the signal for which Sean had been waiting. He breathed a huge, inaudible, sigh of relief. "They succeeded," he thought to himself.

"Now captain fly to the west, circle and land at Nicosia airport, between the lights you can see for yourself."

"But I have no permission. There is no beacon. I do not know the runway, I can't......", he began to protest.

"You have my permission. You can see the lights. It is a flat approach. You will land," insisted Sean, stroking the gun in his hand. "My friend is an experienced pilot, if you are unwilling......"

"No,no. I will do as you say," responded the frightened pilot.

The clear dark night made the lights on the runway clearly visible throughout the descent and approach. The pilot put the plane down gently and without incident, much more softly than had this been a routine landing.

"Turn around and taxi to the west of the runway," ordered Sean.

As soon as the aircraft came to a halt Patrick came forward to relieve Sean who opened the front passenger door with the help of Ruth. A set of rather ancient steps were brought up to the door. When Nicosia airport was closed Boeing 747 jets had just begun operations, so steps had been available to reach the doors of the new generation of wide bodied airliners. The fit was not ideal, but Sean was able to mount the steps and run down to the ground. Philipos was waiting for him.

"Sean O'Neill?" he asked.

"Yes, I was expecting someone else," Sean replied.

"I know," said Philipos handing him a portable telephone which Sean raised to his ear.

"Sean?" said Helena's voice.

"Mother?" replied Sean, the first time he had ever called her by that name, "we have brought the Emerald Aphrodite down for you."

"Sean, my son, thank you," was all she could find the words to say at first, but then she went on, "I have told you of Philipos, he is my brother, he is in charge at the airport, work with him. I'll see you later."

Philipos looked at Sean as he returned the telephone.

"Who were you calling 'mother'?"

Sean said simply, "Helena is my mother. Uncle Philipos I presume?" and he held out his hand.

CHAPTER FIFTEEN

Charles Noble stared into the eastern darkness and saw little. Barbara, together with Steve and John were recovering after the drive from Ayia Napa and could barely focus their eyes to see anything had it been there to see. Charles knew the city of Famagusta lay before him, but his next move was unclear. He could not warn the Turkish army, he had no orders, and in any case that would have implicated his country. Besides, he had no love for the Turks, having lived in Cyprus and enjoyed the hospitality of the Greek Cypriots for his period on the island. His sympathies were with Clare's kidnappers and Richard's killers, not their opponents, despite these events. His objective was to rescue his Prime Minister and keep his country out of a war, however limited it might be. One of Richard's last few words, after he had temporarily regained consciousness, remained on his mind. 'Helena', what was the connection? He knew Helena Haduanois, by reputation. She had organised demonstrations against the green line, but they had all been women's affairs. It was suspected she was a member of the CLM central committee, but why should Richard refer to her in almost his last breath? It didn't make sense, or did it?

"Barbara, did you ever meet Helena Haduanois when you were in Cyprus?" he asked.

"Yes, many times, she is Richard's," she stopped abruptly after speaking his name, "er, Philipos' sister. They are -er were - all partners in Cypropoult. She is the deepest person I have ever met. No one knows Helena. Philipos told us once that she had never been the same after 1974, she had been a student in Ireland and had just finished her finals at the time of the Turkish invasion. Back in Cyprus she rescued Philipos and her mother, then she started to make money. He didn't recognise her as the sister who had left. Whether it was Ireland, or whether it was what she found when she returned here he never knew. Neither did he ever discover where she got her money to begin the business and buy somewhere to live. Apparently she came back, a new graduate, and just bought a house and began importing chickens from Ireland. Without her money Philipos could never have joined Richard to start Cypropoult."

"Where in Ireland did she study," asked a curious Charles.

"Queens University, Belfast, I think."

"Interesting," remarked Charles, much more interested than he sounded.

"Does Major Patriches mean anything to you?"

"Yes, vaguely. It's odd you should mention him in the next breath after Helena, the only time I ever met him, Helena was there too. We were to go out for a meal to the Cosmopolitan with Philipos one evening. He had asked us to meet him at the Cleopatra, I'd never been there before, or since, that's why I remember. Anyway we were early, or on time, it's usually the same to Greeks, and when we arrived, Philipos, Helena and Patriches were totally absorbed in a serious discussion in the lobby. When she saw us she pretended not to notice and literally dragged Patriches into the bar off the lobby. In his own hotel, why would she do that?"

"When was that?"

"Oh, about a year ago, a little more perhaps."

Charles knew that the CLM leader was Patriches, but his investigations, although not thorough enough he now realised, had never suggested anything about him that would suggest him capable of the role. The assumption had been that there must be someone else, a power behind the throne. But since they did not seem a threat to British interests Charles had not paid them enough attention. His resources had been too stretched trying to track and understand the new crop of Muslim Fundamentalists, shadowy figures who did threaten British interests from across the fifty miles of Mediterranean in Beirut.

Richard had wanted to tell him about Helena before he died. It had been that important. Helena had led demonstrations against the Turkish occupation. Helena had studied in Belfast in the early 1970s at the height of the bombing campaign and had returned to Cyprus with money. Helena had been seen with Patriches and had been seen to have some influence over him. Helena's character was very strange and mysterious. These facts were not coincidences. They all pointed to her deep involvement in tonight's events, and much else as well he suspected. He decided to gamble on Richard's last words. Helena may be the key and even if she were not it may be still imperative that they get to her. He made a series of decisions.

"Barbara, do you know Helena's headquarters, where she could quite easily hide herself away with access to telephones, radio telephones, fax and telex?" he asked.

"Yes, her office in Nicosia has all of those. Richard could never understand why she always insisted on duplicating all the systems in the main office by private lines of her own to her own office, but she did. Whenever he raised the cost in Board meetings Philipos always defended her, usually by justifying it on the basis that she needed her own instant communications to get the best currency rates, then changed the subject, usually by suggesting something that he knew Richard wanted, to get Richard off the subject. Most odd he always thought," she replied.

"Right, I want you to take Steve there now, just as quickly as possible. Steve find her, don't get caught, but find out as much as you can. It's a long shot I suppose since she's bound to well guarded. But try, that's all you can do. Use your initiative. I'll call Dhekelia and you can pick up another communicator like mine, then they can patch you straight through to me when you have anything to report. Barbara, just get him to the right office. Don't get involved, it's not your fight."

"Yes," she said, knowing that she would get as involved as possible and necessary, but also knowing that there was no need to tell him that then. "What are you going to do?" she added.

"You can take John and I back to Dherinia before you leave.

Then we will see how far we can get on our press passes. John has his own, I always carry one, just in case, Daily Express actually. If they want publicity then they might just welcome us into the centre, if we get to them there might just be a possibility of helping free Clare Spencer. All we can do is to take it one step at a time. OK John? You don't have to come along, you can go to Nicosia if you prefer. It's my job, not yours."

"Of course I'll come along. I would come with you whether or not I was a reporter, after what we have gone through together already tonight."

"Good, that's settled then. I'll drive to Dherinia, then you can take over Steve."

They retraced their steps, even more quickly than before. After virtually flying through Phrenaros they arrived in Dherinia at ten fifteen. It was clear before they arrived at the junction in the middle of the village, where one road went towards Famagusta and the other towards Paralimni, that something was happening. There were a great many people standing in a crowd near this junction and others were running towards their homes in the other direction. The action was causing some to be curious and others to flee, remembering, as they did, the events of August 1974 when their village had somehow escaped from the Turkish army despite their tanks having travelled the village streets before withdrawing back to Famagusta.

"This is far enough, I'll turn around."

He did this quickly, yet expertly, avoiding some fleeing citizens with courtesy.

"Right Steve, get going now, don't bother with the new coast road, head straight for Liopetri and Dhekelia. I've arranged for you to pick up the communicator at the petrol station in Dhekelia base, someone will be waiting for you. Hurry, but try to be safe. A lot could depend on you. Look after Barbara." Charles ordered his young assistant, before shaking his hand and spontaneously kissing Barbara on the lips through the open passenger window.

John and he watched as the Ford fought its way past an increasing horde of people drawn onto the street. Most seemed frightened, only a few excited.

The ghost town of Famagusta is a Turkish military area. Despite this designation, separating it from the rest of the north which is merely occupied by the Turkish army, few Turkish soldiers had actually patrolled Famagusta during the preceding twenty years. There was no large garrison, merely occasional patrols. No attack was expected in that area because the Greek Cypriot's only route of entry was thought to be through the British base of Dhekelia. Therefore its defence had not been given a high priority.

The UN post on the headland was taken with ease. The surprise had been complete and there had been no time to radio a warning to their command. The Major had taken personal control of the force to attack along the coast. The two other groups were to move directly into Famagusta from Dherinia, one to the north before turning north west towards Ayios Nikolaos, their aim being to hold these roads as a defensive boundary; the other group would head just north of west along the road that led directly to the coast at the Golden Sands hotel, through the former citrus groves which had become an overgrown wilderness during the previous twenty years of neglect. The Major proceeded carefully along the beach. His men advanced on foot. Their intention was to link up with the group approaching across the citrus groves, without, if at all possible, engaging any Turkish army units. They could then consolidate around the deserted beached whale that had once been the Golden Sands hotel, making a fortress of that formidable building which dominated the wide, flat and golden beach.

They had reached a point less than a hundred meters south of the Golden Sands when their observer's infrared night sights spotted activity in front of the hotel.

"Major, there are at least six Turkish soldiers and two jeeps in front of the Golden Sands," he reported quickly.

The Major called up the leader of his second group now only four hundred metres away to the west and told him to encircle three sides of the hotel, but to hold back from the fourth side facing the sea to the east, to call him when his men were in position and not to move out of cover until told to do so. He then ordered a detachment to get themselves ready to make the final hundred metres approach, taking what cover they could at the edge of the beach. The commander of the second group called him up;

"Ready sir, my men are in position."

"Now move, try to get yourselves between the hotel and the sea," he told the detachment.

When they were exactly where he had ordered he gave the order for the Turkish soldiers to be taken, alive if possible.

Five were taken, their officer was not. He was the first Turkish casualty of that night. As the CLM ran the few yards from the beach ordering the Turks to surrender, the officer, a young lieutenant, showed the foolhardy courage that had led to his promotion from the ranks, first to an NCO and more recently into the officer class. He did not raise his hands, he lowered one and took his pistol. Just as he was about to raise it to the firing position he was hit in the side of the chest by a bullet from the second group guarding the north side of the hotel grounds. He fell lifeless onto the hard concrete ground as the burst of fire ceased.

"Damn," thought the Major, "they will have heard that".

It was heard in the military encampment north of the fenced off ghost town. But fortunately for the Major and his men the Turkish soldiers had developed a habit of shooting members of the large colony of rats that had made their homes in the deserted buildings abandoned without any preparation over twenty years ago. The shots were therefore not unusual, except that normally it was during daylight hours rather than in darkness that this sport was practised. The Major did not know this, so he assumed they would be investigated and made no attempt to maintain silence. He called up his vehicles to the Golden Sands and at the same time his men occupied the building and set up an observation and gun emplacement on the roof.

By the time the Turkish army had begun to react to what they had now began to regard as a mysterious shooting, followed by what sounded like unexpected vehicular traffic, the Major had almost five hundred men and the few vehicles available to him, near the Golden Sands. He was now aware that speed was essential and called up his foot soldiers, ordering them to infiltrate the abandoned town, setting-up strategic defensive positions at appropriate points. His objective was to take the town while it remained virtually free of Turkish soldiers presenting them with a 'fait accompli'. Two armoured detachments were sent out, one along the beach towards the Turkish army encampment across the second border fence which separated the ghost town from Famagusta itself. The second was dispatched due west, along the main road to Larnaca, to link up with his third group near the British base at Ayios Nikolaos. Things were going well. The Turkish army had not been prepared and had not reacted strongly, it had merely sent out patrols to investigate. These were relatively easily mopped up by the Major's temporary superiority.

Costas brought Clare to join the Major on the steps of the lobby of the almost derelict Golden Sands, which was well lit by the headlights of two of the vehicles.

"Now Miss Spencer, you see I am a man of my word. This area is under my command and the Turkish armed forces have not responded in strength."

"You mean this is the lull before the storm hits us?" asked Clare sarcastically.

"The reports we are receiving suggest that little resistance is being encountered. I do not believe that they have yet realised the substantial nature and the success of our attack."

"But when they do how long can you resist? I'm not an expert on warfare, but all you have are a few lightly armed men, no artillery, no tanks and no aircraft or helicopters. They will be able to wipe you all out at their convenience."

"Not if we have international opinion on our side this time. Thank you Miss Spencer for being so co-operative. This little meeting has just been recorded onto video tape for the whole world to see. Take her inside for now please Costas."

Clare turned around and lashed out at Costas in a desperate attempt to demonstrate to whoever may be watching that she was not there willingly. But she was too late, and Costas neatly side-stepped her swinging leg and just laughed. All she could see were the four headlamps turned towards the front of the light coloured building, bathing the whole area in light. She could not see that between the two vehicles was a Cyprus Broadcasting Corporation camera team. Neither could she see that one of the vehicles was the CBC outside broadcast unit which the Major had mentioned earlier.

Costas, closely followed by Michalas, led Clare through the open doors into the lobby of what had once been a fine hotel. The Major went across to the CBC vehicle and went inside the mobile studio.

"Now Andreas, what have we got?" he asked.

"We have two minutes filmed at the Golden Coast, your arrival with Miss Spencer, then some very good shots of you eating in the dining room with her. We have some close-ups so there can be no doubt about who she is. The minute or so we taped now should be equally as good, close-ups of a discussion. It was good that your man did not need to restrain her, it looked perfectly natural and normal. We also have some shots of you taking the UN post and taking the prisoners here, but there was not enough light to be able to make much out I'm afraid."

"Good, include a few seconds anyway, it could give it all authenticity, make sure this place can easily be identified. How soon can you be ready to send it?"

"Three or four minutes, then we will be ready to go."

"Right, I'll let them know in Nicosia."

The Major spoke into his radio and Helena's voice answered.

"Major, what have you to report?" she said quickly.

"Everything going to plan here, in fact better. We have taken most of Famagusta, fifty percent of it is ours already. Very few casualties, none on our side that I have been informed of. Thirty minutes more and it will all be in our hands. The CBC unit will be ready in two minutes to send at your command."

"Excellent. Thank you Major. Well done. The airport is secure and they are all safely down on our side of the fence. I will send my messages now, then call back with the order to send the pictures."

"Helena, I must leave here. Call Andreas about the pictures. Good luck."

It was ten thirty. Helena had all the information she needed to begin sending the messages that had already been prepared for instant printing and transmission. After adding a few final details that could not have been included in advance her secretaries began to send fax and telex messages. The destinations had been chosen with care and the correct numbers collected during the previous months of painstaking research. The recipients would include, the White House; CNN in Atlanta; three separate numbers at the BBC; the London Press Association; CBC itself; Reuters; The Greek Prime Minister in Athens; The Cyprus President's hotel suite in New York; the UN Secretary General's office; the foreign Ministry in Moscow; all the foreign embassies in Nicosia; and perhaps most importantly of all the President's office in the Turkish capital, Ankara, together with their armed forces chief's office. Helena had arranged some weeks earlier for sufficient extra lines and fax machines to be installed into a spare room she had kept next to her own office for all the messages to be sent virtually simultaneously. The message read:

"The Greek Cypriot people have tonight taken appropriate steps, in full consultation with the Prime Minister of the United Kingdom of Great Britain and Northern Ireland, one of the guarantee powers of Cypriot independence, to begin to ensure implementation of the mandatory Security Council resolution 361, which endorsed UN General Assembly Resolution 3212, following the invasion and occupation of the sovereign territory of the Republic of Cyprus and never implemented by Turkey. These resolutions called upon the Turkish armed forces to withdraw from the sovereign territory of the Republic of Cyprus.

At 22.00 hrs local time, 19.00 hrs GMT, the Cyprus Liberation Movement (CLM) began to take control of the city of Famagusta which has been held as a Turkish military zone from which the inhabitants have been denied entry since August 1974 in defiance of the Security Council. At 22.30 local time, 19.30 GMT, the forces of the CLM had reasserted legitimate Cypriot control over more than fifty percent of the former Famagusta military zone. At 23.00 local time, 20.00 GMT the whole of this area will be under Cypriot control and the CLM will hand over control to the Cypriot National Guard who represent the legitimate national authority.

The Cyprus Broadcasting Corporation (CBC) has visual news coverage of the beginning of tonight's events. This footage together with additional coverage as it becomes available will be transmitted every fifteen minutes, beginning at 22.45 local time, 19.45 GMT. This video is available to, and may be freely used by, all broadcasting services. It has been widely reported that Miss Clare Spencer, Prime Minister of The United Kingdom of Great Britain and Northern Ireland is in Cyprus. The pictures referred to above include coverage of her in discussion with the leader of the Cypriot forces both during the planning and execution of tonight's actions. It is understood that British forces in the Sovereign bases of Akrotiri, Episkopi and Dhekelia have been placed on full alert.

In addition to these steps action has been taken to enforce the Government of the Republic of Cyprus' declaration that all ports of entry in those parts of the national territory under Turkish military occupation represent illegal ports of entry. A

Turkish Airlines Airbus A310, flight no TK 980, which attempted to land at such an illegal port, instead, on the instructions of the CLM, landed safely at 22.17 local time, 19.17 GMT, at Nicosia airport, now under the control of Cypriot forces. All passengers and crew on board the flight are safe and well and are currently being held by forces loyal to the Republic of Cyprus pending a decision on whether they shall be prosecuted for attempted illegal entry into the Republic of Cyprus.

Further action is currently being taken by Cypriot forces to liberate additional limited areas of the national territory.

The Turkish armed forces are warned not to intervene further. The consequences are there for all to see. The British Prime Minister is currently inspecting part of the liberated areas in Famagusta and the passengers and crew of flight TK 980 are being held at Nicosia airport.

This action has been initiated by the people, not the Government of Cyprus, acting through the CLM. The President of the Republic of Cyprus and other key Government ministers and officials are currently out of the country. Therefore, in view of the immediate situation temporary control of the forces of law and order has been assumed by the National Guard acting for the Government in this emergency. No attempt is being or will be made by the National Guard or CLM to overthrow the constitutional Government of the Republic of Cyprus.

The National Guard have appointed CLM spokesperson Helena Haduanois to speak on their behalf."

Arriving as it did late on a Saturday evening the message caused consternation throughout the capitals of Europe and the Middle East. In Washington, although early afternoon there, the position was no less confused amongst the majority of the officials, who had no information about Costas' covert operation.

Nowhere did it come as more of a shock than in the Turkish capital. By the time it was received no messages had arrived from either the Famagusta military garrison or from Turkish Airlines concerning their missing flight.

A copy of the fax was in the hands of President Zekaibes in Ankara within minutes of its receipt. Before he had read it his armed forces commander was on the line requesting immediate permission to deploy the Turkish airforce and to bomb enemy positions in Famagusta. He also requested permission to order the advance of the Turkish army into the UN airport buffer zone across its northern perimeter around Nicosia airport. The President refused permission and instead called Washington. The two Presidents were connected by their staff only after the Turkish President's Private Secretary had explained that his President had chosen to speak to his US counterpart as an alternative to ordering a full scale counter attack.

President Zekaibes began;

"Mr President, you will have seen the message from Nicosia. I must tell you that I have no alternative but to defend myself against this unprovoked aggression by Greece and Britain. I have no choice. What are your friends the British doing getting involved in Cyprus again? Do they want war with us?"

The American President had to persuade Turkey to hold back long enough to be seen as the innocent party seeking to restore order. But he could not say, "wait 'till they have killed the British Prime Minister, then it will all be yours without much of a fight." He had to be more devious, which to him was not difficult.

"The British have deceived us too. We believe their Prime Minister, Clare Spencer, wants to win a war to show she is made of the right stuff, as the British say. To show she is as determined to protect British interests and as strong as Margaret Thatcher was. The Falklands war saved her and that victory gave her another eight years in office. Clare Spencer thinks she can survive a little longer by winning a war in Cyprus. My advice to you is don't give her the chance. We will play our part. I have ordered the Federal Reserve to tell London that unless they disassociate themselves from this nonsense we will sell every pound sterling we have on Monday morning. Just like Eisenhower said to Eden when he was planning to conquer Egypt in 1956. It stopped Eden then, it will stop Spencer now."

"Mr President, that will be too late. They are advancing now. By Monday morning they could be in Kyrenia unless I send in the air force. I must do so, but I wanted to consult you before I did."

"No, my friend. Their message is limited in its objectives. They state their aim is Famagusta and Nicosia airport. Just as you called I received an intelligence report confirming these were their major objectives. If they try to advance further, or try to take anything else, can't you hold them off and defend your positions with the forces you have in place?"

"It depends on what forces they use. If it's just the Greeks we probably can, but if the RAF join in either with aircraft or even helicopters, we must be in a position to strike back. We cannot afford to be defeated, the army would not allow it."

"That's his main concern", thought the US President. "If he shows weakness there will be a coup".

"Look I tell you what I will do if you will agree to hold the situation and not to escalate it further. I will announce publicly that I am sending a squadron of fighters from Greece to your base in the north as a precautionary measure, to reinforce the peacekeeping force in Cyprus. Once they see the US is involved they will stop."

"That doesn't get them out of Famagusta or the airport."

"No, but it puts you in the best possible position to win the peace. By showing restraint now we may be able to support your objective of an internationally recognised government in Northern Cyprus. Politically you will have proved to your own armed forces that restraint can actually provide a strategic advantage."

"Mr President, I don't like it, but there is wisdom in what you say. If you will announce you are sending your fighters within the half hour then I will do as you say. We will defend our positions without escalation unless it is clear that their advance is continuing towards inhabited areas. I am particularly concerned about the situation on the Larnaca Nicosia highway about which I have just been told while we have been talking."

"It's a deal. Goodnight, President Zekaibes. We shall speak again soon."

President Fowler breathed a sigh as he ended the conversation. He had gained time. He would soon have a more favourably inclined British government. A more reliable one. After all since the events of 1989 and 1990 Continental Europe had become a less hospitable place for US forces and he needed his bases in Britain more than ever. Without them it would become impossible to mount another operation 'Desert Storm', most of those forces had been based in Western Europe and were able to be deployed quickly. Britain was absorbing the best of the front line forces remaining on that side of the Atlantic. He couldn't afford a British government that might decide to order their removal, as one led by a strong and self-confident Clare Spencer might just do. It may also be possible now for him to take the lead in promoting a final settlement in Cyprus by allowing Turkey to impose their own solution if the Greeks could be shown to be little more than a bunch of terrorists. That would be an added bonus.

President Zekaibes was less convinced. As soon as the line was disconnected he began to wonder whether he had made the right decision, or whether he had been talked into one that was not in either his, or his county's, real interests. What if his army units on the front line were over-run. He would take the blame for hesitation. He wanted to complete his term of office without another army take over. He also wanted to get Turkey into a position to join the European Economic Community, an application that the Community had rejected at the end of 1989. He was determined to try again before he left office, but both Greece and Britain had a veto. The only means of preventing them using it was to get a settlement in Cyprus. Perhaps President Fowler was right. Perhaps he could win the peace and find a settlement that the army would find more difficult to obstruct than they had in the past. It was his best option. He would take it. He called his armed forces Chief.

"Permission refused. There will be no airforce involvement without my direct order. The army must defend its positions on the ground, but do not counterattack in Famagusta or Nicosia airport. But, do everything to hold the Nicosia Larnaca highway."

Captain George Spyrou was not having an easy time. His group had encountered heavy resistance just north of the UN checkpoint and the turning to Athienou. His column was pinned down and making no further progress. His deputy, making his way south from Nicosia, was faring even worse. He had not reached the UN checkpoint where the road was closed off at the green line. Unfortunately for his unit it had been spotted by the Turkish army long before the point of first contact. This was because the green line ran parallel with the road for a distance of several miles, only a short distance from the road. The Turkish commander had recognised the danger presented by an armoured column heading south towards his fixed defensive positions. Without waiting for orders he had taken the decision himself to make a pre-emptive attack. His big guns had been ordered to take out the advancing column and had largely succeeded in doing so. Three of the light tanks leading the attack had taken a direct hit and had blocked the road to further advance. To save the rest of the force from similar destruction the remaining units had been ordered to turn off the road and head west, towards Nicosia and away from the Turkish emplacements, into open country. They had not returned fire and the Turkish commander, believing he had prevented any threat to his positions, ceased fire and merely maintained the highest state of alert and observation.

When Captain Spyrou heard the report of this failure from his northern group he recognised that his task was hopeless and that Helena had been right to hesitate about sanctioning his idea. They should never have begun this action. Never a defeatist he was now reconciled to the fact that he could not reopen the road. This was not now his major concern, however. By having started an attack, which he could not win, and would probably lose, he risked being pushed back to the south of the road to Athienou, perhaps as far as the motorway. That would be an unmitigated disaster. His village would be totally cut off from the rest of Cyprus, its inhabitants would become enclaved in the midst of hostile territory. That he could never allow. He was determined to hold his position despite mounting odds against him. His would be the most fearful night imaginable. He had to hold the line at all costs.

CHAPTER SIXTEEN

To the passengers sat in a hijacked aeroplane on the runway of Nicosia airport Philipos' address to them through the aircraft's own communications system came as both a relief and as a shock. It was a relief to learn that they would shortly be allowed to leave the airport and would not have to spend an uncomfortable night in a cramped aircraft seat. It was a shock to learn that it was being considered whether or not to prosecute them for attempted illegal entry into Cyprus. Philipos had begun, reading from the text that Helena had carefully written for him.

"Ladies and gentlemen, welcome to Cyprus, to the internationally recognised Republic of Cyprus. Following the occupation of forty percent of the national territory by the armed forces of the Republic of Turkey in July and August 1974 all ports of entry in the occupied territory are designated by the legitimate government of Cyprus as illegal ports of entry. This aeroplane was scheduled to land at one of these illegal ports - Ercan airport. Had the aeroplane been permitted to land there each one of you would have been guilty of the criminal offence of illegal entry. Since this illegal landing was prevented your crime was attempted illegal entry. Consideration is therefore being given to bringing appropriate charges against each one of you. The crew will be so charged and the aircraft impounded as evidence in their trial before the Cyprus courts. Therefore, whether or not you are all charged, it will not be possible for you to leave the island on this aircraft. It is also understood that many of you had intended, while in Cyprus, to stay at hotels being operated illegally in the occupied area. All tourist hotels in that part of the island are owned by persons expelled at the time of the military occupation and have subsequently been operated illegally by persons loyal to the occupying forces without their owners consent. Consideration will also be given to these facts when considering whether or not criminal charges will be brought against you as an example to others.

"The people of the Republic of Cyprus being a most hospitable people wish however to make your stay in our country as pleasant as possible. Our people wish to demonstrate that hospitality to you. Those of you who can provide evidence that you were travelling to Cyprus on holiday will be accommodated at no cost to yourselves at first class hotels in the Republic of Cyprus until a decision is reached on whether charges are to be brought against you. If no such charges are brought then you will be free to remain for the duration of your holiday and you will be provided with complementary return tickets from Larnaca or Paphos airport, the only two legitimate airports in Cyprus. It is expected that a decision on possible prosecutions will be reached shortly.

"If you will kindly remain in your seats and be ready to show your passports and provide evidence of your intended destination in Cyprus, then we can then arrange for you to be escorted off the aircraft. On behalf of the Republic of Cyprus I can assure you that you will all be treated well and within the terms of international law."

None of the passengers had realised that everything he had said was recorded by a National Guard reservist who was also a radio reporter from CBC. His recording was taken to Nicosia by a motor cycle dispatch rider and was broadcast to the world within sixty minutes of being spoken. It was included in the BBC World Service 21.00 Hrs GMT, midnight local time, news broadcast.

Patrick's place guarding the passengers and crew had been taken over by four Nicosia policemen, also National Guard reservists, wearing their khaki summer police uniforms, not their army ones. As soon as they had come on board Patrick had disconnected his device by removing the detonator, then carefully removing the wires from the razor. He gently replaced the plastic explosive together with the other items into his flight bag before carrying it off the aeroplane.

In addition to his military vehicles and the private cars

lining the runway Philipos had also brought into the airport and up to the aircraft four coaches for transporting the passengers. Ruth and Sarah had been given the task of identifying and handing to each passenger a preprinted card which served as a pass onto one of the numbered coaches. When she reached Helen and Bob Jones Ruth asked politely;

"Can I see your passports, tickets and your accommodation vouchers please."

Bob had become very angered by the whole episode. At first he had been shocked by finding himself the subject of a hijack. Then he had become resentful, asking himself why it had to happen to him, it usually happened only to someone else. He hated to be put into a position where he had no control over events. Eventually this angry resentment had subsided into silent relief. It was therefore Helen who answered Ruth's enquiry. Being a very practical person all she wished to do was to oil the wheels as much as possible by reducing any possibility of friction between passengers and those in control. Like most of her fellow travellers she had become totally confused by the whole affair, but she at least saw the possibility of a happy ending if everyone kept calm.

"Here they are my dear, both British. We are, or were, on a Sunquest package to the Dome Hotel in Kyrenia. Here's the accommodation voucher." Helen replied to Ruth.

After a quick examination Ruth handed the two passports and the voucher back to Helen and smiled as she gave her two cards printed 'coach one'. Then she made a note of their hold baggage claim ticket number.

"Please take your hand baggage and leave the aircraft by the forward cabin door. Show this card to the officers and proceed to the coach displaying 'number one'. Thank you for being so co-operative. I hope the remainder of your stay is more pleasant."

Bob was about to make a remark, but knowing him so well and not wanting him to spoil anything at this late stage by a resentful or unnecessary remark, Helen interrupted;

"We haven't enjoyed it so far, but thank you for making it

much less unpleasant than it could have been. Goodbye."

Then she rose and gave Bob a very hard look, which caused him to remain silent and follow her meekly down the steps and onto the first coach.

Pete Wright was not resentful or angry, but worried. He was very concerned about the effect on his children, how much they had understood, would they suffer nightmares as a result; but he was much more worried about his job. He had not told his employers about his holiday to the North, neither had he told his friends and customers in Greek Cyprus. How would he keep it from them? What would they say if and when they did discover the truth. Lists of passengers of hijacked aircraft tended to be released to the press in such circumstances. The press sought interviews with passengers released. Then there was the possibility of prosecution. He could find himself with a criminal record in Cyprus and barred from future entry into the Republic. What was he to do? He had not spoken of these concerns to Sandra. She had her hands full with Joan for whom it had all become just too much.

When Ruth asked him the same question that she had asked Helen and Bob Jones a few moments earlier, he answered her himself;

"We just have one family passport, for the four of us. We were to have a quiet family holiday at the Salamis Bay Hotel on a Sunquest package. Are there any press reporters outside?"

She glanced at his documents, somewhat puzzled at his question, as she handed him four passes for coach number one, and said;

"No, there are no reporters outside, except for one from Cyprus radio, but he will not be allowed to speak to any of the passengers. But we are expecting a television crew soon and have promised them pictures of some of you, for transmission at a time of our choosing, which will not be for some hours. Why?"

"No reason", he said quickly and unconvincingly, "I just didn't want to find myself walking off the steps into a scrum of reporters, we have to think of the children."

"You needn't worry, there will be nothing like that," she said in her voice designed to reassure. "please take your family off when you have collected your hand baggage. I have made a note of your hold baggage identification. This will be delivered to you as soon as it can be arranged."

"Thank you." Pete said simply.

Ruth and Sarah gradually made their way to the rear of the plane. When they had finished only the crew and the two Turkish officers that Sean had identified earlier, remained on board. They were brought together and escorted to the terminal building by two of the uniformed policemen and two men in National Guard uniform. The remainder of the passengers had been assembled onto the four coaches.

It had been Philipos' intention to remove the passengers as quickly as possible. Although he wanted the outside world to believe they were being held hostage on the plane, he did not want to be responsible for their lives if anything did go seriously wrong. Although a little later than had been intended, he had hoped to remove them within one hour, the four coaches left through the airport gates at eleven thirty five. None of the passengers knew their destination. As they swept left, through the main gates, then turned left again off the spur road, to follow the route that Philipos and his men had used ninety five minutes earlier, the public address system on each coach was switched on. One of the officers accompanying each group began to speak, reading yet another of Helena's scripts;

"Ladies and gentlemen. Thank you all for your patience. It has been decided after all that none of you will be charged with attempted illegal entry into the Republic of Cyprus. The people of Cyprus welcome you as our guests. Once we have arrived at your destination you will be free and will be provided with first class accommodation for the duration of your stay and a return flight for the day you had been due to leave the island."

"In view of the unpleasant experience you have had

during the last two hours we wish to explain a little more to you so you may understand why this has been necessary. Tonight the people of Cyprus have begun to fight for their freedom from the occupation by the armed forces of Turkey. Much of Famagusta, has already been recaptured. The diversion of your aeroplane was an integral and necessary part of this operation, the reopening of Nicosia International Airport. It was necessary to demonstrate that this was possible. It was also useful to make Turkey believe that if they counterattacked our forces immediately then your safety would have been jeopardised since your aeroplane was under our control. I can assure you we would not have harmed you in any way. Since it is useful to us that they continue to believe this to be the case, it will be some hours before you will be permitted access to telephones or to speak to anyone we have not screened ourselves. We are taking you to hotels in the Paphos area. The journey will take three hours. When you arrive at your hotel you will discover that all outside telephone lines to the bedrooms and to public phones have been disconnected. It is hoped that these conditions can be relaxed and that you can be permitted to leave the hotel by tomorrow evening. That will depend upon the situation on the ground."

"I am not prepared to answer any questions. Please enjoy the journey. At midnight I will switch on the radio so that you may all listen to the BBC World Service news which I expect will cover tonight's events here in Cyprus and you will discover that I have been telling you the truth."

The coaches did not turn left towards Nicosia, but instead carried straight on, to the west along the road that had once led to Morphou, a town that had been prosperous and the centre of the citrus fruit growing industry of Cyprus, but now twenty years later remained occupied and poor. After passing Peristerona the coaches turned left at Astromeritis and its roadside cafes, before beginning the long climb, at first gradual, then steeper, towards Troodos in the heart of the island. Rising to more than six thousand feet during daylight hours the journey would have been delightful. Since it was totally dark the passengers saw little through their windows. The southern slopes of the Troodos mountains led towards Limassol. Over the summit they passed through the forest of trees with downward sloping branches. Seeing them in the heat of the summer few tourists believed that the cause of these bent branches was the weight of snow that they held for several months each winter. These trees featured on many picture postcards bought even by the summer tourist who was fascinated to learn that the heart of a mediterranean sunshine island became a winter sports resort during the winter months and that sufficient snow actually fell to cause this alpine phenomenon. The coaches headed due south as quickly as they safely could down what could be treacherous mountain roads, which had claimed the lives of more than one unsuspecting motorist who had underestimated the dangers and the gradient, becoming victim to the steep, long cliffs to the valleys below. Once Limassol was reached they turned right and followed the coastal road to Paphos, passing Pissouri and the Temple of Aphrodite en route. Then a few miles after the Cypriot home of Turkish Delight, Yeroskipos, unlike Turkish coffee, still an appreciated delicacy in Cyprus, they reached the town of Paphos, where they turned left down the hill towards Kato Paphos and the sea. All four coaches arrived at the same hotel. One whose owner had been only too happy to accommodate the requests of the CLM leadership and re-book his guests into other nearby hotels, leaving his free of ordinary holidaymakers and ready to accommodate four coach loads of very special guests. Being an active member of the CLM and National Guard reservist he would rather have been in Famagusta that night, helping to free his own small hotel that he had not seen for so many years. But instead his role was to receive these guests, provide them with every possible comfort, but to make absolutely certain none were able to contact the outside world until he was given the word. He did not relish his task. He was a soldier, not a prison camp commandant.

The Cypria Maris Hotel was about two miles from the harbour and had 237 rooms, more than enough for tonight's purpose. Being so far from the harbour was one reason it had been chosen, the temptation to stray was that much less than had, say, the Paphos Beach Hotel been chosen. It was just after two in the morning when the passengers were ushered, one coach at at time, into the lobby. Formalities were kept to a minimum, passports and accommodation vouchers were collected, and room keys handed out. A note was taken of which guest occupied which room. They were told that it was hoped their luggage would be brought to them by breakfast and if not they were assured that the hotel shop would offer them complementary beachwear.

It was only after closing their room door behind them, after settling Joan and Adrian, that Pete Wright began to understand the significance of the BBC broadcast they had heard when approaching Troodos summit.

The implication was that his own Prime Minister was involved in providing assistance to the Greek Cypriot advance into Turkish occupied territory. If this were true then it must also be true that the British Government was a party to the hijacking of a plane load of British holidaymakers. Whatever he thought of politicians, and it was not a great deal, he did not believe this could be true. Apart from being senseless, which he could understand, it was political suicide. That was one thing of which, even he, thought no politician capable.

As soon as Ruth and Sarah had finished processing the passengers off the Airbus sitting idle on the tarmac at Nicosia International Airport, Sean and Patrick led them to the waiting taxi that Philipos had provided for them. After leaving the airport by the same route as the coaches, instead of heading west, they turned towards Nicosia itself. It took them thirty minutes to reach the city. The suburban streets were deserted, but Sean noticed that despite the hour every house was lit. Few in Cyprus had gone to their beds that historic night. Some because they were following events on the radio and television, others fearing a Turkish response, perhaps an attempt to take the city itself, were packing their most cherished possessions and getting ready to flee to the south, to Limassol or Paphos, to put the Troodos mountains between themselves and any advancing Turkish army.

Sean and his companions had a well planned escape route. It was not in any of their interests for their involvement to become public. After spending two nights at the Hilton they were booked on the Monday morning flight from Larnaca to Athens, were to spend a few days in company with a group of holiday makers from Ireland on the coast to the east of Athens, before taking a direct holiday flight to Dublin as part of that same group. Helena had told Sean to remain at the Hilton and that depending upon the situation she would make contact with him sometime during the Sunday.

The taxi followed the old airport road into the city, past the late night cafes and bars where Cypriot society tended to congregate after eating out at one of the city's many fine restaurants. It went past the Cosmopolitan night club, following the road commonly known as the 'by-pass' - like Limassol's, now integrated into the city - as far as the Cyprus Airways' building on the left and Woolworths across the junction with Makarios III Avenue. They crossed the junction and the flashing yellow traffic lights, since no right turn was now allowed, before turning right parallel to Makarios Avenue, prior to joining that road half a mile from the Cyprus Hilton. The driver entered the hotel grounds and stopped outside the front entrance. They were ushered through the main doors and directed to the front desk, around the corner to the right.

The check-in formalities were minimal. Patrick and Sean each signed for one twin room. None of them had any luggage other than their shoulder bags they were carrying and they went straight up to their rooms along with Sarah and Ruth, in the lift across the lobby from the check-in desk.

As soon as Sarah and Sean had closed the door of their room behind them Sean let out an audible sigh of relief. What a day. Although the IRA had been active for twenty five years in its present form it had never before been responsible for hijacking an aircraft. He had no experience in the organisation to learn from, and for security reasons it had been impossible to seek explicit outside assistance. All he had been able to gain from outside were some of the tools, the iron and the razor, without providing any details of the use to which they were to be put. He had planned the operation virtually alone and it had succeeded, totally and completely. That was surely reason for some self satisfaction and perhaps even celebration. He hoped Sarah felt the same. He was determined to find out, now.

But first he struggled to open the mini-bar. When he found the right key, he opened it and took out half a bottle of sparkling wine, the nearest thing to champagne it contained, opened it and poured two glasses. He walked over to Sarah, who had collapsed onto the edge of the bed, and handed one glass to her. She smiled back to him as she stood up and touched her glass against his.

"I'm still shaking, I never thought I could stay as calm as I did for so long. Look I can't hold the glass still now," she said as she raised it to her lips and took long slow drink.

When she had finished Sean took the glass from her and placed both empty glasses down on the chest.

"You are in a state, that's for sure. There's no chance of you sleeping for a while yet," he said taking her into his arms and drawing her close. "You need to forget the last few hours and remember something more pleasant before you can get any rest my girl."

He undressed her slowly and carefully. By the time he had finished, undressed himself and joined her under the cool yellow sheets she had begun to catch his mood. Gone was her edgy nervousness that had characterised her behaviour since leaving the airport. Instead she was becoming again that passionate, intelligent and attractive girl he had found six months ago on a return flight from Amsterdam. Tonight was to be special, he decided. They would make love slowly and caringly, he would temper her passion. As she began to stir, trying to climb all over him, or pull him onto her, he kept her at a distance, for, what seemed to them both, hours. Then gradually they moved together and were, for the first time, real lovers mentally, as well as physically.

Later, much later, long after Sarah had fallen into a deep sleep of satisfied exhaustion Sean found himself wide awake. He looked at his watch. It was almost three. He got out of bed, put his clothes on and left a note on his pillow for Sarah to find when she awoke.

The lobby of the Hilton was far from deserted, despite the hour. People were standing around in small groups, some had heard the news and were fearful to leave in case there was trouble on the streets, others had arrived at the Hilton believing it to be safer than their own homes, and others were representatives of the press, many of them Middle Eastern correspondents who had chosen to cover the region from the safe distance and comfortable life-style of Nicosia, following the demise of Beirut as the centre of their world. Now they found themselves virtually in the middle of a new war, a war that none of them had predicted and would, therefore, find difficult to explain to their masters, just as they had failed to predict the Iraqi conquest of Kuwait in 1990. Now their priority was information. Few had the right contacts in Cyprus, that was their base, not their source, so they talked to each other, each one hoping someone else may know more than him or herself. In fact none had the perspective of the night's operations, they had little more than they had learnt from the television and radio.

Sean quickly recognised what was happening and walked across to one group, one member of which he recognised from his television screen back home.

"What's the latest?" he innocently enquired of noone in particular, but of the group in general.

"It's terribly confused," offered one young man eager to engage someone else in conversation, his relative youth and inexperience having prevented his gaining the full confidence of his fellow journalists.

"From what we can gather three things have happened. The Greeks have taken part of Famagusta, hijacked a Turkish aircraft to Nicosia airport, and failed in an attempt to open the direct road from here to Larnaca, we hear there was fierce fighting in that area. The surprising thing about it all is the British involvement. Clare Spencer was shown in Famagusta on television, but there have been no reports of British forces moving out of the Bases, nor can we get any sort of statement out of the High Commission here at all. They won't say anything to anybody."

"What about the Turkish forces? Are they trying to kick the Greeks out of Famagusta? Why aren't you all there seeing for yourselves instead of standing around in here?"

"That's another strange thing about it all. There are no reports of a Turkish counter attack, except on the Larnaca road. All we can assume is that they are waiting until daylight to launch some air strikes, or else they believe they are really up against the British."

"Might it not be that the airliner is being held hostage against a counter attack?" Sean contributed, since that was exactly why he had risked his own life.

"Possibly, yes, but we have an unconfirmed report that all the passengers have been taken off and away from the airport. The truth is we just don't know what is happening. Do you want a drink?" offered the young reporter.

"No thanks, I just came down to find out the latest. Have you been outside? Is it quiet or is there a lot of activity?"

"It's much quieter than I would have expected, perhaps many people are too frightened even to try to get away from here."

"I think I will go outside for some air and see for myself," said Sean casually.

"Do you mind if I come with you. I've stood here for too long, I need to get out," asked the reporter.

Sean decided reluctantly, but without showing his reluctance, to agree. He intended to walk down Makarios Avenue into the city to see if there was any activity outside Helena's offices. He hadn't decided whether to call on her or whether just to observe. But if he was not alone he couldn't try to contact her as easily. On the other hand if there was any trouble he would be safer with a reporter than he would be on his own. After all he could always find an excuse and lose him if necessary.

"Yes delighted for the company, I'm sure. Provided you vouch for me as a fellow reporter, say the Irish Times if you like, if there is any trouble."

"OK, where do you want to go?"

"Let's just see where the mood takes us," answered a confident Sean.

They walked down Makarios Avenue towards the centre of the city and were immediately impressed by how quiet it was in that part of the capital at least. There was virtually no traffic at all on the road except the odd taxi returning a late party-goer home. It was still no busier when they reached Woolworths, a store that in Cyprus represented the opposite to that of the well known name in Britain. Here it was one of the top class stores with the best food department of any Cypriot town. They paused at the lights, which were still flashing amber in every direction as they had been doing a few hours earlier when Sean's taxi had crossed that junction.

They walked on towards the very heart of the city, past Grindley's Bank on the right, before turning left at Sean's prompting when they reached the Nicosia Wimpey franchise. At the end of the narrow street Helena's office block faced them. Much of it was in darkness, but the entrance and the top floor were a blaze of light. As they stood there, Sean having suggested a pause to decide where to go next, he thought of his mother across the street, succeeding in her first step towards setting her people free from Turkish occupation. He had to be with her, one day he planned to be in her shoes, not in Cyprus, but in his own divided island.

CHAPTER SEVENTEEN

The people in the small Whitehall room had spent the last hour in the sort of purposeful and direct activity of which few outsiders would have thought the British Foreign Office capable. The air force chief had arrived at eight, he was closely followed by his fellow service chiefs. Everyone who had been informed of the meeting, except Dr Evans, was present. Then they began. Edmund Stead let Sir Rodney outline events as they were known at the time, then he took over. The one thing he knew they must not do was to do nothing. They had to give the impression that something was being done. His mind flashed back to 1982, to April 1 1982, All Fools Day. They would have all been made to look fools if they hadn't acted. Then they had taken the heat out of the public reaction to the events in the South Atlantic by sending a task force, even if no one, with one crucial exception, had ever expected it to go into action and win a war. This time he needed action and to concentrate minds onto things actually under their control, not on actions by others totally outside his Government's control or even influence, about which they may not even know the true facts.

"Gentlemen. Sir Rodney has given you the current position to the best of our knowledge. Let me tell you what I conclude and what we shall do."

The faces around the table looked straight at Edmund, seriously. None had expected him to be positive, they had their own views to put and solutions to offer.

"It's quite clear that the Greek Cypriots have become impatient. Just about everyone else in Europe has democracy and freedom, why should they alone still be host to an army of occupation. Their President told me as much earlier this week on his way to the United Nations General Assembly in New York. He almost hinted at something like this happening. Too many of his people were losing patience. He told me he was surprised there had been so little trouble around the twentieth anniversary of the invasion last summer. He had thought something was brewing from information he had received. It seems now that his instincts or his intelligence was right, but the timing was wrong. Clearly the CLM discovered Clare was going to be in Cyprus now and took advantage. I don't know how they discovered it since we didn't know," he said sharply looking straight at Sir Rodney, "but it was probably through her friend Richard Rowland. They have kidnapped her, partly to put pressure on both the Turks and ourselves, but probably more importantly to get more publicity. We cannot leave her to their mercy, from what Noble tells us they have already killed Rowland. None of us knows exactly what they plan, but it seems safe to assume with my knowledge of the island, that they intend to have a go at the Turks' weakest point, Famagusta."

"We must do two things now. I shall go to Cyprus tonight, by the quickest possible means of transport. I don't want anyone to get the impression that we do not have a strategy and have left our PM isolated. Secondly I want an SAS team in the Dhekelia Base before dawn. If there is one there already, fine. If not they must leave before midnight".

The phone rang. Sir Rodney picked it up and listened, then said, "Bring it in, now please".

A secretary brought in copies of a facsimile that had just been received from Cyprus. It was Helena's first statement. They all read it in silence, several of them having to share one of the three copies that had been made. Edmund was the first to speak.

"This confirms most of what I have said, it makes it even more important that I leave straight away". He turned to the air force chief. "See what you can do. I want to be there in the shortest possible time. See if you have a suitable fighter that could get me there in a couple of hours. No, don't do that, requisition Concorde. They must have one at Heathrow overnight. Tell them I wish to leave by ten tonight. Speak to the French and the Italians. Tell them anything, mercy flight, whatever you like, but find the shortest route for it to fly me there directly at top speed".

"Secondly I shall need our SAS team to be on hand. They can travel with me if necessary, but must be told to stay in the background, to shadow me and to be ready to act instantly, without question, at my command". He turned to the army chief, "Understand?" The army chief nodded his agreement. "Why argue now?" he thought to himself, "it wouldn't get me very far with him in this mood, after all he may be right, and the commanding officer I shall send would not attempt anything that he was not certain he could successfully achieve."

"Now," Edmund turned to his Private Secretary, as the army and air force chiefs left the room to implement his decisions, "now that we have the mechanics in place let us set up the diplomacy. You see gentlemen, the Services can only provide the conditions favourable to a negotiated settlement, you cannot provide that yourselves, the Turks thought they had done that in Cyprus twenty years ago. Get me the Cyprus President in New York, President Zekaibes in Ankara, the the Greek Premier in Athens, in that order."

"It's time Cyprus was sorted out once and for all. If we do nothing the Government probably won't survive. Clare will be discredited even if it is proven she was an innocent hostage she will be condemned for going in the first place, so we might as well use the whole business as an opportunity, an opportunity to settle it once and for all." He looked up. "no one in this room must say or do anything outside to give the impression that we had no knowledge of all of this and that we are not involved. Let them all think we are, that way we may have some influence."

Fortunately the leaders he had asked to speak to were just as anxious to talk to him as he was to talk to them. President Zekaibes made no reference to his conversations with Washington and agreed to the request, made to each of the leaders, and that their agreement remain confidential in view of the serious situation on the ground. When he had finished he ordered his airforce chief to facilitate the agreements he had made and to requisition a second Concorde, likely to be parked overnight at Kennedy airport in New York. The others around the small table could not help but view this man with fresh admiration. They all began to see him in a new light.

Charles Noble led John out of Dherinia towards the Green Line and was stopped at gun point by a group of six men dressed in National Guard uniform and asked in Greek where he was going. He replied in English;

"We are both reporters here in Cyprus to cover the Clare Spencer story, but we heard there would be some activity here tonight so we came to see if there was anything interesting."

An older man stepped forward, he was clearly in command and spoke to them in English;

"How did you know about tonight? Who told you? There has been no announcement."

"You must know journalists never reveal their sources." Charles attempted to joke, realising the attempt had failed and thinking quickly he continued;

"No, actually we tried to get down to the coast from Paralimni and we were turned around. Just put two and two together, made five and came here to see if we could see anything. Pure chance officer I can assure you. But it seems we were right."

He took out his press card and John did the same. The officer examined them under his flashlight and handed them back, apparently satisfied.

"What is happening here? Isn't this a UN check point? Why are the National Guard manning it?" asked Charles innocently.

"An announcement will be made by the proper authorities shortly. Until then I must ask you to remain here as my guests. We will release you as soon as this activity is no longer secret, then you can return to your hotel and turn on the television and radio and learn more."

"No way," said Charles, "we are here to report the news as

it happens, not watch it on television. Can I speak to your commanding officer, please?"

"He's far too busy to waste his time talking to a couple of nosey reporters, sorry that will not be possible."

At that moment there was a burst of gunfire from the direction of the coast, from the southern edge of Famagusta, about a mile away across the citrus groves.

"It sounds to me as if someone has just started a war around here. Don't you think your commander might welcome the opportunity of putting his side directly to two leading British newspapers. Don't you think you should give him the chance? He might not like to read in the London Times that he was denied this facility by the initiative of one of his own officers."

"You win, but you'll have to wait a few minutes. I'm due to call in just after ten thirty, I'll mention you to him then," the officer reluctantly agreed, after all one of their main objectives was to place the Cyprus issue right back on the front pages of the world's press, just where the quarter of a million refugees believed it should have always remained. This particular officer had only joined the CLM after reading an article in the Christmas 1989 edition of the London Economist magazine. It had been an article that had so angered him that he had determined to do something about it himself. All the world's refugees, some fifteen million, had been listed, but despite his own and almost a quarter of a million others' existence there was no mention of a single refugee in Cyprus. It particularly enraged him that Cyprus was mentioned and listed in the table of European countries, but only as a refuge for forty thousand Lebanese refugees.

Charles agreed, good-naturedly to wait for a few minutes and turned his attention to the spot from which he had heard gunfire. The officer hurried the hundred metres further down the road to the guardhouse. Charles did consider going it alone, going back towards Dherinia, then heading across the fields. Then he thought better of it. He had John with him and something in the officer's manner led him to believe that if he was patient he would be escorted to the front line, getting him exactly where he wanted to be.

Soon after the Major had finished speaking to Helena and had left the television unit the officer called in to report on the situation at Dherinia. After learning the good news that progress was being made in the face of only light resistance with no sustained counter attacks he was fascinated to learn that two British reporters had arrived on the scene. Not wanting to waste time consulting Helena again and believing such a decision to be within his competence, after all publicity was a prime objective, he ordered that they be escorted to him at once.

"See if you can spare a vehicle and drive them here to the Golden Sands straight away," was his direct order which was overheard by the men in the guard post. The officer, together with another soldier, hurried towards Charles and John a few moments later, speaking into his field telephone as he walked. As soon as he was close enough he called to them,

"This way, quickly." He turned to the side of the road where his 4x4 was parked. "Get in, my driver will take you to Famagusta, my commander wants to talk to you there."

Charles looked at John, his expression did not change, but to John he seemed to be saying, "round one to us."

They sped across the flat coastal plain through what had once been the citrus grove. All three of them were less than confident that they might not be mistaken for a Turkish patrol by their own defensive positions that had taken up their stations along the line of the road. Their concern was unfounded, they arrived at the Golden Sands command centre at ten forty five, at which time pictures of the beginning of the operation and of Clare Spencer's presence, were being fed by CBC at the speed of light around the globe and into the satellite receiving dishes of the world's media.

Before they arrived the Major realised that he was treading on very dangerous ground. He had at all costs to prevent them discovering that Clare Spencer was not present of her own free will. They must not be allowed to report that she was a prisoner, not yet. But if he could feed them the story their very presence would give added weight to their reports of the events. He met them cordially.

"Welcome to the liberated Golden Sands gentlemen. This is a battle zone and I can't allow you to remain here for more than a few minutes, but let me explain what we have achieved."

The Major described the state of the action against a background of intermittent shooting and rocket fire. They had now taken virtually all of the southern part of Famagusta, by virtue of the element of surprise they had achieved. He went on to explain that they were busily consolidating their hold on the strategically important points. He did not explain that there was no real resistance, but implied that they had been victorious through superior force and strategy. Neither did he mention the real vulnerability of his forces and positions to air attack from the north. Charles saw through everything he was told at once, but went along with the misrepresentation to gain the Major's confidence, only beginning to ask carefully phrased questions when the Major had finished and had taken them to the television van and replayed to them the pictures and statement that had just been put out by CBC.

"Major, the statement refers to British support, are any of the British forces here in Famagusta, or are you keeping them in reserve?"

"No, they are in support a few miles to the east, defending the southern border of the Turkish zone of occupation."

Charles knew the geography well enough to understand that this meant the British forces had not left the Sovereign Base, but he did not press the point.

"Didn't they come to protect the Prime Minister, she was here when you shot those pictures we have just seen?"

"No, the Prime Minister is our guest, she has every confidence in the Greek Cypriot forces supported as they are by her own."

For the second time in five minutes he recognised his mistake, his use of the word 'is'.

"Can we talk to the Prime Minister before we leave?" asked Charles.

The Major thought quickly. He wanted to retain their confidence, it was important that their suspicions were not aroused, but he could not allow a free interview, not after her demonstration in front of the cameras. He had an idea.

"Gentlemen, please wait here a moment and I will see if she will grant you an interview." He turned to his sergeant and added pointedly, "Look after our guests."

The Major entered the Golden Sands and found Costas, Michalas and Clare together in what had once been the cocktail bar, just off the lobby. He began by addressing Clare sharply;

"Miss Spencer, your demonstration in front of the cameras was foolish. You leave us no alternative but to be very careful to whom you are allowed to speak, and what you are allowed to say. This gives me a problem, and it puts the lives of two of your citizens in real peril. We have two British journalists outside requesting an interview with you. We cannot let them leave without granting them one, that would make them suspicious. Neither can we let them leave if they learn that you are not here of your own free will and part of the operation. This leaves me a choice and provides you with an opportunity to save the lives of two of your people. I could have them shot now, we could easily make it look like an unfortunate accident of battle. Or I could let them meet you first and only shoot them if you do not co-operate fully. I have decided to give you a chance to meet them and save their lives. Costas, look after her, I'll bring them in straight away."

Clare did not speak. She had no choice. "But," she kept thinking to herself, "is there a way I could give them a sign that only they will recognise, without arousing the suspicions of the Cypriots?" If there was she couldn't work it out. Perhaps something would come to her.

The Major returned with John and Charles who recognised Clare instantly, although neither had met her personally before. After the introductions and the Major's instructions that they had two minutes only, but not a second longer, Charles began, not knowing of the Major's conditions for the interview he had decided to try to throw her off guard straight away with a totally unexpected introductory remark:

"Good evening Miss Spencer, although we have not met before we do have mutual friends, Barbara Rowland is a personal friend of mine, I understand both her and her husband are friends of yours."

As he spoke he watched Clare very closely and she seemed to shrink visibly when he mentioned the name 'Rowland'. She did not know what she could say, all she could manage was;

"Yes I had dinner with Richard last night...."

"We have more in common than I thought, I had cocktails with Barbara earlier tonight..."

Now Clare knew there was more to Charles Noble than an Express reporter. "He knows...he's come to get me out.." she thought, visibly, to Charles, regaining her stature.

The preliminaries over, now that they understood each other, Charles continued;

"Miss Spencer can I ask when the British involvement was agreed and whether the cabinet as a whole endorsed the plan?"

"No Mr Noble, that is something I cannot comment upon, it is something I must report on first to the House of Commons."

"Were the Americans consulted?" interjected John.

"I cannot add to my answer to Mr Noble's question."

"How many troops do we have in Cyprus?" asked Charles taking up the questioning again.

"I am afraid that is a military secret. The Turkish command would be interested in the answer to that question," she replied, then her brain sprang into action automatically, "but of course you know we have contingents from all three services based here in Cyprus, the Army, the Royal Air Force and the Navy." the she looked at Charles straight in the face and added, willing him to read more into what she was about to say, "and of course that includes the Marines."

Charles caught on in a flash. He was sure she was trying to say "tell it to the Marines", in other words that she was not able to speak freely to them and wanted them to know it. Could he confirm it without risking her life? Richard's death may be enough in itself, but there had been no certainty that he had just not found out more that he was expected to, unless Clare confirmed it herself.

"Have you been in touch with London since the action began?"

Clare's hesitation was enough, her reply didn't matter. It was clear that if British involvement had been real she would have spoken to London. If she was a hostage she would not. She had not known what to reply. The Major interjected in an attempt to cover up her hesitation.

"The Prime Minister's discussions with her Government must remain a matter for her, not the press."

"Of course that is so, but we would like something we could quote, to demonstrate that we have not fabricated this meeting."

"What I can say, on the record," Clare began, recovering her composure, "is that I have every confidence in the ability of my country's armed forces to meet every eventuality. despite the reductions of recent years, which I intend to take much further as I made clear at the election, their quality remains second to none, the airforce is exceedingly well equipped with both aircraft and innovative human resources, the army superbly trained, the navy remains the most professional in the world and the Marines, well what can one say about the Marines....?"

"Yes indeed, what can one say..." answered Charles, projecting an imperceptible sign straight through her eyes with the force of his own, as he wished he could have added, "especially to an ex-Royal Marine Officer."

They both now knew that the other knew the truth. She made a mental note to find out more about Charles Noble, if she ever got out of this mess.

"Right gentlemen, you have had your time, please come with me," the Major ordered, leading them towards the door. They both turned and thanked Clare as she turned away towards Costas, who had been closely following every word. Something bothered him, but he couldn't quite work out what it was.

When they were outside in front of the Golden Sands again Charles said;

"I congratulate you Major on a very impressive operation. Can we file our stories from the CBC van, that way we might just catch the late editions of tomorrow's Sunday newspapers back home?"

The Major looked concerned. He had been about to bring their visit to an end and ask them to return to Dherinia with the driver who had brought them across. "Why not," he thought, "their independent confirmation of the CBC reports might make a difference to the credibility and coverage."

"Yes, that would be a pleasure. Follow me please, this way."

He led them to the CBC van for the second time and explained to those present that his guests were to be given every facility and that he would return in thirty minutes to escort them to their vehicle so they may leave. He closed the door behind him after leaving them in the unit and explained to the driver that he was to stand guard and was not under any circumstances to allow them out of his sight until he, the Major, returned.

After the Major had closed the door John looked at Charles for a signal. He did not know what was expected of him. Charles didn't need prompting. He knew exactly what he would do now that he had to some extent lulled the Major into a false sense of security.

"John, your deadline is earlier than mine, you go ahead and file your story first." Charles began in a voice loud enough to be overheard by those present in the unit. "Is it alright to telephone the story straight through?" he continued, directing his question to the man he assumed to be in charge.

"Yes, give me the number. I will make the connection." came the rather grudging reply.

John handed over one of his cards, pointing out the number to dial. As soon as the call was answered the phone was handed to John. He desperately needed to ask Charles what he should say, but how could he with the CBC staff present. Charles had read his mind.

"John, to save time let's make it a joint report, for our two papers. Just tell them where we are, who I am, then I'll take over and give them a story for the two of us."

John got a rather startled Sunday Times news editor on the line. He explained who he was, where he was - that he was with the victorious Greek Cypriot forces in Famagusta. He confirmed the story that had just been put out by Cyprus television and introduced Charles, as Charles Noble from the Express.

By this time the news editor had pressed his panic button and he was not the only person listening to the call. His editor James Dudley-Foster had taken over and had begun to shout questions down the line. Since John was not finding the situation easy to handle he was relieved to hand the phone to Charles. As he took it the Harrow educated voice was booming;

".....is she still there, have you seen her, what is she doing, that is the real story...."

Charles interrupted.

"Charles Noble here sir, check that name with the Foreign Office straight away to be certain of my credentials. John has been tremendous, we are covering the story together in a pooled report, so it is important that you pass all this to my paper. The Foreign Office will confirm that I am a registered foreign correspondent with the Express."

Charles did not have to wonder long how quick Dudley-Foster would be in recognising his signals and take the point since no foreign correspondent was or needed to be registered with the Foreign Office. He silently pleaded with the man at the other end of the line to give him a return signal that he understood. He did not have to wait long.

"Certainly Mr..er Noble, will the office be open tonight to check credentials?"

"Without doubt, but if there is any trouble try one of these numbers..." he then quoted Sir Rodney's numbers.

"By the way, John forgot to mention that this is entirely a land based operation so far, no sign of activity in the air, and although we are on the coast, no sign of an amphibious landing by the marines. When we spoke to the Prime Minister a short while ago she was full of praise for the marines, so I would not be surprised if she had been talking to them about the reasons for her presence here in Famagusta."

He dared not say anymore, but hoped it might be enough, especially if every word was passed to Sir Rodney.

Dudley-Foster was no fool. He had realised the significance of what he had heard and he replied cautiously.

"I have taken note of what you have said, I will contact the FO and play them a tape of our conversation so they can confirm your identity."

Charles was grateful, "Thanks mate, we will be in touch just as soon we can with any further news. Just pray the Turks stay at home until we all get out of here."

"Phase one completed, now for phase two, how to get her out'" he mused as he opened the door for John and he to leave the van. They had about fifteen minutes to get rid of the driver, release Clare from the two men guarding her, and get away, before the Major returned.

CHAPTER EIGHTEEN

When Steve Bradshaw and Barbara Rowland emerged from the village of Dherinia a little after ten fifteen they confidently expected to be in Nicosia soon after midnight. Their route took them through the potato villages. Villages that had grown rich from the lucrative trade in that vegetable to Great Britain. The villagers lifted their main crop in March and April and had been able to sell onto a high priced market at the end of the British season, when that country's crop, lifted the previous autumn, was looking its age, and before the new season's crop began. It had been a niche market. That was until restrictions and quotas had begun to be established by the Brussels machine during the integration of British agriculture into Europe. Then there had been the determination of the continental member countries to seize the opportunity of taking the market previously enjoyed by members of the British Commonwealth and former Empire. All the headlines had concentrated upon New Zealand lamb and butter, but the situation was just as serious, if not more so, for the less industrialised Cypriots, as it was for the more sophisticated New Zealanders. Potato growers in Spain, Italy and Greece saw their opportunity to grab the early market that had been the domain of the Cypriot. That had been one of the main reasons for Cyprus' application to join the European Community, one that had been deferred and side-stepped, first by the division of the island and the Community's desire not to offend Turkey, and later by the restructuring of the Community that had been necessary to accommodate the new democracies of central Europe and the dominant inward looking Germany.

Once they had passed through all these villages they entered British Sovereign territory, the Base at Dhekelia, then left it temporarily to pass through the Cypriot island that accommodated the Dhekelia power station. Re-entering the Base they turned left onto the main road through a piece of

England transplanted onto the southern shore of Cyprus. Houses and streets that would not have looked out of place in Aldershot or Colchester. Half way through Steve slowed down and turned into the BP petrol station. He got out and walked towards the Land Rover parked at the side, was met half way by a young soldier, identified himself and was handed one of the latest two-way communicators, identical to the one Charles Noble always carried on his person.

They completed their journey through the Base at high speed and after joining the former main road to Famagusta at the foot of the hill, continued along Larnaca Bay as far as the Nicosia motorway junction. Until the early 1980's there had been little or no development between the British Base and the industrial estate and oil installations to the east of the town of Larnaca. The loss of the tourist areas in the North had changed that situation totally. After a much slower start than had been the case at either Limassol or Paphos or even Ayia Napa, Larnaca Bay had raced to catch up and take its share of the enormously increasing tourist revenues. Both sides of the road, which itself had not changed, had become a continuous concrete resort of sorts stretching for about five miles. This was the least tasteful of all the developments that had taken place in Cyprus during the previous twenty years. It was just a mass of hastily designed and constructed hotels, apartments, shops and tavernas, typical of the Spanish Costas of the 1960s. It was not Cyprus, it was the Mediterranean. Fortunately for Steve a motorway by-passing this new development had opened in 1990 and he was able to turn right onto it soon after joining the coast road. But unfortunately four miles towards Larnaca it had been blocked by one of the many accidents this fast, straight stretch had seen. not being prepared to wait for the problem to clear he crossed the central reservation and returned to the old coastal route.

Like that of Limassol and Nicosia the Larnaca bypass had become just another street in the town as the town had expanded and jumped into open country to the east. Once they had negotiated it successfully they turned right onto the main road north to Nicosia. It was now almost eleven and they listened silently to the BBC News on the hour. It carried the first news of the night's events in Famagusta, but nothing to warn them of what was in store for them as they sped towards the capital. At Aradipou Steve made the wrong snap decision. He decided not to rejoin the motorway and risk another blockage, instead he stayed on the old main road. They passed the junction of the narrow old road to Lymbia and were near the next junction, where the main Lymbia road left the old Nicosia road that now only led to Athienou. There was a bright flash straight in front of the car, followed by three more, much closer. Steve had no choice but to stop, as he was braking he said urgently to Barbara;

"We've got to get out of here fast. There's a battle raging and we are less than a mile from the front, and it's getting closer. Let's get back and join the motorway"

He threw the car into reverse and was across the road when there was a loud explosion to the south of them."

"Quick, get out!" he almost shouted at her. He got out himself and raced around the car, grabbed her arm and literally pulled her into the ditch at the side of the road, throwing her to the ground and himself half on top of her.

It took only a few moments to work out what was happening. The Greek Cypriot forces must have struck north in an attempt to take the Turks by surprise as in Famagusta. But it had not worked and the Turks were striking south from their base between the Lymbia hills and the Nicosia road itself.

"They must be intending to take the road junction and cut off the Cypriot forces who must have advanced to the north," he surmised. Sure enough another barrage of shells landed near the junction. Their aim was improving. Then another landed just to the south of their car. It was clear they had to get out, fast.

"Barbara, we can't stay here. We've got to try to reach the old Lymbia road or the motorway on foot. Do you think you can make it?"

Her reply was drowned by the explosion as their car burst into flames. It had received a direct hit. Steve reacted, just in time, he had been in the process of lifting himself off the ground to decide the best route to take away from the trouble. Instinctively he recognised the danger a millisecond before it happened and once again had thrown himself down onto Barbara. Although debris from the explosion fell around them and he was showered with dust and small pieces from the crater made in the road, they were both largely unhurt. He was temporarily deafened in one ear and she was badly bruised on her back from the impact he had made in falling on her for the second time. He took her arm, almost dragged her to her feet and they set off as quickly as they could over rough ground towards the west and away from danger.

They had to be cautious. The battle was raging to their right and behind them as they made their way towards the old road. Between taking cover from the intensive barrage that had developed it took them more than an hour to reach their objective. Barbara was exhausted, even a fit Steve Bradshaw was ready to rest. As they sat on the edge of the narrow road they saw little sign of the battle they had left behind. Neither knew why. Whether the Turks were advancing against no resistance, or whether a stalemate had been reached. He took a decision to be cautious. Instead of heading towards Lymbia, hoping to find transport there to Nicosia, he decided instead to follow the safer course and Larnaca. Then he remembered his communicator. He still had it with him and called Dhekelia. He was put straight through to the commander after mentioning who he was and Charles Noble's name. During their scrambled conversation Steve explained what had happened and that he must nevertheless get to Nicosia without any further delay. It was agreed that the commander would send a car and driver to collect and take them to Nicosia. They would attempt to reach the motorway and wait at the edge of the northbound carriagway.

Steve kept looking at his watch for the next few hours. Delay compounded delay. It took longer than he had anticipated for the car to reach them. The roads from the villages were becoming busier as many began to flee to the comparative safety of Larnaca. It had been yet another accident this time at the junction between the coastal road and the temporarily closed motorway that had delayed the car at first. Then an accumulation of problems, with the motorway still closed there was an ever increasing number of vehicles. Finally they had to find an alternative cross-country route to Nicosia to avoid Lymbia. The result was that it was almost three thirty when they reached the centre of Nicosia. They asked the driver to stop outside Grindley's Bank on Makarios Avenue and to wait for them there however long that might might be. They cut through a side street and approached Helena's offices, from the south. As they got nearer they noticed two young men talking to the security guard outside the main doors to the building. Whatever they had said to him caused him to take out his personal radio and speak into the mouthpiece. When he had finished speaking he ushered one of them through. The other walked across the street and watched and waited.

It was nine in the evening in London, eleven in Cyprus, when Dudley-Foster dialled Sir Rodney's number. Not that he had any idea who he was calling. Sir Rodney picked up the phone and answered simply, "yes".

"Dudley-Foster here, Sunday Times".

Sir Rodney feared the worst. First, how had they got his red number, and secondly he concluded they must be trying to obtain his comments on some in-depth investigation that they were publishing that night, in the late editions, to avoid the possibility of an injunction. But he was not a naturally rude man so instead of merely hanging-up, he began to explain,

"I am in-conference, I shall have to cut you off......"

Not to be put off Dudley-Foster shouted;

"Wait, for God's sake wait, I've just had a man called Charles Noble on the line from Cyprus, told me to call you."

Sir Rodney jumped and stood bolt upright startling everyone, including the Foreign Secretary and the service chiefs, around the table. He pressed a button on the phone to switch on the speaker so they could all hear the remainder of the conversation.

"What did he say? Why was he calling you?" demanded Sir Rodney.

"My man called in first, Charles Noble was with him and took the phone. I'll play you a tape of the conversation if that would help."

"Yes please, do you know to whom you are speaking?"

"Not exactly, but I can guess and will find out later."

To save him the trouble Sir Rodney told him that he represented the security services and that it may be necessary to ask that nothing of this be published. Then he asked for the tape to be played. They all listened carefully and appreciated the significance of what they had heard. When it had finished Dudley-Foster asked what exactly was going on in Cyprus, he had seen the tapes, but that was all he knew, apart that was from the Clare Spencer in Cyprus story that had been running all day.

Edmund Stead took the telephone from Sir Rodney, he knew Dudley-Foster well.

"James, how good to hear from you, Edmund here. You are quite sure he didn't say anything else before you switched on the tape?

"Hello Edmund, no nothing at all. I can vouch for that."

"Look you are sitting on quite a story there."

"Yes, it was quite clear that Noble couldn't speak freely. He was being very careful to chose his words. Is there really any British military involvement, why should we want to reopen that old wound?"

"Look you know the score James, we are officially refusing all comment. In return for not disclosing Noble's call I can give you an exclusive for your latest editions. I am going to Cyprus tonight on Concorde to join the Prime Minister there. We are after all one of the guarantor powers, we have a lot of men in the UN peacekeeping force there, and we do have several Sovereign Bases, so we are involved in anything that happens there. Unofficially and off the record I'm going to try to find out what the hell is going on. Have you any idea how your man and Noble got to Famagusta?"

"No, none. Look this is dynamite. I can't sit on it for ever. If I agree will you agree that we will be the first to know if there is any change? - and," Dudley-Foster suddenly added, a new thought had just occurred to him, "I want my man on Concorde with you, after all I have a reporter in the middle of it over there who is probably in great danger and who is obviously working with your people."

"Damn," thought Edmund, knowing he had no real choice, but that he could control communications.

"Yes of course old man, provided he signs an undertaking to accept military orders. Tell him to be at the VIP lounge Heathrow in forty five minutes. We won't wait."

"Thanks Edmund. You can rely on us to be responsible. I'll call if either of them contact me again"

When Edmund had replaced the phone Sir Rodney asked him;

"Was that wise, to tell him so much and to agree to taking one of them with you?"

"Unavoidable. Far better to have them with us under an obligation and some control, than leaving them to speculate on the basis of half the truth. Noble spoke to him. He has every right to publish, he knows it and knew I knew it."

As far as Edmund was concerned the fact that he was travelling to Cyprus to join his Prime Minister could be given full publicity, provided the story broke after he had arrived there. Publicity was one of its prime objectives. He had to deflect domestic attention away from events on the ground and to provide the appearance of action and that matters were under control. He had to gain a few more hours to find out the exact position and to find a way to rescue the Prime Minister who, he was now totally convinced, was being used as a hostage and was in real danger. She was being used to prevent British condemnation and a Turkish response. The visit would also draw attention towards him, and would the hide the simultaneous arrival of the special forces he had ordered to Cyprus. If they could link up with Noble then there was still a real chance.

It was very true that Dudley-Foster was no fool. Knowing that anything his man on Concorde could get back would be too late for his paper, he decided to send someone else, and secure his own future in the media megacorporation that paid his salary. Not only did it control the Sunday Times and Times, together with several down market titles Dudley-Foster would rather forget belonged to the same stable, it controlled two television networks, one in the United Kingdom and Europe and another in the United States. Instead of sending his man from the Sunday Times or one from the Times, which would be difficult in any case, that was why John had had to go to Cyprus in the first place, he called Sky News. That would give them the opportunity to be to the Cyprus story, what CNN had been to Bagdad in the early days of the Gulf War. Being close to Heathrow they could make the deadline. His only slight worry was that his agreement with Edmund only allowed for one extra passenger, not two or three. He gambled that there would be no argument about numbers, but told his opposite number in Sky that he must send only two and that they must state that they were representing Times Newspapers and Sky, and not just Sky.

A little after ten thirty London time, half past midnight in Cyprus, Concorde took off from the number one runway of London's Heathrow airport. It headed west, shattering the peace of a quiet, late September Saturday evening. It disturbed diners and residents alike amongst the Thames Valley high society. The airport switchboard was swamped with angry calls of complaint about this breach in the night hours noise regulations. These had only recently been amended after a long fight, to allow quiet aeroplanes to use the airport during the night, but as a concession restricted the noisiest planes, of which Concorde was the most blatant example, to the middle of each day. The flight plan had been hastily put together and had involved high level agreement with France and Italy. It permitted a direct flight across the French heartland, before reaching the Mediterranean west of Marseilles, crossing the tip of Sicily and then heading directly for Akrotiri. The estimated flight time was two and a half hours. Touchdown for the dozen or so passengers, including a two man Sky News team, was expected at one in the morning London time, three in Cyprus.

In addition to the two from Sky News, there were eleven other passengers. Edmund Stead, his Private Secretary and a senior eastern Mediterranean diplomat who had been hastily collected and brought to Heathrow from his Wimbledon home, made up the skeleton Foreign Office team. Sir Rodney had sent two men from the security services to form a link between Charles Noble, the Foreign Secretary and the special services team. The remaining six were a crack SAS team who had flown into Heathrow by helicopter from Hereford minutes before Concorde was due to leave. In true SAS fashion, much to the horror of the Heathrow authorities, the helicopter had landed less than twelve feet from Concorde, the men entering only when the arc lights flooding the steps had been switched off. That was only done very reluctantly after the helicopter pilot had been ordered to radio the tower a message to the effect that unless they were switched off immediately they would be shot out. Major Colin Brightwell had not been joking when he had made the order. He did not joke.

The French authorities had been very co-operative. Although they were not told officially, they knew the score. That trouble had erupted in Cyprus and the British were in a mess with their Prime Minister in the middle of it. Relations between the two countries had improved immeasurably since the French had rescued the channel tunnel project and completed it with government money, something the British had refused to do, thereby allowing it to be controlled and owned by France. To help out the British they had readily agreed to clear a military corridor through the less populated heart of their country, usually reserved for supersonic exercises.

Before Concorde had crossed the coast of Normandy Edmund had begun to reflect upon the arrangements he had constructed in haste for the next day. Everything was in place except for the clearance of the venue. Since Concorde carried an excellent communications system this was easy to remedy. It provided for businessmen to make secure telephone calls while in flight. He decided to take advantage of the scrambled satellite link and asked his Private Secretary to place a call to the United Nations Secretary General in New York. He was lucky. It was only six in the evening there and the Secretary General had not left his residence for the evening of receptions which always preceded the annual General Assembly starting on Monday morning. He was instead locked in talks with his staff about the situation that had arisen in Cyprus in the last few hours. When he heard of the arrangements that Edmund had made he was relieved and agreed to send his deputy and was delighted to add his endorsement to the chosen venue. He was less relieved to learn that he was expected to treat the matter as confidential for the next seven hours. Seven hours during which he was likely to be the object of intensive lobbying to do something, when there was nothing more he could do, it had been done for him, but he was unable to say so. Eventually he agreed to a compromise in which he could say that appropriate steps were being taken to restore the situation, but that in order to save lives an announcement could not be made before five hours GMT, which was one in the morning in New York.

Edmund then put through a call to his High Commissioner in Nicosia. To protect security this call was patched through London to the building close to the Green Line in central Nicosia. The High Commissioner was the most relieved man he had spoken to that evening. He was besieged with enquiries about the situation, but had known no more than he had seen on television or heard on the radio. After outlining his arrangements for the next day Edmund told him to get some sleep and to expect him between four and five the next morning when they would be able to brief each other more fully.

Edmund then decided to make the call he had been avoiding making all evening. To Washington. Previous governments in which he had served had always had good relations with Washington. Since the last British election, however, these had deteriorated sharply. They clearly did not trust Clare Spencer. True they had some reason to be suspicious, Clare had made no secret of her desire to remove the last remaining US forces in Europe from her country. She had promoted that as a moral crusade. But that was no more than other European countries had been doing since the turn of the decade, and France had done the same nearly thirty years earlier. There was something else, a real hostility was developing, especially when the Prime Minister's name was mentioned. It reminded Edmund of the attitude of the Americans towards Nicaragua during the Regan years. He himself had tolerably good relations with his opposite number, it was as if they were trying to separate him and his party from their coalition partners whom they had willingly joined after the election.

He was unable to reach the President, the Chief of Staff took his call and explained, somewhat unconvincingly Edmund thought, that the President was otherwise engaged. "Probably listening on the extension," thought Edmund. The conversation was brief. Briefer than he had intended. The American had not contributed anything useful to the dialogue, so Edmund had restricted the information provided to the minimum he considered courteous. He told the Americans that he had decided to join his Prime Minister in Cyprus. He did not say he was on board Concorde and only two hours away from the island. He did say that it was the British intention to take a new initiative over Cyprus. He did not say what that initiative was, nor that it was already in hand. He did not mention Clare Spencer by name, nor what she had been doing in Cyprus, neither did Washington. Before the call ended the Chief of Staff did however attempt to keep the channel between Edmund and the White House open. He said that he would report to the President, asked Edmund to contact him again the following day, when he hoped that the President would be in a position to speak personally to him to put the United States' position directly and offer any personal support he may request. "They are playing their cards close to their chest, and waiting to see which way the wind blows. I wonder what he means by 'personal' support?" thought Edmund.

The remainder of the flight passed uneventfully. Concorde landed at RAF Akrotiri at three in the morning Cyprus time, one in London, and eight in the evening in the eastern United States. A convoy of cars was waiting for them. Before getting into his own Edmund walked over to Major Colin Brightwell and shook him by the hand.

"Major, as we agreed you will go to Dhekelia and wait for further orders. One of Sir Rodney's men is to go with you as liaison with his colleague who will stay with me. As soon as we hear anything more from Noble we will try to put him in touch with you.

"I want you to understand one thing very clearly," he continued, "Clare Spencer is important to me - and the Government and people. Her safety is paramount. We must rescue her, but not risk her life. There is no doubt she is in great danger. It would be very convenient for her captors if there was an unfortunate 'accident' so that she could not tell anyone the circumstances of her capture. You may consider me a political opponent of hers. That is nonsense, I regard her as a personal friend." Edmund spoke with such sincerity that even the hard SAS man believed him to be genuine. A man of few words, he merely shook Edmund by the hand, saying;

"Yes sir, I understand."

Pete Wright could not settle his mind and go to bed as his exhausted wife Sandra had done. He sat outside on the balcony of his Paphos hotel looking south towards the sea. It was tranquil and very quiet. It was impossible to imagine that less than one hundred miles away across the island to the east a small war was being fought. As he was meditating, his mind was dazed, not concentrating on anything in particular, just revolving in the haze of the night's events, he began to hear an aircraft approaching. "I hope they are luckier than we were," he thought to himself. The noise became louder and he assumed it was coming into land at Paphos airport, a few miles further down the coast to the east. Then it became a roar, but although it was too dark to see the shape of the aircraft itself, it was clear from the navigation lights that it was too high and too near to attempt a landing at Paphos after all. The only plane he had heard make such a particular noise was Concorde. "Could it be?" he asked himself. He could not know, but if it was why was it flying so low over Cyprus? As he watched the lights flashing they were definitely getting lower, but heading out to sea again, not towards Larnaca. Then he realised, it was aiming for Akrotiri. Often he had sat on the beach at Pissouri, half way along the coast to Limassol, watching jets exercise over Akrotiri Bay. Yes it was definitely preparing to land there.

Then his mind really did begin to concentrate. "What really was going on? Were the British really involved in hijacking the flight? Were the hijackers not Irish? Did the British know? How could they since no passengers had been allowed to speak to anyone?" He stood up and looked over the balcony and could see a contingent of National Guard. They were not taking their guard duties too seriously. Just standing around patrolling the car park in front of the hotel entrance. He took a decision, went inside, found some 10 cent coins that he had carried with him in case they were accepted in the North, took his diary, looked across at his wife who was sleeping peacefully, pocketed the room key and left the room, closing the door silently behind him. As he stood in the corridor he pictured the floor plan that he had seen fastened to the back of the door to the room. He walked away from the direction of the lift and main stairs towards one of the emergency exits. It was easy. He just pushed it open and carefully and silently went down four floors to the ground. He was lucky, it was the western end of the hotel. A guard had been stationed to watch that end, but was instead one of a huddled group of three other men a little way across the car park. He heard sounds. Yes they were listening to the BBC News on the hour, it was three Cyprus time, but midnight GMT. He had put more than a hundred metres between himself and the hotel before the group of National Guard broke up and returned to their stations.

In less than ten minutes he was outside the Paphos Beach hotel. He did consider entering and using one of their telephones, but he would be obvious to the night duty staff. No, he walked on and in five minutes he found what he was looking for. A public telephone box in the new development of shops and apartments in Kato Paphos centre. Being a frequent visitor to Cyprus he kept the British High Commission's telephone number in his diary. He dialled that number and after some delay it was answered by one of the duty officers manning what had become a very busy switchboard during the last few hours. Pete was polite and was not put off by the automatic answer that was being given to all callers. His voice contained a determined edge and eventually it was listened to;

"I am a British citizen. A passenger from the plane hijacked to Nicosia earlier tonight. We are being kept prisoner in Paphos. I escaped. Please let me speak to the High Commissioner, I have some important information which I will only give to him."

The duty office had received many dubious calls, both that night and during his career, but he recognised this one to be genuine.

"Certainly sir, give me your number in case we get cut off."

Pete did so. The duty officer called the High Commissioner, who took the call by his bed. The duty officer began to tape the call.

"Julian Metcalf here, please give me the details."

"My name is Wright, Peter Wright - and before you ask, not

the infamous one of the same name. You have heard most of the details on the radio, but all the passengers were brought here to Paphos, to the Cypria Maris Hotel. The hotel is under armed guard. I got out through an emergency exit. The plane was hijacked by four people with Irish accents who said they were doing it for their Greek Cypriot friends. As soon as we landed Cypriots took over from them. They still have the crew and two Turkish passengers they gave a hard time to on the flight. I thought you ought to know this. The radio implied that the British Government were involved, it isn't, is it?"

"Of course not. No civilised government would allow itself to become involved in something like this. You are certain the hijackers were Irish?

"Yes two young men, and two girls, all around twenty I should guess. By the way was that Concorde I just saw making an approach to land at Akrotiri?"

Julian Metcalf thought, "they really have arrived then." Then said, "I really couldn't comment. I am sure there will be movements, military and civilian as a result of what is happening tonight and certainly I will not be informed of them all. Mr Wright thank you very much. Your information could be most useful. Please get in touch again as soon as you can to make a full report."

"Look, I must go now. Someone may see me and get suspicious. It seems most Cypriots in uniform are involved in this somehow. Bye."

It was three thirty.

Pete made his way slowly back to the hotel-prison. He waited a safe distance away until just before four. Then he edged a little closer. Just as he had hoped the guards gathered together around their radio for the news. He took his opportunity and was back in his room before the news summary was over. Sandra was still fast asleep.

CHAPTER NINETEEN

The President looked puzzled as his Chief of Staff replaced the receiver after talking to the British Foreign Secretary Edmund Stead.

"Why didn't you tell him about the fighters we promised Zekaibes? We told Zekaibes we would announce it publicly."

"Because he didn't tell us everything. He didn't tell us what his initiative was. More importantly he didn't tell us that he has invited the Greek Premier to meet him in Nicosia in the morning."

"What? How do we know that?"

"Just had an intelligence report from our bureau in Athens. They picked up the call. We'll have a transcript soon. The point is we can't show our hand to him. Let him get in out of his depth first. Then when we've got rid of that woman for him we can drag him out of the mud, prove it was the Greek Cypriots and that there was nothing he could have done to prevent it, then he'll be in our pocket. We mustn't give him any assistance, after all he may be intending to try to rescue Spencer."

"What's our man doing. Hasn't he finished her off yet. When will we hear?"

"Unfortunately we don't know exactly. It's all up to him now. He has his orders. To do the job and be at his rendezvous at the agreed time. We're in his hands. Don't like it, but we've no choice."

"You don't think he will funk it do you?"

"No we are quite sure he won't do that. Physcologically he's up to it alright. We checked that for sure. Our only worry is that he might wait too long for exactly the right moment, stick too strictly to his orders. You see he has to allow her enough rope to really be seen to be involved. Firstly, it's no good bumping her off before its easy for us to prove beyond all doubt she's in it up to her ears. Secondly he has to make it look like an accident. There must not be any possibility that anybody could suspect an assassination. Got to be a pure accident, in the battle itself, or probably a vehicle gets hit and explodes. Something like that, we've given him lots of alternatives, but left him some discretion over the detail."

"How will we get to know?"

"Athens has arranged an escape route for him to get out. If he uses it, he has succeeded. He might think it is an escape, but we've made sure he won't survive it to tell the tale, as it were."

"What if the Greeks gain ground? Won't it be difficult for the Turks to get them out again, especially if Stead is arranging a peace conference?"

"Don't worry, once he discovers they have murdered his Prime Minister there's no way he can continue to side with them. He'll have to adjourn and join with us in urging the Turks to finish the job."

"Good. I'll have to get ready. The first lady and I have promised to turn up at a reception for the Emperor of Japan. Never thought I would see the day when an American President would be expected to pay homage to the Mikado's son. The world's changing too fast. We knew where we were when we had the evil empire, as one of my predecessors used to say. Now we don't even know who's the enemy. But I suppose we've still got Castro, must be thankful that some things never change."

Dismissed from his audience the Chief of Staff left the President and returned to his own room which he expected might become the centre of attention during the next few hours and perhaps days. He was still waiting for news when the President called down before leaving the White House for the Japanese Embassy. It was eight thirty in New York, three thirty in the morning in Cyprus.

Charles Noble recognised that it was a very tall order, after all they had shown no mercy to Rowland when he had escaped. He must do better. Nevertheless it was worth the risk. Otherwise British forces could be drawn into a war, a war which they could not influence, of that he had no doubt.

No country could allow their Prime Minister to be held in such a helpless position. If he succeeded then the worst need not happen. The thought of failure was not something he normally allowed to enter his mind. But this time it was different. Much more than his own life and that of men under his command depended on his judgement. He hesitated, then remembered that hesitation was a far greater danger than the enemy. He considered his plan as he followed John out of the CBC van. Deliberately he remained two paces behind his companion as the driver, now ordered to serve as their guard, approached.

"Their third mistake," he thought to himself. "First they let us into the Golden Sands and see their position, then they allowed us to phone London, now they trust a driver to be our guard. Not very professional."

Hidden from the driver by John he made himself ready. He slipped his belt off his trousers and placed the two ends together in his right hand. Noticing that the driver did not take his duties too seriously, his rifle was pointing to the ground, not towards either of them, he closed the gap between John and himself, but was careful to keep his right arm hidden behind John's left shoulder. Then he made his move. He pushed John hard to the right with his hidden arm still clutching his belt. His gamble was working, the driver's eyes followed John. In an instant the rifle he was raising was snapped out of his grip with a violent twist. Before he could even think the driver found himself suffocating from a tightening leather loop around his throat. He could not speak, only to listen to Charles.

"John pick up the rifle. You.." he turned to his captive, "any noise at all and this belt is your noose. If you understand lift your right foot."

He fractionally loosened his grip when the signal followed. Then he spoke to John.

"John take off your shirt and tear off a strip about six inches wide. Then come over here with it."

John did exactly as he was asked. Expertly, Charles, with

John's willing, but unskilled, assistance, immobilised their captor with a variety of John's clothing torn and tailored to meet its new purpose.

They did not have time to search for a suitable hiding place for the driver and had to be satisfied with leaving him behind the CBC van, guessing that anyone entering or leaving would walk straight up to the door and would not venture around it. Charles dressed himself quickly in the National Guard uniform taken from the driver, telling John to put his discarded clothes on as necessary to replace those used on their captive.

"Right, cover as much of your head as possible with his cap, try not to let anyone see your face. I'll use the helmet and the rifle. Act as if you were a prisoner being taken into the hotel by me. When we get there take your lead from me and do exactly what I say without question. OK?"

"Fine. But how are we going to get away, have you thought about that?"

"Leave that to me my friend, don't worry, you and I will be out of here with Miss Spencer in ten minutes." Charles answered confidently. Remembering his own thoughts of a few minutes ago he added, "whatever you do don't hesitate. Don't hesitate if you see anything unexpected. Remember you are being guarded by me and taken into headquarters. Don't hesitate when I tell you to move. Just do it. Ready?"

John nodded.

"Good, let's get started."

They walked across towards the entrance to the Golden Sands. The night was dark, and had it not been for the sound of gunfire, mostly small arms, but with intermittent deep roars from larger weapons, accompanied by bright flashes, to the north east, it would have been a still night.

Although technically the field headquarters of the operation this was largely symbolic. Charles had recognised this earlier. Only two men were guarding Clare Spencer and two more were posted on the front steps, those on the roof were observing more distant activity than that around the building itself. Otherwise the derelict hotel was empty. There was some vehicle traffic around the forecourt and in the overgrown car park.

"So it was two against four", thought Charles, "four armed men against one."

But they had the element of surprise on their side, or so he hoped. The major problem he believed were the two men on the steps. Unless they could be taken silently the two inside and possibly those on the roof would hear the danger and be prepared.

They were only ten yards away when one spoke to them in Greek. Charles understood enough to recognise what had been asked. He did not answer, but he was close enough to whisper to John:

"When I poke the rifle in your back fall to the ground."

After they had taken three more steps towards the guards Charles pushed the rifle butt between John's shoulder blades. Exactly on cue John fell to the ground, a little dramatically perhaps, but effectively enough. As Charles had expected and planned the two guards stepped forward to investigate. As they bent over the prostrate John he struck, reaching into the depths of his training of more than ten years ago, he hit the backs of both their necks almost simultaneously, one with his bare hand, the other with his rifle butt. Both guards joined John on the ground virtually silently. He checked their motionless bodies for consciousness, found none, then signalled to John to follow him in, dragging the two silent National Guardsmen away from the main steps and into the overgrown shrubbery to the side. The removal of their final obstacle had taken less than thirty seconds and had been completed without any unwelcome attention having been drawn to their demise. Charles said quietly to John:

"Well done, now follow me, let's get this finished quickly."

They entered the lobby quietly and quickly, and most importantly, unseen. Charles knew he had the advantage of surprise. There were only two men guarding the Prime Minister and he doubted whether they were mentally prepared for a determined rescue mission, certainly not yet, he believed. The lobby was empty. The little group had remained in the cocktail bar and with the lobby itself in darkness the storm lanterns showed clearly their position without revealing his own. So his advantage was doubled, not only surprise, but darkness to hide their presence.

Slowly and carefully he moved along the wall towards the former cocktail bar, being careful to try to avoid stepping on any of the debris that had accumulated during the past twenty years of Turkish neglect. It was too easy. Clare's minders were separated from her by at least ten feet and neither of them was holding a weapon. They may have been able to prevent Clare from escaping herself, but they were in no position to do anything to prevent her from being rescued.

Charles lifted his rifle, held it out in front of his body and threw himself clear of the side wall so that the two men and Clare were in his full view with a clear path, free of obstacles, between them.

"Don't move. Freeze," he shouted. Seeing they had obeyed his command he continued. "Miss Spencer, please come here quickly, get behind me and in the cover of the wall. John, keep her there."

When she had done as he asked, and John had safely taken her arm and led her to comparative safety, Charles continued speaking to her two amateur guards, Costas and Michalas.

"Now, very slowly, raise your hands above your heads, and put the palms on your heads. You." he pointed to Costas, "kick away that rifle, this way. Slowly, remember I have you in my sights." Costas did as he was told.

Recovering a little from the shock and trying to buy time to think of a way out of this real problem Costas said,

"Who are you, how did you get here tonight. I knew there was something odd about you when the Major brought you in earlier. Whoever you are, and you are not a reporter that's for certain...." he stopped suddenly, quickly realising that he spoke with an American accent, which might make his captor suspicious. Then he went on, thinking as he spoke,

"Have you thought about how you are going to get away

from here? The whole area is full of our forces. No one will let you past. Look what happened...." He stopped again as he had been about to say "Richard Rowland."

Charles said it for him, "You mean Richard Rowland. Yes I know all about that murder. What you don't know is that I found him and talked to him before he died. Yes I know all about you. Everything", he added pointedly.

"What you don't know is that I tried to stop this part of it. I insisted on taking charge of them both, even then at first I was told to kill Rowland as soon as we had captured them. You don't think they intend to let Miss Spencer out alive do you? No they would have killed her before it was over, as soon as she ceased to have any more use to them alive. When you burst in Michalas and I were just deciding when to make an attempt to get her away safely. I have it all planned, with an escape route in place from. Look, why don't we all go together. Take us with you and we'll get you away. After all if you take Miss Spencer now and leave us here they'll shoot us anyway."

If Charles had any real idea about how he was going to get away, if he had a convincing plan of his own worked out, he would have treated Costas' offer with the contempt he believed it deserved. Unfortunately he had no idea how he would escape, but had been confident that an opportunity would present itself to him, it usually did.

"Perhaps," he thought to himself, "this is that chance. I can't trust him an inch, but if he helps us put some distance between ourselves and this place, then I'm sure I'll find a way to deal with him."

He had to decide quickly. The longer they remained inside the less chance they had of making their escape. That he knew to be a fact, one of the very few hard facts he could count on. Not a gambler with his own life, but nevertheless he would take a chance, that his own instincts were correct. They had no time to lose, and it was almost eleven.

"John, come over here please," Charles called. When he had walked the few steps from behind the safety of the wall

Charles saw that Clare was with him.

"Miss Spencer, please stay out of sight," Charles implored her.

"No, I'm safer here if any more men come inside than over there by myself."

Charles had to acknowledge that she did have a point and nodded silently, but slightly irritated that his orders had not been obeyed without qualification.

"In any case," she added, "do stop calling me Miss Spencer, it wastes time and makes me feel ancient. I'm just as capable as most men in this situation."

Charles tried to ignore her and said to John as he handed him the rifle, still pointed at Costas' heart.

"Cover them, if they move fire."

Then he walked over to the point where Costas' rifle had come to rest and picked it up, then he found Michalas' automatic and he collected it too. He quickly removed the ammunition from them both and put it into his pocket, then pulled the trigger on both of them just to be certain.

"Keep them covered John. You two, keep your hands above your heads, both of you."

He then walked over and searched them both, pocketing more ammunition he found on Costas and a small loaded pistol Michalas had hidden above his ankle. He made no comment, but did begin to think that perhaps Costas had been telling the truth. Perhaps he had not been trusted and Michalas was his minder, why else would the junior man have the hidden pistol?

"Now how would you get us out of here?" he said, directing his question towards Costas.

"I told you I have a route planned. Before we left Pernera I arranged to have the yacht Salamis Dawn brought here to arrive by eleven. I knew the area would be cleared by then if we were going to survive at all. It's just a case of walking across the beach and climbing aboard.

"How many men on board?"

"Two, the same two Miss Spencer saw when we were on

the yacht earlier."

"Are they armed."

"Yes, of course."

"Right, this is how we proceed. Do exactly as I say. Costas is my hostage now. You." He pointed to Michalas, "what's your name?" Michalas replied quite brightly.

"Michalas, come here. Now take this," he said handing him one of the empty rifles. "You will lead the way with..er..Clare & John, just as if you were leading two prisoners away. Costas, you will follow them, and remember I will be right behind you, but I have bullets in my rifle, you don't. Right, let's move out of this place, now."

There were half a dozen of the National Guard busy moving stores and ammunition from vehicle to vehicle, but there was no sign of the Major, and to two guards had been neither missed nor found. Charles and John had been inside the hotel for less than five minutes in all.

Michalas led the little group across the southern edge of the car park, then turned left, towards the sea. They left the CBC van some eighty feet away to the north. That area of beach was now clear, just as Costas had predicted to himself when he had ordered the Salamis Dawn north from Pernera. They were not challenged and had no difficulty in crossing the beach to the small jetty that had been roughly maintained by the Turks as a useful place for their Famagusta Bay patrol boat to moor for short periods.

Sure enough the outline of the Salamis Dawn became clear as they approached. Charles said quietly into the back of Costas' head. "Call halt." When he had done so Charles ordered Costas to call the two men on board and tell them to bring their weapons. This he did.

"Now Costas we will see what respect they have for you. Tell them to come ashore with their weapons, then order them to drop them in into the water. If they don't obey I will shoot you first, so I can can get a clear shot at each of them. The two of you will be dead in the sea before either of them can fire a shot. You had better believe me."

Costas was inwardly shaking now. He believed every word only too well. Nevertheless he followed Charles' instructions to the letter, and the two men from the Salamis Dawn did respect Costas enough to obey his commands. Half a minute later all seven were aboard the yacht. Charles had the only loaded gun and Michalas handed John the empty one as soon as he was told to do so.

"I want to be able to see all four of you at all times," Charles said as he handed John some spare ammunition and pointed to him to load his rifle. John's ignorance in handling even the simplest rifle was clear not only to Charles, but to Clare, who took it from him and expertly loaded the ammunition she took from John's hand.

"I once went on a weekend assault course and rifle shooting in my youth," she replied to the unasked question.

"Clare you had better keep hold of it yourself. If you have to fire, shoot to kill, the boat's too small to risk a wounded man driven to desperation," Charles said, having concluded that after John's performance Costas could not be certain he would know how to fire it if necessary, but would have no doubt that Clare could and would.

Costas had little doubt that to play along was his only option. He would have the opportunity to complete his mission. Not exactly as planned, but complete it nevertheless. He and his three companions quickly got the engine started, cast off and headed south as near the coast as they safely could for the first part of the journey.

"We cannot land anywhere before Cape Greco, do you want to go to Ayia Napa or all the way to Larnaca?"

Dhekelia will do nicely. I'll take over the helm when we are round the Cape," replied Charles. "In the meantime no tricks. I'm watching carefully."

They all settled down to pass the time as best they could. Since there were no reasons for secrets between any of them Charles talked freely and asked Clare for her version of the night's events. Costas knew most of it so it didn't matter that he heard it again. For his part he was determined his captors, and particularly Clare Spencer, never set foot on land again. Clare spent the time learning everything she could about what had happened. The only thing Charles kept back was Barbara's attempt to find Helena. He was determined to try to protect her for as long as possible.

Costas was very quiet during the voyage south. His concern was to steer a course a little to the east of the direct route and to reduce speed to arrive at his rendezvous three miles off Cape Greco on time. Two hours had passed before Charles began to become suspicious that they were not travelling as quickly as they had earlier during their journey from Limassol. It was well after one before they reached Fig Tree Bay. When challenged Costas protested that they had only sufficient fuel for a reduced speed since it had been his intention to call into Fig Tree Bay to refuel, but he was sure Charles would not allow him to do that now. He also pointed out that this way they were making less noise and there was less chance that they would be discovered. He promised Charles that they would reach Ayia Napa by four, and if he still wished to go on to Dhekelia they would be there by five.

Costas kept edging further offshore as they approached the Cape. He had calculated that a long shallow turn to the west would almost intercept his rendezvous. He was right. At three precisely the radio came alive, it was switched to the prearranged frequency.

"US Minesweeper Atlantis calling motor yacht Salamis Dawn. You are on collision course, please steer to port."

"What was that? How could he know the yacht's name?" asked an unstartled Costas in a startled voice.

"These days their night sights give them as good a view as in daylight for several miles," answered Charles.

"Salamis Dawn calling US Minesweeper Atlantis, we read you loud and clear and are following your advice," Costas replied into the radio.

"Please identify your business and those aboard."Before Charles could intervene Costas replied,

"Costas Koumides and guests returning to Ayia Napa

from Pernera."

There was silence. Charles was still furious that he had left his communicator in his clothes when he had changed into the National Guard uniform. He felt helpless.

Captain Ronald Bennett had been surprised to have been ordered to take the Atlantis into Pireus ten days earlier. It was unusual for single minesweepers to leave the fleet for port visits unaccompanied by the capital ships they were protecting. Nevertheless, he had been quite looking forward to a few days leave in Athens for his hard working crew. It was therefore most unwelcome to find it would not be a long stay, just long enough to pick up a mysterious civilian. No naval commander likes civilians aboard, especially one who demanded the best cabin, his own, and had no sea legs, even in the relatively calm late summer Mediterranean.

They had left port eight days ago and he was under orders from Washington to obey any orders given to him by the civilian. Because he had spent most of his time in his cabin the civilian's presence had become almost tolerable, but very strange. The only order he had issued until one hour ago was to be at this precise location, three miles south east of Cape Greco, at midnight GMT, three in the morning local time.

After leaving the Oval office the civilian had travelled to Athens, then had visited Larnaca for an important meeting, then had returned to Athens to join the Atlantis. He was no ordinary civilian. He took his orders directly and only from the Director of the CIA, from no one else.

"Captain, turn off that frequency", the civilian ordered after listening to the radio conversation, "please note that I have made a positive identification of Costas Koumides, Greek Cypriot terrorist, enemy of the United States. What is their position?"

"Five hundred yards to the north-east."

The civilian looked at his notes.

"Captain, you are ordered to launch rockets, then open fire to remove that vessel; from the ocean. There must be no survivors."

"But, we cannot fire on civilian vessels without warning...."

"No 'buts' Captain. Do it now."

"Yes sir," the captain answered, but please record that I only obey this order under protest."

"There will be no record of this engagement captain," the civilian said flatly. "Proceed to open fire, then ensure there are no survivors. You are wasting time captain."

The Captain made his decision. He could be court-martialled for disobeying orders, but it would be much more difficult to prove incompetence.

Costas, meanwhile was busily calculating exactly how to make his move. His orders were to kill Clare Spencer, then to rendezvous at this point. It had not been his fault that he had been prevented from carrying out the execution. The right opportunity had not presented itself. Michalas had never left his side, he now knew why Helena had agreed to his handling Clare Spencer, she had Michalas as her insurance that nothing went wrong.

The Americans would have to do it themselves, or let him do it when they were all aboard. Unseen by Michalas or Charles Costas had mustn't to dump most of their fuel while at sea, there was only enough for another five minutes at most when the Atlantis had called them on the radio. Costas decided it was now or never.

"Look Michalas, the fuel, look it's nearly empty." Turning to the two men who had brought the Salamis Dawn from Pernera he added, "Why didn't you take on enough fuel?" Then he added, attempting to be convincing, "Oh yes I'm sorry we were going to refuel....I forgot"

Charles looked for himself. Sure enough both gauges registered 'empty'. Costas turned to the radio.

"I'm going to ask the Americans for help."

He could not raise them, despite trying repeatedly in an increasingly, now genuine, voice for almost two minutes.

"Now what?' asked a deeply suspicious Charles. It was

too coincidental for them to have run out of fuel and have made an 'accidental' rendezvous with an American warship.

"At least we have the dingy in tow," offered Clare, having noticed this addition since leaving the yacht in Pernera earlier. "Is it large enough for us all?"

"Yes, it will take up to eight," answered Michalas, "and I made sure it has an outboard and a radio on board.

Costas shot him a puzzled look. That was not something he had arranged, Michalas had done it on his own initiative. Before he could reply there was an explosion forward of where Clare, Charles and Michalas were sitting. The two crew men had caught the full impact, their shattered bodies making a gruesome sight. Costas had fared better, but his left leg and left arm were badly mutilated as could be seen as he crumpled on the floor.

Charles was stunned for an instant. Then his training took over. He recognised a rocket had entered the cabin, but instead of exploding it had turned through forty-five degrees and left through the floor, under the water line. In the chaos it was clear that they had two dead, and one probably dying in a rapidly sinking motor yacht. It was time to leave. He took command.

"John, Michalas, leave the other two, there's nothing we can do for them, but bring Costas, he's too valuable to leave behind."

He took Clare by the arm and they made their way to the rear of the saloon, closely followed by their companions struggling with an unrecognisable Costas. The floor was rapidly tilting as the yacht listed to thirty degrees as it took on water in increasing quantities. There may have been time to haul in the dingy alongside, but Charles was not certain, and in any case he feared a second rocket, one that exploded on impact. Without waiting for any discussion he shouted.

"Take your shoes off and jump in the water. Try to bring Costas, but save yourselves first," he added as he looked towards John.

Clare was in the water first. She didn't need a second

invitation. Being a strong swimmer she had scrambled on board the dingy first so she could help pull the others over the side. John joined her, Charles remaining in the water to help Michalas push the almost lifeless Costas over the side. As Michalas was lifting himself over the side and was about to be grabbed under the arms by Clare there was a tremendous explosion that brightened the night. Clare was thrown flat on her back into John and Michalas found himself back in the water. Somehow the turbulence that rocked the dingy did not capsize it, but it was Charles who had the sharp enough mind to grab the rope attaching the dingy to the yacht and release it, so the dingy was not dragged down to the same watery grave to which the Salamis Dawn was now destined to sink in several pieces. He also had the presence of mind to keep hold of the rope so that he was not cast adrift as the dingy was pushed away by the force of the waves caused by the explosion. Michalas was not so lucky. They did not see him again. They hoped he might find some driftwood to cling to and be washed ashore, but somehow they doubted it.

"Will they try again?" asked John.

Clare was busying herself with tending to Costas. Despite him having held her captive, her humanitarian instincts were paramount. In any case as Charles had observed, there was a lot Costas could tell them, if she could save him. Perhaps more than any of them could imagine... Charles began struggling with the outboard as he answered John.

"It depends whether they saw the dingy cut free. If they did they are bound to try again if their aim was to kill everyone on board. They won't want any witnesses. See if you can find the radio Michalas mentioned. It must be somewhere, perhaps in one of the side-pannels..........."

His last words were lost in an explosion less than a hundred yards away.

"What was that?" shouted Clare.

"Depth charges, it must be a minesweeper."

The engine started, just as what seemed like a lethal wave hit them.

"Let's get away from here and as close to the shore as we can."

A second depth charge helped them on their way, this time there seemed to be a second explosion. John was most scared. He was sure they had no chance, but at least he had found the radio and if they could make it work their loss may not be a mystery. They could get their story out, and after all that was the most important thing to a good journalist.

CHAPTER TWENTY

As Edmund Stead released his hand from Major Brightwell's firm handshake on the Akrotiri concrete apron he was tapped on the shoulder by Sir Rodney's man with the party.

"We've just had a message through from Dhekelia. Charles Noble has Miss Spencer in a small craft of Cape Greco. and they are under attack requesting immediate rescue. We need your authority to go in to a battle zone with our forces."

Colin Brightwell overheard the conversation and was the first to speak.

"Sir, request permission to requisition a Wessex and collect them."

Since that is why he had brought the best men to Cyprus he had no hesitation in agreeing.

"Don't provoke the hostile forces, but get them out safely." Knowing the geography of Cyprus thoroughly he added, "Bring them to Dhekelia base military hospital. I'll be waiting for you there. Good luck."

There was a frantic, but not chaotic, period of five minutes before everything was in place. A Wessex air/sea rescue helicopter for Brightwell's team complete with the best possible equipment, a thorough briefing to a member of the team on the exact location Noble had reported their last position to be, and their radio frequency; a second Wessex to enable Edmund and his team to get to Dhekelia. Edmund had now postponed leaving for Nicosia, believing it to be more important to be waiting for his Prime Minister at the hospital. Nevertheless the SAS team took off before three fifteen, less than fifteen minutes after Concorde had touched down.

Edmund and his party, including the Sky News crew, left ten minutes later for their shorter, less dangerous, journey to Dhekelia.

Charles looked fractionally relieved as he looked up from

speaking into the microphone above the roar of the powerful outboard.

"At least they know where we are and help should be on its way soon," he shouted towards the others in the rear of the boat.

Clare had done all she could for Costas, with no medical equipment or bandages. For the second time that night John had lost his shirt for more useful purposes, this time the torn strips, soaked in salty seawater as a rudimentary antiseptic, had allowed Clare to temporarily stem the bleeding. She had now taken over steering the dingy to allow Charles to go forward as far from the noise as possible to use the radio, while John took over from her in tending to the injured Costas.

There had only been one more depth charge explosion. This time it was more than two hundred yards away. They all began to hope that the worst may be over, that they might reach land safely. Clare headed the small craft straight towards the Cape Greco lighthouse. Charles believing their best chance was to get as close as possible before deciding whether to land or skirt the coast, waiting for help to arrive.

They all had some time to reflect on the events of the day, and in particular on the last thirty minutes.

Had it been an American vessel? If so why had it fired on them? Or had it been Greek Cypriot? Why would they fire on Costas? Perhaps it was a Turkish vessel passing itself off as American and firing on anything Greek. Perhaps this was the most likely explanation. It was the one Charles hoped was true, since if it was Turkish it would be less likely to follow them inshore.

Charles was keen to get as far away as possible, not only from their attacker, but from the Protaras area, so as they approached the shoreline he got Clare's attention and passed a message to her via John.

"Turn towards the west, keep as close to the shore as possible without running aground."

As soon as he had passed the message he turned to the

radio again and attempted to call Dhekelia, knowing the batteries were only designed to provide enough transmitter power for emergency messages and may not last much longer. Reception was bad now that they were close to the shore and under the cliffs. But he did manage to get his new position out when a new voice came over the air.

"Rescue mission calling Noble. Wessex helicopter will be overhead within eleven minutes. Do you have flares, if so fire one to denote position when you hear us."

Charles could not make them hear his reply. Perhaps his batteries were too low. But he shouted to John,

"They are almost here, helicopter on its way."

His watch was still functioning and he noted the time, then took a distress flare that had been packed into the side panel of the dingy with the emergency radio. He made it ready. Nine minutes later he shouted again.

"Tell Clare to cut the engine."

The silence was deafening as they drifted very slowly towards the shore on a flat calm sea. Then they heard a sound. The sound they had each been longing for since they began their escape. The sound of help, an approaching helicopter. The moon had just crept over the horizon and had begun to cast a pale shadow along the shore. Charles saw an opportunity. They were off a small, shallow, sandy bay with a flat area above a low smooth cliff.

"Clare see if you can start her up again and run aground on that sand."

Charles waited another thirty seconds, then he fired the flare at 45 degrees directly towards the point on the coastline to which they were heading, pointing the helicopter to read his intention.

A few minutes later Charles and Clare, leaving John with Costas, climbed up the rocky shoreline to the flat cliff top where the Wessex had been landed in expert fashion between boulders that would have rolled it over had the landing not been so precise. Colin Brightwell was the first to jump down and identify himself, recognising Clare Spencer, despite her appearance and bloodstained clothes, instantly.

"Ma'am, I'm honoured."

"Major Brightwell, how can we ever thank you. This is Charles Noble, do you know him?"

"Not personally, but he has been an example to us all. We know his record and his achievements."

"Major," interjected Charles, "we can congratulate each other later. Send a stretcher party down to the sand we have a wounded man, lucky to be alive. He's a Cypriot, was holding Clare, but it is vital we keep him alive. He has information we need. Badly need."

It was three thirty local time.

On board the US Atlantis the past half hour had been one of controlled confusion. Captain Ronald Bennett had personally handled with great reluctance the initial attack on the Salamis Dawn. But he had not been prepared to murder its occupants mercilessly without giving them some chance. That is why he had ensured the first rocket launched had not been armed, but was instead selected from those used for target practice containing a dummy explosive head.

But even he knew that he could not justifiablely pull the same switch twice, not after the first had failed to explode to the consternation of the civilian under whose orders he was now operating and who was watching the Salamis Dawn closely through his powerful, infrared binoculars. As the second rocket was fired the civilian shouted in alarm.

"They have a dingy, they're trying to reach it. Quick. Take the dingy out as well before they get away."

Captain Bennett had great delight, but didn't show it, in replying.

"We can take the yacht." As he spoke the second rocket exploded. "look it's a hit. But the dingy is too small from this distance. We could never hit it from here even if we fired rockets at it all night."

"You will pay for this. We must destroy it," said an increasingly agitated civilian. "What do you suggest?"

"Depth charges, set to explode at zero depth, should do the trick." replied Captain Bennett, knowing they would look impressive, but that the dingy would have to be very unlucky to be hit or capsized. He ordered the Atlantis to manoeuvre into position, calculated the range, then added two hundred yards.

"Fire!"

The walls of water created by the exploding depth charges hid the dingy from view as it made its escape. He believed it should have made its escape. The civilian was, however, more impressed by the foaming ocean they had created and convinced himself they had succeeded in their ugly task. It was three thirty when the civilian finally said,

"Hold your position Captain. We will wait for daylight to examine the wreckage and search for bodies."

"Yes, sir", replied Captain Bennett, smiling to himself, knowing they would find little, but pleased that he had followed his own conscience, without destroying his career.

Steve Bradshaw had been correct in his assumption. Following the abortive attempt by George Spyrou's forces to take the Larnaca-Nicosia road to the west of Athienou, the Turkish forces had counterattacked in force. Neither did they stop at the old cease-fire line now cleared of many of its United Nations peace-keeping forces. Instead the local Turkish commander saw his opportunity to break through to the sea east of Larnaca and force the Greek Cypriots around Famagusta to surrender or remain cut off from the rest of the island.

At first their progress was rapid. They took the strategically important road junction with the new Lymbia road with relative ease. The shell that destroyed Steve Bradshaw's car was just one of an intensive barrage that cleared the junction and the road for a mile to the south, almost as far as the motorway. But despite their superior force the terrain was no longer to their advantage as they continued to advance. The regular National Guard units based in the former Turkish

Cypriot village of Goshi which straddled the road a mile from the junction had not been initially involved in what had begun as an action by reservists on exercise. When their positions became threatened they did involve themselves. The threat they faced was exactly what they prepared for. Their very position, at the head of the narrowest point of the valley was no accident. The plan they had exercised constantly to alleviate the boredom of twenty years' passive defence was put into action immediately they recognised the threat. They commanded the hillsides on either side of the road. Any attempt to pass along it was doomed to failure, as was discovered by the leading formation of Turkish light armour. Destroyed and blazing it made an impenetrable barrier to further progress.

After accurately warning the regular units of the threat they faced George withdrew sideways into Athienou itself. If he couldn't succeed in achieving his objective then he could at least attempt to defend his native village, now totally cut off from the rest of Cyprus by metalled road. The expected attack never came and he was able to spend much of the early morning hours regrouping what was left of his forces and developing a strategy to evacuate the civilian population of the small town to the south-east, towards Aradipou and the coast, over the rough bare, small, mountain terrain. Finally at three thirty he was at last able to reach Helena and to tell her his bad news.

The Major returned to the Golden Sands at eleven fifteen. It had taken him longer to resolve the front line positions than he had expected, but all was now well. Short of intensive house to house, apartment block to apartment block fighting, or sustained air attack, he believed his front line secure. As secure as anything could be, but knowing the lessons the Syrians had learnt across the short sea crossing to the east in Beirut he believed it would not be simple or feasible for the Turkish forces to dislodge his men from their defensive positions in the concrete jungle that was the southern suburbs of Famagusta. He was even confident that he could hold the line in the west, where much of their defence had to be in open country. There the Turkish army could not surround his men. To the west was the British base and to the east Famagusta itself. No he had achieved most of his objectives within little more than one hour.

Just as he was congratulating himself and contemplating walking over to the CBC van two of his men ran up to him.

"Sir, we have just found one of our men tied-up behind the CBC van. He says it was the Englishmen, and they have disappeared."

"Good God. Clare Spencer and Costas are they still there?"

He did not wait for an answer, but turned and ran towards the steps of the hotel, noticing as he approached that the guards were no longer on the steps.

"Wait, careful, it may be a trap, the Englishmen may still be inside," he said abruptly, halting on the bottom step. "Let's work this out."

Very carefully, and as silently as possible, the three of them entered. They waited and listened. Nothing. Then they gradually edged forward until the light from the storm lantern demonstrated conclusively that the area was empty. Clare Spencer had escaped, or had been rescued and both Costas and Michalas had disappeared. There was no sign that there had been any struggle. Everything was exactly as it had been when he had last seen it more than thirty minutes previously. Except that two men and one woman had vanished.

"They can't have got far," offered one of the men.

"Probably been picked up by now," suggested the other.

As much as he wanted to believe them, he didn't. There had been something about Noble, something that did not quite fit. Now he began to piece it together, but too late. If he was a British agent he would have had his escape planned before attempting anything. But why leave the driver tied-up, but take Costas and Michalas? With no conviction at all he went outside to his mobile communications centre at the far end of the car park and systematically called up all his units. None had seen Costas or Michalas. He did not want to spread a rumour that two British agents had left him for a fool, so he merely enquired about his two trusted lieutenants, as if it were a matter of routine.

Not wishing to interfere with the operation itself, he asked the two men to take him to the driver who was recovering in his 4x4. He could shed no further light on the matter, except that one of his attackers was a real expert. The best in his opinion. The three of them agreed to keep the matter to themselves so as not to prejudice the operation and began a search of the surrounding area. It was not long before the two guards were found. Both still unconscious, but alive. The Major realised he was not going to repair the damage quickly so he told the two men and the driver to get the guards to the forward field hospital that had been set up in a hotel closer to the front. He slowly, reluctantly and fearfully, walked over to the CBC van. He would have to inform Helena because if Clare Spencer got free and announced she had been kidnapped it would undermine their credibility and leave them open to air attack, an attack he dreaded.

"Sir," one of his staff said running towards him, "we have a report that the Salamis Dawn is heading out across the bay towards the headland."

"You are sure? You mean away from here?"

"Yes, looks as if she's bearing south south east, we expect at the speed she's travelling she'll be about a mile off Fig Tree Bay by midnight."

The Major couldn't believe his luck. It must be Costas. But who was with him? Why had the Salamis Dawn left Pernera and sailed to Famagusta? Who had ordered it north?

Believing his positions were secure he left his deputy in charge and the four of them left hurriedly in the 4x4 for Protaras, where they arrived, after negotiating his forces' road blocks and obstructions set to deter any attempted Turkish breakout, soon after midnight.

Using his authority, the Major commandeered the only

suitable boat in the small marina, leaving an extremely angry German owner and his wife on the quayside in their night clothes with a half packed suitcase. Part of the suitability of this craft to the Major was its radar. He could shadow the Salamis Dawn from a distance without being seen or heard and remain totally out of sight knowing that it was never out of reach. He was very surprised by the Salamis Dawn. It hardly seemed to be making any progress at times, but nevertheless he shadowed it faithfully until at about two thirty a second vessel began to show on the radar screen. Fearing that it was a British vessel with whom Noble had arranged a rendezvous he began to close in a little hoping there would be an opportunity to intervene before it was too late.

His problems were confounded by the uncertainty. Who was directing the Salamis Dawn? Noble or Costas? What was the other vessel? Was it coincidental, or was it there for a purpose? He just did not know.

Suddenly, just after three, there was a streak of light that seemed to begin near the larger vessel and end near the Salamis Dawn. Within a minute there was another, but this time the Salamis Dawn exploded in front of their eyes and disappeared from their radar screen.

His instinct was to flee, but his curiosity and determination not to miss an opportunity led him not only to stay, but to edge closer. Then there was a series of explosions near to the point where the Salamis Dawn had exploded and sunk. The driver suddenly shouted,

"Look, there's a small boat getting away. Can't see how many there are in it."

The Major turned his night glasses towards the larger vessel.

"He's still not moving, this way or that."

Then, when they were within a few hundred yards of the small boat, which the Major had set off to pursue, their world disintegrated. They received a direct hit. The explosive force tore the luxury cruiser into thousands of pieces.

CHAPTER TWENTY-ONE

The Wessex helicopter carefully lifted off the low cliff-top ridge and began to head west towards the Dhekelia base less than 20 miles away. In addition to Major Brightwell's team it was now carrying three passengers, one of whom was their Prime Minister and therefore technically their commander. It made no difference to their professionalism, nor to their language. Clare Spencer had been told unceremoniously to lie on the floor, although they had more respect for Charles Noble's reputation and had not attempted to subject him to the same treatment. Not that he would have willingly obeyed had he been so ordered. Costas' condition had stabilised, but he was in urgent need of surgery to his arm and leg, otherwise he would lose both. Clare's attention had saved his life, she had virtually stopped the life threatening loss of blood.

It had been the most traumatic thirty seven hours in Clare Spencer's thirty seven years. Since her arrival at Larnaca airport the previous afternoon she had been subject to every possible emotion. She had fallen more deeply in love with Richard Rowland than had ever been true previously, and it was more than the effect of being reunited after a long absence. Much more. Then at the height of this emotional attachment to Richard there had been the trauma of the kidnap and several hours of feeling totally helpless and angry. This had been followed by the contrasting relative excitement of the dinner with the CLM leaders and the politics that went with it, together with the drama as Richard escaped. The last few hours had merely been the culmination. Lying on the floor of the helicopter she had begun to cry uncontrollably. Although she had been close to it the previous night during her small sob with Richard, and again when she had first heard of his death, it was the first time she had allowed herself the luxury of real human distress, last night most of it was the wine. Now it was for real.

It was only now that the realisation of Richard's death

came flooding into her mind. No one had fought harder or campaigned more vigorously for peace than she throughout her adult life. Not because she was frightened for herself or those near to her, but to be true to her humanitarian instincts. Now the very forces in the world against which she had fought so hard, the inability to settle differences by peaceful means, had shattered her own personal world. During those few minutes lying on the floor of the helicopter, the deafening noise allowing her to remain totally enclosed in her own thoughts, she became more determined than ever to rededicate herself to continuing her lifelong struggle against the forces of destruction and despair. No longer would she contemplate leaving the scene to enjoy her own personal fulfilment. She would continue, and now she had the added advantage of personal experience of the indiscriminate effects of violence being used as the primary means of achieving what might otherwise be worthwhile objectives. Although deeply distressed by the loss of Richard she would ensure he, unlike millions of others, had not been sacrificed in vain. From his death would come her purpose.

The short flight neared its end and it dropped quickly, but surely, towards the military hospital. The final approach was deliberately at low level, since the hospital was close to the border between British territory and Turkish Cyprus. As they landed they noticed under the floodlights a second Wessex a short distance away. A small group were standing close to it. They began to approach as soon as the helicopter was on the ground. When the engines had been switched off Major Brightwell approached the prone Clare and said.

"I am very sorry we had to be so ungentlemanly with you, but we had to treat you as we would any civilian. Our training tells us any exceptions are dangerous. The risks we run mean every possible element of danger, however remote, must be eliminated. I hope you can understand."

Clare realised then that she had not been made to lie in such a miserable and uncomfortable fashion for her own safety, but to protect the SAS team from her!

"I'm no danger to you now that we have landed then?" she asked sarcastically.

"Miss Spencer, please understand that some persons who we may be called upon to rescue in such circumstances as you have suffered may become hysterical with relief. A helicopter such as this is too small to allow for the possibility of anyone being in that state. It would endanger my men, the aircraft and the mission. Therefore we always, without exception, eliminate the potential source of any danger."

This was not the place to pursue the matter, she decided. Charles intervened, his time in civilian life having tempered his own previous instincts. He offered her his arm.

"Come on Clare, let's get down and find out what's happening."

She took his hand and allowed him to help her to her feet and then he put his arm around her shoulders. He jumped down to the ground, turned and caught her in his arms to soften her fall. He released her as soon as he was sure her own legs were strong enough to bear the weight. As he turned round he noticed with astonishment the Foreign Secretary approaching. Clare did the same and let out a delighted cry.

"Edmund, how did you get here?"

She ran the few steps separating them and threw her arms around him and hugged him. This time she really meant it, and had extreme difficulty in preventing the tears starting again. She couldn't find any words, but he began to explain.

"When we learnt about your predicament thanks to Mr Noble I had to come. We requisitioned a Concorde to get here as fast as possible. Major Brightwell and his team came with me. I brought the best men possible to get you out, but it seems Mr Noble achieved it himself."

"Charles has been marvellous. I don't know about Major Brightwell, but Charles is the best," Clare said with conviction.

"How are you yourself. You must be totally exhausted. Let's get you into hospital for a rest and thorough check up."

"No." she said defiantly. "All I want is a change of clothes and a shower, then I'll be fine. Then I want to talk this whole situation through with you from beginning to end. Surely there must be something we can do?"

"Clare are you sure you are up to politics now? We can manage until tomorrow."

"If this has taught me anything it is that I must involve myself, because now I know what others have to suffer when politicians fail. That means I have a new determination. No, Edmund, I want to know everything that has brought you here. You wouldn't have come just for me. Brightwell would have done that if Charles hadn't got to me first."

Recognising he had no choice, Edmund saved his energy for the discussion she wanted and was bound to achieve, however long he fought her.

"Very well Clare, where should we start, at the beginning?"

"What I would really like are my own things - let's talk to Charles about Costas - the Cypriot we brought in on a stretcher. Then your helicopter can take us back to my hotel. We can talk while I shower and change, then we can take it from there."

Edmund was too polite to ask whether she really meant for them to talk while she was actually taking a shower and getting changed, or whether she had meant it figuratively. He looked at her. What a contrast between the sophisticated young woman dressed in a tailored business suite last time he saw her, to the young woman dressed in a soaking wet shirt with several buttons missing, that left nothing to the imagination, worn with a torn, rather short, equally wet cotton skirt. Was this really his Prime Minister? Was he really in Cyprus on the edge of a shooting war? Or was he dreaming? It was after all the middle of the night. He smiled.

"You win Clare, you usually do anyway. Let's go inside and find Charles Noble, your Knight in shining armour!"

"Really Edmund, it wasn't like that," she smiled back to him, taking the arm he offered her to help her avoid walking anywhere too rough for her bare feet. That was one reason they had developed the personal affinity they had, even at the most serious moments they could each understand the human dimension of life.

"He is conscious. They are examining him now, but I expect they will want to operate within the hour. I would really like to talk to him before then, otherwise it could be another twelve hours or so," Charles said to them both when they found him on the edge of casualty waiting with Major Brightwell. Clare looked at Edmund, becoming serious.

"That's too long to wait. We need to question him now. There was something very curious about the radio conversation he had with the ship that later tried to sink us and blast us out of the water depth charges. We must find out everything he knows right away. Edmund, you must speak to the medical staff. Explain that talking to him could save numerous other lives. Stress how important it is. Even at some risk to his life."

Edmund nodded and walked off with the senior foreign office official who had accompanied him, to see what he could achieve.

"Charles," Clare began, turning to him and Major Brightwell who were standing together. "I am leaving shortly with Edmund. We are going to try to work out what should be done and probably talk to other capitals. We have to decide among other things, whether to announce my kidnap and escape or whether to keep that under wraps for the moment."

"What about John? Can we keep him quiet? Where is he?" asked Charles.

"Leave him to me. He's outside with the TV crew Edmund brought. We can keep them quiet. We are in a military base, after all. But I think after all he's gone through he'll co-operate a little longer if necessary. Now, if, or when, Edmund arranges for someone to be allowed to question our friend Costas, I want you to do it. Find out everything. Secondly," she continued, glancing at Major Brightwell, " I am asking you to take personal command of the Major's SAS team. You have my full authority as Prime Minister to take any action you believe necessary after talking to Costas. Charles, after all we've been though together tonight I have to have confidence in you and your judgement. I do and I am sure you will not let me down."

"Is that clear and understood Major?" she asked, finding it very difficult to prevent her voice and face from betraying the pleasure at paying him back for his treatment and comments in the helicopter.

"Yes, ma'am," he replied, without showing his anger at being placed under the command of someone not active in the regiment.

"Right, that's settled. Keep us informed as best you can. Edmund's aid will look after communications".

After Edmund had left the medical staff in no doubt what their respective duties were towards their patient and their country; and after Clare had spoken to John and gained his agreement to keep the lid on everything at least until eight thirty, when they agreed to meet at the High Commission in Nicosia, they left for the short flight to Limassol and the Amathus in the second Wessex.

Helena had spent much of the time since the dispatch of the prearranged series of fax and telex messages very frustrated because everything was out of her hands. All those on the CLM central committee had important tasks to perform and she had no reason to believe any of them were failing in their duty towards the future of Cyprus. But her thoughts focused upon four of these men. Her brother Philipos and the diversion of the Turkish airliner to Nicosia. Major Patriches' task was the most important by far. Everything else tonight was subsidiary to taking and holding Famagusta. That was the central task. Then there was George Spyrou. She was sure that was a side issue which she should have rejected. But she hadn't. The emotional connection to her own village and its locality had persuaded her. Why had she allowed herself to listen, hadn't she spent most of her life since Sean was killed rejecting emotional considerations and concentrating on reality. Finally there was Costas. What did he want with Clare

Spencer? She did not know. At least he was with the Major and she had placed Michalas to watch his every move. There was little more she could do.

She received every message herself or through one of her secretaries, and followed events on the board room table which had been covered with a large scale map of Cyprus, showing every detail on the island. Self adhesive coloured stickers were added and removed as new reports were received.

It was almost eleven when the news first came that something was going wrong on the Nicosia-Larnaca road. The news was not totally unexpected, but it was no less unwelcome for that reason. However, she recognised that it was out of her hands now and in those of George, who was in command. Delegation had never been her strength.

An hour later the news was worse. Not from George, but from Famagusta. The Major's lieutenant called her personally and explained that Clare, Costas, Michalas and the two Englishmen had disappeared. It was possible, but not certain, that the Englishmen had overpowered Costas and Michalas and rescued Clare Spencer. It seemed that they had sailed on the Salamis Dawn, which had unexpectedly appeared off Famagusta, instead of staying in Pernera. The Major had set off in pursuit, he had just learnt, in a German cruiser taken from Protaras.

Helena was at first shocked, then worried that any announcement that Clare Spencer was no longer in Famagusta, or even worse, that she had not been there of her own free will, but as a hostage, could place the whole operation in jeopardy. Her concern was not for the people, or that Clare Spencer was free, she had nothing personally against her and had hoped to meet her and apologise, but for the operation itself. Its success was paramount. Again there was little she could do herself, but she ordered that news must not be passed onto the CBC staff, although part of the operation they were still journalists and a good story could tempt one of them to be less than discreet. The lieutenant's other news was extremely encouraging. They had succeeded far beyond their initial expectations in taking Famagusta and consolidating their positions. The lieutenant even suggested to her that they were already far less fearful of air attacks as their positions were so well established, several hours ahead of their most optimistic expectations. These had been to be in a position to suffer attack from the air by dawn without damaging losses or the need to retreat. The lieutenant believed they had already achieved that objective some five hours early. She asked him to keep her informed. Particularly should they hear anything significant from the Major.

Helena was very pleased with her brother's part in the nights operations. The least qualified and least motivated of her inner circle, he had delivered a perfectly managed operation at Nicosia airport. She knew, above all, he had done it for her, and her alone. That had given her added satisfaction. She had chosen him for the task against opposition from the Major, who had little confidence in Philipos. She knew it was, or should be, a management task, not a military operation. Philipos was the ideal man for the job she had thought, and had been right.

Soon after George had spoken to her and explained his retreat to Athienou. She agreed he had done exactly the right thing and explained that after his earlier news she had contacted the regular National Guard camp at Goshi, who she had been told would mobilise immediately and prevent any further advance by the Turkish forces. It had been one of her great disappointments that despite the efforts of herself and other members of the Central Committee it had not been possible to persuade the senior officer at that camp to become actively involved in the CLM. He had remained totally committed to constitutional Government and was not prepared to become associated with a para military organisation, or as he saw it, with an alternative Government. It had not therefore been thought wise to advise him in advance of that night's plans. He was told at ten, but it was not until he had been advised, just over an hour later, by Helena that the

Turkish forces were advancing towards his unit, that he agreed to mobilise and fight. He could then justify it to himself as defending the national territory, not merely supporting the CLM.

From midnight until three Helena had little to do. Regular reports were received, but little changed. The Major had established contact with his staff and was continuing to shadow the Salamis Dawn on which Costas and Clare Spencer were believed to be. No news had leaked that Clare Spencer had been a hostage and was no longer in Famagusta. The airport operation was completed, only the Turkish crew and the two persons believed to be Turkish army officers were being held at the airport. The National Guard had, however, remained, and intended to continue to occupy the area and keep the airport open if at all possible. Famagusta remained secured and stalemate, or a stand-off, had occurred on the Nicosia-Larnaca road. She began to relax and wondered whether she could take a short rest. Then she received the first direct reaction to her initial message on behalf of the CLM. It was from her own President, whom she had met at several business events and Embassy receptions in Nicosia over the years, but did not know well.

"Miss Haduanois, Miss Helena Haduanois?" she recognised his voice. "Do you know who I am?"

"Yes sir," after all he was still her Head of State.

"I am calling from an aircraft, from a Concorde, and expect to be in Cyprus in less than two hours."

"Your message came as a great disappointment, coming as it did on the eve of such an important debate on the Cyprus question. For all these years we have been able to present our case as the innocent party. Now you and, what can I call them? I suppose mutinous, yes mutinous National Guard, have changed that dramatically. A mutiny in the National Guard caused the invasion in the first place, have you forgotten that? Turkey can present us again as aggressors, as posing a renewed threat to Turkey and Turkish Cypriots. Nevertheless I am a realist, as you know. My information is that you have virtually full support and I must recognise this, much as I deplore it. I have to regard tonight as a coup against my authority as President, so I am considering my position."

"The British have called a conference at the Ledra Palace for tomorrow, Sunday, for you it must already be today. They have invited my friend the Greek Premier, UN Deputy Secretary General, who is travelling with me. They have also invited President Zekaibes, who I understand has agreed to attend, along with the Turkish Cypriot leaders from the north. The British Foreign Secretary is also arriving in Cyprus shortly, hoping to discover the truth about his Prime Minister. I have advised the Greek Premier to accept his invitation to attend."

"I must ask you four or five questions. It might be easier if I ask them separately so you can answer each one. Firstly, in view of the Conference, will you announce an immediate cease-fire?" he waited for Helena to answer.

"Mr President, it is excellent news about the Conference, if it can achieve more than Geneva 1974, which was also held during a cease fire, which Turkey used to prepare to attack us again. How do we know they will not do the same again?"

"There is one difference this time," the President answered, "the British Foreign Secretary has agreed to tell Turkey in no uncertain terms that for them to break any cease fire they agree to would be regarded as an attack to which as a guarantor power Britain would respond. This time time they would not stand by and do nothing as they did in 1974."

"In that case," Helena continued, "yes I will order and announce an immediate cease-fire. We have achieved our primary objective. But I will make it clear we intend to hold everything we have won."

"Thank you. That is very wise. Secondly I do not believe that the British Prime Minister was in Famagusta of her own free will, however convincing you managed to make her presence seem. Neither does the British Foreign Secretary, who has an intelligence report confirming his view. Release her to the British Foreign Secretary directly he arrives in

Cyprus. Since he has called the Conference, partly from his concern for her, he would see her release in a favourable light. I am sure he would not wish to make an issue of her kidnap, if that is what it was, and would be likely to persuade her to remain silent for a few more hours."

"I would willingly agree to your suggestion," began Helena, "but it is not that simple. You are correct she was taken against her will, but very strict instructions were issued that she was not to be harmed. The problem is she has disappeared. We think she has been rescued by two British agents, posing as reporters, but her two captors have vanished too. This happened about four hours ago and we still have no news of her or them."

"I understand," said the President thoughtfully, "but if the British have taken her back it's likely she will join her Foreign Secretary before making any announcement. We shall have to hope that is the case."

"My next point is the disgraceful hijacking. That is the worst thing you have done tonight. It is not done by civilised peoples...."

"It was not really a hijacking. All we did was to divert an aircraft from an illegal, to a legal port of entry. The passengers are already settled in a hotel in Paphos. We have only kept the crew and two Turkish officers found to be on board."

"When you announce the cease-fire, announce you will return them across the Green Line at the Ledra Palace in the morning and that the passengers are free."

"Yes, you are right, I will agree to do this. It will be done as you suggest."

"Finally, and this is a very hard thing for me to ask, I am seriously considering my position as President. You staged a Coup in everything but name. The forces of law and order seem to be loyal to you, not to me, or to my Office. If I resign I want it to be done so no power vacuum is left. We must avoid another Nicos Sampson at all costs. Cyprus must have an internationally recognised President. Who is your candidate to replace me, to whom could I hand over?"

"It would be better for our country for you to remain in office and accept the fruits of our action. This is something we have discussed and considered. However, if you cannot be persuaded to remain, then we would wish to see Major Savvas Patriches become interim President, until fresh elections could be held. But we all hope you will not resign at least until a new equilibrium is reached."

"Thank you for your frank and honest answer. I shall consider the matter further and decide before the Conference."

One further point. Will you please agree to have breakfast with me at the Presidential Palace at eight in the morning. This is very important. Your safety I personally guarantee. You could be accused of treason, but these matters will all be suspended and I shall not attempt to have you arrested by the forces remaining loyal to me."

"Thank you Mr President, I shall be delighted to join you at eight."

"Goodnight Miss Haduanois."

Helena thought quickly to herself and decided to make one call before arranging the cease-fire. This was to the commander of the regular unit now plugging the the halted Turkish advance towards Larnaca. Although he had not been with her initially, he was now crucial. He was also intensely loyal to the President. He would be pleased she had agreed to his cease-fire request. He was, but she needed something more.

"The cease-fire will take effect in thirty minutes, to give us chance to inform everyone, including the Turks. Can you recapture the Lymbia road junction and safeguard the motorway before then? I know you cannot relieve Athienou, but to lose the roads from Nicosia to Larnaca airport would be a disaster."

She told him how reluctant she had been to agree to the attempt to force a corridor to Nicosia in the first place. He agreed to consider whether it was possible, and if so to try. He could say no more.

She spent the next twenty minutes finalising all the cease-fire details. All her commanders were contacted, except the Major who could not be contacted personally. All were told that there was to be a unilateral halt to all offensive operations from three thirty to provide the right atmosphere for a peace conference to be held in Nicosia in less than seven hours time. She emphasised that they must nevertheless continue to defend their positions. A new general news release was prepared and sent to all those who had received the first at the opening of hostilities. It read:

'The Cyprus Liberation Movement is pleased to announce that it has agreed to cease all hostilities unilaterally at midnight thirty GMT, three thirty local time on Sunday 2 October. This action has been taken in response to a request from British Foreign Secretary, Edmund Stead, who is now in Cyprus. He has called a peace conference between the three guarantor powers, Greece, Turkey and the United Kingdom, together with the United Nations, the Government of the Republic of Cyprus and representatives of the Turkish Cypriot minority community. This Conference is to be held at the Ledra Palace Hotel, Nicosia at 7.30am GMT, 10.30am local time, Sunday 2 October 1994. It is emphasised that all territory restored to the legitimate authority of the Republic of Cyprus will be defended by forces loyal to the Republic. Helena Haduanois, spokesperson for the CLM, has been invited to breakfast with the President of the Republic in preparation for the Conference, following his return from New York aboard a Concorde airliner put at his disposal by the British Government. All passengers aboard TK 980 diverted to Nicosia airport have now been released from protective custody and are beginning their holiday in the Republic. The crew of the airliner and two further Turkish citizens aboard will be handed to the Turkish authorities at the Ledra Palace immediately before the commencement of the Conference.'

Deliberately she made no mention of Clare Spencer, nor

the extent of the gains made. Equally deliberately she linked the return of the crew of the aircraft and the other two Turks to the beginning of the Conference, and also made the point that the President, by meeting with herself, was legitimising the action taken by the CLM.

Helena began to relax again after the stress of the last half hour when another call was put through to her. It was from the guard posted outside her offices. She had a visitor, her son Sean.

"Why didn't he stay out of the way at the Hilton," she asked herself. "Why risk further exposure."

But secretly she was pleased. Even Helena had feelings, despite their being well below the surface.

"Send him up. I'll meet him myself at the lift."

As Sean was travelling up to the top floor two more potential visitors approached the guard. Barbara and Steve had crossed the road as soon as they had seen Sean satisfy the guard outside the door. The guard made another call on Barbara's insistence, despite his reluctance to put through yet another call so quickly. Helena took it as she was about to walk out to the lift to welcome her son. This time her shock was greater. Although Barbara had been into the building many times, with, and to see her husband Richard, Helena had had no idea that Barbara was even in Cyprus, especially since Richard had been with Clare Spencer. There was only one possible explanation for her visit. She must now know the truth about her husband's death and her, Helena's, involvement in it. What was she to do? Barbara was the last person she wished to see. But she could not just send her away. Neither did she know who Barbara's companion was. It was all very unexpected and concerning. But she had to bring them up, if only to keep them there for the moment. Reluctantly therefore she told the guard to send them up, but that they must be searched first and accompanied.

It was not therefore a happy smiling mother who met her son out of the lift. She was more worried than she had been at any time during the previous twenty-four hours.

CHAPTER TWENTY-TWO

A Wessex helicopter is not the quietest means of transport, a fact that became clearer to a number of guests of the Amathus Beach hotel as one landed on its green lawns at 4am. Not considering the protocol, nor waiting for an escort, Clare leapt from the helicopter, turned to help Edmund, then set off up the slope, dragging him by the hand.

The duty manager looked questioningly at her shocking appearance as she calmly asked for the key to her room. Seeing the hesitation on his face Edmund, who had his papers with him, quickly identified himself and the key was handed over. She turned to Edmund and said,

"This way, we can talk in my room."

As she closed the door behind them she was pleased the connecting door to Richard's room had been closed by the housekeeper. Leading Edmund to the lounge area she gave him the keys and told him to help himself to a drink from the mini-bar and to pour her a gin and tonic.

"I won't be more than a few minutes. I'll just get out of these things and take a shower."

As he began to do as he was told Edmund couldn't help noticing in the mirror above the mini-bar that she did not wait to remove what was left of her clothes until going into the bathroom. He was lost in his innermost thoughts for the next five minutes. The still and silent night was only broken by the sound of Clare's running water. He opened the patio doors and walked outside and began to reflect on his day. What a day it had been. In all his years in politics, in Government, he had never known one quite like it, Neither was it over yet. His thoughts were only broken by two arms suddenly clasping his waist. He turned, somewhat startled to find Clare, now respectably covered in a white, tied, bath robe, looking refreshed.

"Where's my drink, I need it."

They went inside and he handed it to her. Then she became

serious again.

"Edmund, tell me what you have arranged. What's this about a conference?"

Edmund explained quickly, but calmly everything that had happened since they had spoken the previous morning on the phone.

"What time have you arranged to be in Nicosia?" she asked.

"By eight at the latest. I must get to the High Commission and sort out our delegation and agree our position. Are you coming with me?"

"Just try to keep me away. Anyway I agreed to meet John."

"Clare, exactly what happened to you since we spoke?"

Clare told him. She left nothing out, not even the afternoon 'siesta'. She spoke calmly until it came to Richard's escape. Then she started to break down again, recovered and completed the story to the point they had been reunited at Dhekelia. Then she continued.

"All my life I have worked for peace. That's how I got into politics, that's what motivates me more than anything else. Peace and security, removal of fear, fear of violence and poverty. But mostly to remove the need for men, and it's usually men, to kill other men and women to further their cause. Today it's no longer an abstract emotion. It's real, it has affected me personally. Edmund we must find a way to end it."

"It's not that easy. It's part of human existence - to want power, land and wealth. You can't change it overnight, too many others have tried and failed. All we can do is to try to control it, we cannot end it."

"Yes, I know that, but I can try. I can do everything possible to settle this, to solve our own problem in Ireland..." Oh, Edmund, I'm so tired. Can we afford a couple of hours' rest?"

"Yes, we should leave by six-thirty, that will give us plenty of time to drive. We can't risk flying a military helicopter into Nicosia, someone may see it as a provocation."

Edmund called the High Commission and asked for the

embassy car to collect them for the drive to Nicosia at 6.30 a.m. When he had finished the call he looked across to the bed. Clare was fast asleep. He did not want to leave her alone so decided to stay, and after calling reception for a call at 6.15am he laid on the sofa and tried to rest. Although he too was tired, he could not sleep.

Had it not been a military hospital Charles Noble would have been unable to keep the medical staff at bay long enough to have got the truth out of Costas. It took him two hours and it was only the increasing pain and the promise of immediate relief once Charles was satisfied that had eventually broken him into submission. It was not torture, Charles told himself, but merely judicious use of favourable circumstances. The momentus nature of what he had learnt from Costas relieved his guilt somewhat as he left the room and nodded to the waiting medical staff who could now prepare Costas for the operation to try to save his life and limbs.

Charles went outside as the dawn was breaking. He gestured to Major Brightwell.

"We must talk. Can you get one of your men to find us a drink, anything will do."

As one went off in search of something to revive him Charles led Colin Brightwell away from the main group around the helicopter.

"Major, I'm going to confide in you because I need to talk this through before deciding anything, and we may be able to work something out together. By the way, I may have been put into command, but I'm not going to attempt to order you to do anything we cannot agree upon."

"Thanks. I know your reputation, your legend, well enough to respect what you might suggest, sir," Major Brightwell said genuinely.

"Ok, cut the 'sir', this chat is confidential and informal, for now."

Charles relayed Costas' story. His entrapment into the CIA in 1984 and his service as an agent for the last ten years. Then he hesitated. How credible would it sound to explain that the CIA had planned to assassinate the British Prime Minister? He had to try.

"Colin, the CIA ordered our friend Costas to kill the Prime Minister last night. They knew she was to be kidnapped and ordered Costas to get himself the job of holding her and to find a convenient opportunity to kill her. It seems we got to her just in time."

"Why? Why? It doesn't make any sense, does it to you?"

"Yes, I suppose it does in a way. They have a very right wing Administration now. They've been kicked out of Continental Europe and Clare Spencer had made it clear she intended to kick them out of Britain. They know as far as she is concerned it's been a lifelong crusade, they know they couldn't talk her round as they may be able to do with anybody who replaced her. For her it's personal as well as political. By getting the Cypriots to do it for them they would also give Turkey the justification to take the rest of Cyprus and finish the job the Americans encouraged them to start in 1974".

"Good God, you could be right."

"Anyway, that's not the end of the story. It's all a bit conjectural, but Costas was to kill her, then escape and be picked up at an agreed rendezvous. Once we got to him he had no alternative but to take us on his escape route, hoping to get an opportunity to finish the job and get rid of us on the way. Then as soon as he was identified at the rendezvous they assumed he had carried out his task and they shot him out of the water, not realising we are all there too. Mind you, they would have done the same even if they had known we were with him. Seems they didn't want any witnesses."

"That ship, what was it called?"

"Atlantis, minesweeper, why?"

"Let's find out if she's still there. HQ at Dhekelia down the road will tell us. Shall we?"

"Yes."

Colin Brightwell called his lieutenant and told him to

enquire the location of the US Atlantis, but not to offer any reason for wanting to know. It only took a couple of minutes.

"It's off Cape Greco. Been there since midnight. Now she's circling over a radius of two miles."

Charles turned to Brightwell and half smiled.

"Can we?"

"You bet."

"Right. How soon?"

"Give me ten minutes to brief my men and we'll be ready." he paused, then added, "Charles we'd be honoured if you would accompany us. No heroics, that's our job, but you will be welcome."

Charles had intended to pull rank and go in any case, perhaps because Brightwell knew that, he offered first. But Charles was pleased that it had come as an invitation rather than him having to insist. He nodded his thanks and went inside the helicopter to put on some more appropriate clothes.

Less than fifteen minutes later. 6.30am local time, they were airborne, heading due south. Their pilot had orders to navigate a huge semicircle to their destination. Then to make the final approach from the south east. Twenty minutes later they spotted their objective. Descending rapidly they were above and behind the Atlantis before its radar operator had become fully alerted, so involved was he in their current search for bodies and wreckage in the water.

In fact alarm had already begun to spread through the minds of both the civilian and the Captain. Yes, they had found wreckage, not from the Salamis Dawn, but from what appeared to be a German motor cruiser, having found a life belt bearing the name 'Hamburg'. The implications were only just beginning to surface when the sound of the helicopter became louder than that of their own engines. Before they had time to react five ropes dropped from the hovering machine and simultaneously black clad figures slid down the ropes and covered the decks with exploding canisters of CS gas. Three of the SAS team then expertly searched below deck and brought up the rest of the crew to join their recovering ship mates and the civilian. Major Brightwell spoke to the Captain:

"Captain, this ship is under arrest on grounds of carrying out hostile activity in the territorial waters of Her Majesty's Sovereign Base territory off the island of Cyprus. You will order her to head for Dhekelia, where you will anchor while a full investigation is carried out."

The Captain did not answer. The civilian answered for him.

"This is an act of aggression against the naval forces of the United States of America...."

"Save the bullshit. You know why we are here so cut it out," Major Brightwell said sharply. "Captain who is this man not in uniform?"

"Refuse to answer any questions," the civilian barked at the Captain.

"So you and not the Captain are in command of this ship. Interesting don't you think Major Noble?" said Brightwell as Charles joined him having climbed down from the helicopter which had now landed on the ship's helipad on the stern.

"Captain, you and your boss, whoever he is, will accompany us in the helicopter to Dhekelia. Four of my men will stay aboard while your ship is brought inshore."

The Captain was quite relieved that it had become clear that he was not responsible. The civilian had identified himself as being in charge by his own foolish protests. He had no intention of endangering his own life or liberty by resisting or adopting a hostile stance and allowed himself to be led aboard the helicopter voluntarily. The civilian was not so placid and his futile resistance only resulted in a more uncomfortable journey than may otherwise have been the case. He was thrown on the floor and Major Brightwell himself took great pleasure in keeping him prostrate by sitting on his immobilised body for the whole duration of the short trip to Dhekelia. Charles, however, allowed the Captain to sit relatively comfortably, covering him lightly himself. It had become clear to Charles that the Captain resented the civilian and rather enjoyed seeing the way he was being treated by Major Brightwell. He hoped this may encourage him to talk more freely than he might otherwise do.

This time the helicopter did not land at the hospital. Instead it went directly to the military police headquarters on the base, which had been forewarned by radio and had been ordered to place their facilities at the disposal of Charles Noble and his team. The civilian and Captain Ronald Bennett were taken separately to individual interview rooms. The civilian was locked in his room and left. Captain Bennett however received a more civilised welcome. Knowing that the US Navy was 'dry', Charles provided a much needed supply of scotch and an American breakfast, complete with steak. He began:

"Look Captain, we know what happened. I was on the Salamis Dawn myself. So was the British Prime Minister, Clare Spencer. I recognise your voice as the one I heard on the radio. Why did you attack us, was your target Costas Koumides, who spoke to you, or was it Clare Spencer?"

"Major, I appreciate your treatment of me, but you must know I can't answer those questions, even if I knew the answers, which truthfully I do not."

Charles knew he was going to have to work hard, or wait for the scotch to do his work for him, although he needed quick answers. But he was already beginning to succeed. Clearly Captain Bennett didn't know why he had opened fire or who his real target had been.

"Look, this isn't official, yet. I decided myself to take your ship without asking anyone. You fired at me. I want to know why. You can regard it as personal interest."

"Like I said, I don't have the answers you want," the Captain began, then loosening a little, continued, "all I know is that I was ordered to open fire. I didn't like it. In fact I fired a blank first time, that's probably why you are still alive."

Recognising that he was telling the truth and guessing the rest Charles changed tack.

"Why were you still there? If I'd been you I would have

been a long way away before now."

The Captain decided to tell the truth. They would find out soon enough. A search of the Atlantis would produce the evidence.

"We began looking for wreckage. Then we found some from a German motor cruiser, couldn't understand it, so we continued to look, and found one body and one alive. Your boys must have missed him."

Charles guessed that they must have been pursued and their pursuers had been hit.

"Any identification?"

"The one alive is in a bad way, most of his clothes torn off, but he still had a wrist chain, Major Patriches."

Charles made a call and ordered the Wessex to make another trip to the Atlantis and take an injured man to Dhekelia hospital.

"Quite a night to remember then Captain. Please excuse me for a few minutes. If there is anything more you would like to eat or drink please call one of the guards. They have been asked to treat you as our guest, not our prisoner."

Charles left and joined Major Brightwell in the otherwise empty interview room that had been set aside for their exclusive use.

"Any joy?"

"A little. Trouble is I don't really think he knows much more than he has told us. Our friend next door seems to have left him in the dark as far as reasons are concerned. We can try again after the scotch has had time to have more effect and may have loosened him up a bit more, but we're not going to find the answers we really need from the Captain. Have you any ideas as far as the pro next door is concerned?"

"Not really, unless he isn't a pro at all, but just a faceless wonder boy. All we can do is to try the usual approach. I'll try first if you like."

"Ok, but make sure you don't kill him."

Although the cells were virtually sound proof, Charles listened to the noise with mounting horror and concern as the

Major attempted his brand of unorthodox interrogation.

"He hasn't talked yet, but he will, he's not a real pro, now it's your turn." Brightwell said five minutes later after he had returned to Charles' interview room.

Charles was shocked, if he could any longer be shocked by anything, by the smell, by the vomit and worse. 'What have they learnt in Hereford since my period there', he thought to himself.

"Now, my friend," Charles began, in a quiet friendly voice, "what has been going on here? I'm sorry if your treatment has been anything less than civilised. Let me order you an American breakfast, steak, scrambled eggs, tomatoes, the lot, with a large scotch and dry to top it off."

The thought of it was enough to start the civilian retching again, although thankfully his stomach had no more contents to spill.

"While we wait for your breakfast," Charles continued, not appearing to have noticed the distress the mention of food had brought to his captive,"I can tell you that your Captain thoroughly enjoyed his, we've just been eating together. He's a very bright young man. He's learnt that there is nothing to be gained from trying to cover-up a failed mission, far better to come clean straight away, causes less problems in the long run, don't you agree?"

The civilian was silent.

"Let me tell you what happened. You arranged for Costas Koumides to be involved in holding Clare Spencer prisoner, then to kill her and to make it look like an accident, then to escape and rendezvous with the Atlantis. As soon as he was in range you ordered a surprised Captain to open fire and explode the yacht to remove any evidence of your involvement. Instead your man failed to kill my Prime Minister and she and I were on the yacht you sank. We escaped and the British forces helped us to take you into custody."

The civilian remained silent.

Charles got up, turned as he was about to leave and said, "My colleague, the one who was with you earlier, will be back in a moment with your breakfast. I hope you enjoy it."

The thought was finally too much for the civilian. A week at sea, now this, however hard he tried he couldn't face any more. Knowing his own government would attempt to disown him, he had nothing to lose, and a great deal to avoid, if his dread of the first interrogator was correct.

"You win, I confirm that your understanding is essentially in accordance with the facts of the situation as they appear to be consolidating."

After translating that rather convoluted statement, especially in view of the circumstances, Charles smiled.

"Co-operation with us will be wise. Thank you. Who are you, what is your rank?"

The civilian remained silent.

Charles continued, "That is something we can quite easily find out. If you are who I think you are you are probably already in our files."

He was bluffing, but the civilian knew his details were with MI6, he had served at the London embassy earlier in his career. He concluded that there was no further point in resisting.

"Dean Lawson."

"We'll check that out. I'll send in someone to clean you up and provide some fresh clothes."

Charles then did leave him alone to reflect on the disastrous end to his first important active service mission after half a lifetime of sitting behind a desk. He had decided exactly what he would do to make the maximum impact. It would finally destroy the last remaining remnants of the special relationship. But in his view this had been largely a vehicle for spreading American economic imperialism into Europe. He had never forgiven them for killing the economic prospects of Concorde, just because they could not compete with its excellence. Now they had tried to overthrow his Government. Not some corrupt dictatorship, but the British Government.

Helena embraced her son as he stepped out of the lift and

into her arms.

"You shouldn't have come here. Not now."

"How is it going?" he asked seriously

"Very well. We've gained our major objectives on the ground and more importantly a major conference here in the morning. We could never finally win militarily, but only politically, if anything gained was to last. But there's no time for that now. I have two other visitors on the way up. You remember I talked to you about Richard Rowland? Well he was with Clare Spencer as we knew, but the fool escaped and got himself killed. His wife and a companion have arrived to see me. She must know I am behind it all. What am I to say to her? You must keep out of sight."

"No, Mother, I want to be with you when Richard's wife tries to express her anger towards you."

She nodded, "Now I've agreed to a cease-fire, and Clare Spencer seems to have escaped, there's nothing I need hide any longer, except your role. She can know the whole story."

The elevator lights told her it was on its way up. Her visitors were nearly with her. What she saw when the doors opened surprised her greatly. Barbara Rowland looked quite calm and serene. Her young companion looked totally exhausted and ready to collapse. Her personal bodyguard stepped out after the two visitors and handed Helena three objects. An identity card listing Stephen Bradshaw as a member of HM forces on Cyprus, a small service issue revolver and the latest two-way communicator, which she knew to be service issue. Having noted what the items represented, she brushed them aside, not taking them from the guard's outstretched hand, instead she took a step towards Barbara and said.

"Hello, Barbara, aren't you going to introduce me to your friend?"

Instead Barbara introduced Steve to Helena.

"Steve, this is Helena. The same Helena who arranged to have my husband killed a few hours ago. You remember, he was the man who died in your arms telling you about this woman, the same man whose body you carried from the car and hid in a hotel bedroom."

She made this introduction in the calmest, most matter-of-fact voices, displaying not a trace of emotion. Helena was far more nervous now than at any time during the night's events. All she could think to reply was:

"Barbara, er...Steve, this is Sean, he has been helping me for the past few months with the business with a view to him taking over some of the exporting to Western Europe. We can't stand here, let's go inside."

She turned and led them into the boardroom, whose table had been quickly cleared of the large scale map of Cyprus.

"Barbara, it's no good apologising for what has happened, but I do owe you an explanation. If you will listen I will try."

Steve looked at Barbara. Although he was tired, he was recovering somewhat, and the coffee he had just been handed would help. She now looked awful, the change had been sudden. All feeling seemed to be draining from her, she was almost in a trance. He answered for her.

"We're listening, go on."

Helena spent the next ten minutes explaining the plan they had executed earlier that night. She emphasised how important Clare Spencer had been in the first hour in making the Turks believe the British were involved. She tried to explain that both Clare and Richard were to be treated well and that they had not been in any danger. She accepted that she had not planned for Richard to make an escape and prejudice the operation together with many lives, and that the commanders on the ground had dealt with that using their own initiative with tragic consequences. She went on to explain that Clare had apparently been rescued and had disappeared, but that it didn't matter now since she had called a cease-fire and there was to be a peace conference of the guarantor powers in the morning.

As she was finishing Steve smiled. Charles had clearly succeeded in finding Clare and getting away. Then Helena was called out to the telephone. When she returned she too was smiling.

"I am pleased to say that I have just been told that Clare Spencer has been taken to Dhekelia by a British military helicopter. My informant tells me she is unhurt, but a Greek Cypriot, my cousin Costas actually, is seriously injured. It appears they were rescued at sea after their yacht was fired on by a warship, not ours, we don't have any."

At this Barbara became alive, all the tension and anger surfaced and she stood up shouting.

"That bloody woman tries to take my husband, then gets him killed by you." pointing at Helena, "then she comes out of it all unhurt and smelling of roses. Why? Why?"

She was about to continue, but instead she threw her hands out in a vain attempt to catch the table, missed and fell heavily to the floor, catching her head on the corner of the table as she did so. She did not move.

After the drama of Barbara's sudden appearance, followed by her equally dramatic collapse and dispatch to hospital, Helena had been able almost to relax for a couple of hours with her son. Sean had remembered the reporter who had walked down from the Hilton with him when they called the ambulance. Realising that its appearance would make him even more curious he had arranged with Helena for him to be picked up by the National Guard and returned to the Hilton on the pretext that he was breaking a curfew. That way he would delay having to explain his own disappearance. Later Sean took a taxi back to the Hilton, and Helena grabbed an hour's rest, took a shower and changed ready for breakfast at the Presidential palace north of the city centre.

She arrived on time, as was her practice, and was escorted to the small private dining room, where the President was waiting for her.

"Good morning Miss Haduanois, welcome."

"Mr President. I am honoured to be your guest."

"What is the position on the ground? What is your information about the cease-fire, is it being honoured by both sides?"

"As far as we can tell, yes. We hold the south of Famagusta and Nicosia airport. We have lost some ground around Athienou, but were able to cut our losses there in the final minutes before the cease-fire. We have regained the Lymbia-Larnaca road junction, but not the road north from there to Athienou, that remains cut, but all we have lost is the road, no villages, and very little land."

"What about the British Prime Minister and the passengers? I hear Miss Spencer was rescued from the sea. How did that arise?"

"She was rescued by two British agents. After that it is a mystery. It appears they escaped by sea and there are reports that they were fired upon and sunk by a warship. We have no knowledge of that. The passengers are now free, the Turks will be handed over at the Ledra Palace at 10am."

Good. Perhaps the British will throw some light on the warship incident."

The President offered Helena coffee and invited her to help herself from the buffet that he had laid on for his guest.

"You must explain everything to me if I am to continue. I cannot go into the conference representing my country if I do not at least appear to be in control and on top of things here, do you not agree?"

"Certainly Mr President, let me begin by explaining how I first became involved in our struggle and why, then you may begin to understand what my country means to me."

Helena told her President almost everything, only omitting the IRA connection and her son's involvement in the hijacking. He listened in silence, with growing understanding and admiration.

"You know we can only achieve a settlement here if it is politically acceptable to Turkey. You may have secured short term gains, but you must know as well as I do that they could take the whole island in a few days if they really tried. It was a tremendous gamble you took last night."

Helena smiled, "No, Mr President, it was very carefully calculated. The timing of the British Prime Minister's presence in Famagusta and the Turkish airliner were crucial in buying us time while the Turks were unsure what they faced. The real risk comes if we cannot use the cease-fire to win a settlement."

"What sort of settlement would you accept?"

"A federal Cyprus. It is probably inevitable that we shall have to allow the Turks their own area, but it must be much reduced in size. We shall also probably have to concede some restriction on cross state settlement rights, but there must be a right to travel. I have some more ideas which we can discuss later. The main essential is to determine whether or not Turkey wants to see a solution, or whether they seek to maintain the stalemate. It must be our priority to get Turkey out of it, and to achieve this we must keep Greece at arms length, being too close to Greece has been a major mistake."

"Miss Haduanois, or may I call you Helena, I won't repeat my rebuke to you. You know how difficult my position is politically. I will remain for the sake of continuity and appearances on one condition."

He handed her a press announcement, then continued,

"If you agree I shall release this at 9am, alternatively I shall announce my resignation, the choice is yours."

The statement read:

'His excellency President Spiros Theodoulu has announced the appointment of Miss Helena Haduanois to his cabinet as Minister with special responsibility for Constitutional Affairs. Miss Haduanois will take up her appointment at once and will accompany President Theodoulu to the Emergency Conference to be held at the Ledra Palace later today.'

CHAPTER TWENTY-THREE

Although he had not slept Edmund Stead was startled by the telephone. He looked at his watch, saw that it was more than five minutes before he had asked for the alarm call, but nevertheless answered it at Clare's bedside as she began to stir. He noticed, but she was not awake enough to notice, that her robe had become untied and had fallen open during her sleep, revealing that it had been all she had worn.

It was Charles Noble. He asked for Clare, but was satisfied with her Foreign Secretary. He did not go into details, but made one determined request: that the United States Ambassador be invited to the Conference as an observer. Edmund agreed to discuss this with Clare during their journey to Nicosia, thanked Charles once again for his efforts and suggested he get some rest and join them later in the day at the High Commission.

As he was replacing the receiver Edmund noticed that Clare was now almost fully awake and diverted his eyes from her body. This time she did notice and laughed.

"Really Edmund don't be so embarrassed, I haven't time to seduce you now, perhaps later..." she added cheekily.

He ignored the remark and suggested she get dressed as the car was due in fifteen minutes. He felt it would be better if he left while she dressed, so agreed to meet her in the lobby. Clare dressed in the most formal and attractive dress she had brought with her. It was not entirely appropriate for an international conference, but then she had not packed with the intention of attending one.

Their breakfast meeting at the High Commission was a formality, Clare and Edmund had agreed on Clare's insistence that they would not predetermine their position, but would only do so on the basis of the statements and positions of the parties more directly involved. Not being experienced in diplomatic affairs she was sure a radical approach was necessary if anything useful were to be achieved. She was very conscious that every more conventional idea had been tried and rejected during the previous twenty years. She was also sure that her own team would try to talk her out of any new initiative if the were given the chance. Edmund had become more reliant on his officials for his ideas, so he was not wholly convinced that her approach was correct, but he accepted that this was a matter on which he had no alternative but to be content with his number two role in government. The High Commissioner, Julian Metcalf, told them both about Peter Wright's call from Paphos a few hours earlier. They took particular note of his reference to Irish accents and wondered if this was a new dimension to which they might have to pay particular attention, but were pleased that there did not appear to be any suggestion of hostages.

The Sky News team, following discussion between Clare and John when they had met as arranged at 8.30am, had got into position early. They were ready to transmit live pictures of the arrival of the delegations to the Conference. The speed at which the Conference had been called meant that they were the only foreign television team that had been able to get into position in time and their live feed was in great demand from around the world. Because they had arrived with a reduced team John found himself on television screens explaining the background to the calling of the Conference, Clare and he having agreed how much it would be wise to report concerning the previous evening. They had agreed to withhold, for the moment, only Richard's killing, the manner of Clare's escape and the Atlantis affair. Just after they came onto the air they received news of Helena's appointment to the Republic's Cabinet. Knowing some of the background John was able to speculate that this was perhaps a concession the CLM had demanded in return for allowing the President to remain in office. He was able to conclude that it did mean that the Cyprus Government delegation was now truly representative of the vast majority of Greek Cypriots, comprising as it did both the legitimately elected government and the movement that had taken action the previous day.

Everybody had assembled by 10.30am local time. Rarely, if ever, had an international conference been called and begun within twelve hours. The immediate urgency, the kidnapping of the head of government of one of the parties, had already been resolved happily, so happily that the subject of the initial concern was present and was determined to use the conference that had been called to secure her freedom to achieve freedom and peace for a Cyprus that had been brutally divided for more than twenty years. In doing so she wanted to atone for the guilt of her country, in particular that of one of her predecessors, who had abandoned Cyprus to its fate for domestic political considerations in the summer of 1974, between the two British General Elections of that year. She was convinced that determined diplomatic efforts, and if necessary the threat of military intervention, would have prevented much of the misery that its absence had undoubtably caused.

Clare Spencer had, as a preliminary action, taken steps to ensure that she had the freedom to use the conference for the purposes she intended, and not allow herself to become a diplomatic referee.

"Edmund, you called the Conference. It is your initiative. You must chair it," she had said earlier. "I will be the British spokesperson, but I do not have your experience to preside over the debate. So I am delighted for you to relieve me of this task."

Put like that Edmund had readily agreed, although he had certain misgivings about leaving her free to lead the British delegation and make policy spontaneously herself. He hoped he would be able to control events from the chair to make that less likely.

Edmund looked around the round table at the assembled dignitaries. To have succeeded in bringing the President of Turkey and the Prime Minister of Greece to the same table had been an achievement in itself, owing much to his own reputation as an honourable man. They were separated by the Deputy Secretary General of the United Nations; between the Greek Premier and himself was the President of Cyprus and his team, and on his other side, next to the Turkish President, was the President of the self-styled 'Republic of Northern Cyprus'. The American Ambassador, the Soviet Ambassador and the French Ambassador, the latter representing the European Community, were seated at a rectangular table behind the UN team. The scene was set. Edmund opened the Conference by explaining why it had been called and what he hoped it might achieve. He continued;

"I am not prepared to see Cyprus, an Associate member of the EC, and a Commonwealth country, slide in to the sort of anarchy and destruction that we have seen in Lebanon. A new round of fighting began here last night. Fighting that has been waiting to happen for twenty years. It is not the purpose of this Conference to apportion blame for last night, nor for that matter for the division of 1974, nor even the ill-fated 1960 Constitution. We must begin again from the position we find today and find solutions to prevent one more man or one more woman dying in a fight for his or her idea of the future of this island. We all have a responsibility to ensure our ideals and beliefs, our prejudices and our honour is not paid for by any further rape of this beautiful island. The time has come for the people of this land to show the maturity and self confidence to secure their own destiny in peace."

Each of the delegations then made their own opening statements. Disappointingly they all largely reiterated their own long held positions. Turkey and the Turkish Cypriots expressed their fear for the minority population in a united unitary Cyprus, claiming that separation and self determination of the two nationalities under a weak central government was the only real solution. Greece concentrated its contribution to the occupation of forty percent of the island by Turkish armed force, making this the central obstacle to a solution. The Greek Cypriot President advocated a strong central government, freedom of movement and settlement, and restoration of property rights as being essentials for a solution. These positions had largely remained unchanged since the post-invasion accord between Makarios and Denktash. The fact that so much time had passed without these ideas having led any closer to a lasting peace had not reduced the vigour with which they were put by each party to the problem.

Clare was very tired, but the frustration of the predictability of the discussion, if it could be called that, kept her wide awake. She saw her opportunity to intervene, but after making Edmund aware that she wished to speak, he introduced her properly, making particular reference to her kidnapping and suffering. All the delegates applauded her before she could begin.

She used the goodwill shown towards her to analyse each opposing position with some sarcasm, pointing out the total incompatibility of one to the other, allowing her anger to become transparent.

"We need vision. The sort of vision the freed Eastern Europe in 1989 and 1990. Artificial compromises cannot succeed without real determination on all sides, reluctant acquiescence would render future trouble inevitable. What is required is a new beginning as my Foreign Secretary quite rightly said in his opening remarks. We have a divided island. One part totally isolated from the other. One side rich, the other poor. Let us remove the division, just as was done in Germany. Let the money flow north and avoid over development in the south. Let us remove all our forces, and I include the British forces. Let us try to be imaginative for once."

Edmund shot her a glance, it was no part of British policy to consider giving up the sovereign bases. Why had she made such a statement? Helena had not spoken yet, but took her cue from Clare;

"Miss Spencer, you lecture us here in Cyprus about removing the division from our island. If it is so simple why have you not ended the division of the island off your coast? Why has your country's governments not ended the misery of Ireland? If you cannot even achieve that how can you come here and try to tell us how to organise our affairs here in Cyprus? Your position in Ireland is just the same as Turkey's position in Cyprus. Each of you have used your military force to partition the island on the grounds that you are protecting the minority from becoming oppressed by the majority of the island's population, when all you are effectively doing is suppressing the rights of the majority of the people of each island. End your partition of Ireland and set an example to Turkey, then we might listen to you."

Edmund intervened as Chairman;

"We are discussing Cyprus, not Ireland. Let us try to keep to this one issue. We cannot solve all the world's problems in this forum, and we have less chance of achieving anything if we try."

President Zekaibes quickly followed. He explained that Turkey was indeed protecting the minority, but that they held no antagonism towards the majority and wanted the two communities to live in peace side by side in partnership, but separately. He tried to blame the British action in the 1950s for the current state of affairs, contending that by recruiting Turkish Cypriots to help them in controlling the Greek Cypriots who were engaged in a terror campaign trying to achieve Enosis, they had set one community against the other from which the relationship had never recovered. He concluded that he had only agreed to the temporary cease-fire to enable the meeting to be held and that if real progress towards a lasting settlement was not reached then he would not be bound by the cease-fire, nor agree to its continuation.

Clare was beginning to feel even more frustrated by the concentration of delegates on history at the expense of progress. She proposed an adjournment for refreshments and bilateral informal discussion. Edmund began to seek the opinion of other delegates to that suggestion when the doors at the rear of the conference room burst open. Three men and a two man television crew entered, having brushed aside in a determined manner a contingent of Austrian United Nations troops who although theoretically guarding the conference delegates would only act in self defence.

Charles Noble was the first to speak;

"Please excuse this interruption, but before you reached any conclusions I thought you should know a little more about the events of last night. This man," he pushed Dean Lawson roughly on the shoulder, "is an American CIA agent. To cut a long and very complicated story short he had arranged for Clare Spencer, the British Prime Minister, to be murdered last night while she was a captive of the CLM. His Government, the most powerful nation on earth, does not like the British Prime Minister and decided to take advantage of the opportunity offered to it by its advance knowledge of the kidnapping of the Prime Minister, not to warn her or her Government, but to have her killed. Fortunately we were able to rescue her first."

Edmund stood up and almost shouted;

"This might be true or it might not, but it is not the subject of this Conference. Please leave Mr Noble."

"No, sir. It is very relevant to your discussions. It is relevant in this sense. The American Government knew the Turkish army was to be attacked. Did they warn you President Zekaibes?"

The President shook his head.

"The Americans knew the British Prime Minister was to be kidnapped. Did they tell your Government?" he addressed his question to Edmund who remained rigid.

"They knew the authority of the Cyprus Government was to be challenged. I need not ask, we know they said nothing."

"What is very important for each of you to understand is that you were all being used. It used to be said of the British in the days of Empire that they liked to divide and rule. But they never took it to the extremes practised by America. America intended to discredit the Greek Cypriots by making it appear that they, not the Americans, the real culprits, had murdered the British Prime Minister. This would have enabled them to encourage Turkey to seize the whole island, then impose a solution on their terms, a solution favourable to the United States' interests, not the Cypriots', Greek or Turk. In fact both communities would be far better off uniting in their own self interests. We came very near to a real war last night involving Turkey, Greece and Britain as well as Cyprus itself. Why, because America wanted it that way. You are all pawns. Be your own men and women. Settle your differences today."

Every word had been filmed by John and his team. There was a hushed silence as the camera turned and followed Charles out of the room, before it turned again making one last sweep across the faces, the thoughtful faces, assembled. Edmund said simply;

"I propose we adjourn for forty-five minutes."

He ignored Clare, who had a blank look on her face, a look that was hiding anger. Anger because what she had heard confirmed her view of the United States, a view she had held for more than twenty years, and one that had almost cost her her life.

Edmund caught the United States Ambassador as he was attempting to leave without speaking to anyone. Although Edmund thought it most unlikely he would have known, only a very few would have ever known the truth, that did not lessen his contempt. He had the least diplomatic conversation he had ever held with a diplomat. He too was angry. Angry enough to tell the Ambassador to advise Washington that the United Kingdom would be announcing a break in diplomatic relations just as soon as he could arrange to make a statement. Edmund was as shocked as the Ambassador to hear himself say what yesterday would have been unthinkable.

President Zekaibes got up from the table. He did not attempt to leave the room for a break, but instead walked around and sat down next to Clare, who had not moved.

"Please let me say how shocked I was, and my country will be, to hear that. We have both been accused of dividing and ruling this morning so perhaps we have something else in common, you remember how I survived an assassination attempt last year. It is not easy to forget. But it can help you to be clear about the future."

Clare turned to him and smiled weakly.

"Thank you Mr President. Can we not find a solution to make this all worthwhile for the people?"

Helena looked at the two of them talking quietly to each other as she was about to leave with her President. She hesitated, thought 'why not?', and walked slowly round the table towards them both, sitting on the other side of Clare, who turned to acknowledge her arrival. Helena began, loud enough for President Zekaibes to hear.

"We never meant you any harm. Costas is my cousin, but I never trusted him and only allowed him to take charge of you to get him off my back, even then I sent my best man, Michalas, to watch his every move."

Clare knew then that she was telling the truth. She had rather liked Michalas, and remembered well how he had watched Costas so very closely. She put her arm on Helena's and replied simply;

"I know," then she added, "I don't suppose the two of you have ever met?" Helena Haduanois, meet President Zekaibes. Look," she continued with renewed life, "if the three of us could agree on the future then everyone would have to support us now. We have a few minutes, let's try. What exactly do you want Miss Haduanois?"

"Ideally one Cyprus, with one government and one people. But I know that isn't possible, at least not at first, but it should be the ultimate aim and no settlement should be built so that fundamental objective becomes an impossible dream. I would settle for much less now, provided it was a big improvement on the last twenty years. I am sorry to bring this up again, but I would have much more confidence in you if you would agree to do something about Ireland. I lived there for three years and the situation is so similar."

Putting Helena's final remarks to the back of her mind, but knowing she was right, Clare turned to President Zekaibes;

"What exactly do you want Mr President?"

"It may be easier to tell you what we do not want. We do not want all of Cyprus, as some, even, it seems the Americans, suspect. We do not want to have to keep our army in Cyprus. We do not want to have to continue to support part of Cyprus financially, we need that money at home. Neither do we want to see the Turkish Cypriots discriminated against in their own country just because they are Turkish. In particular we do not want the Cyprus problem to remain the obstacle that it is to our relationship with the European Community that we wish to join. We will only ever begin to be regarded as truly European if we remove this problem. That is why I agreed to the cease-fire and why I came here today."

"So you both really want a settlement. Let's use the rest of the day to make a start. I will ask my Foreign Secretary to announce an adjournment until four this afternoon. We can find somewhere quiet to go and talk."

They agreed. Clare called over an aid from the High Commission who had just returned to the room to ask what refreshments they required. At her request he arranged for them to be taken to a small conference room away from the main hall. He took her message to Edmund and finally arranged for refreshments to be sent in to them.

As news of their meeting circulated there was intense speculation and jealousy. Speculation about what they could possibly be discussing, and jealousy by the others that they had been excluded. The Turkish Cypriot and the Greek delegation were particularly upset that they had not been included in what they suspected might be a genuine attempt to achieve some agreement. As the afternoon wore on and they had not emerged the feeling turned to nervousness. What would they learn at 4 p.m. By 3.59 p.m. the remaining delegates had reassembled, but the key delegates had not returned. At 4.05 p.m. Edmund decided he had to say something, so he began to attract the attention of those present, but before there was complete silence a side door opened and the three absent delegates returned to their seats. Clare whispered something in Edmund's ear, then he began.

"Welcome back. I trust you all had a useful break. Some of you have had individual meetings, perhaps we can now attempt to make progress. Our first priority must be to prevent any further fighting, so we should not leave until we have at least extended the cease-fire, but I hope we will be able to achieve very much more. I understand Clare Spencer, the United Kingdom Prime Minister, wishes to make a statement."

Helena and President Zekaibes had insisted Clare make the statement. Because of her position and because of the sympathy for her recent experiences, they felt she would carry more weight in presenting their conclusions than either of them could have achieved. Clare began;

"By agreeing to my Foreign Secretary's invitation to attend this meeting you all demonstrated how important it is to each of you to find an acceptable solution to the apparently intractable and long standing problem of Cyprus. I was not invited initially, for reasons which you all know, but I was greatly relieved to find that this conference had been called. Since you all came partly to save me it is only right that I repay that goodwill by doing everything I possibly can to contribute to a successful outcome. President Zekaibes, Helena Haduanois and I have spent the afternoon in informal discussions seeking common ground and a meeting of minds. I was asked to make a statement to you on behalf of the three of us."

Glances were exchanged around the room, it seemed that she might be leading up to reporting an agreement, however unlikely that might have seemed just a few short hours ago.

"None of us can do other than speak for ourselves, none of us, not even a Head of State or a Prime Minister, nor even the leader of a popular movement, can commit our colleagues. Nevertheless we commend our conclusions to you all."

"The fundamental problem is not uncommon in the late twentieth century; different national groups sharing the same territory or country. As has been said here we have a similar situation in Ireland. Belgium is another country which has existed despite an uneasy cohabitation between two nationalities. The United States survived a racial crisis in the 1960s, Nigeria has been plagued by this problem since independence, even before the Biafran civil war. Lebanon is only a few short miles away from here, and Israel/Palestine only a little further away. The Soviet Union is a patchwork of disputed national authority and Russian settlers."

"Colleagues, such problems can never be totally solved. They can only be defused and substituted by peaceful coexistence. This is what we believe should be the aim in Cyprus. The people of Cyprus have had plenty of experience of the alternative."

"We propose that Cyprus becomes a genuinely federal state consisting of five States. Yes five. These States should radiate from the capital, Nicosia, which will nominally be divided, so that the appropriate sector belongs to one of the future States, but it will effectively be controlled by a second tier municipality, thus becoming a unitary capital city, the hub of the country. The borders of the five States will need to be carefully worked out, and we have not attempted to do this in detail today. All we have done is illustrate broad principles. The first State will be a Turkish Cypriot State, this will be to the north of Nicosia, with one boundary reaching the sea at Cape Kormakiti, and its eastern boundary reaching the coast at Cape Elea. The second State will be the largest. It will be in the south west of the island and include both Limassol and Paphos, it will primarily be a Greek Cypriot State, as will the third State in the south east, which will include Larnaca. The final two States will consist of the remainder of the island. One of these will include Morphou and Nicosia airport, its southern boundary will reach the coast at Kokkina Point and it will border the Turkish Cypriot State to the north. The fifth State will contain Famagusta and the rich agricultural land to the east of Nicosia. Its southern boundary will cross the coast at Cape Pyla. Neither of these final two States will be dominated by either community. They will represent the model upon which we all hope the future of Cyprus will be built, peaceful co-operation between the members of a multiracial society."

"The Central Government will have competence over external affairs, defence and the economy. The States will deal with most domestic matters and will have powers of local taxation. The structure of the Central Government will be based largely upon that of the United States. There will be a President, a Supreme Court, which we all hope and expect will uphold the Constitution in a totally impartial and non-racial manner, and two houses of Parliament. There will be a Senate, to which each State will send ten Senators elected by proportional representation, together with a house of Representatives elected by constituency. If the demography remains as we believe it will then the proposals I have outlined would be likely to produce 16 Turkish Cypriot Senators. Thus important legislation and constitutional change will require a 75% majority in the Senate."

"Rights of property and settlement will be laid down in the Constitution. This will permit the three ethnic States to restrict the right of settlement and property, but will prohibit such regulation in the two multiracial States in which pre-1974 property rights will be restored."

"We propose that the European Community and the United States together agree to provide aid to enable those not permitted to regain their pre-1974 property rights, to be properly and fully compensated as a final settlement of their claims. In such circumstances the United Kingdom Government would consider restoring relations with the United States following the break which I understand my Foreign Secretary will be shortly announcing."

"I now wish to turn to external relations. If these proposals were to be acceptable then Turkey would agree to withdraw its forces from Cyprus within a twelve month period. Greece would also not be permitted to keep armed forces in Cyprus. The United Kingdom proposes to withdraw its forces from the Dhekelia base and reduce the 99 square miles of the bases to less than 50 square miles. We would agree to sell all property on the land vacated and to donate the proceeds to the compensation fund. In the remaining base area we will provide facilities for the forces of Greece, Turkey and Cyprus to train and exercise together to promote goodwill and greater understanding. Finally the United Kingdom will take steps to persuade its EC partners to accelerate the acceptance reiterated membership of the Community of both Turkey and a united Cyprus. Accession would provide further safeguards to the people of Cyprus against discrimination on racial grounds since the people would then be under the added protection of the Court of Human Rights and the European Court itself. Successful accession would eventually require Cyprus to accept the freedom of movement and settlement of all EC nationals. At that point it would become necessary for the three ethnic states to allow such free movement of peoples regardless of ethnic origin as part of the accession process. Then within the European Community Cyprus would again become united in the true spirit of that word."

"Lastly, if I may turn to another issue. One that is not directly related to the problems of Cyprus, but one that is of direct personal concern to one of the participants to our discussions, and of great political concern to me. Particularly, I might add, since I have reason to believe that there may have been some co-operation between those seeking a united Ireland and those seeking a united Cyprus in respect of some of last night's events. However I shall not pursue that particular point now, but, as Prime Minister of the United Kingdom of Great Britain and Northern Ireland I shall be making proposals to the House of Commons in London designed to bring the present constitutional anomaly of Ireland to an end. There the problems may appear similar, but history requires the solution to be different. I shall propose that Northern Ireland be granted full independence within both the Commonwealth and the European Community. This will provide the people of Northern Ireland with a common self interest to manage their own affairs. Those who want the British out will be able to claim a victory. Those who would fight to prevent any control from Dublin will also be able to claim a victory. Belfast will gain equal status to Dublin. Since within the EC they will both look to Brussels they will be partners with London. I have believed for many years that such a solution is the only practical one that has any chance whatsoever of general acceptance by all the parties involved. They all gain at least part of their objective."

"Fellow delegates. We have outlined our ideas to you. If this Conference can agree then I propose we establish a small working group charged with meeting here in continuous session until a Constitution is completed. I propose the timetable be kept very tight. The Constitution should be ready for adoption by the first week of November, my Foreign Secretary and I will come to Cyprus for the formal signing ceremony. Elections should be held before Christmas, with the new structures and the newly elected President being in place on 1 January 1995."

CHAPTER TWENTY-FOUR

Saturday 1 April 1995 was a special day. Twelve months earlier the stories that appeared in the newspapers that spring morning would have been treated with the scepticism that some stories published on that date usually attract.

President Helena Haduanois had arrived from Nicosia the previous evening, still barely able to believe everything that had happened since that crucial October weekend the previous year. The constitutional proposals she had devised with her new trusted neighbour President Zekaibes and her now trusted friend Prime Minister Clare Spencer, had been developed very rapidly into a final document following the historic Ledra Palace Conference. The principal parties to the Conference had returned to Nicosia early in November for the formal signing ceremony and this agreement had then been approved by the people in a referendum held later that month. Helena had allowed herself to be nominated for the office of President following the referendum campaign in which she had played such a key role. She had been elected unopposed, Clare Spencer and her Foreign Secretary, together with President Zekaibes, had returned for her Inauguration in which she had insisted she would be sworn-in standing on a section of the old city walls of Nicosia that had previously been in the 'dead zone' between the former cease-fire lines. This she hoped would demonstrate the new unity she would bring to her country. She had also been pleased that Barbara Rowland and Charles Noble had accepted her invitation and they, together with Clare Spencer and Edmund Stead, were to stay as her guests at the Presidential Palace and attend the inauguration Ball. Her visit to London was only the second time she had been abroad since becoming President, the first having been to Brussels to successfully present the case for an accelerated entry of her country to the Community.

Clare Spencer rose early that unusually bright and warm April morning only to find her house guest was already in the kitchen making herself tea. Barbara Rowland had been delighted to accept Clare's invitation to spend the night at No. 10. It would be an important day for both of them and they had been able to spend the Friday evening together re-living their separate parts of the drama of last year. Barbara had accepted Clare's affair with her dead husband as history. She held no resentment towards her. Barbara's life had begun again. When she remembered Clare now it was the totally exhausted young woman who had insisted on visiting her in hospital in Nicosia, then breaking down in tears at her bedside. From that moment she began to understand Clare better than she had since their days together in Bristol. She understood that it was Clare's desperate need for companionship that had led her to seek out Richard again, something she could now well understand. Clare was very relieved to have been able to relax the previous evening after a very tiring week, as the House had sat very late each night with numerous divisions on the committee stage of the Northern Ulster Independence Bill.

The two of them had a relaxed breakfast together, then went off to their rooms to dress and prepare themselves for the day ahead.

President Sam Fowler was paying his first visit to London as President, but it was kept a very low key affair. He had not even met the Foreign Secretary, and certainly not the Prime Minister. He had however, out of respect for his position and the American people as a whole, been invited to Buckingham Palace for lunch the previous day. It had been made very clear to him by senior Foreign Office officials that diplomatic relations would only be restored when his Government made a substantial donation to the Cyprus Compensation Fund. But after the public fiasco of the Costas Koumides and Atlantis affair he was having problems of survival in office, and certainly could not get approval from Congress for what they saw as money to pay for his mistakes and worse. He had hoped to be able to use his visit to London, and the fact that he had accepted the invitation, to make progress in halting the withdrawal of US forces at British insistence. Already only two bases remained, those at Mildenhall and Bentwaters in Suffolk. However, it had been made clear to his officials that there was little hope that anything could be achieved. His second objective had been to try to make some progress in securing the release of Dean Lawson whose trial was to begin shortly. Lawson had been taken from Cyprus to England by the British military authorities on Charles Noble's orders before he became subject to any extradition dispute. Possession was nine tenths of the law Charles had decided. Although treason was still a capital offence in Britain that was not the President's major concern. The disclosures that Lawson could decide to make were, especially if they revealed his own real involvement and led directly to his impeachment.

The dignitaries had all assembled in Westminster Abbey and were awaiting the arrival of Her Majesty the Queen and other members of the Royal Family. The lead reporter covering the event live for Sky News was talking into his microphone, just as he had done outside the Ledra Palace in Nicosia. As his camera panned around the guest's faces. He pointed out Presidents Zekaibes, Haduanois and Fowler, as well as those less well known, including Sandra and Pete Wright, and Helen and Bob Jones, although none of his audience knew the real significance of some of the names he mentioned. Following his starring role the previous October in Cyprus John had abandoned his attempt to climb the ladder in the Times newsroom and had instead accepted the well-deserved offer of a transfer to Sky News that his reports from Nicosia had fully justified. As he spoke the Queen and her entourage entered and took up their places just below the choir stalls.

Finally all heads turned as the music changed to welcome the arrival of the most important personalities of the day. The Archbishop had co-operated in turning the event into one that would be long remembered alongside other ceremonials that had been hosted by the Abbey. It was some thirty minutes before he reached the central part of this particular ceremony.

He turned to his left and spoke a few words.

Edmund Stead replied;

"I do."

He turned to his right, a few moments later Clare Spencer replied;

"I do."

The Archbishop went on.

"I now pronounce you man and wife."

Then he turned to his left once more.

Charles Noble replied;

"I do."

A few moments later Barbara Rowland responded;

"I do."

After pronouncing them man and wife the Archbishop continued;

"I ask you all to kneel."

At that prearranged signal Her Majesty stood and walked the short distance from her seat towards her Archbishop, who handed her a sword. As she touched Charles Noble on each shoulder with the sword, she said simply:

"Arise Sir Charles."

Ten hours later after a four-hour flight and a drive in the Presidential limousine, escorted by a detachment of the integrated police force, the four newlyweds arrived at their honeymoon destination. As soon as their car had come to a stop at the foot of the steps outside the main entrance the door was opened for them and they stepped out. A man approached them on crutches, clearly still in considerable pain, and being helped by a woman his own age. He handed Clare Spencer a pair of silver scissors and said in a faltering voice;

"Welcome. Mrs Haduanois and I can never express our thanks for what you have done. Can I ask one more favour. Will you cut the tape and perform the reopening. You are our first guests.

Clare smiled at him, took the scissors and said in a mock royal voice;

"I have great pleasure in reopening the Golden Sands

Hotel. Long may she stand in peace and tranquillity; and may I wish you, Major Patriches a complete recovery from your injuries."

He smiled back weakly, "My country is more important than one man's legs."

POSTSCRIPT

It was Friday 1 September 1995. The Airbus crossed the lough and headed across the rolling green hills of the Antrim countryside, towards the largest fresh water lake in the British Isles. There were no vibrations as this modern aeroplane circled over Lough Neagh, to remind one of the passengers that it was almost exactly twenty-four years to the day since she had first landed at Aldergrove airport. Then she had been arriving for the first time in a foreign land and had to find her own way through immigration and to the city. This time she would be met by a guard of honour on the tarmac and whished away in an official car.

Prime Minister, Clare Spencer's Northern Ulster Independence Bill had received Royal assent in May and the elections it required had been held in June. Clare was grateful to Helena for suggesting the name of the new country. None of the old names would have been acceptable to the whole community, but Northern Ulster at least stood a chance. The election result had been far more encouraging than Clare could have expected when she determined to solve the historic problem that had brought about the downfall of many more experienced politicians than she. The Democratic Unionists, who had represented many of the Protestant community who would have voted socialist in a less sectarian society, and who had always been more opposed to Dublin, than loyal to London, had accepted the new Constitution and had combined with the old Social Democratic and Labour Party to fight the election as a new style Democratic Party. The Democrats had gone on to win a majority of the seats at Dundonald Palace, as the Stormont Parliament building had been renamed. However, they had not been as successful in the Presidential election, this had been won by a leading member of the old Unionist Party, which itself had merged with the local Conservative Party, and had taken that name.

Clare was satisfied. The French-style Constitution that had been adopted provided for a semi-executive President, with more than mere ceremonial duties, elected by the people, and an executive Prime Minister, elected by Parliament. After tomorrow's Independence Day ceremonies Northern Ulster would have a Protestant President and a Catholic Prime Minister. But, Clare noted, equality only went so far, both were men.

The next day, after the formal ceremony at Dundonald, the principle guests were taken in a motorcade to the new Presidential Palace for an informal reception, before they had to leave for Aldergrove. Hillsborough House had been the home of the British Governors of Northern Ireland, but since the abolition of the Stormont Parliament in 1972, it had been little used. Now it was to be the home of the President. Today, Heads of State and Heads of Government of more than fifty countries graced its lawns. Clare had until then been involved in the formal aspects of the hand-over of power, so she had not spoken to the President of Cyprus, but now that her work was finished she found Helena standing, and talking quietly to one of her own people. They approached each other, hesitated, then embraced as warmly as any two long-lost sisters.

"Clare, you may remember Michalas....," Helena began hesitantly, as she was about to re-introduce them.

"Yes, of course. Did they ever find any trace of him? I was so sorry about what happened as I am sure he didn't like or trust Costas either."

Then, the man who had been talking to Helena turned to face Clare, and she realised. They looked at each other and were speechless. Helena continued.

"Yes, he did manage to swim ashore that night, but it seems one of the explosions must have caused him to lose his memory. He was taken to Larnaca hospital soon afterwards and for months the only thing they ever heard him say was to ask for me. By then I was in the news and soon President, so they thought he had just got my name from the television which he was allowed to watch in case it helped him. Eventually a young student nurse thought there might be something in what he was saying, but no one would listen to her, so she wrote to me herself. The next day I went to Larnaca and found him. A week later he had almost fully recovered, so I appointed him Head of the Presidential Palace Household and Guard, a sort of General Manager of the place."

"Oh, I'm so pleased Michalas, I always knew you weren't like Costas," Clare said as she stretched up to kiss him on the cheek.

"Be careful with him, Clare. He's done such a good job as Head of Household that I've decided to make sure he stays. We're to be married at Christmas, in a double ceremony, like the one you had, with Mamma and Major Patriches. Do you and Edmund want another New Year in Cyprus, like you had last year?"

"Clare embraced a beaming Helena, this time they both wept.

THE APHRODITE PLOT

by michael jansen

THE APHRODITE PLOT tells the story behind the headlines...

Between Easter and August of 1974, a series of events shook the island of Cyprus. The result was the division of this beautiful island, a great loss of life and 200,000 Greek Cypriots became refugees in their own country. This tragedy still lives on today.

"This is the story of the people of Cyprus whose lives were shattered by events not of their making and beyond their power to control."

Published by KYRIAKOU

CYPRUS
in colour

The Cyprus Magical Bestseller

226 photos, 128 pages

"As a gift for someone who knows the island, or indeed to intrigue those who do not, or merely to spoil oneself, "Cyprus in Colour" would be hard to better. It's a pictorial gem of a book that seeks to introduce its reader or transport him back to the warmth and magic of this Mediterranean island."

BOOK REVIEW EXTRACT from SUNJET,
the in-flight magazine of CYPRUS AIRWAYS